## Praise for Laura Caldwell's
## IZZY McNEIL novels

### Red, White & Dead

"A sizzling roller coaster ride through the streets of Chicago,
filled with murder, mystery, sex and heartbreak. These
page-turners will have you breathless and panting for more."
—*Shore Magazine*

"Chock full of suspense, *Red, White & Dead* is a riveting
mystery of crime, love, and adventure at its best."
—*New York Times* bestselling author Gayle Lynds

### Red Blooded Murder

"Smart dialogue, captivating images,
realistic settings and sexy characters... The pieces of the
puzzle come together to reveal the secrets between the sheets
that lead Izzy to realize who the killer is."
—*BookReporter.com*

"*Red Blooded Murder* aims for the sweet spot between
tough and tender, between thrills and thought—
and hits the bull's-eye. A terrific novel."
—#1 *New York Times* bestselling author Lee Child

"Izzy is the whole package: feminine and sexy, but also smart,
tough and resourceful. She's no damsel-in-distress from a
tawdry bodice ripper; she's more than a fitting match
for any bad guys foolish enough to take her on."
—*Chicago Sun-Times*

### Red Hot Lies

"Caldwell's stylish, fast-paced writing grips you
and won't let you go."
—Edgar Award–winning author David Ellis

"Told mainly from the heroine's first-person point of view, this
beautifully crafted and tightly written story is a fabulous read.
It's very difficult to put down—and the ending is terrific."
—*RT Book Reviews*

"Former trial lawyer Caldwell launches a mystery series that
weaves the emotional appeal of her chick-lit titles with the
blinding speed of her thrillers... Readers will be left looking
forward to another heart-pounding ride on Izzy's silver Vespa."
—*Publishers Weekly*

# LAURA CALDWELL

## CLAIM OF INNOCENCE

MIRA®

ISBN-13: 978-0-7783-2932-9

CLAIM OF INNOCENCE

# 1

"Izzy," my friend Maggie said, "I need you to try this murder case with me. Now."

"What?" I shifted my cell phone to my other ear, not sure I'd heard her right. I had never tried a criminal case before—not even a parking ticket, much less a murder trial.

"Yeah," she said. "Right now."

It was a hot August Thursday in Chicago, and I had just left the civil courthouse. I had taken three steps into the Daley Center Plaza, looked up at the massive Picasso sculpture—an odd copper thing that looked half bird, half dog—and I actually said to it, "I'm back."

I'd argued against a Motion to Dismiss for Maggie. She normally wouldn't have filed a civil case, but she'd done so as a favor to a relative. I lost the motion, something that would have burned me in days of yore, but instead I was triumphant. Having been out of the law for nearly a year, I'd wondered if I had lost it—lost the ability to argue, to analyze information second-to-second, to change course and make it look like you'd planned it all along. I had worried that perhaps not going to court was like not having sex for a while. At first, you missed it deeply but then it became more difficult to remember what it was like with each passing day. Not that I was having that particular problem.

But really, when I'd seen the burning sun glinting off the Picasso and I stated boldly that I was back in action, I meant it figuratively. I was riding off the fact that although Maggie's opponent had won the motion, and the complaint temporarily dismissed, Judge Maddux had said, "Nice argument, counsel" to me, his wise, blue eyes sparkling.

Judge Maddux had seen every kind of case in his decades of practice and every kind of lawyer. His job involved watching people duke it out, day after day after day. For him to say "Nice argument" was a victory. It meant I still had it.

As I walked through the plaza, the heat curling my red hair into coils, I had called Maggie. She was about to pick a jury at 26th and Cal on a murder case, so her voice was rushed. "Jesus, I'm glad you called," she said.

Normally, Maggie Bristol would not have answered her phone right before the start of a criminal trial, even if she was curious about the motion I'd handled for her. But she knew I was nervous to appear in court—something I used to do with such regularity the experience would have barely registered. She was answering, I thought, to see how I was doing.

"It went great!" I said.

I told her then that I was a "lawyer for hire." Civil or criminal, I said, it didn't matter. And though I'd only practiced civil before, I was willing to learn anything.

Since leaving the legal world a year ago, I'd tried many things—part-time assignments from a private investigator named John Mayburn and being a reporter for Trial TV, a legal network. I liked the TV gig until the lead newscaster, my friend Jane Augustine, was killed and I was suspected in her murder. By the time my name was cleared, I wasn't interested in the spotlight anymore.

So the reporter thing hadn't worked out, and the work with Mayburn was streaky. Plus, lately it was all surveillance, which was a complete snooze. "I miss the law," I told Maggie from the plaza. "I want back in."

Which was when she spoke those words—*I need you to try this murder case with me. Now.*

I glanced up at the Picasso once more, and I knew my world was about to change. Again.

# 2

Over the years, it became disquieting—how easy the killing was, how clean.

He had always lived and worked in an antiseptic environment, distanced from the actual act of ending a life. They were usually killed in the middle of the night. But he never slept on those nights anyway, even though he wasn't there. He twisted in his bed. The only way he knew when they were dead was when he got the phone call. The person on the line would state simply, "He's gone."

He would thank them, hang up and then he would go on, as if he hadn't just killed someone.

But then he'd reached a point when he wanted to make it real. He wanted to see it.

And so he went to watch. He remembered that he had walked across the yard, toward the house. In the eerie, moonless night it seemed as if he heard a chorus of voices—formless cries, no words, just shouts and calls, echoes that sounded like pain itself.

He had stopped walking then. He listened. Was he really hearing that? Something rose up inside him, choked him. But he gulped it down. And then he kept moving toward the house.

# 3

Ah, 26th and Cal. You could almost smell the place as you neared it—a scent of desperation, of seediness, of excitement.

Other parts of the city now boasted an end-of-the-summer lushness—bushes full and vividly green, flowers bright and bursting from boxes, tree branches draping languidly over the streets. But out here at 26th and Cal, cigarette butts, old newspapers and crushed cans littered the sidewalks, all of them leading to one place.

Chicago's Criminal Courts Building was actually two buildings mashed together—one old, stately and slightly decrepit, the other a boxy, unimaginative, brownish structure better suited to an office park in the burbs.

The last time I'd been here was as a reporter for Trial TV, covering my first story. Now I flashed my attorney ID to the sheriff and headed toward the elevators, thinking that I liked this feeling better—that of being a lawyer, a participant, not just an observer.

I passed through the utilitarian part of the building into the old section with its black marble columns and brass lamps, the ceiling frescoed in sky-blue and orange. As I neared the elevator banks, my phone vibrated in my bag, and I pulled it out, thinking it was Maggie.

But it was Sam. Sam, who I nearly married a year ago. Sam, the guy I'd happily thought I'd spend the rest of my life with. Sam, who had disappeared when we were engaged. Although I eventually understood his reasons, I hadn't been able to catch up in the aftermath of it all. I wanted more time. He wanted things to be the way they'd been before. We'd finally realized that the pieces of *Sam and Izzy, Izzy and Sam* no longer fit together.

I looked at the display of the phone, announcing his name. I knew I had to get upstairs. I knew I was involved with someone else now. But I hadn't talked to Sam in a while. And the fact was, his pull was hard to avoid.

I took a step toward a marble wall and leaned my back on it, answering the phone. "Hey. How are you?"

"Hi, Red Hot." His nickname for me twinged something inside, some mix of fond longing and gently nagging regrets. We had a minute or two of light, meaningless banter—*How are you? Great. Yeah, me, too. Good. Good.* Then Sam said, "Can I talk to you about something?"

"Sure, but I'm in the courthouse. About to try a case with Maggie." I told him quickly about Maggie's phone call. I told him that Maggie's grandfather, who was also her law partner, had been working extra hard on the murder case. Martin Bristol, a prosecutor-turned-criminal-lawyer, was in his seventies, but he'd always been the picture of vigor, his white hair full, his skin healthy, still wearing his expensive suits with a confident posture. But that day, Maggie said he'd not only seemed weak but he'd almost fainted. He'd denied anything was wrong, but Maggie sensed differently. And now here I was at 26th and Cal.

"You're kidding?" Sam had always been excited for me when I was doing anything interesting in the legal realm. It was Sam who had reminded me on more than one occasion over the last year that I was a lawyer—that I should make my way back to the law. "This is incredible, Iz," Sam said. "How do you feel?"

And then, right then, we were back to *Sam and Izzy, Izzy and Sam*. I told him the thought of being back in a courtroom was making my skin prickle with nerves but how that anxiety was also battling something that felt like pure adrenaline. I told him that adrenaline was something I had feared a little, back in the days when I was representing Pickett Enterprises, a Midwest media conglomeration.

"You've always been a thrill seeker," Sam said. "You jumped in with both feet when Forester starting giving you cases to handle."

We were silent for a second, and I knew we were remembering Forester Pickett, whom we had both worked for, whom we had both loved and who had been dead almost a year now.

"You didn't even know what you were doing," Sam continued, "yet you just charged in there and took on everything."

"But when I was on trial or negotiating some big contract and the adrenaline would start surging, sometimes it felt like too much. And now…" I thought about trying a case again and I let the adrenaline wash over me. "I like it."

"You're using it to fuel you."

"Exactly."

This was not a conversation I would have had with Theo, my boyfriend. It was not a conversation I would have had even with Maggie. It felt damned good.

I looked at my watch. "I need to go."

A pause. "Call me later? I kind of…well, I have some news."

I felt a sinking in my stomach, for which I didn't know the reason. "What is it?"

"You've got to go. I'll tell you later."

"No, now."

Another pause.

"Seriously," I said. "You know I hate when people say they want to talk and then don't tell you what they want to talk about."

He exhaled loud. I'd heard that exhale many times. I could imagine him closing his green, green eyes as he breathed, maybe running his hands through his blond hair, which would be white-gold now from the summer sun.

"Okay, Iz," he said. "I know this isn't the right time for this, but…I'm probably moving out of Chicago."

"Where? And why?"

But then I knew.

"It's for Alyssa," I said, no question mark at the end of that statement. I suddenly knew for certain that this *news* of his had everything to do with Alyssa, his tiny, blonde, high-school sweetheart. His girlfriend since we'd called off our engagement.

And with that thought, I knew something else, too. "You're engaged."

His silence told me I was right.

"Well, congratulations," I said, as though it didn't matter, but my stomach felt crimped with pain. "So when is the big date?"

He didn't say anything for second. Then, "That's why I had to call you. There's not going to be a date."

I felt my forehead crease with confusion. Across the foyer, I saw a sheriff walking toward me with a stern expression. I knew he would tell me to move along. They didn't like people standing in one place for too long at 26th and Cal.

"There's not going to be a date," Sam repeated. "Not if you don't want there to be."

# 4

I got in the elevator with two sullen-looking teenagers. I needed to focus on Maggie's case and put my game face on. I couldn't think about my conversation with Sam right now, so I tuned in to the teenagers' conversation.

"What you got?" one said.

The other shrugged. "Armed robbery. My PD says take the plea."

"Why you got a public defender if you out on bail?" The first kid sounded indignant. "If you can get bail, you can get a real lawyer."

The other shook his head. "Nah. My auntie says she won't pay no more."

"Damn." He shook his head.

"Yeah."

They both looked at me then. I tried to give a *hey-there, howdy* kind of look, but they weren't really hey-there, howdy kind of guys. One of the teenagers stared at my hair, the other my breasts. I was wearing a crisp, white suit that I'd thought perfect for a summer day in court, but when I looked down, I realized that one of the buttons of my navy blue blouse had popped open and I was showing cleavage. I grasped the sides of the blouse together with my hand, and when the elevator reached my floor, I dodged out.

Although I was still in the old section of the courthouse, that floor must have been remodeled a few decades ago, and its hallways now bore a staid, uninspired, almost hospitalish look with yellow walls and tan linoleum floors. I searched for Maggie's courtroom. When I found it and stepped inside, I felt a little deflated. Last year, when I'd been here for Trial TV, the case was on the sixth floor in one of the huge, two-story, oak-clad courtrooms with soaring windows. This courtroom was beige—from the spectators' benches, which were separated from the rest of the courtroom by a curved wall of beige Plexiglas, to the beige-gray industrial carpet to the beige-ish fabric on the walls to the beige-yellow glow emanating with a faint high pitch from the fluorescent lights. A few small windows at the far side of the benches let in the only other light, which bounced off the Plexiglas, causing the few people sitting there to have to shift around to avoid it.

Maggie was in the front of the courtroom on the other side of the Plexiglas at one of the counsel's tables. She was tiny, barely five feet tall, and with her curly, chin-length hair, she almost looked like a kid swimming in her too-loose, pin-striped suit. But Maggie certainly didn't act like a kid in the courtroom. Anyone who thought she did or underestimated her in any way ended up on the losing end of that scuffle.

No one was behind the high, elongated judge's bench. At another counsel's table were two women who must have been assistant state's attorneys—you could tell by the carts next to their tables, which were laden with accordion folders marked First Degree Murder, as if the verdict had already been rendered. The state's attorneys were talking, but I couldn't hear them. The room, I realized, was soundproof. The judge probably had to turn on the audio in order for anything to be heard by the viewers.

I walked past the spectator pews and pushed one of the glass double-doors to greet Maggie. The door screeched opened half an inch, then stopped abruptly.

Maggie looked up, then pointed at the other door. I suddenly remembered a law professor Maggie and I had at Loyola Chicago. The professor had stood in front of an Advanced Litigation class and said the most important thing she could teach us, if we planned to practice in Cook County, was *Always push the door with the lock*. I'd found she was right. At the Daley Center, where most of the larger civil cases were held, there were always double doors. One of them always had a lock on it, and that one was always unlocked. If you pushed the other, you inevitably banged into it and looked like an ass, and in the world of litigation, where confidence was not only prized but required, you didn't want that.

From what I had learned through Maggie, though, Chicago's criminal courts didn't run like anyone else's, so I hadn't thought about the door thing. More than anything, though, I was probably just out of practice. I gave Maggie a curt nod to say, *I got it,* then pushed the correct door and stepped into the courtroom.

The state's attorneys turned and eyed me. One, I guessed, was in her forties, but her stern expression and steely glare made her seem older. She wore a brown pant-suit and low heels. The woman with her was younger, a brunette with long hair, who was probably a few years out of law school—enough time to give her the assurance to appraise me in the same frank way as her colleague, but with a lot less glare.

Maggie stepped toward me, gesturing toward the

woman in brown who had short, frosted hair cut in a no-nonsense fashion and whose only makeup was a slash of maroonish lipstick. "Ellie Whelan," she said, "and Tania Castle." She gestured toward the brunette. "This is Izzie McNeil. She'll be trying the case with us."

Both the women looked surprised.

"With you and Marty?" Ellie said, referring to Maggie's grandfather.

Maggie grunted in sort of a half agreement.

"Haven't I met you?" the brunette said to me, her eyes trailing over my hair, my face.

"Yeah…" Ellie said, doing the same.

I used to have to make occasional TV statements in my former role as an entertainment lawyer for Pickett Enterprises. But after Jane Augustine's murder last spring, my face had been splashed across the news more than once. Sometimes I still drew glances of recognition from people on the street. The good thing was most couldn't exactly place me.

I was about to explain, but Maggie said, "Oh, definitely. She's been on a ton of high-profile cases." She threw me a glance as if to say, *Leave it at that.*

I drew Maggie to her table—*our* counsel's table, I should say. "Where's your grandfather?"

Maggie's face grew serious. She glanced over her shoulder at a closed door to the right of the judge's bench. "He's in the order room. Said he wanted a little time to himself." She looked at her watch. "The judge gave us a break. Let's go see how Marty's doing." Maggie called her grandfather by his first name during work hours. Maggie and her grandfather had successfully defended alleged murderers, drug lords and Mafioso. They were both staunch believers in the constitutional tenets that gave every defendant the right to a fair arrest and a fair trial. Those staunch beliefs had made them a hell of a lot of money.

I put my hand on her arm to stop her. "Wait, Mags," I said, my voice low. "Tell me what's been going on."

She blew out a big breath of air, puffing her wheat-blond curly bangs away from her face. "I really don't know. He's been working around the clock on this case. Harder than I've ever seen him work."

"That's saying something. Your grandfather is one of the hardest-working lawyers in town."

"I know!" She bit her bottom lip. "This case just seemed to grab him from the beginning. He heard about it on the news and told me we had to represent Valerie even though she already had a lawyer." Maggie named an attorney who was considered excellent. "My grandfather went to the other lawyer and talked her out of the case. And he's been working on it constantly for the last ten months. I'm talking weekends and nights, even coming into the office in the middle of the night sometimes." Maggie shook her head. "I think he pushed himself too much, and he's finally feeling his age."

"That's hard."

Maggie nodded, then shrugged. "So that's basically it. I was ready to handle the opening arguments today after we picked the jury. And we had all the witnesses divided. But we got here and he started talking to our client, and his knees just buckled. He almost went down. I had to catch him." More chewing her bottom lip, this time on the corner of it. "It was so sad, Iz. He gave me this look... I can't describe it, but he looked scared."

I think we were both scared then. Maggie's grand-father had always held a tinge of the immortal. He was the patriarch of the family, the patriarch of the firm. No one ever gave thought to him not being around. It was impossible to imagine.

"Shouldn't he see a doctor?" I asked.

"That's what I said, but he seemed to recover quickly, and he said he wouldn't go to the hospital or anything. You know how he is."

"Yeah. It would be tough to force him."

"Real tough."

"Okay," I said, putting on a brusque voice and standing taller. "Well, before we talk to your grandfather, update me on the case. Who is your client?"

Another exhale from Maggie sent her bangs away from her forehead. She looked over her shoulder to see if anyone was near us. The state's attorneys were on the far side of their table now, one talking on a cell phone, the other paging though a transcript.

"Her name is Valerie Solara," Maggie said. "She's charged with killing her friend, Amanda Miller."

"How did the friend die?"

"Poisoned."

"Wow."

"Yeah. It was put in her food. The state's theory is that Valerie wanted Amanda out of the way because she was in love with Amanda's husband, Zavy."

"Zavy?"

"Short for Xavier."

"Any proof Valerie did it?"

"The husband will testify Valerie made overtures toward him prior to the murder, which he turned down. A friend of Amanda and Valerie's will testify that Valerie asked her about poisons. Valerie was the one cooking the food that day with Amanda. It was her recipe, and she was teaching it to Amanda. Toxicology shows the food was deliberately contaminated and that caused Amanda's death."

"What does your client say?"

"Not much. Just that she didn't do it."

"What do you mean not much? How are we going to mount a defense if she won't say much?"

"We handle this case the same as any other," Maggie said. "First, we ask the client what happened. Then the client chooses what to tell us. Usually we don't even ask the ultimate question about guilt or innocence because we don't need to know. Our defense is almost always that the state didn't meet their burden of proof."

"So you never asked her if she did it or not?"

"She says she didn't. Told us that first thing."

"If she didn't, who did?"

"She hasn't given us a theory."

Just then, a sheriff stepped into the courtroom. "All rise!"

The judge—a beefy, gray-haired guy in his early fifties—zipped up his robe over a white shirt and light blue tie as he stepped up to the bench.

"The Circuit Court of Cook County is now in session," the sheriff bellowed, "the Honorable—"

The judge held his hand out to the sheriff and shook his head dismissively. The sheriff looked wounded but clapped his mouth shut.

"Judge Bates," Maggie whispered. "He hates pomp and circumstance. New sheriff."

I nodded and turned toward the judge, hands behind my back.

"Counsel, where are we?" the judge said.

Maggie stepped toward the bench and introduced me as another lawyer who would be filing an appearance on behalf of Valerie Solara. That drew a grouchy look from the judge.

"Hold on," he said. "Let's get this on the record." He directed the sheriff to call the court reporter. A few seconds later, she scurried into the room with her machine, and Maggie went through the whole introduction again on the record.

"Fine," the judge said when she was done, "now you've got three lawyers. More than enough to *voie dire* our jury panels." The judge looked at the sheriff. "Call 'em in."

"Excuse me, Judge," Maggie said, taking a step toward the bench. "If we could have just five more minutes, we'll be ready."

Judge Bates sat back in his chair, regarding Maggie with a frown. He looked at the state's attorneys for their response.

Ellie Whelan stepped forward. "Judge, this has taken too long already. The state is prepared, and we'd like to pick the jury immediately."

The judge frowned again. I could tell he wanted to deny Maggie's request, but Martin Bristol carried a lot of weight in Chicago courtrooms, even if he wasn't present at the moment. "Five minutes," the judge barked. He looked pointedly at Maggie. "And that's it." When the judge had left the bench, Maggie nodded at the door of the order room. "C'mon. Let's go see how Marty's doing. It will help that you're going to try this case. You're one of his favorites."

We walked to the door, and Maggie swung it open. Martin Bristol sat at a table, a blank notepad in front of him. He was hunched over in a way I'd never seen before, his skin grayish. When he saw us, he straightened and blinked fast, as if trying to wake himself up.

"Izzy," he said with a smile that showed still-white teeth. "What are you doing here?"

"Izzy's looking for work, so I'm going to toss her some scraps." Maggie shot me a glance. She wanted it to seem as if she was hiring me as a favor, not as a way to save her grandfather.

"I'd really appreciate it," I said.

"Of course," Martin said. "Anything for you, Izzy." His posture slumped again, the weight of his shoulders appearing too much to hold.

"Mr. Bristol, are you all right?"

Maggie took a seat on one side of him. After a moment, I sat on the other side, a respectful distance away.

A moment later, when he'd still said nothing, Maggie put her hand on his arm. "Marty?"

Again, he didn't respond, just stared at the empty legal pad, his mouth curling into a shell of sadness.

There was a rap on the door and the sheriff stuck his face into the room. "He's had it," he said, referring to the judge. "We're bringing in the prospective jurors now."

Maggie's eyes were still on her grandfather. "Izzy and I can handle the *voie dire*. We may not open until tomorrow, so why don't you go home?"

He sat up a little. "What have I always told you about jury selection?"

"That it's the most important part of the trial," Maggie said, as if by rote.

"Exactly." He straightened more but didn't stand.

"I think you should go home. Get some rest."

His gaze moved to Maggie's. I thought he would immediately reject the notion, but he only said simply, "Maybe."

"Let us handle it." Maggie nodded toward the courtroom. "I've already told the judge that Izzy was filing an appearance."

Again, I waited for swift rejection, but Martin Bristol nodded. "Just this one time."

"Just this once," Maggie said softly.

Martin pushed down on the table with his hands, shoving himself to his feet. "I'll explain to Judge Bates." He slowly left the room.

Maggie's round eyes, fringed with long brown lashes, watched him. Then she met my gaze across the table. "You ready for this?"

My pulse quickened. "No."

"Good," she said, standing. "Let's get out there."

# 5

"How's Theo?" Maggie asked as the sheriff led a panel of about fourteen potential jurors through the Plexiglas doors and into the courtroom. Theo was the twenty-two-year-old guy I'd been dating since spring.

"Um…" I said, eyeing the potential jurors. "He's fine. So what's your strategy here? Did you do a mock trial for this? Do you know what kind of juror you want?"

As was typical, the possible jurors being led in were a completely mixed bag—people of every color and age. I remembered a story my friend, Grady, once told me about defending a doctor who had been sued. As they were about to start opening arguments, the doctor had looked at the jury and then looked at Grady. "Well, that's *exactly* a jury of *my* peers," the doc had said sarcastically.

When Grady told me the story, we both thought the doctor arrogant, but we understood what he meant. Chicago was a metropolis that was home to every type of person imaginable. As a result, you never knew what you were going to get when you picked a jury in Cook County. "Unpredictable" was the only way to describe a jury in this city.

"We talked to a jury consultant," Maggie said, answering my question, "but tell me, what's going on with Theo?"

I turned to her. "Why are you asking this now?"

"My grandfather always taught me to have two seconds of normal chitchat right before a trial starts."

"Why?"

"Because for the rest of the trial you become incapable of it and because it calms you down." She peered into my eyes. "And I think you could use some of that."

"Why? I'm fine." But I could feel my pulse continue its fast pace.

She peered even more closely. "You're not going to have one of those sweat attacks, are you?"

I glared at her. But she had a right to ask. I had this very occasional but acute nervousness problem that caused me to, essentially, sweat my ass off. It usually happened at the start of a trial, and it was mortifying. I'd always said it was as if the devil had taken a coal straight from the furnace of hell and plopped it onto my belly.

I paused a moment and searched my body for any internal boiling. "No, I think I'm fine."

The sheriff barked orders at the jurors about where to sit.

"If it's a tradition," I said, "the chitchat thing, then we should do it."

Maggie nodded.

"So Theo is good," I said. I got a flash of him—young, tall, muscled Theo, with tattoos on his arms—a gold-and-black serpent on one, twisting ribbons of red on the other. I could see his light brown hair that he wore to his chin now, his gorgeous, gorgeous, gorgeous face, those lips...

I shook my head to halt my thinking. If I didn't stop,

my internal heat would definitely rise. "Actually, I have more to talk about in terms of Sam."

"Really? I thought you hadn't seen him much."

"I haven't. He called this morning."

"Hmm," Maggie said noncommittally, her hands tidying stacks of documents. "How is he?"

"Engaged."

Maggie's chin darted forward, the muscles in her neck standing out. Her eyes went wide and shot from one of mine to the other and back again, looking for signs, I supposed, of impending sobbing. Finding none—I think I was still too shocked—she asked, "Alyssa?"

I nodded.

"Oh, my gosh. I'm so sorry, Iz."

Maggie's gaze was worried. She knew the ins and outs of Sam and me from start to finish. After Sam and I broke up, she was one of the few friends who understood that I still adored him, even as I felt I couldn't continue our relationship. Eventually, I put that relationship away, in my past, likely never to be seen in my future. But here it was in my present.

"Where are they getting married?" Maggie asked. "And when?"

"Well, that's the thing. He says he won't set a date. Not if I don't want there to be a date."

And then I saw something remarkable, something I'd seen only once or twice before—Maggie Bristol, who was never at a loss for words, stared at me, her mouth open. Not a sound emanated from within. Not even when the judge shouted at her.

"Counsel," the judge called to Maggie again, this time very loud. "Is. Your. Client. Here?" he said, enunciating.

Maggie finally dropped her eyes from me, picked up

a cell phone and glanced at it. "Yes, Your Honor. One moment please." Maggie gestured at me to walk with her.

"Where *is* your client?" I whispered.

"*Our* client," Maggie whispered back. "She gets emotional when she's in the courtroom so we try to keep her out until it's absolutely necessary. I have someone from our office sit with her in an empty courtroom, then I text them to get her down here." She put her hand on my arm. "We'll have to table this discussion of Sam."

"Of course. Forget I said anything."

She scoffed as she led us past the gallery pews, all filled with more prospective jurors. I knew what she meant—it was hard for me to think of anything but Sam. Sam's voice. Sam, saying he still wanted to be with me after everything.

I forced myself to focus instead on all those people in the pews, watching us like actors on a stage. And in a way litigation was a performance. I knew exactly what production Maggie wanted us to act in right now. She wanted us to make a show of solidarity—the two women lawyers about to greet their female client.

I threw my shoulders back, banned Sam Hollings from my mind again and smiled pleasantly at a few of the potential jurors as I followed Maggie to the courtroom door. I spied a couple of reporters scribbling in notepads. "I'm surprised there isn't more media," I whispered to Maggie.

"We've been trying to keep it low-key. We haven't made a statement to the press, and Valerie hasn't, either."

As we stepped into the hallway, Maggie was stopped by a man with bright eyes who must have been at least eighty. I recognized him as a famous judge who had stepped down over a decade ago but was always being profiled in the bar magazines as someone who spent his retirement watching over the criminal courthouse where he had presided for so long.

"Hey, Judge!" Maggie said casually, shaking his hand and patting him on the arm. "How's the golf game?"

"Terrible this summer!"

"It's always been terrible, sir."

The judge laughed. Maggie was like this at work—irreverent in a respectful kind of way. But she had an immediacy to her and a clear-cut way of speaking to people like judges, other attorneys and politicos, as if she had been intimately involved on their level for decades.

The judge moved on. A few steps later, I saw Maggie's receptionist, whom I knew from my frequent visits to Martin Bristol & Associates. "Hi," I said to her, but stopped short in my greeting when I saw the woman next to her.

Valerie Solara was a beautiful woman. She had golden-brown skin and eyes that were so dark they were almost black. Her gleaming ebony hair was pulled away from her face, showing her high cheekbones, her elegantly curved jaw. She wore a brown dress with tiny, ivory polka dots and a wide leather belt. But it wasn't so much her beauty that struck me. It was the feel of her—some kind of powerful emotion that hung around her like a cloak.

And suddenly I knew what that emotion was. I'd felt it for a large part of my last year, after my fiancé disappeared, after my friend died, after I was followed, after I was a suspect in a murder investigation. The emotion was fear.

# 6

Back in the courtroom, Maggie explained to Valerie that I would be helping on the case. Valerie looked confused, but nodded. Maggie then took the middle of the three chairs at our table so she could speak to both Valerie and me during jury questioning.

The state had the right to question potential jurors first. Tania Castle flipped her long brown hair over her shoulder as she looked at the jury questionnaires. She began calling on potential jurors, asking them whether they or their family members had been victims of a violent crime, whether they were members of law enforcement, whether they could be fair. When she was done, she consulted with Ellie, the other state's attorney, and they booted two of the jurors, who were replaced by two others from the gallery.

Maggie held out our copies of the questionnaires. "You're up," she said.

"You're letting me go first?"

She nodded, then leaned in and whispered instructions to me.

When she was done, I took the questionnaires from her hand. "Got it."

I glanced at Valerie, whose face seemed to war between calm and dread. I gave her my best *it will be fine* expression.

Wishing desperately for that expression to be true, I strode toward the jury box, exuding what I hoped was a composed, authoritative air, even though my skin felt tingly, as if my nerves were scratching against it.

We wanted to present Valerie Solara, Maggie had said, as a mom, a Chicagoan and a friend. Valerie had lost her husband some years back and in order to be able to afford her daughter's private school, they'd moved from their upscale Gold Coast neighborhood to the west side of the city, into a cheaper apartment. We wanted jurors who were devoted parents, or jurors who lived either north or west as Valerie had, or even widowers. Basically, we wanted people who seemed as much like our client as possible.

I looked at one potential juror and smiled. "Ms. Marshall. You mentioned on earlier questioning that your husband is a police officer, is that right?"

She nodded. She was a heavy woman with faded blond hair and splotched skin. She looked annoyed about having to be here, but her previous answers had shown she had some interest in being on the jury. She was also obviously in support of anything law enforcement; one of those people who believed the police could do no wrong.

*I want her out,* Maggie had said fiercely. In Illinois, an attorney can ask that a potential juror be dismissed for "cause"—meaning a situation where it was evident that a potential juror could not be impartial—as many times as they wanted. But what if it wasn't evident that person was unfair? What if the lawyer just had a *feeling?* Then you had to use a "challenge." But each side only got a certain number of challenges. My role was to try and get the juror to say something that would rise to the level of "cause."

"Given your husband's job," I said, "do you believe you would be able to stay fair and impartial throughout the trial?"

"Of course," she said, clearly annoyed. Exactly what I wanted.

"It could be days, even weeks, until Valerie Solara will be able to present her own evidence. Will you be able to wait until you hear all the evidence before you decide whether the state has proven their case beyond a reasonable doubt?"

"Yeah." She crossed her arms and glared. She struck me as someone who wanted to be on the jury for the sake of being able to say so to her friends.

"Do you have children, Ms. Marshall?"

She shook her head.

"You'll have to answer out loud for the court reporter, ma'am."

"No," she said loudly.

"Have you ever seen your husband testify in any cases?"

Now her face lightened. "Yes."

"And have you ever encountered a situation where your husband testified in a case where the defendant was not guilty of the crime of which they were accused?"

"Oh, no," she said immediately. "He wouldn't."

"Why is that?"

"Because he's a policeman."

"And police officers know who is guilty."

"Right."

"Is there a situation you could imagine where a police officer might testify and that person might end up being innocent?"

"No."

I had her. I didn't want to look triumphant in front of the whole jury, so I asked a few more questions, all benign, before I turned to Judge Bates. "Your Honor, I'd request that Ms. Marshall be excused from the jury for cause."

He nodded. "So granted."

Judge Bates looked at the jury. "Ms. Marshall, we thank you for being here today. You may leave." He nodded at the sheriff to show her the way out. "Continue, Ms. McNeil."

I picked out a thirtyish guy with hair flattened to his head in a way that was technically stylish but not on him, and who had been staring at my legs since I'd been in front of him. "Mr. Heaton."

He raised his eyebrows in a suggestive kind of way.

I asked a couple of questions, enough to see that this guy would say yes to whatever I wanted. I thanked him and wrote *W* on the questionnaire, my shorthand for *I-want-this-one-on-my-jury*.

I turned to the woman next to him and questioned her, then another.

During the process of *voie dire*, you needed to not only pick out the jurors you wanted dismissed, but also win over the jurors you wanted to keep. You had to chat and crack a couple of jokes and respond to the judge and read one juror's face while you read another's body language out of the corner of your eye and keep your ears open for a *C'mere a sec* from your cocounsel—and you had to do this all at the same time and make it look smooth. I loved *voie dire*.

By the time I was done with the panel of jurors, I felt great. I walked toward the table and saw Maggie give me a pleased nod.

I glanced at Ellie Whelan, who regarded me for a second before she returned her gaze to the questionnaires in front of her. If I was correct, her eyes had held grudging respect.

I sat next to Maggie. "I want to do it again."

# 7

Maggie let me handle two more panels of jurors before she took over, but the judge kept the jury questioning surprisingly quick compared to civil court. Once the jury was sworn in, the judge gave them directions about reporting for duty the next day. Then they were dismissed.

Maggie, Valerie and I went into the order room where Martin Bristol had been that morning. We sat at the same table. Valerie looked more shaken than earlier. "It's really happening," she said.

Maggie nodded but didn't appear worried. I was sure she'd heard such sentiments from other clients before.

Just then, Maggie's phone buzzed. She grabbed it from her pocket and looked at it. "It's my mom. She never calls when I'm on trial. It must be about my grandfather."

Valerie's eyes closed at the mention of Martin Bristol.

Maggie left the room and shot me a look over her shoulder. *Take charge.*

I turned to Valerie and put on my best lawyer face. "So Valerie, let's talk a little bit and let me explain why I'm here."

She nodded fast and looked into my eyes, clearly wanting to be reassured.

"As you apparently saw this morning, Marty is feeling ill. He's never really shown his age, but he is in his seventies."

Valerie gave a short shake of her head. "But he doesn't *seem* old."

"You're right."

"He came to me so certain we would win. He believed me, and I found myself trusting him, which is unlike me." Her small, dark-skinned hands flew to her face again, and she looked as if she might cry. "He promised to win my case."

I sensed she wanted to say something else, so I remained silent.

"And now..." She looked at me, then her eyes darted to the door, and I could almost hear her words. *Now, I have you two.*

I leaned forward, my hands on the table, wide apart. "Valerie, I'll ask you to do something right now. Please don't underestimate either Maggie or myself. Maggie is one of the best criminal defense lawyers in the city, and in large part that's because she was trained by her grandfather. I've also done a lot of trial work. We are both much more experienced than we look. And—well, I was thinking about this during jury selection—frankly, I think it gives a good impression for two women to represent you on this particular case."

"What do you mean?"

"You're accused of killing your friend." I sat there and let the words sink into the room, as much for Valerie as myself. I was sure that Maggie and Martin had engaged in numerous conversations with Valerie before, but now that I was one of her attorneys, we needed to have an honest discussion ourselves. "Anyone would want Martin Bristol on their case. But I have to tell you, it's not bad that you now have two young women whom the jury may see as the friends we are, representing you when you are accused of killing *your* friend."

She said nothing, a look of concentration settling into her face.

"Our presence tells the jury we believe you." I didn't mention that Maggie had told me many times that she didn't always believe her clients; she didn't need to.

Valerie took in a large breath, seeming to gather strength from somewhere inside her. Her eyes softened. "I'm glad you are here. I thank you for it. And yes, I understand what you are saying. By the way…" She paused. "I did not kill Amanda."

I nodded. "Maggie told me you've said that."

Her mouth pursed. "I want you to believe me."

I nodded. I wanted that, too. "Look, I don't try criminal cases often, but the fact that I'm not usually a criminal lawyer is a benefit to you because I bring other things to the table." I thought about it. "Maybe when we're outside the courthouse, you and I could talk about what happened. Maybe if I hear everything from you, I could see other avenues for this case."

I would have to see if Maggie was all right with that. Maggie had always said she didn't *need* to have that kind of discussion with the clients, and maybe there was a little bit of protecting herself from hearing too much. But now that I was back in the law, I didn't want protection from it. I wanted to be hit with it.

"Okay." Valerie's eyes looked deeply into mine, and I thought I could read a message there. *Thank you.*

Suddenly, I remembered something that pleased me about being a being a lawyer. It wasn't just the excitement of a trial. I liked helping someone who truly needed it. I liked finding solutions that a person wouldn't be able to reach themselves.

"Do you have any restriction for your bail?" I asked Valerie.

"No. The state's attorneys asked that I be required to stay at home and wear an ankle monitoring bracelet, but Martin put up a fight."

We both smiled. Marty Bristol was fairly unstoppable once he put on the gloves.

"But essentially," Valerie said, "I've just been going home every day. It's been very hard. Amanda was my best friend, along with Bridget." She saw me raise my eyebrows in question. "Bridget is—was, I guess—a friend of Amanda's and mine."

"The woman who is going to testify against you."

Her face twisted as if seized by something. "Yes. So now I don't have Amanda *or* Bridget. My daughter, Layla, has been living with me. She just started her sophomore year at DePaul University, but she's moved back with me because of this…" She raised a hand and waved it around the room. She looked down and smoothed her dotted dress, crossing her lean legs demurely. "Sometimes I wonder if it will be the last time we ever get to spend any time alone together."

The pain of her statement hit me. "I don't want that to happen to you," I said. "Let's make some time to meet outside the courthouse. Either at night or this weekend."

She met my eyes, nodded and gave me a small smile. In that, I could see a tiny sign of life—the life Valerie Solara used to have.

"Tell me," I said, turning to Maggie when she returned and Valerie had left, "what do you want me to do tonight?" On a big trial like this, there was always so much to do—contact witnesses, draft motions, prepare direct exams and crosses, research issues that had arisen that day.

"Do whatever you had planned," Maggie said, lifting her trial bag, a big, old-fashioned, leather affair handed down from her grandfather. "I'll give you transcripts to read to get you up to speed. But you could do that this weekend. We've got openings tomorrow, and I'm ready to handle that." She furrowed her brow. "My grandfather was going to cross the detectives next week. I'll get his notes."

"How did your mom say he's doing?"

"Same." She slid some grand jury transcripts across the table to me and snapped the trial bag closed, a frown on her face. "I may have you handle one of the detectives on Monday."

"Really? Do you think I can? I've never crossed a detective before."

"Yeah, well, I think this detective in particular might be the best place for you to start."

"Why?"

A pause. "It's Vaughn."

It took a moment for the name to register, then my voice rang out. "*Damon* Vaughn?"

The bailiff walked into the room, apparently to retrieve something from the judge's desk. He stopped at the sound of my indignant voice, lifting an eyebrow.

I turned back to Maggie and dropped my voice. "I can't believe you didn't tell me that the detective who made my life a living hell is testifying in your case."

"Well, before today I was going to let Martin massacre him on the stand, then tell you all the gory details. I didn't think you would be trying this case with me."

I thought about Vaughn, a lean guy in his mid-forties.

The first time I'd met him was at the office of my old firm after Sam disappeared. The next time was at the Belmont police station after my friend died and I realized that Vaughn suspected me of killing her. Usually, I hated no one. But I hated Vaughn.

"That mother trucker," I muttered.

Maggie rolled her eyes. "You're still on your not-swearing campaign?"

I nodded. I was trying to quit swearing. I didn't like it when other people swore. The problem was it sounded *so* good when I did it. Still, I replaced *goddamn it* with *God bless you* and *Jesus Christ* with *Jiminy Christmas* and *motherfucker* with *mother hen in a basket*. Maggie was forever mocking me about it. "But I think this requires the real thing," I said. "That mother *fucker*."

"So you want a shot at crossing him?"

I thought about it, then smiled a cold smile. "Let me at him."

# 8

When Maggie and I left the courthouse, the city was hot and humid, and the air crackled with a Thursday-night near-weekend buzz.

"I wish I had my Vespa here," I said. I had driven a silver Vespa since law school. I found it cathartic and freeing.

Maggie nodded at a sad-looking parking garage across the street. "I'll drive you home."

I glanced up and down the street. "Can't I get a cab?"

"Not in this hood."

"Just drop me off somewhere I can get one." Maggie lived on the south side, while I was Near North in Old Town. "You have too much to do tonight to be schlepping me around."

As we crossed the street, Maggie said, "Don't you think it's time to get rid of the Vespa?"

My head snapped toward her. "Get rid of the Vespa?" My voice was incredulous.

She looked at me with sort of an amused air. "Yes. Honey, I think it's time."

"What do you mean, it's time? Gas is expensive, and it's an easy way to get around."

She gave me a look that was more withering than amused now. "How did you get to court this morning?"

"The El."

"Then how did you get to 26th and Cal?"

"Cab."

"And now I'm driving you home."

"You're driving me to get a cab."

We entered the parking garage and took a stairway— one that smelled like urine—to the second floor. "Whatever," Maggie said. "My real point is you are too old for a scooter."

"Too *old?*" The indignation in my voice was strong. I huffed. "And it's not a scooter, it's a *Vespa*."

We found Maggie's black Honda and got in it. It was blazing hot, and we both rolled down the windows.

"You're thirty now," Maggie said.

"So? You're thirty, too, and you're driving this crappy Honda."

"But I have a reason. I don't want to go into this crappy neighborhood with a nice car. What's your excuse?"

"Why do I need an excuse?"

Maggie backed out and headed for the exit. "Well, there's more than just you being thirty. There's also the fact that you have been followed by thugs and investigators and such more than once over the past year."

I fell silent as Maggie turned from the garage onto the street. When Sam disappeared last year, I had been tailed by the feds—and by other people, as well. We were back to Sam.

"So, what did he—" Maggie said before I cut her off.

"I don't know anything more than I told you. Literally, he said he was engaged, but he wouldn't set a date if I didn't want him to."

Maggie whistled then added, "Holy shit. Or as you would say, 'Blessed poo.'"

"Oh, shut up."

"So do you want Sam to cancel the engagement?" she asked.

Confusion seemed to swirl around me, seemed to make the heat thicker. "Doesn't your air-conditioning work?" I fiddled with the knobs on Maggie's dashboard. "I don't want to talk about it. Not until I talk to him."

"Why?"

Good question. I talked to Maggie about most everything. "Because I don't want you to shoot it down. Because I don't want you to be pragmatic or to remind me what happened before. Because I want to hear what he has to say."

We were both quiet for a second.

"Fair enough," Maggie said. "Getting back to the Vespa…"

I shook my head. "I'm just not willing to give up something I love so much like the Vespa."

Maggie nodded. "Well, if you won't get rid of it, maybe you can borrow Theo's car sometimes. What does he drive?"

I paused. I blinked.

"You don't know?" Maggie asked, laughing.

I felt myself blushing a little. I looked at her. "I don't. I really don't. When we go out, he gets a cab and picks me up, or we meet somewhere."

"I can't believe you don't know what kind of car your boyfriend drives."

I looked out the front window, mystified. I used to know everything about Sam. "I don't even know if Theo *owns* a car. He has a plane. He must have a car, right?"

"Ah, the plane," Maggie said with a wistful tone. Theo and his partner had a share in a corporate plane, and

Maggie and I had been lucky enough to use it earlier that summer.

"You know what's nuts?" I said. "I haven't even seen his apartment."

Maggie braked hard, making the car screech. "Are you kidding me? You've been dating him for five months."

"I know." I shrugged. "He always stays at my condo."

Maggie shook her head and kept driving. We passed a bar where an old motorcycle hung from the sign out front.

"He never wants me to come over," I continued, "because he says his place is awful, and he's been there since he was nineteen. I think the word he used was *hellhole,* which didn't make me want to see it very badly."

Although he was only twenty-two now, Theo was mature in many ways, having run his own business for a while, but in other ways he was still in the throes of those postteen years where you could live in a hovel and have just as much fun as if it were a mansion.

Maggie started driving again. "Jesus, your life is fucked up."

"I know." I couldn't even take it personally. "But in an interesting way, right?"

When she didn't respond, I pulled out my phone and I texted Sam three words. Meet me tonight?

# 9

The restaurant was called Fred's. It sat atop the Barney's department store like a little sun patio hidden amidst the city's high-rises. The roof had a geometric shape cut into it so diners could gaze up at the sky-scraping towers blocks away, their lights twinkling against the blue-black sky arising from Lake Michigan behind them.

Fred's was more formal than Sam usually liked. I wondered what this meant. He had decided the rendezvous point.

I watched Sam across the table from me as he searched the room for the waiter. It was as if he could hardly look at me. Was that because being together was overwhelming, emotionally speaking? Because he was nervous? What? I used to be able to read him so well. I understood him in ways he didn't even see himself. Like the fact that he had been wounded by his family, even though his mother and siblings were all very nice people. When an abusive dad finally moves out, and you're the oldest and only son, some male instinct kicks in and you become the dad. You take over. And that will wound. Nobody's fault.

Finally, the waiter arrived, and Sam ordered a Blue Moon beer.

"Sorry, sir," the waiter said congenially. They didn't have any.

"A different Belgian white?" Sam requested.

The waiter apologized and helpfully offered other options, but Sam stalled, seeming a little off-kilter somehow. I jumped in and placed my order to give him time.

"I'll have vodka and soda," I said. "With two limes."

Sam's eyebrows hunched forward on his face. "When did you start drinking that?"

I thought about it. "A few months ago? My friend introduced me to it."

Sam searched my eyes. "Your boyfriend."

I nodded.

He laughed shortly, gruffly.

The waiter still stood at attention. "Sir...?" he asked Sam.

Sam looked up at him. "Patrón tequila. On the rocks."

"When did you start drinking that?"

"Just now." He smiled a sardonic grin. "You inspired me to change."

A few moments of silence followed. They felt like a settling of sorts, a shifting into us with a recognition that *us* wasn't the same. But somehow, it felt okay. It felt normal.

"I don't want to screw things up with you and your boyfriend," Sam said. I could tell by the way he pronounced *boyfriend,* in sort of a lighthearted, almost dismissive way, that he didn't think much of my new relationship.

"Very little could disturb our relationship," I said, giving a little more weight to Theo and me than might be accurate.

Sam looked at me, blinking a few times.

When I said nothing, he spoke. "I'm just gonna put it out there. Alyssa and I decided to move out of the city.

And that was okay with me, because…" He drifted off. Then he slowly nodded. "It was okay because sometimes it's hard to be here without you. Because Chicago is you. And me."

He looked at me, and this time I didn't hesitate to save him. I nodded back. I knew exactly what he meant. Sometimes Chicago without him was not exactly the city I knew before. It was a little more exciting. A little more dangerous. Less consoling than it used to be.

"So anyway," Sam continued, "we decided to move. Then somehow we started looking for engagement rings. But we couldn't figure out what we wanted. Everything she sort-of liked, I didn't. Everything I kinda liked, she didn't."

I nodded at him to continue.

"I just kept thinking about our engagement ring," he said, swiftly unloosening the bolts of my heart with the words. *Our* engagement ring.

"Remember?" he said.

"Yeah, of course. You saw it in that jeweler's window."

"I couldn't find anything better. Not even close." He stared at me with a heaviness in his eyes, which momentarily made me sad for him. For me. For us both.

But then I thought of something. "You found a ring eventually, right? Because you're engaged."

"Yeah. Sapphire cut." Sam rattled off a few more specifics that made it clear that a hell of a lot more money was spent on Alyssa's ring than mine. But the truth was, I couldn't have cared less.

Sam spoke up. Just one raw sentence that filled me with warmth. "It doesn't feel the same with her."

We nodded in silence. Kept nodding. And nodding.

Finally, I spoke. "A minute ago, you said I inspired you."

Sam nodded.

"Meaning?"

"I want to take a page out of your book. I want to be able to start all over like you did, with grace."

The emotional warmth I'd felt at his statement—*It doesn't feel the same with her*—turned into an angry heat. I could feel my face turning pink, then ruddy, then redder still. Instead of being embarrassed, I let it lift my anger up until I could really feel it. "You think I started over with *grace?* Do you think I could possibly handle you disappearing *two months* before our wedding gracefully? I know by taking off you did what you felt you had to. You were fulfilling the dying wishes of a man you thought of as a father. You made a promise. But don't forget that you'd also made me a promise when we got engaged, and do *not* assume I handled it well. Do not assume that, Sam."

I took a gulp of the cocktail, the taste reminding me vaguely of kissing Theo after he'd been out with friends. I wanted that right now. I did not want to be *assumed*— assumedly fine, assumedly good-natured, assumedly graceful, assumedly a roll-with-the-punches kind of girl. I wanted to be consumed. And so I stood from the table, tossed back another gulp and I left.

# 10

Sam walked up the flight of steps to his apartment. His legs felt heavy, the way they did when he'd been playing a lot of rugby. Izzy's anger and her abrupt exit had shocked him. And yet it had made him love her more, respect her more.

When he reached his apartment and opened the door, Alyssa was there. He knew she would be, and yet he felt surprised. He always did when he saw her, as if he couldn't force himself to remember on a regular basis that they were together.

He kissed the top of her blonde head. Felt a wave of guilt. But it wasn't just Izzy that was causing the guilt. There was more. More that he hadn't told either of them. Hadn't told anyone.

The decision he had to make was technically easy. It could be communicated quickly, by phone or email. But the ramifications were bigger. Much, much bigger. Life-changing bigger. He couldn't believe he was considering it. Would never have believed this of himself.

Which scared him. And thrilled him. He hated himself a little. But he couldn't deny the thrill.

# 11

When I got to my condo — the third floor of an old three flat in Old Town—I stomped up the stairs and slammed the door. Silence answered. A minute later, when Theo buzzed and I hit the intercom, I heard him make a growling sound, telling me he was in the same mood as I was. Or at least the same ballpark. I hit the buzzer, felt lighter already.

I heard his heavy footfalls on the stairs. With each one—*thump, thump, thump*—my stomach clenched and unclenched in anticipation. And then there he was, opening the door, standing there for a second, his six-foot-two body taking up most of the frame. He grinned, looking at me, and still he just stood there. He wore a powder-blue T-shirt that had some kind of white lettering writhing across it. The shirt had been washed so many times that it looked incredibly soft. It also couldn't hide his body underneath—the chest, the rippling stomach muscles. He took a step toward me and I flushed, every cell of my body alive and dancing with a desire that ramped up every time I saw him.

My reaction to Theo was so intense each time I saw him that I had begun to wonder if I was... God, I could hardly think it. Well, here was the thing—I had been starting to wonder if I was falling in love with him. Because it seemed nothing else could explain the constant ratcheting up of longing and emotions.

Yet it was hard to judge whether Theo was in the same place. And now there was something else. Now there was Sam.

Looking up at Theo, imagining lifting up that blue T-shirt, I reminded myself that whether Theo and I had perfect timing or not, it didn't matter. Because here he was. Now. And where was Sam? With his *fiancée*. I felt rage again. My face flushed as an ever-so-slight tremor ran through my body. Was the tremor caused by the thought of Sam with Alyssa or the sight of Theo? No idea.

"Girl," Theo said simply, what he always said. "What time do we have to be at your mom's?"

His large body moved toward me, his chin-length hair, shiny and brown, swinging with the movement.

I banished Sam from my thoughts. I grabbed Theo's T-shirt and used it to pull him around, shoving him into a seated position on the couch. I climbed on top of him, my legs on either side of his. "We've got time."

# 12

The first time he had gone to see the killing, the first time he had walked in that house, there was no emotion. That was what he noticed. The people there nodded at him. As if it were simple.

Everyone knew who he was. They seemed to expect him to know where to go, too. When he stood and looked around, feeling helpless—an unfamiliar emotion—someone pointed. He walked the hallway, trying not to think, trying not to blame himself. Other people were as responsible for the imminent destruction of this human being. The killing didn't rest on his shoulders.

But he dropped the rationalizations quickly. He had been telling himself these things for years, especially about this killing, planned meticulously. And still he had done nothing to change it.

He kept walking. In his mind, his feet sounded like drums on the hard floor—*bang, bang, bang*—heralding something momentous, something terrible.

He had wanted people killed before this, had told others to kill. But he had never been there for the act.

Now, back in the present, that house a mere memory, he shook his head, tried to shake away the memories. It did no good for him to remember, no good at all. He told himself this all the time, and yet he kept slipping into these thoughts of the past. They sucked him in whole, so that he was entirely removed from today.

He sat up straighter in his chair now and shook his head again. In the back of his brain he heard a low *bang, bang, bang*—the drums still in the distance.

"Go away," he said softly.

He had been trying to make retributions. But it hadn't made a difference. He kept hearing the sounds, kept trying to wrench himself from that memory. But there was one thing in particular that wouldn't leave him—the words the man had said in the minutes before he died. The feel of those words hitting his ear as he bent over him.

He sat even straighter now. Once again, he shook his head, trying to jar loose the recollection, wondering if the man had known his utterances would stick with him all these years. Was that what he intended? Or were they just more lies falling from the lips of someone who had already caused so much pain?

He tried to believe the latter. He had gone about his business after that day, although he became curious as to whether people saw it in him, whether they saw what he had done. All those years, he walked the streets of Chicago, a city as human as those living inside its borders, and he had wondered.

# 13

When my mother opened her front door, I saw again the change in her.

To say our family had gone through a lot in the past year was an understatement. My mom's first husband—my father, long-presumed dead—had returned to this world and to our city. I had expected this to flatten my mother, as it surely would have in the past. But instead, she was stronger, more self-assured, her eyes more vivid than I had seen since I was eight years old.

But as I stood on her stoop with Theo, I was struck by a void—an empty space of words. I didn't know what to say to her these days. This woman, so alive, didn't seem to be the mom I had always known. So I stepped up and hugged her, wordless. Then I waved a hand behind me and introduced Theo, reminding her she'd met him briefly a few months ago, and she led us through the big front door and into the cool of her home.

The living room was a large space with ivory couches, ivory walls and gentle golden lighting. Soft Oriental rugs guarded over wide-planked, honey-colored wood floors, glossed to a high sheen. By this time of the night, my mother and anyone with her would usually be at the back of the house. The living room faced east and when it got dark in the afternoons, it increased my mother's "melancholy," as I usually called it in my head. But today, the room's lighting blazed brighter. Charlie, my younger brother by a few years, and Spence, my mother's husband, sat at a grouping of couches and chairs around a fireplace tiled in white marble. Inside the fireplace, my mother had placed a flickering candelabra.

I blinked a few times, unused to the sight. I glanced at Charlie, with his brown curly hair that had tinges of red. He gave me a shrug, as if to say, *Don't ask me.*

Spence was a pleasant-looking man with brown hair now streaked with white. It fell longer on the sides to compensate for the balding top. He had on a blue button-down shirt rolled up at the sleeves and sharply pressed khakis.

"Hello, darling girl," he said, standing and giving me a firm embrace. He pulled back and looked at me with his powder-blue eyes, his most striking feature. He appraised my face, and then moved to Theo. "Spencer Calloway," he said, shaking Theo's hand. "What can I find you to drink, son?"

Theo glanced at the coffee table where there was a plethora of food—artisanal cheeses surrounded by grapes and water crackers, prosciutto and paper-thin slices of melon, little croquettes that I knew likely held chicken and sun-dried tomatoes. Next to the food was my mom's glass of white wine, my brother's glass of red wine and a cocktail glass with clear liquid and a large chunk of lime in it.

"What are you having?" Theo asked Spence.

"Helmsley gin with a splash of tonic."

"I'll join you in that."

I smiled, pleased. The truth was, I'd never known Theo to drink gin, but I loved that he was making an effort with my family. I squeezed his hand. When I had dated Sam he'd never joined Spence in a cocktail, and this fact, although meaningless, made me beam at Theo more.

"Good man!" Spence pounded Theo on the back and went toward the kitchen, calling over his shoulder, "Isabel, I'll get you a glass of wine."

Theo looked at my brother, who had stepped up to us. "Good to see you," Theo said.

"Yeah, hey," Charlie said pleasantly. They shook hands and started chatting about Poi Dog Pondering, a local band we'd seen a few months ago when Charlie and Theo first met. Charlie saw live music frequently, and he started rattling off other band names, then Theo told him about a bunch of British bands he followed.

Soon, Spence was back with our drinks, and we were all seated around the fireplace without even one second of that awkward, *So, Theo, tell us what you do for a living* kind of conversation. Instead, it flowed from one thing to another, from Theo's company to Charlie's job as a radio producer—after years of living happily off a worker's comp settlement—to the trial with Maggie. At some point, my mom asked Theo where he was from.

"We moved around a lot for my dad's work," he answered. "California, Oklahoma, New York. Then we moved to Chicago when I was in high school."

"Brothers and sister?" my mom asked.

"Just me."

"And if I could ask, Theo, how old are you?"

I shot my mom a glance. She already knew the answer to that question.

"Twenty-two," Theo said unapologetically.

I'd wondered if my mother would think Theo too young for my thirty years. Sam had been a perfect age, she'd told me once while we were engaged. But now she only said, "So young to own a business."

"Yeah, I went to Stanford for a year," Theo said. "I met my partner, Eric, who was a senior, and we started working on this software. By the end of that year, we were selling it. My dad helped us form the company, and we've been growing strong ever since."

"Where exactly is your office, son?" Spence asked, loving anything that had to do with commercial real estate. That drew Theo and Spence into a new conversation.

We listened for a while, then my mother stood and gestured at me to follow her to the kitchen.

When we were there, she pulled me toward a counter and put her hand on my shoulder. Her blue eyes, more fair than Spence's, were clear and striking. "I like him," she said.

"You do? I'm glad."

She nodded. "For many reasons. And my God, he is gorgeous."

My mother rarely, if ever, commented on men's looks, but I wasn't surprised because nearly everyone mentioned Theo's. When I'd introduced Theo to my former assistant, Q, short for Quentin, he'd commented—crudely, yes, but accurately—that every person in the room, male or female, gay or straight, young or old, wanted to fuck him. Everyone lit up for Theo, got a little red in the face, a little flustered. And the adoration only grew when people realized that he didn't notice those reactions. Theo knew he was good-looking, sure, but he really didn't know *how* good-looking. Or maybe he just didn't like to identify with his hotness. Theo was a working guy, someone who ran his own web-design software company, and I think he liked to be connected to that more than anything.

Now, in my mom's kitchen, I sighed a bit. "Yes, Theo is gorgeous."

"Has your father met him yet?"

"I don't think they need to meet."

My mother's eyes narrowed a little. "He is your father. And he lives in Chicago now."

"When did you start advocating for Dad?"

My mom looked pensive, but her thoughtfulness appeared to have some curiosity about it, as if she were looking inside herself and interested in what she found there. This was different from how she usually did things; usually she shut down, became depressed and we all tiptoed around her.

In the living room we heard Charlie guffaw and Theo saying, "Exactly, dude," laughing with him. A good sound.

"Your father deserves your respect," she said.

"Does he?"

She looked at me, her blue eyes slicing into mine. "Yes." A slight bob of her head. "And you should make some attempt to give him that."

I'd seen my dad occasionally, but it was always awkward. More than awkward. For most of my life, he wasn't around. We had believed him dead, when in truth he'd been working undercover for years. When I'd first seen him again, it was shocking. I was hunted by a faction of the Italian mob that my father had worked most of his life to shut down. As far as I knew, those particular dangers were gone now. But then again I knew that only because my father had told me so. The truth was, I didn't entirely trust my father. Mostly, we made small talk, as if we weren't ready to go into the big things yet. Lately, I'd avoided him. I didn't know where to place him in my life, in my emotions. Avoidance was unlike me, but it had seemed the only workable option as of late.

"I'll ask again," I said to my mom, "when did you start being his advocate?"

The air was prickly as we stared at each other. We were in a minor spar, new territory.

A rueful smile came to my mother's face, accompanied by—*what was it?*—a look of contentment, it seemed. It was that contentment, more than her smile or our spat that shook me somewhat. *So unlike her,* I thought.

"Do you know what it's like to lose your sense of intuition?" my mom asked. Without waiting for my answer, she shook her head. "No, you have always been so good at following your gut instincts."

"That's not true. Last year, when Sam disappeared, I had no idea if my gut instincts were right or wrong. I was confused all the time." I let myself feel the grief of that situation again, the whallop of confusion that had hit me over and over.

"But ultimately you followed your intuition," my mom said. "Your intuition told you Sam was a good man and he had a reason for doing what he did. And you were right."

"I still lost him." *But now he might be back....*

"I know how hard it's been." She gave me a sad face. "Really, Isabel, I'm sorry. I shouldn't have brought this up. This isn't the time for that conversation."

In the other room, Charlie said something about preseason football, followed by the sound of a TV being turned on. My mother shook her head a little. Spence had insisted that they put a TV in the living room. It was hidden behind a painting that would slide away, but my mother still firmly believed TVs had no place in a formal living room. Spence had won.

"What conversation are you talking about?" I asked.

An exhale. "Well, I was just going to say that what I've learned lately, or maybe what I've decided—" she paused, seemed to be regrouping her thoughts "—is that someone can have a gut instinct and struggle with it, just as you did when Sam disappeared. That wasn't easy, but you were smart enough to think of all the options, to play them out, and ultimately you stuck with your intuition."

I thought about it. "Okay." I searched for my intuition about Sam now and found my head empty.

"When your father died so many years ago, I lost that ability. I knew he was alive. I *knew* it in my soul. But everything told me I was wrong. And so I had to shut down that instinct. Because he was dead. Because I buried him. Or so I thought."

Her blue eyes shone bright against the white backdrop of her skin, more animated than I'd seen in years. Maybe ever.

"Over the years I would see him occasionally," she said.

"What do you mean?"

"Here and there, in a crowded street or a busy restaurant, I'd see him like a ghost. And I convinced myself that that's what it was—a ghost. I really came to believe in those things—spirits and such—because there was no other explanation." She gave a brittle laugh. "And because I kept doing that—closing down my instinct—I ended up shutting it down in other areas of my life, too."

I said nothing. I was mesmerized by getting behind the curtain of my mother's mind.

"I drifted wherever life took me," she said, "rarely making decisions, rarely thinking I had any control or any part in this." She waved her hand around her kitchen.

"But you ultimately ended up somewhere you wanted to be, with Spence."

She nodded, gave a little smile. "You're right about that."

Just then Spence came in the room. "Need anything, ladies?"

Classic Spence—always trying to help out, always catering to my mother. And yet when I looked closer, there was something not so classic. I saw he had a nervous edge to him I'd never witnessed.

My mother walked to him and kissed him tenderly on the cheek. She touched his face. "We're fine."

"You're sure?"

"I'm fine," she said. *"Fine."*

Spence didn't look like he believed her. I wasn't sure I did, either.

Spence made a face I couldn't read and left the kitchen.

When he was gone, I looked at my mom. "What's going on?"

"I'm not entirely sure."

"What does your gut instinct tell you?"

My mother laughed, and it was a beautiful sound. But she didn't answer.

# 14

Someone was in her house. Valerie Solara knew it as soon as she stepped through the front door, her arms around a brown grocery sack of baking supplies.

It had made her feel normal, going to the store. She'd decided to make a *torta de chocolate,* the Mexican dessert her father had taught her. It would be a treat for Layla, and baking the *torta* would make her feel normal, too. She wasn't exactly sure what had given her the motivation to bake for the first time in at least a year, but she knew it had something to do with the new lawyer. Izzy, her name was.

At first, when Maggie had told her she wasn't sure if Martin would be back, terror had flooded in. Martin was one of the few men that Valerie had ever trusted in her life, and once the feeling of terror had covered her, it was hard to see or hear around it. Technically, her eyes watched Izzy sparring with a state's attorney about some objection. But the image of Izzy's white suit, her red hair—all that was far away, as if seen through a telescope. The sound was muted, like it was in the next room.

But then Izzy—so charged up and cheerful—had started verbally tussling with a juror, a muscled man in a baseball cap that read *Semper Fi,* and she was distracted away from her panic. Izzy had won, the man was dismissed, and Valerie felt oddly optimistic. Later, Izzy talked to her, really talked to her, suggesting they meet outside the courtroom. And just like that a bolt of something—air? space?—had come in. The optimism flamed.

But now this feeling. The front door opened into a hallway and she moved down it, listening, hearing nothing. She stepped into the small living room, walked past the stairs that led up to the bedrooms and entered the small kitchen. Again she felt it—that sense that someone was there or had been there.

"Layla?" she called loudly into the still of the room.

"Yeah?" she heard her daughter's faraway reply from upstairs.

She felt relieved. "Nothing," she called back.

She expected the feeling to go away then, but instead it returned.

She put the bag on the linoleum counter and looked around. Everything seemed fine, the same as she'd left it—the ugly brown linoleum countertops, the old, yellow fridge—but then she saw it; a black crack running alongside the bottom of the back door.

The door was open, she realized. As if someone had just left. She felt her mouth form an O. Startled and wordless, she made her feet move toward the door. That door was always locked, something Valerie insisted upon, because it led to an alley behind the apartment, a squalid, unlit space where a person could easily hide behind the electric posts or in darkened doorways. The alley had spooked her since they'd moved in, so much so that she'd forbidden Layla to go out there. It was always Valerie who took the garbage to the Dumpster and hurried back into the kitchen.

Yet the door was open. There was no doubt about it. Quickly, she moved to it and opened it farther, ignoring her fear, and looked out at the alley. As usual, she could see little and so she slammed the door shut.

Should she call the cops? But that was the last thing she needed during a murder trial—more problems with the police.

She turned her head. "Layla!" she yelled again.

"Yeah, Mom?" She could tell Layla was at the top of the stairs, closer now.

"Did you go outside in the alley?" she asked, not needing to yell any longer.

"No."

"Was someone here?"

Silence. Then, "No."

Valerie locked the dead bolt. She yanked at the door once, then again to make sure it was locked.

She turned back to the horrid kitchen, so different from the one she had when Brian was alive. She looked at the sack of baking supplies, hoping, somehow, they would calm her. She thought of Izzy. But nothing could soothe her. The panic, the nerves, the questions; they were all there to stay.

# 15

I should be embarrassed to say this—I *should,* I know this—but I was thinking about Sam that night as Theo moved inside me. I didn't like myself for those thoughts, but I let them take me over. I saw the hallway light glinting off Sam's blond head, felt his shorter, muscled legs connecting with mine, each time.

"Set me up with one of Theo's friends," Lucy said. Her blue eyes were wide and excited. It was early in the morning, but Nookies, the diner where we'd met, was already open.

Lucy DeSanto and I had planned this breakfast date a month ago. Originally, we'd planned to be there at nine, after her kids were gone for the day. When I'd texted her to say I couldn't meet because of the trial, she quickly offered to meet me beforehand, promising to be quick. I could tell she needed to talk to me about something. But I hadn't expected this.

"Set you up with Theo's friends?" I said incredulously. "But you're in love with Mayburn."

"I know." The excitement disappeared, a crease appearing on the usually smooth skin between her eyes. "But I don't want to roll into another relationship." She looked out the window. Across Wells Street, people left their brick three flats and headed for the bus, en route to work.

Lucy and John Mayburn, the private investigator I sometimes worked for, had fallen for each other when he'd been hired to conduct surveillance on her husband, Michael. At first, it was a crush on Mayburn's part, spent from afar. But when Michael was charged with money laundering and sent to a federal prison, Mayburn and Lucy had met and begun to date. Then Michael got out on bail, causing Lucy to feel she should give their relationship another shot, both for her and her kids. That shot had failed, and recently, Michael was returned to prison when new evidence was received, and he was charged with additional crimes. Lucy and Michael's relationship was finally over and it had seemed a happy ending was in store for Mayburn and Lucy.

The other happy ending was Lucy and me. When Mayburn was watching her husband, he had asked me to befriend her as part of the case, but we really did become friends.

"Here's the thing," Lucy said. "I *think* I love John, but I can't just move from a ten-year marriage right into another serious relationship."

I didn't say that I understood, that I had wondered if it was wise for me to have moved from something with Sam right into something with Theo, something that felt very real. I didn't mention Sam's offer to return to my life. I felt reluctant to discuss it at length with anyone before I really knew why it was happening or how I felt about it. I'd expected him to call or text me after I'd stalked out of the restaurant the night before. But so far my phone, and Sam, had been silent.

"You know John wants a serious relationship," Lucy said.

I nodded. "He wants to be a stepdad to your kids. A very involved one."

That desire of Mayburn's was unlike what I had known of him before. I'd met him when I worked at the law firm of Baltimore & Brown, which often hired him to conduct private investigations—digging up info on corporations or plaintiffs who found themselves opposing our clients. When Sam disappeared, I'd turned to Mayburn for help. When he was too expensive he'd proposed a tit-for-tat relationship. I would work for him when he needed a woman to conduct surveillance work a man simply couldn't do.

When I said yes to his offer, I assumed Mayburn was a straightforward, by-the-books investigator. He had nondescript looks—brown hair, brown eyes, medium build, a forty-year-old face that looked younger. Mayburn had always said that those vague looks had helped him in his line of work, helped him to stay under the radar. As we worked more closely together, I discovered Mayburn was a sarcastic, Aston-Martin–driving renegade. But now we were friends, and I realized that at his core, he was a softie. At least when it came to Lucy DeSanto.

"John would be a great stepdad," Lucy said, "but I can't do that to the kids. Michael is the only dad they know. I can't push another man into their life right when their father has been yanked out."

"So why would you want to date one of Theo's friends?"

"That's exactly it—I don't want to date! So don't even fix me up exactly, just take me out with a bunch of young guys who want to drink and flirt."

"You want to drink and flirt?"

"Yes. I don't want to be part of a couple. I've been part of a couple for more than a decade." She nodded at me pointedly. "I want to do what you're doing."

"What *am* I doing? Is it embarrassing that I'm dating

someone younger than me and so different than me?"
*Should I go back to Sam?*

Lucy shook her head fast. "No, I think it's exciting and
fun. And that's what I want." Her eyes dropped. "Because
my life is not going to be fun and exciting for a while. I'm
going to have to divorce Michael, then deal with the kids
while he's in jail waiting for a trial, and then help them
deal with the outcome of the trial, and then I'm going to
have to decide if I stay in Chicago."

"But Mayburn is here."

"I know." A sad cast appeared on her face. "And that's
why I can't get too deeply involved with him right now.
I'm not ready and I don't know when or if I will be." She
blinked, as if batting away tears. She cleared her throat,
then her eyes focused on mine. "Can I ask you a legal
question? How long will it take until Michael's case goes
to trial?"

"A federal indictment having to do with organized
crime? That's a biggie. It could take a year or two, easy."

The sad cast returned.

"Hey," I said, "did you ever learn what evidence sent
Michael back to prison?"

She shook her head. "Since I've told him I want a divorce, he doesn't tell me anything. All I know is that the
feds received some kind of anonymous information that
linked him to that group from Italy who were trying to
establish themselves in the U.S."

"The Camorra."

"Yeah." She ran her fingers across her forehead, as
if trying to rub away some thought. "I still can't believe
that the man I married got involved with any of that. It's
so hard to wrap my head around, and I don't know what
to say to the kids…."

I didn't know what to say, either. The Camorra was

the group my father had spent much of his life trying to shut down. It was what had taken him away from us. But Lucy didn't know all that.

Lucy looked at me. "Don't you see why I want to go out with Theo's friends? I want to be with people who are younger. I want to go backward."

*Was that what I was doing with Theo? A better question—was that what I'd be doing with Sam? Going backward?*

"Theo and I are supposed to go out tomorrow night with his friends," I said. "But I have to warn you—a couple of them aren't the brightest tools in the shed. Once I saw one of them wearing a T-shirt that said, Things are smaller than they appear." I threw my hands up. "What does that mean? That his penis is smaller than it seems?"

Lucy laughed. "Was he cute?"

I nodded grudgingly.

"Great! This is exactly what I want. Cute, young and not-so-smart."

I shrugged. "Tomorrow night at nine."

# 16

When I got to the courtroom, Maggie was raring to go. I could see that even through the Plexiglas wall. Her cheeks were tinged pink, the way they got when she was excited.

I pushed open the door with the lock and walked to our table. "You're ready?"

"Oh, yeah." She grinned.

"You look a little revved up."

"I found out Bernard is coming into town next week to sub with the orchestra." Maggie actually clapped her hands.

Maggie and I met Bernard in Italy in June. He was a French horn player with the Seattle Symphony. And he was also a huge, huge Filipino guy, which was sort of funny when you paired him with little, golden-haired Maggie. But they had become a couple, despite their odd appearance together. The minute we'd returned to the U.S., she was on the phone with him a few times a day, emailing about ten times a day and texting even more.

"That's fantastic!" I said.

"I know. My grandfather is going to flip. He loves the CSO."

She went quiet. We both thought of Martin.

"Where is he?" I asked.

The grin fled her face. "I went to his house this morning, and he's not doing well. He's just kind of…fading. I don't know how else to put it."

"Your grandmother must be worried."

"She is. I am, too, but I told him we could handle the openings and the first witnesses."

"We can." I wanted to keep up her spirits, so I changed the topic and told her I'd seen Sam after court yesterday and how I'd stormed from the restaurant.

"Interesting," Maggie said. "But that doesn't really help you figure anything out, does it?"

I gave her an irritated look. "No." I changed the topic again. "Who's handling our exhibits and graphics?"

Now Maggie gave me an annoyed glance. "What do you mean? I'm handling the exhibits. Or *we* are now. And we don't have any graphics. I've got some blowups of a couple photos, but nothing else."

"Holy mother of Elvis."

Maggie looked even more annoyed. "You know, that stop-swearing thing of yours has got to go. Those curse word replacements are ludicrous, and you always end up swearing anyway to explain it. Just *say* it."

"Fine. *Holy shit,* are you serious?" When I was at Baltimore & Brown, if I was on trial, I not only had my assistant, Q, to handle the exhibits and the graphics, I usually had command of one or two paralegals, as well.

"Yeah, I'm serious," Maggie said.

"Do you have records from this case scanned into your computer?"

"Yeah."

"Any exhibits in your laptop?"

"Yeah."

"Then you should be putting them on a screen or on

the wall. Everyone is used to looking at a TV or a computer. They can't just listen anymore. You've got to show the jurors something."

Maggie chewed her lip. "I know one of the attorneys in my office has the equipment for all that, but he's a personal injury lawyer. We never use that kind of stuff."

I shook my head. "You criminal lawyers are so weird." I took my cell phone out of my bag. "I'll call Q to do it."

She shook her head. "No, no. I just brought you in on this case. I can't add anyone else. It will throw me off. Plus, we're in a small courtroom, and there aren't many exhibits needed right now."

I sighed. "Keep it in mind."

"Done."

I looked around the courtroom again and saw more people filing into the gallery. "Where are Amanda's family members?"

Maggie jutted her chin toward the right side of the spectator benches. "That's the husband, Zavy."

I followed her gaze. I saw a handsome man, mid-fortyish, I guessed, but he looked younger. He wore a navy blazer over a white shirt. His hair was blond-brown and thick. His face bore slight creases around the eyes and mouth, but he was a type of man on whom facial lines looked handsome. From what I could see, he was in shape, probably a weekend athlete. If Valerie had wanted him for her own, I supposed I could understand why.

As I looked at him, Zavy raised his head and gazed through the glass to the front of the courtroom. He stared at the state attorneys' table, at the lawyers there. It seemed to me as if he was waiting for them to glance at him, to give him some direction or ask him questions. He looked sad, helpless.

"Shouldn't he sit at the counsel's table?" I asked Maggie.

She shook her head.

"But he's the victim of the crime." I saw the look Maggie shot me. "*Alleged* crime."

"He's the victim's spouse, not the victim," Maggie said. "And even if he were the victim, he's not a party to the lawsuit. The state is. Technically, the case has nothing to do with him."

In a civil trial, Zavy would be sitting with the attorneys. He would be an integral part of the case. I felt a wave of pity for the guy. His wife had died and yet the case didn't have anything to do with him? "I'm going to say hello and introduce myself."

Maggie looked startled. "Why?"

"Because I think it would be polite. It seems the right thing to do."

"I don't think Zavy Miller wants to hang out with us."

"I'm not going to hang out with him. I just think civility demands an introduction."

"The state's attorneys won't like it. He's their witness."

"But he's not their client. Like you said, he's not a party. And anyone can talk to lay witnesses."

Maggie's face scrunched in concentration.

"What?" I said in response to her expression.

"I'm trying to think of what my grandfather would say." She looked around the courtroom, her eyes stopping on the state's attorneys and then Zavy Miller. When she looked back at me, she was grinning. "I think he'd say go ahead. You're an adult and a lawyer, and you should do what you think is ethically right." She laughed quietly.

"I also think he'd say go ahead and piss off the state's attorneys. It'll throw them off their game."

"Great." I turned, pushed open the Plexiglas door and stepped into the gallery.

More people had gathered now for the opening arguments and all eyes went to me. Zavy Miller looked at me expectantly, too.

I stepped into the pew where he sat and took a seat, making sure to be a respectful distance away from him. "Mr. Miller," I said, my voice low, "I want to introduce myself. I'm Izzy McNeil. I'll be representing Valerie Solara, along with the Bristols."

I held out my hand to him. He looked at it, then back up at me.

I waited for a look of hatred or maybe revulsion. But he only nodded, as if he respected the gesture. He stuck out his hand. Our shake was firm, friendly even.

Out of the corner of my eye, I saw the state's attorneys staring at us. Ellie was giving Tania a shove on the arm, pointing to me. Tania headed for the Plexiglas door.

"Mr. Miller," I said, "I don't know if this will make sense, but I just wanted to tell you I hope that whatever is supposed to happen here, whatever is right...well, I hope that happens."

He nodded. Sadness crossed his face and he swallowed, as if gulping something down. "Thank you. That's very kind."

I stood and almost ran into Tania, who had a stern look on her face. "Excuse me," I said, trying to move around her.

But Tania didn't move. "Everything okay?" she said to Zavy.

He gave a simple nod.

"Mr. Miller," she said, "I'm sorry but you're going to

have to step out of the courtroom until we call you as a witness. After that you can stay. I know that's difficult, but those are the court rules."

"That's fine." Zavy Miller stood. "Nice to meet you," he said to me with a kind smile.

"Likewise."

When he was gone, Tania leaned in and whispered to me, "Ellie wants you to know that we looked into your background last night."

"Excuse me?" I pulled away.

"Your background." As if that explained everything.

"Okay."

"You're not a criminal defense lawyer."

"Just a lawyer," I said with an easy tone. I shifted toward her, sure she would move now, but again she didn't budge.

"Things are different here than they are at the Daley Center." She said *Daley Center* with a mocking air, as if she were saying, *Things are different here than they are at that day care center.*

Normally, I took the high road. But not when I was on trial. "Yeah," I said, "the difference is that attorneys there intimidate with talent."

*Zing.* Tania actually took a step back, and I moved around her. As I pushed through the Plexiglas wall, Ellie Whelan was glaring at me.

I smiled in return and went to the defense table. "See," I said to Maggie, "that wasn't so bad."

# 17

"For most of us, best friends are safe havens. Best friends provide a place where we can let ourselves be who we really are, where we are supported, where we are loved." Ellie Whelan paused, as if having a hard time with her words. "But this woman…" She turned and pointed at Valerie. "This woman is pure poison. For her friendship was merely a disposable relationship where she could shop for a new husband. And kill any obstacles. Any at all."

Valerie sat on the other side of Maggie, but even from that distance I heard her whimper. Maggie put her hand on Valerie's forearm for a brief second. I saw a couple of jurors notice the movement.

Ellie Whelan patrolled the courtroom, moving back and forth in front of the jury, often pointing at Valerie and combining the gesture with damning words. She told the jury that Valerie and Amanda were best friends, or at least Valerie let Amanda think that. She told them that they would hear all about the friendship from another best friend, Bridget. They would hear how Bridget and Amanda and Amanda's husband, Zavy, had supported Valerie after her own husband, Brian, died years ago. They'd become her second family.

"Because for Bridget and Xavier, and especially for Amanda, friendship meant something," Ellie said.

She gestured toward Tania, who strode forward with a few poster-size exhibits. Tania placed them on an easel and went back to their table.

"Friendship and family," Ellie said. "That's what was important to Amanda Miller."

She turned the first exhibit to face the jury. "This was Amanda Miller."

I stood and walked to a side wall, where I could see a photo of a lovely brunette with green eyes and a big smile.

"You will hear from Amanda's husband about the importance of friendship to Amanda Miller. He will tell you how much she loved her two girls, Tessa and Britney." Ellie put the first exhibit on the floor, revealing a blown-up photo of Amanda and two toothy, gorgeous girls. "Xavier will tell you how the girls are now motherless. He will tell you they are having a very, very hard time of it. And all because of…" She didn't have to say her name this time; she just turned and pointed toward Valerie.

From my vantage point at the wall, I could see the jury from the side. I was standing not just to see the photos, but also to try and determine the jury's reaction to the state's opening. For now, they were calm and attentive. But if I was looking for a reaction, I was about to get it.

"Here," Ellie said, beginning to slowly remove the photo of Amanda's kids, "is Amanda Miller on the day she died."

As the next blown-up photo was revealed, the jury gasped.

I couldn't help it—I winced. Maggie shot me a dirty look from across the courtroom, and I composed my face.

The photo was a "death shot." Amanda, naked on a stainless-steel counter, a sheet draped across her lower half, her skin white as pearl, her mouth open, rigor mortis making her neck look stretched and rigid, like she was screaming into eternity.

I couldn't take my eyes away from the photo. Out of my peripheral vision, I could tell that the jurors couldn't, either. *That poor woman,* I heard one say. *Horrible,* murmured another.

"Quiet, please," the judge said.

I glanced at Valerie. Had she killed Amanda? Had she done that to her friend? And if she had, constitutional rights or no, what was I doing representing her?

The courtroom felt chilly suddenly, as if sinister air had entered through a back door and wound its way through the place.

"You will hear from the coroner who examined Amanda's body after her death, and you will hear how he came to the diagnosis of death by poisoning." Ellie took a step away from the photo, letting the image of the dead woman speak volumes to the jury. "From Bridget, you will hear that just weeks before Amanda's death, Valerie asked her about poisons, which Bridget had researched as part of a novel she was writing. And you will hear Xavier Miller tell you about the day…" A heavy pause. "About the day he came home from work and saw Valerie put something crushed, something *blue,* into the food she was cooking. She said it was an herb. It was not. It was a drug that, given at high doses, acted as a poison, and that poison would kill Amanda Miller before the day was done."

Another pause to let all the information settle.

"Why would Valerie want to kill her 'best friend'?"

Ellie asked the jury. "I'll tell you why. Because she was husband hunting."

There seemed to be no more exhibits forthcoming, so I went and took my seat again next to Maggie.

Ellie continued. Brian, she told the jury, was Valerie's husband, although not the father of her daughter. He had died of Lou Gehrig's disease. He was only forty-eight at the time, Ellie said, which was strange because the disease didn't usually exhibit itself until people were over fifty.

I looked at Maggie. "Objection," I whispered. I saw Valerie's pained face on the other side of her. I dropped my voice even further. "Are they trying to imply she killed her husband?"

Maggie frowned at Ellie. "We already dealt with this in motions before the case started," she said under her breath. "If she says one more word…"

But sure enough, Ellie moved on, just short of drawing an objection. She told the jury how Amanda and Xavier had helped Valerie care for Brian. She told them that Valerie had fallen for Xavier during that time and shortly after had tried to seduce him.

A number of the jurors furrowed their brows and openly appraised Valerie.

I glanced at her. She seemed to nearly tremble in her black dress, but she didn't blink, didn't flinch.

Ellie Whelan was nearing the close of her argument. "At the end of this trial," Ellie said, "I will have an opportunity to get in front of you again, and at that time, I will ask you to do the only thing that justice will allow. Find Valerie Solara—" again she pointed at our client "—guilty of first-degree murder."

Maggie popped up from her seat even before Ellie had found hers. She waited for a minute, then when Ellie was in her chair, looked at the judge. "Your Honor, I'd request that the state remove their exhibits."

"Granted." The judge nodded at Ellie Whelan. "Counsel?"

I saw Maggie cover a small smile. Ellie had tried to leave the autopsy photo in front of the jury, a good move, but Maggie had countered it, not just taking it down, which she could have done, but getting the judge to make the state do it after Ellie had taken a seat.

Ellie shot an annoyed look at Tania Castle, who jumped to her feet and removed the photos.

Maggie introduced herself quickly to the jurors, then said, "Boy, that was a good story, wasn't it?" She nodded. "Kind of like watching a soap opera, am I right? All that stuff about coveting someone else's husband, about poisoning someone? That's really interesting, huh?" She nodded as if to concede the point. "But that's *all* that was—a really interesting story. A story concocted by the state in order to lay blame for the tragic death of Amanda Miller. But this woman—" she moved behind Valerie and placed a hand on her shoulder "—is not to blame."

She took her hand off Valerie's shoulder and went to a podium, placing her notes on it and crossing her arms. "And do you know what? The state can't just spin a good story. They have to prove that Valerie Solara was guilty beyond a reasonable doubt." She intoned again, *"Beyond a reasonable doubt."*

Maggie looked at the state's table for an uncomfortable, quiet second, then back at the jury. "But how are they going to do that? They told you you'd hear from Mr. Miller about some…what did they call it? A seduction. They told you you'd hear from other witnesses. But isn't it interesting that they are accusing Valerie Solara of planting poison in her friend's food…and yet they *didn't* tell you that you would hear any evidence of Ms. Solara buying the medication. You know why?"

The jury waited for the answer.

"Because there isn't any evidence of her acquiring it. None. They couldn't find any link between Valerie and the drug that killed Mrs. Miller. That's interesting, don't you think?" She huffed out loud, as if expelling disbelief.

"And they want to talk about friendship? Well, let's talk about it." She put a blown-up photo of three women on the easel.

"These women met fifteen years ago at a gym here in the city. Amanda Miller was newly married to her first husband. Valerie was a single mom. Her daughter, Layla, who is nineteen now, was just four. And Bridget was a surgical nurse. Usually, Amanda was busy with charitable events, Valerie was busy being a mom and Bridget was always working. Usually, they wouldn't have had time to make new friends. But on that one day, they all had time for one reason or another. After they met at a gym, they went to a restaurant nearby to talk. It was a Tuesday. And for nearly every other Tuesday after that, up until the time Amanda Miller died, these women met to share their lives. They were immediate friends. They were like sisters. There was no one who supported Amanda more than Valerie and Bridget and vice versa. That continued to the day she died.

"You will hear from witness after witness who will tell you how close these women were. You will hear Amanda's husband, Xavier, tell you that himself. He will tell you that he never would have suspected Valerie Solara of wanting to kill her friend. Her *best* friend. Their other best friend Bridget will tell you the same thing. They will all tell you that Valerie wasn't like that. She wasn't jealous, she wasn't violent, she couldn't hurt anyone. You will hear this over and over. Because it's true."

Maggie picked up her notes and reviewed them. She explained that Valerie Solara didn't have to put on any evidence herself. She didn't have to prove anything at all.

Maggie stopped, dead center of the jury. "A woman died. By all accounts, a lovely woman, a good mom. When someone like that dies, we all want someone to pay for it. But the *right* person must pay for it. We cannot allow them—" she turned and pointed at the state's attorneys "—to rush to judgment and pile up inconsequential tidbits to make it appear they have the person who committed this when they *do not*. That's not how the American criminal justice system works. You are the upholders of that system. Your job is large. Your responsibility is massive." She looked up and down the row of jurors. "Do it," she said. "Do your job."

# 18

A mother's words can soothe. But just as easily they can sting.

Recently, I had been hearing my mother's words about my father, about how I owed him respect, how I should make "some attempt" to give him that. They had hurt at first, but then the sting wore off. Yet they kept winding through my head, then into my heart, creating a slow-building guilt that, once it had taken hold, could not be released without me doing what she wanted me to. What I needed to do, I suppose.

And although I still hadn't spoken to him, Sam's offer to cancel his wedding—his ultimatum, if I was honest—was reverberating through me. I needed my dad's cold, unflinching analysis.

As soon as court was over for the day, I called my father.

He answered on the first ring, as if he'd been waiting all day or maybe all month, for this call. I told him that I wanted to see him. I thought about asking him to have dinner, but none of my usual places, the ones where I might step out on a Friday, seemed right. Twin Anchors, Marge's, Benchmark—they all seemed too casual, places to meet a friend.

"Can I stop by your place?" I asked.

There was no pause before he said yes.

My father lived in a nondescript midrise building on Clark Street, just south of North Avenue. Although I'd known the location of his building, it wasn't until I pushed through the revolving glass doors that I realized that it was nearly equidistant between my mother's house and my own. Did that mean something? As always with my father, I had no idea.

Likewise, I didn't know what to expect from my father's apartment, but I sensed it would be worldly and interesting, something like my father himself or the person I thought he was.

But when I got there, I saw the apartment was a place for someone transient, a place where no one would live for long.

The gun-metal-gray couch was dark enough to hide any stains and looked like the type rented from one of the furniture places on Milwaukee Avenue. To the left was a reading chair that had once, maybe, been interesting. But now the wood arms were nicked and scarred, the formerly ivory paint across the top yellowed. My guess was that it was the fruits of Dumpster-diving or a visit to a secondhand store. A squat old table, too low, sat in front of the couch and chair.

The living room held little else but a small desk in the corner, which faced the wall. If the apartment had been mine, I would have put the desk near the window, in order to look outside and get a glimpse of the world. But my father was different from me. Maybe he didn't need to see anything at all.

We stood at the threshold of the room, my father quiet, letting me study it. I looked at him then. It still startled me to see him, a handsome man in his late fifties, instead of the younger version of him, forever memorialized in my brain. His wavy hair was now salt-and-pepper-gray instead of chestnut-brown like Charlie's. He was still trim, but he was more refined than when he was younger. After living in Italy, he dressed like an Italian—slim-cut linen trousers, an expensive white shirt, open at the collar, a beautiful gold watch. His eyes were still the same green, still intensely focused through the copper glasses he'd always worn. But there was rarely life in those eyes.

He gestured to the couch. "Have a seat."

I sat. The couch was stiff. I shifted back and forth, trying to get comfortable. I now faced the open kitchen, which held nothing on the counters save an espresso machine.

My father followed my eyes and gestured at it. "Can I make you some espresso?"

I shook my head. "No, thanks. I drink tea."

"That's right. Green tea."

I couldn't remember if I'd ever told him that or if it was one of the things he'd learned from watching me. I was just coming to understand how much he'd observed me, on and off, for most of my life.

"Mom told me she used to see you sometimes," I said.

If he was surprised by the shift in topic, he didn't show it. He said nothing.

"That must have been intentional," I said.

"It was. But it was also a failure, a weakness."

Now neither of us said anything.

"I'd give you a tour—" he gave a little polite laugh that sounded unlike him "—but it's just this room and the bedroom." He gestured toward a short hallway.

"That's okay."

The apartment made me profoundly sad. My father had lived an incredible life—incredibly tragic, incredibly exciting. This empty shell of an apartment didn't fit him.

He seemed to sense my thoughts. "I'm just here until I decide…"

I nodded. I understood what he was saying—until he decided what to do with himself.

"Let me get you some water."

I watched him go into his kitchen and open and close cabinet doors as if unsure where the glasses were. Or if he even owned them.

Finally, he found one made of orange plastic. "This is all I have," he said over his shoulder in an embarrassed tone.

"Anything is fine."

I heard him opening some drawers. When he came back with the water, he put it on the table, then placed two other items there.

I looked closer. My old cell phone and my old ID.

"Those were in the building. The one we were in with Aunt Elena." *The one that exploded.*

There had been an explosion in Chicago earlier that summer, and my Aunt Elena, my dad's sister, had been one of the last people in the building that was blown to smithereens. Long story. Really long story. My dad had told me he got word that she was uninjured and in Italy. The body found after the explosion was male, likely either Dez Romano, the boss of Michael DeSanto, or the guy who worked for him. Dez was a gangster I'd gotten mixed up with thanks to a gig from John Mayburn. Dez had once made it clear he'd wanted to kill me, and so although *I'd* never wanted anyone dead before, there was a part of me that hoped that he was enjoying himself in gangster heaven. But it was more than likely that the body was that of Dez's lackey. I tried not to think about the fact that Dez could still be out there.

My father's head bobbed in a single nod toward the items on the table. "I retrieved them before we got out."

"You're just giving them to me now?" I made an irritated sound. "Do you know what a pain in the ass it was to spend half a day at the DMV and the other half at the cell phone store?"

Without pausing, without expression, he said, "Do you know what a pain in the ass it would have been if the police learned you were there that day and confiscated them as evidence? Or if they had tracked a call from your phone and then you'd used it again?"

"That's why you told me to get a new phone number."

He nodded.

I looked at the phone and ID. So he'd been protecting me. "Thanks."

Again, he said nothing.

I put the cell phone and ID in my purse. "So…" I looked around. "It must be strange to be so out in the open now. I mean, since you were almost—" what was the word? "—invisible before. Mostly."

I regretted it as soon as I saw the strange expression on his face.

"I don't mean that in any critical kind of way," I said quickly. "I guess I was just thinking about it because Mom and I were talking and…" I shrugged. "I'm just wondering how you're doing."

My father looked around his new apartment, then back at me. "I still feel invisible."

I felt the weight of his words, and it nearly flattened me. "What do you mean?"

"I'm used to either blending into the background or starting over. But this is different. This feeling I have, it's more about Chicago."

I scrunched my face in confusion.

"Chicago is one of those towns," he said. "One where you need to know people. More than any town I've ever seen, even in Italy. You Chicagoans are part of your city. Either you have family here or your friends become your family, and you all seem to move forward together."

The statement was left unsaid—*and I have neither friends nor family.*

"Do you know the best thing about Chicago?" I asked.

He shook his head no, looked hungry for my response.

"The best thing is that people *want* more friends and more family. They want to grow. They want the city to grow. They're not trying to keep people out."

My father frowned. "I don't know if that's true."

"It is. For the most part. People want to know interesting people. They want others to be a part of their web. It's not exclusive."

He crossed his arms. "So what would I do to join a web?"

*Was he asking me personally because he wanted to know my world and Charlie's? Or was he just looking for advice about making it in the city?* The answer to either, I figured, was the same. "It's up to you to stick your foot out and stop a couple of people from walking by."

"My whole life, I have tried very, very hard to blend. I kept myself closed off."

I saw how uncomfortable his admission made him and I knew then we were talking about more than the move to Chicago.

I nodded. "I know. But other people have done that,

too. Maybe not in the way you have, but they've closed themselves off just the same. And they've gotten past it. Maybe this is your challenge now. I'm sure it's one you can handle."

"When did you get so wise?"

"Oh, I've got tons of this stuff. I just need to apply it to myself now."

I thought about asking him about Sam, but now that I knew my father was having his own struggles, it seemed somehow wrong.

He smiled with one corner of his mouth then. "I think you're doing fine, Izzy."

I shifted on the stiff couch while my father just sat there, looking contemplative and sad. I wished I could help him become less invisible.

And then I had an idea.

I reached for my bag and took out the notes that Detective Vaughn had made in Valerie's case. "I have to cross-examine a detective on Monday. I'm helping Maggie on a murder trial..." My words died off when I saw recognition in his face. "You already know all of this."

He gave a slight bow of his head.

"*How* do you know this? I didn't even know I was trying this case until yesterday."

He didn't look sheepish or embarrassed. He said nothing.

I felt a flicker of anger. I thought about telling him that I no longer needed him to follow me around, to see if I was okay. I thought about telling him that he should be a normal person. But the anger fizzed when I realized he was looking after me in the only way he knew how. And really, when I thought about it, was it so bad to have someone looking over my shoulder?

When I was younger, zipping through the city on

my Vespa, never bothering with a helmet, I felt I hadn't needed protection. When I was in a relationship with Sam, I hadn't felt any desire for that, either. But when I learned Sam was going strong with Alyssa, I had suddenly liked the idea of someone else keeping an eye on me.

Thinking of Sam, I lifted my current cell phone from my purse and glanced at it. Still nothing. A flash of annoyance lit up my brain. How could he walk back into my life and then not call or text me? It was true I'd walked out on him, but still…

My dad cleared his throat. I looked at him, at his woeful expression, and the urge to help him feel less invisible returned. "Would you review these records for me?" I held out the Chicago Police Department notes for the Amanda Miller murder. "They're written by the detective I'm crossing on Monday."

"Of course." His expression turned hopeful. "What do you want me to look for?"

"Anything, basically. Any inconsistencies, anything lacking."

"Of course."

I handed him the records. "Thanks. I guess I can leave those with you, and I'll get another copy from Maggie."

He looked momentarily confused. "I just need a few minutes."

"What do you mean? You only need a few minutes to analyze the records of a Chicago homicide detective?"

"Probably less than that." His face was flat. He wasn't trying to be funny or impressive.

"Oh. Okay." I stood. "Can I use your restroom while you look those over?"

He nodded, waved at the hallway.

In the bathroom, I ran the water, wanting some kind of buffer in the quiet apartment. I used the toilet, then washed my hands. I couldn't help it then. Trying to be silent, I opened the medicine cabinet. On a slightly rusted metal shelf was a can of shaving cream, an expensive-looking chrome razor, deodorant, a wood-handled brush and nail clippers. I had more toiletries in my purse than my father had in his whole apartment.

Back in the living room, my father was still in the chair, the notes in his hand. As I came into the room, he put them on his lap. He said nothing. Although I was somewhat used to his silences, I wondered if his quiet was because he knew I'd been snooping in the bathroom.

I decided I could be just as unreadable. I sat and pointed at the notes. "Got anything?"

He smiled, and nodded.

# 19

Valerie walked around her lifeless apartment. It felt that way, she supposed, because she herself had grown more and more like that, as if she were in a walking coma, getting ready for her mind to shut down. Because prison seemed real. Imminent. And the only way she could imagine surviving that was to become someone else and put away the person she was now.

She walked into the kitchen and turned on one small light. Although she had enjoyed wine before, in her other life, she had not had a glass of wine or a cocktail for months now. She had no taste for it, had little taste for anything. But now there was a pinprick of light in the flat existence in which she had been living. It was the light of possibility.

The reason for the slice of optimism was Izzy McNeil. She completely trusted the Bristols, but neither Martin nor Maggie had wanted the whole truth. She was fine not to give it. The whole truth would cause so many more problems. But still. But still, it cheered her somehow that Izzy wanted to know, wanted to understand. She had told Valerie again today—*I want to believe you.*

Valerie opened the door of the refrigerator, the light from inside making a bold entrance into the dimly lit kitchen. Although the sun still shone outside, it was always dark in her home these days. She had gotten used to closing all of the blinds and drapes to keep herself away from the curious eyes of her watching neighbors.

The refrigerator was old and mustard-colored. It had been here when she'd rented the West Side apartment after Brian died. Despite her hopes that she would come into some kind of salary stream, that she would find her calling and be able to replace the appliances, maybe even move back to the Gold Coast near Bridget and Amanda, such a bounty had never happened.

Her refrigerator, as well as her cupboards, was only spottily inhabited, aside from the supplies she'd bought the other night for the chocolate *torta*—the one she'd never made. Neither she nor Layla was particularly interested in grocery shopping lately. Or food. But she knew she should eat. She looked at the random contents of the fridge—ketchup, eggs, a slightly shriveled pear, a bottle of grapefruit juice, ground flax seed, a folded piece of foil with an old tortilla in it, half a carton of graying mushrooms, a few teaspoons of milk in the bottom of a carton, and a container of leftovers Layla must have brought home from a restaurant. She opened it—half-eaten strip steak. Where had Layla gone and ordered this? She looked at it a moment longer, then put it on the counter.

*Amanda.*

*Amanda.*

*Amanda.*

Valerie tried to keep her friend at bay, tried not to let the memory ravage her. But everything led her back to Amanda. To Bridget. Her life had been led with them, next to them, for so long.

She knew she had to eat. She let herself think of

Amanda then, tried not to let the memory cut her. What would Amanda do?

Like her, Amanda had loved to cook. She was always reading recipe magazines, taking classes at the Chopping Block or asking Valerie to teach her one of the Mexican dishes she had learned from her father.

If Amanda had been standing here at her fridge, what would she do, Valerie asked herself?

She permitted herself a short laugh. Amanda, whom they often called "Demanda" because she always knew what she wanted, would put her hand on her hip and consider the food and the leftovers. She would be wearing designer jeans, a casual shirt and lots of the blingy accessories she loved and pulled off with aplomb. She would have said something like, "Don't you have any potatoes? What about some fresh herbs?" Then she would have turned around before Valerie even answered and said, "Never mind."

And then what would she have done?

Valerie looked at the contents of the refrigerator again and concentrated in a way she knew Amanda would have. She scanned all the random bits, putting them together in different ways.

She took out the tortilla, and steamed it back to life. She cracked open a couple of eggs and whipped them with the milk, then scrambled them. She sliced the strip steak into thin ribbons and sautéed them with the mushrooms and garlic. Then she put everything in the tortilla, wrapped it tight the way her father had taught her, dug some salsa from the back of her refrigerator and sat down with her steak-and-egg burrito.

"Thanks, Manny," she said out loud to the silent house. "Manny" was the other nickname Amanda had. One only

Valerie used. She couldn't even remember how it had started.

As Valerie took her first bite, she heard the front door open and footsteps in the hallway. She felt herself smile and her face open up, as only one thing could make her do so these days. "Hello, Layla."

Her coltish, beautiful daughter smiled as she entered the kitchen, then came forward and kissed her on the cheek. Layla slid her tall frame into a chair.

"How are you doing, little one?" Valerie asked, even though Layla wasn't little anymore. Far from it.

Layla looked worried. She *always* looks worried now. How horrible for her child to have to agonize about her. It was what Valerie had hoped to avoid as a mom. But there was no way around it, and the truth was that she appreciated the concern. She had learned to relax around her daughter, to let Layla see her frailties. They had been through so much.

Layla didn't answer the question. "How was today?" Layla asked.

Layla had three classes that day at DePaul, and although she'd been in court every other day of the trial, Valerie had refused to let her miss school.

"Today…" Valerie dialed her mind back, saw Maggie Bristol facing the courtroom. She liked the spitfire spirit of that girl. Then she saw Izzy McNeil and that tiny pinpoint of light got a little bigger. She wanted to talk to her, to tell her the truth.

But then she remembered that even if she told the truth, even if Izzy believed her, she couldn't prove it. And the truth was…well, the truth was something she could not let anyone know.

# 20

I called Mayburn as soon as I awoke on Saturday morning. "Meet me for breakfast?"

Theo was still asleep. I heard him mutter a soft, "No, stay here," felt him slide across the bed, weaving his arm around my waist. His body felt warm as it cupped mine. He angled himself so we were puzzle pieces that fit perfectly. Had Sam and I ever felt like this?

"Yeah, fine," I heard Mayburn say. "Where?"

Theo pushed himself against my back. I felt all of him now, felt him growing hard. I couldn't think. "You decide," I said into the phone.

"Salt & Pepper Diner. On Lincoln. Half an hour?"

Theo's lean, muscled body curled tighter around me. He lifted my hair and began to kiss the back of my neck.

"An hour," I said. Theo pushed his pelvis into mine and began to nudge my legs open. "An hour and a half," I said.

Salt & Pepper Diner looked like Chicago in the 1950s—red leather booths and a shiny silver counter where you could sit and watch men in white paper hats cooking pancakes.

After my time with Theo, I was famished. "I'll have the Popeye omelet," I said to the waitress, handing her my menu.

"Toast or grits?"

They sounded delicious. "Both."

Mayburn handed over his menu. "Scrambled eggs. Egg whites only, please."

"Toast or grits?"

"Neither."

"Fruit?" the waitress offered.

He shook his head silently.

"Sliced tomato?"

He didn't even look at her. Just shook his head again.

I gave him a once-over. He was thinner than usual. His brown hair, which he'd been wearing stylishly messed over the last year, was hidden under a Blackhawks baseball cap. The dark blue jeans and the polo shirt he wore hung on him, when he usually wore things more fitted. Mayburn was at least ten years older than me, I knew, but right now he looked more than that. The lines around his eyes were set deep.

"What's up?" Mayburn said.

I thought about asking the same thing, but I knew he preferred to deal with work first. He wasn't someone who disclosed his personal business very easily. I told him how Maggie had recruited me to work on Valerie's case, that we needed his help.

"What can I do?" he asked.

"I'm not exactly sure." I thought about Valerie's face when she said, *I didn't do it.* Maggie said we didn't have to know such things as Valerie's criminal lawyers, but I was having trouble separating myself as a person from myself as a lawyer. I'd never had such a struggle when I was a civil lawyer.

"Let's break it down," Mayburn said, leaning forward. "Just start at the beginning."

I took a sip of water, and then I told him everything I knew, which wasn't that much, really. I wondered how Maggie could do this on a regular basis. How did she work with such a relatively limited amount of information from her clients? When I was a civil lawyer and I had a trial, I knew exactly what every witness would say because I'd taken their depositions or I'd made them fill out interrogatories or both. The trials there were more about shading the information, drawing out some bits and burying others to persuade the jury that your side was right. But this criminal thing was a whole different matter. There had been no depositions and little other pretrial testimony to plan our trial strategy. We had no idea what was going to happen. We couldn't plan, couldn't pretend we were in control of anything.

It struck me that the same was true of life—you could attempt to be in control of all the information that came at you, could even attempt to control the direction of it, but ultimately, you realized that life was unpredictable as a jury in Cook County. Control was an illusion.

Mayburn listened. He leaned toward me when he seemed to need clarification; he nodded when he got it.

When I came to the end of what I knew about the case, I said, "That's it, basically. Our client says she didn't commit the crime. So far, she won't say who did, or if she even knows who did. We don't know if she's lying, and Maggie tells me none of this matters. But I want to know. So I guess we need to look at everybody in the case. *Everybody.*"

"What if I dig up something bad about Valerie? Something that's not out there yet? Do you have to tell Maggie?"

I chewed my bottom lip the way Maggie did when she was thinking hard. "I think so. But I'm not sure. I just know that I might have to take a backseat on the case or maybe get off it altogether if I don't personally believe Valerie."

"You sure you want to go down this road?"

The waitress delivered our food. We thanked her, but neither of us picked up our forks.

"I have to." I nodded, then repeated, "I have to. Can we start with background checks on all the players?"

"Sure." Mayburn pulled out a pen and a tiny notebook from his back jeans pocket. "Name 'em."

"Bridget and Valerie and Amanda, the victim." I thought about the photos the state had used during opening arguments. Amanda appeared to be the kind of person Maggie and I would be friends with. The fact that I was representing someone who had allegedly killed her was jarring. I *needed* to know the real story. "Zavy, the husband. They had a live-in nanny named Sylvia Zowinski." I spelled her name for Mayburn. "And…" My voice trailed off as I thought hard. "Those seem to be the people who might know something."

"If you can get social security numbers, the states they've lived in, birth dates, anything…" Mayburn said.

"I'll collect what I can from Valerie and the police records. I'm going to be studying the records all weekend to get ready to cross Vaughn."

"Detective Damon Vaughn?" That drew the first smile of the day from Mayburn. "I gotta be there to see that."

"Monday morning."

He gave a smile and a long nod. "If you give me Maggie's files, I'll read them and see what I can find."

"There's not much there. But hey, you're the one who

always says investigations are like puzzles, and you just have to start collecting the pieces, right?"

He raised his eyebrows with a grudgingly impressed expression. "I thought you didn't listen to me."

"I don't listen to you when doing so will get me in trouble."

He scoffed. "Like when?"

"Are you kidding? What about when you made me get into Lucy's house and download Michael's hard drive and Michael came home? There was no time for the series of checks you told me to run. I *couldn't* listen to you."

He chuckled a little. We looked at each other. I think both of us heard the words—*Lucy, Michael*—hanging there.

"How are you doing?" I asked.

"How am I doing?" Mayburn echoed. "I am doing distinctly shitty."

"Will you be okay?"

"No." He said it simply, not like he was feeling sorry for himself, but rather like he was being matter-of-fact. "I've always wondered what was wrong with me, why I didn't want to commit to someone before this."

"You wanted to commit to that gallery owner you dated. What was her name? "

"Madeline Saga. I guess you're right. I did want her to commit. I even bought my house in Lincoln Square hoping she'd move in. But in retrospect, I think I wanted that because she told me she didn't. It was the ultimate challenge."

I looked at Mayburn, at his sad face, his eyebrows drawn together. His skin appeared grayish now that I looked closer, as if he wasn't hydrated.

"Have you been boozing?" I asked.

A sharp glare. "What do you think, McNeil? The love

of my life left me. Yeah, I've been drinking. Wanna talk more about it?"

I shook my head, raised my hands in surrender. Mayburn's show of emotion was unlike him, so much so that I suddenly felt a need to help. Aside from when he was with Lucy, Mayburn seemed happiest to me when he was involved with work. "Why don't you do some investigating for me?"

"I am. You've got me on this poison case."

"Yeah, I know. But I need you on something else. It's Sam."

His narrowed eyes went wide. "Your ex-fiancé, Sam? The one who disappeared?"

"He's reappeared."

"What does that mean?"

"He's engaged now."

"Well, that doesn't sound like much of a reappearance for you."

"He said he'll break off his engagement if I want."

Now, Mayburn's face turned to disbelief. "Are you telling me that you've got a boyfriend *and* you can get your other boyfriend back?"

I thought about it, agreeing that my situation probably was unhelpful when set up against his. "I'm a mess!" I said, which wasn't exactly true. "More than anything, I'm confused," I said, which was precisely true. "I need you to help me with…"

"With what?"

"I want to know how serious he is. About me. About Alyssa."

"Well, ask him."

"I will. But tell me what to look for. Tell me what to ask. You work on all these infidelity cases. I mean, c'mon!" My voice had risen. I realized then that I was anxious to make the right decision—Sam, Theo, or none of the above?

Mayburn's face softened. "When are you seeing Sam next?"

"I...I don't know."

Now Mayburn looked concerned. "Let me know," he said. "Let me know where you're going and what you're doing. And then I'll help you. I promise."

# 21

I parked my Vespa in my garage, thinking about Mayburn and Lucy, thinking that the most important thing about relationships, it seemed, was *timing, timing, timing*.

What that meant for me and Theo, or me and Sam, I had no idea.

I put my silver helmet on the shelf and left, locking the door to the garage behind me. I juggled the keys, looking for my house key as I walked from the detached garage down the brick pathway at the side of my house. I was slightly distracted, thinking about Theo and Sam. But right as I came to the corner, exactly at the point where I would turn and be twenty feet from the front door, I felt someone.

I thought of my mother's words about gut instincts. I stopped. I leaned my ear toward the front of the house. Heard nothing.

I took a tiny step, then another and another until I could ever so slowly peek my head around the side of the building.

There was a man sitting on my front steps, his back to me, his head hanging low, as if to get his face out of the August sun that scorched the stairs. Or to hide who he was?

I pulled myself back behind the building. *Should I leave? Maybe get back on the Vespa and drive by to see who it was?*

I peeked my head back again. His face was still obscured. He was a big guy, but I could see love handles under the white shirt he wore. I could probably outrun him if I had to.

I stepped into clear view. "Can I help you?"

The man turned.

"Spence?"

He stood and smiled weakly. His face was flushed from the heat, but otherwise he looked like the usual Spence. But the fact that he was here, at my house, was unusual. Occasionally, Spence and my mom came for dinner, especially when I'd dated Sam, but their house was nicer and larger than mine, and it was the place they were most happy.

"Darling girl," Spence said.

"Is something wrong?" Suddenly, I felt a lightning-flash of pain. *What if someone had died?*

"No, nothing's wrong. I don't think." A pause. "I just came to talk to you."

"Oh. Okay."

I led him upstairs. By the landing of the third floor, Spence was huffing with exertion. The stairs were another reason they didn't often visit.

Inside, Spence sat on the couch while I retrieved glasses of ice water. I handed one to him, then sat on my favorite yellow-and-white chair. "What's up?"

"I was just at church." Spence went to Old St. Pat's frequently, sometimes during the week and on Saturdays, like today, in addition to every Sunday. My mother usually opted out. She always said she'd lost her taste for religion after my father died—or after we *thought* he was dead. "During the homily," Spence continued, "the priest talked about asking for help, about how it was important to do that. So, I guess I came here for...for some help."

"I'd do anything for you, Spence. You know that. What do you need?"

A sheepish expression. "I believe I just need to talk. To someone who understands your mother."

"Well, I don't know if anyone really *understands* her. Even her."

He laughed. "She is an enigma. It was what drew me to her initially."

"You're the person who knows her best now."

He gave a single nod in acknowledgment. "After we met, she flowered. At least that's how I saw it. She let me in. I understood her moods, and I didn't mind them. In fact, I loved her for them."

I felt a searing regret. I used to feel like that about Sam's failings, and he felt the same way. I knew what it felt like to have someone love me for *me*. Early in our relationship, I saw that Sam was enthralled with me. I had feared if I showed him too much, that enthrallment would turn to irritation and maybe even disgust. Allowing him to see my flaws had been terrifying. But when he didn't flinch from anything, it was thrilling.

"You've been wonderful for my mom, Spence. You know that. So what's happening?"

He took a long sip of water, then placed the glass back on the white plaster coaster I'd given him. He sat back and sighed, looking straight ahead. "She's different." His head turned, and his eyes met mine. Those blue eyes looked tired, weary and a little frightened. "You've seen it, too, I know."

"I've noticed it since he came back."

We didn't need to say who "he" was.

"Yes," Spence said.

"It's a confidence she didn't used to have, don't you think?"

He nodded.

"But Spence, I don't believe that's such a bad thing."

His face went stricken. "I feel terrible saying this, but it's bad for me." He hung his head, shaking it back and forth. "I don't know how I fit into her life when she's... when she's like this."

I sat forward and reached across the table to grab his hand. "You will always fit into her life." I squeezed his hand tighter. "She loves you."

"Of course she does." He pulled his hand away and sat back on the couch, rubbing his face as if he could not open his eyes, as if he didn't want to see what was there. "But the way that we have always worked is that I have taken care of her. I have been there through all those moods—the ones that are beautiful and the ones that are darker."

"She's always going to have moods. We all do."

He dropped his hand and opened his eyes. "No, you're right. But the moods are different now. This confidence you mentioned..."

"We *want* her to become more confident, to become more alive."

"I know that, darling girl. But don't you see? Before, *I* was the one who gave her confidence. I was the one who held her up when she didn't know what to do. I was the one who took over and made things better. Now, she doesn't want my help."

"Yes, she does."

"No. She's made it quite clear. She wants to handle things herself. And as much as I want that for her, I no longer see where my place is."

I paused a minute, looking at him. I could tell that Spence didn't want simple, meaningless reassurances. "I know what you mean," I said. "Sam and I went through something…not the same thing exactly, but…" I stopped again and thought of Sam. "Sam and I tried to adjust after he returned to Chicago, but we weren't able to get our relationship back to the way we had it before."

I was hit by a wave of sadness so strong I could almost feel it dousing me. I felt suddenly bleak. *Why hadn't we tried harder? Was I being given the chance to do that now?*

"I guess what I'm saying," I continued, "is I understand some part of what you're going through because Sam and I couldn't do it. We had changed, and after that happened, we couldn't make the alterations. Not then, anyway. We'd become different people, in a sense. But I think you and Mom *can* do it. You're seeing changes in Mom, sure, but maybe it's an opportunity for you to make some changes, too. Maybe you need to see yourself in a different light. Maybe you need to start looking at ways you can support the person she is now."

He nodded, seemed to be considering this. "What you say is true. We are all different people at different times in our lives. I suppose the success of a marriage isn't about years but about whether each person can adapt to each new one."

"Yes."

My mother had gone through a lot after my father "died." She had met someone else and fallen in love. I wondered how much Spence knew about that. But it didn't matter. Only now mattered.

"Spence," I said, "I think you need to keep reminding yourself how much she truly, truly loves you."

He looked at me. "I do know that she loves me, darling

girl. Thank God, I do know that." He exhaled and clapped his hand on his knees. He stood. "Thank you, Isabel. That was exactly what I needed, a pep talk from a beautiful and smart woman."

I stood, too. "You sure you're all right?"

"Much better."

I hugged him.

"I like that I can come to you for help," he said, his voice soft.

"Anytime."

I felt a bloom of something inside of me, some kind of pride. I'd been able to give back to Spence, a man who had made it his job for years to do anything he could to help the McNeils.

As we stepped away from each other, my cell phone rang. I lifted it from the coffee table.

It was Maggie. I answered. "Where are you?" she asked.

"At home. With Spence." I looked at my watch. "I'll head over to your place now." Maggie and I had decided to get together to divide the trial tasks we needed to accomplish that weekend.

"Good, because Valerie is coming over, too. She just called and she wants to talk."

"About what?"

"I don't know. She just said that she wants to talk to *you*."

# 22

Maggie's apartment was a sleek tower just south of the Loop in Printer's Row. The view from her seventeenth-floor apartment, which faced west, was of Roosevelt Road leading to the highway and the multitude of buildings that peppered the Loop. At the end of the day, the sun set over all of that, washing it clean.

Maggie had left her front door open, and when I entered her place, I could hear her speaking to someone. A guy.

I walked down the small hallway and into her living room—a sophisticated space with circular, glass-topped tables and Swedish-style couches. Her apartment, so clean and contemporary, seemed unlike Maggie in some ways. I'd always envisioned her living in an old-school apartment with moldings and slanted, hardwood floors. But Maggie liked her home to be Zenlike. Her office was a mess, her practice was crazy and she'd said that home had to be minimalist, somewhere she could escape the rest.

I found Maggie in her kitchen, a place filled with stainless-steel appliances. She sat at a bar stool at her kitchen island, talking at her computer. I could hear the guy's voice again. He was laughing now.

"We're on Skype," Maggie said. She swung the computer around to show Bernard.

"Hello, Izzy!" he said when he saw me.

"Hi, Bernard. How's Seattle?"

"It's great, except that I miss my Maggie."

I looked at Maggie, whose eyelids fluttered with happiness, as if she might swoon.

"She misses you, too."

Bernard was a huge guy, and his head took up most of the screen. His black hair was thick and spiky, as if he had just gotten out of bed.

"Will you be in Chicago next week?" he asked.

"I'll be here. You're coming in for the CSO?"

Bernard smiled big. He had a front tooth that was slightly crooked, but it seemed to suit him. "Yes, that's right. I'll get two of my favorite things—the Chicago Symphony Orchestra and Maggie—so I'm a happy man."

Maggie swung the computer back to face her. "We have to get to work now. Love you."

"Love you," he said.

Maggie logged off Skype and looked at me.

"You're using the *L* word?" I asked.

"Oh, yeah."

"Wow. Congratulations. When did that start?"

"About two weeks after we met him in Italy."

"I guess it's meant to be."

"It is."

Just then the doorman buzzed, and his voice came over the intercom. "Valerie Solara to see you."

A minute later Valerie was in Maggie's living room, and there was no denying her presence.

Instead of the elegant dresses she'd worn to court, today she had on jeans, a light blue T-shirt and a white linen jacket. A tiered necklace made of silver chains hung against the dark skin of her chest. The effect was still elegant, but it was softer, more casual. Her hair was loose, dark, and carried a brilliant sheen as it cascaded around her shoulders.

"Thank you for seeing me." She looked at Maggie, then me, and smiled, her eyes staying on mine. We sat on the couches that faced each other, Valerie and me on one, Maggie on the other.

"Thanks for coming here," Maggie said, "instead of the office. Izzy and I had planned to work today, and everything was already here." Maggie waved at a black dining table behind her, which was covered with transcripts and pleadings that she'd brought from the office.

Valerie nodded. "Of course. To be honest, I much prefer this. Your office is lovely, but it has come to remind me of…" Her voice trailed away.

Maggie spoke up. "Sure. I know what you mean."

Maggie had a few legal pads on the table in front of us. She handed me one along with a pen, then one to Valerie, then placed one on her own lap. "So, Valerie, should we tell you what we're working on today or is there something you'd like to address specifically?"

Valarie clasped her hands together, as if she was praying, and stared down at them. When her head rose again, her eyes stayed on mine. "I know Martin spoke with me about this once, but could you explain to me again what attorney-client privilege means? I want to know, I guess, how much I can tell you as my attorneys and what you'll have to keep confidential."

"Well, it's pretty simple," I said. I glanced at Maggie to see if it was okay that I take the lead.

She gave me a nod.

"Essentially, you can tell us—" I pointed between

Maggie and me "—anything you want. Ethically, we can't repeat that information to anyone. No matter what it is. Now, there are one or two exceptions. For example, if you told us you planned to harm yourself, or someone else, we would then have to do something about that. But if you told us that in the past you *had* harmed yourself… or someone else—" I paused and let that possibility hang out there "—we would not be able to speak of that to anyone."

Valerie wore a look of concentration. "Okay."

"There is one more thing to consider, though."

I saw Maggie shooting me a look, and I gave her a quick nod to let her know I understood the message she was trying to send.

"If you did tell us you had harmed someone, we couldn't allow you to take the stand and say you didn't. In other words, we can't knowingly allow you to perjure yourself." I turned my attention to Maggie. "Mags, have you decided whether Valerie will testify?"

"No. We wanted to see how the state's case came out first."

"I don't want to," Valerie said.

Neither Maggie nor I asked why. For the first time, I really understood why Maggie and her grandfather didn't want clients to tell them everything—they didn't want to have to maneuver their defense around in a situation where someone might lie on the stand.

Yet still I wanted to know. Part of me felt I *had* to know before continuing on this case.

"So those are the parameters of the attorney-client privilege," I said.

Maggie's cell phone, which was sitting on the table, rang. She picked it up and looked at the display. "It's my grandmother." She answered it and listened for a minute or two, then raised a hand to her face and covered her eyes. "No, I'm glad," she said. "He had to go. I'm just so glad you convinced him. I'll be there in..." She looked at her watch. "Fifteen minutes. I'm with Valerie and Izzy. But Izzy can handle it."

She glanced at me, and I nodded.

Maggie hung up. "My grandmother finally got Martin to go to the emergency room. He's definitely dehydrated, and they're looking into what else might be going on with him. I'm going to head there."

Valerie stood. "Can I go with you? I've been so worried about him."

"It would be better if you stayed with Izzy until I find out what's going on." Maggie's eyes took on a film of worry. "I just hope he's okay."

"Me, too," Valerie said.

Maggie turned and headed for the kitchen. "I'll call you as soon as I know anything." She stopped. "Damn, I don't have any extra keys. I gave them to Bernard last time he was here, and the front door doesn't lock when you close it."

"That's okay." I stood. "Valerie, why don't we go somewhere and have a cup of coffee?"

"Where are you thinking?"

I shrugged. "Maybe a Starbucks? Or I think there's a coffee shop on Dearborn, not too far from here."

She seemed to be mulling over the options.

"We could go someplace else, too." I shrugged. "Whatever you feel like. Are you hungry?" I was at a loss.

"I'm sorry, Izzy," she said. "I'm just a nervous person. I always have been and now, this whole thing..." Her gaze turned to the window and the city beyond that. "Sometimes I don't feel safe in public places. Especially since the trial started. Sometimes people notice me, and I don't like that."

"I've been there," I said. "I know what you mean." I thought about where I went when I needed to feel safe. "Would you like to go to my mother's house?"

# 23

My mother's home was a cool haven from the humid August air. As we stepped inside, Valerie glanced around at the ivory living room. She gasped a little. "It's beautiful."

I looked around. "Isn't it?"

I had left my scooter at Maggie's, gotten in a cab with Valerie and texted my mother on the way. I heard her footfalls on the front stairway now.

"Hello, hello," she trilled. She stepped into the living room wearing crisp khakis and a white sleeveless blouse. Gold bangle bracelets tinkled as she raised her arms to give me a hug.

She turned to Valerie. "I'm Victoria Calloway, Izzy's mother."

Valerie held out her hand. "Lovely to meet you."

Both women smiled as they shook hands. When they broke apart, my mother gave Valerie a kind look and a reassuring smile. "I'm stepping out in a minute, but you two go into the kitchen. I put some tea and treats for you at the bay table."

We led Valerie to my mother's kitchen, the place where the McNeils did most of their socializing. A large octagonal table was tucked into a bay window. Beyond it was my mother's garden, bursting this year with red hibiscus trees and yellow-and-white perennials.

"I'd love to sit outside," I said to Valerie, "but it's just too hot."

"This is fine."

"Izzy, can I talk to you for a second?" my mother asked.

"Sure." I pointed toward the table and said to Valerie, "Help yourself. I'll be right back."

"Yes, please," my mother said. "Do help yourself to anything, anywhere." She gestured around her house as if saying, *Help yourself to the artwork, and the TVs, too.* My mother always had been utterly generous.

She led me to the doorway between the kitchen and the living room. "So, sweetheart, do you need anything else?"

"No, we're good. Where are you going?"

"Well…" She laughed nervously. "Actually I'm off to talk to someone."

"Someone?"

She gave a little smile, almost with a hint of mischief to it. "I'm going to see a therapist."

I tried not to blink madly in surprise, but it was nearly impossible.

My mother saw my expression and laughed. "I know, I know, you've been telling me for years to do this." She gave a little shrug. "Well, now I'm doing it."

Charlie and I had recommended more than once that she see someone for her "melancholy." It was easy to see now that it was depression. When I was growing up, though, depression wasn't talked about much, not in the no-nonsense, keep-your-head-down-and-do-your-job confines of Chicago. In time, I think we all came to accept my mother's perpetually morose attitude. But here she was, *off to talk to someone.*

"Well, I'm…I'm happy for you." What was the correct response when someone told you they were going to therapy?

"Thank you." She sounded pleased. "Good luck with your client. She seems a lovely woman. Hard to believe she could have…" My mother looked past me toward the kitchen. "Well, she didn't do it, did she?"

I glanced over my shoulder. Through the doorway, I could see that Valerie had settled herself at the table and was looking at all the snacks my mother had laid out.

I turned back. "I honestly don't know."

Her brows drew together. "Should I be leaving you alone with her?"

"Mom, she's not a deranged, roaming-the-street killer. If she did kill someone, it was an act of passion." I wasn't even sure the statement was accurate, but I was hoping there was some moral high ground in all of this.

My mom exhaled swiftly. "I trust your judgment."

"Good luck at the therapist."

"Thanks!" She beamed. I wished Charlie were here. The situation was so weird.

She gave me a kiss and moved toward the door, another version of Victoria McNeil Calloway I had never seen before.

I took a seat at the bay window table and began pouring tea. My mother had laid out a series of small cucumber sandwiches and scones. Valerie and I put food on the dainty china plates. I noticed that Valerie chose her food carefully, only after studying it. I couldn't help but think of the meal she'd allegedly poisoned and fed to Amanda Miller.

But then Valerie spoke. "Sometimes when I eat now," she said, "I wonder if these are the last times I'll ever be able to choose what I put in my body."

I had a cucumber sandwich halfway to my mouth, but I froze. When I'd been falsely accused last year, I'd been scared, but I'd never let myself go so far as to imagine landing in an institution, eating prison fare for the rest of my life.

I didn't know if Maggie and Martin would want me to say this, but I couldn't help it. "You must be very scared."

"I am," she answered simply. She chose a small cranberry scone and placed it on her plate next to a small sandwich, then wiped her fingers on a white napkin.

I didn't know how to address her fears. Should I tell her it would be all right? I had no idea if that was true. My former client, Forester Pickett, the CEO of Pickett Enterprises, was a pro at this. He'd been through hundreds of lawsuits, assumed he'd see hundreds more, and he didn't let them get to him. But this was personal. This was Valerie's life.

I decided to tell her the only thing I knew for sure. "Maggie and I—and Martin, if he's able—will do everything possible to give you the best defense. Everything. We will follow up every angle, we will work very hard."

"Thank you." A small smile. "I believe that."

We fell silent, taking a few bites and sipping some tea.

"Your mother seems like a nice woman," Valerie said.

"She is. Do you have any family in the city other than Layla?"

A short shake of her head. "Layla is my only family. I once considered Amanda and Bridget family, too, but..."

Silence. "What about your parents, your sisters and brothers?"

"I'm an only child. My parents are both dead." She closed her eyes, as if stopping herself from seeing something horrible. She opened them again. "I'm glad my mother isn't alive to see this."

"When did she die?"

"About a year after my father. They were an unusual couple. My mom was black, my dad Mexican. No one really supported their relationship, but she was very much in love. After he was gone, she was never herself again. She simply withered away."

"That's what happened to my mom, too, for a while, after my father died. Or, we thought he did…"

Valerie looked at me with a question in her eyes.

"It's a long story," I said.

Valerie made a rueful smile. "So I'm not the only one with a checkered family history."

"Oh, no. You've got company."

We both laughed a bit. I liked connecting with her, especially on something that didn't have to do with the trial.

"For some reason, that makes me feel better." She looked at me, her expression eager, as if hungry for this kind of conversation.

"How did your father pass away?" I asked.

A long exhale. "Well…" She turned her face slightly, as if she didn't want to see my reaction to what she was about to say. "My father left my life a long time ago for prison. He was… He was a convicted murderer. And he was executed."

# 24

My mind whirred with questions.

"Can you talk about it?" I asked Valerie. "I mean…" I had so many questions, I didn't know where to start. *Who did your father kill? Does violence run in families? Does evil?* So many more suspicions had presented themselves now. "So this happened before the moratorium on the death penalty in Illinois?"

"Yes. He was accused of killing my neighbor. Her name was Marilee." Her eyes drifted away, as if seeing the girl. "I always thought that was such a pretty name. She was fifteen, three years older than me. I thought she was the most beautiful girl around. Everyone did."

"Where did this happen?"

"We lived in an unincorporated area of Cook County. It was south of the city, near a big forest preserve. They called it Timsville back then." She pursed her lips, then kept talking. "When it happened, it was terrifying. There was a killer on the loose, they said, and so everyone kept their children inside. They closed the schools for weeks. And then…" She swung her head back and forth, back and forth. "And then they came for my father. The police said he did it. He denied it. I believed him. So did my mom. He wasn't violent. He wasn't like that at all."

"But there was evidence?" *The way there's evidence against you?*

"Two people testified they saw him near Marilee's backyard, but of course that was true, because our yard was right next to theirs. He had a couple of old cars that he worked on back there." Still she shook her head. "Someone said they saw the two of them later in his car, but that was normal, too. Marilee's parents were gone a lot, and we would pick her up and drive her home or take her to town when she needed." She sighed. "Then Marilee's mother said she'd been suspicious of my father after Marilee babysat for me a few times. *My* mother said it was crazy—if that were true, why hadn't this woman said anything at the time? And why did she keep letting her daughter come to our house after school to watch me?"

"Was there a murder weapon?" *Poison?*

"Marilee was stabbed. The police never found the knife, but they said the stabbing had been done with a very sharp knife, one with a rounded edge instead of a pointed tip. My father was a cook—not as a career, but he was always cooking *tamales* and *moles* and *tostados*. *Nopalitos* were his favorite." As she spoke the names of the dishes, you could hear from her pronunciation that she spoke Spanish fluently.

"What's that?"

"*Nopales* are a flat plant, like a cactus. When my dad could get his hands on some, he loved to make *nopalitos*. But you had to use a special knife to get the thorns off. It was a very sharp knife."

"With a rounded edge?"

She nodded. "The police took pictures of all the knives in our house. There wasn't blood on them or anything, but they showed his *nopalito* knife at trial. But even then, I didn't believe it. Javier Solara was not that kind of man."

I thought of my mom. She had said the same thing the other night—that she had known my father wasn't dead, and yet she had buried him, she had forced herself to go on. And so she ignored that voice that told her his death wasn't real. Ultimately, she found out she was right. And yet I knew that many people believed their family members incapable of committing crimes, even when everything pointed to the contrary. Was the same true for Valerie?

I looked at her. "Maggie said you wanted to talk to me."

She paused a moment, as if considering something. "Yes, that's true. I've been thinking of what you said yesterday, about wanting to know anything that could help with the case. I kept thinking how you said you wanted to believe me. And I loved hearing that. Because I did not kill Amanda."

I held my teacup near my mouth, but didn't take a sip, hoping to keep her talking.

"So far, no one has said that to me, Izzy," she said. "About believing me. Not even Martin, although I know he does."

I put the cup on the saucer. "Maggie and Martin are exceptional criminal lawyers, the best. But sometimes it's easier for them not to hear every little detail. They want to ensure your constitutional rights are being upheld. They want to give you the best defense possible. And if they hear every detail, they might not be able to do that."

"I understand." Valerie held one of my mother's thin, light blue teacups. "I really do. Because of my dad, I've had experience with the criminal justice system before."

Valerie played with the dainty handle on the teacup, drawing circles inside it with her finger, lost in thought.

Just then the back door opened and Spence came into the room. "Darling girl!" He came to the table and gave me one of his bear hugs. "Twice in one day. A delight!"

"Hi, Spence."

He beamed one of his big, patented smiles at Valerie, who blinked rapidly.

I introduced them, glad that Spence seemed to have recovered his buoyant personality.

Valerie, however, said little and shook his hand lightly.

"What can I get you two?" Spence rubbed his hands together, then glanced at his watch. "Let's see. Is it too early for wine?"

In Spence's world, it was always five o'clock somewhere.

"It's a little early for us. We're trying to get some work done."

"Work? What? It's a Saturday."

Spence had retired from his real estate developing business years ago. His profession now was to enjoy life, and to make sure everyone else did, too.

"What are you working on?" he asked. He stopped. Surprise and recognition appeared on his face. "Oh. The trial."

"Yes," I said, "we're discussing a few things. We didn't feel like going to Maggie's office."

Spence clapped his hands together. "I'll get out of your hair then."

He patted me on the back and grasped Valerie's hand for another quick pump. "Help yourself to anything. Anything at all."

When he was gone, I turned back to Valerie. "Sorry

about that. I guess he didn't know we were coming. He really is the most wonderful man."

Valerie didn't look so convinced. She said nothing.

"Listen," I said, "I'm sorry if that made you uncomfortable when he brought up the trial."

"It's not that. It's just that men tend to make me uncomfortable. Well, except for Martin. And Brian."

"Your husband?"

Valerie let a small smile take over her face. "Yes. Brian was my husband." She sat there, as if she wanted the words to sink into the room, into herself.

"They mentioned him in openings, right? He passed away of Lou Gehrig's disease."

"Yes."

I noticed Valerie twisting a platinum band around her finger. I pointed at it. "Your wedding ring. You still wear it?"

She nodded. "I'll never get married again. I don't want to. Brian was all I ever wanted."

*What about Zavy?*

She shrugged, twisting her wedding band once more. "Brian was one of the only men I've ever been able to trust in my life. If I'm honest, he's one of the few *people* I've been able to trust."

I didn't know what to say to that. If anything, I had the opposite problem. I tended to trust people, maybe more than I should.

"What about girlfriends?" It was out of my mouth before I remembered that Valerie was on trial for killing a girlfriend. *Nice, Iz. Very nice.*

"Actually," Valerie said, "I'm glad you mentioned that. Two of the people I did trust, implicitly, were Bridget and Amanda."

I watched her face for some reaction when she mentioned Amanda. There was none. *What did that mean?*

"Maggie said in her opening statement that you and Bridget and Amanda met at a gym?" I asked.

She nodded. "It was like the stars aligning—us in that class, talking afterward, deciding to have coffee. God, thinking back on that, I feel so different."

"What do you mean?"

"Layla was four, and I was happy being a mom."

"Did you have help from Layla's father?"

She shook her head. "He sent occasional checks, made occasional efforts to visit, but he didn't want to be a father. Eventually he ceased to be anything to either of us. It was Brian who changed everything."

"When did you meet him?"

A smile. "The day before I met the girls. I think that's why I was so open to them, because I'd just met Brian and it had lightened my world a little. We met at a park. Layla was in the sandbox, and Brian's dog ran up to Layla and we both panicked, thinking the dog could bite her. But he just bowed his head and Layla petted him." She laughed. "The dog's name turned out to be Kayla."

"No way. Kayla and Layla?"

"Yes. Brian and I let them play and we talked and…we had a wonderful thing until he died eight years later."

"That must have been awful."

She raised the teacup again and put it to her mouth, took a sip. "It was. He got Lou Gehrig's disease very young, and it took him fast." She shook her head as if trying to dislodge a vision of her sick husband. "But I had Amanda then, and Bridget and Zavy. They were wonderful." She stared ahead now, blankly, her teacup suspended, and for a moment it seemed she'd disappeared, as if only the shell of Valerie Solara were sitting there. "They took care of so many things. We called Amanda 'Demanda' because she could be bossy, but boy, she knew how to get things done. I don't think I could have handled it without them."

"But still, the loss of a husband." I thought of the time when Sam had disappeared and shivered. "That kind of thing is hard to get over." *Could I get over it if I needed to? Where was Sam now? Why hadn't he called?*

"Yes." She put the cup back on the saucer and looked at me. "But that wasn't when everything went wrong." She looked to be fighting tears. "It was later. And then I had to tell Bridget and Amanda about it."

"I'm sorry, I'm confused. Tell them about what?"

Her eyes were a little glazed, staring at the tabletop. "It was horrible."

# 25

That night she went to Bridget's house. It seemed a lifetime ago. Things were so different now. Yet she remembered easily how she walked into the house, unannounced, on that November night. They never knocked at each other's homes, always simply strolled inside.

They'd been meeting every other Tuesday night for so many years by then. Amanda was usually on time, sometimes even early. Valerie tended to run a little late, but those nights in Bridget's blue room were the sun in her life, for many reasons.

"You're late," Bridget had said good-naturedly when she walked in the kitchen.

Valerie had paused then in the kitchen, her eyes suddenly filmy. Neither of her friends seemed to notice anything amiss right away.

Bridget handed Valerie a waiting glass of cabernet and kept talking to Amanda, apparently about a doctor at work who had hit on her. "He actually said, 'C'mon, all surgical nurses sleep around.'"

"He didn't!" Amanda said. She put down her glass and turned to Valerie. "How are you?" She pulled Valerie into a hug.

Valerie remembered how she had embraced Amanda

tight with her one free arm. When Amanda started to pull away, she pulled her friend back to her, squeezing her again.

When they finally broke apart, Amanda looked into her eyes. "What's wrong?"

Valerie didn't even try to say, "Nothing," because it wasn't true, and both Amanda and Bridget would see that.

She took a gulp of the cabernet. It tasted rancid. She put the glass on the counter and reached into Bridget's cabinet for a water glass.

When she turned on the faucet, Bridget said, "There's filtered water."

Valerie said nothing in response, just filled up the water glass, drank it down, then filled it up again.

She turned to her friends, glancing back and forth between them. Then her gaze rested on Amanda and stayed there. "Let's go to the blue room."

November had just turned cold and Bridget had a fire going, as Valerie knew she would. Bridget had grown up on the Upper Peninsula of Michigan, and her family room looked more like a cabin in the woods than a Chicago apartment. The walls were painted Wedgwood blue, but the color was muted by the battered brown leather chair which sat to the right of the fireplace, a velvety couch, chocolate-colored ottomans, the wide-planked wood floors.

Bridget took her seat in the leather chair as she always did, stopping to stoke the fire with a huge iron poker. Amanda and Valerie sank onto the couch, Amanda putting her feet on the old trunk that served as Bridget's coffee table.

They both looked at her.

"What is it?" Amanda said.

"Oh, God," was the only thing Valerie could say. She stared into Amanda's eyes.

She had thought her tale would reveal itself in a rush, since it had been waiting and waiting in her mouth. She looked at Amanda, and found no words would come.

"Hey!" Charlie bounded into the kitchen with a loud series of footsteps.

I had heard the front door open while Valerie talked about that night at Bridget's house, but I hoped it was my mom and she would quietly slip up the front stairs. Valerie had been absorbed in her words, telling me about Bridget and Amanda and how she had to tell them…something. *What?*

She clearly hadn't heard the door open.

Now she flinched as Charlie entered the kitchen, looking at him in a fearful way.

"Charlie, this is Valerie," I said. "Valerie, my brother."

"Hey," Charlie said again. He loped over to Valerie and shook her hand. She seemed to suffer the gesture.

"So how do you guys know each other?" Charlie asked.

"Valerie and I are working on something."

"Cool," Charlie said.

I knew, with Charlie's inquisitive nature, that the next words out of his mouth would be a flurry of questions about what, exactly, we were working on. To distract him from talk about the trial, I searched my mind for a topic shift. "How's work?" I looked at Valerie to explain. "Charlie has been working for a few months at WGN. You know, the radio station on Michigan Avenue?"

She gave a barely perceptible nod of her head.

"Yeah, I can't believe how much I love it," Charlie said. "But it's exhausting. I mean today is my day off and

I *just* got out of bed. I've been sleeping since last night at seven-thirty." He opened the fridge. "I'm starving."

Valerie was silent.

"You're okay with being up early every day?" It still seemed odd—Charlie's sudden devotion to his professional life.

"It's killing me, but the job is great." He lifted a small roasted chicken and turned to us. "Do you realize that some people get up at 5:00 or 6:00 a.m. for work every single day for, like, twenty years?"

I laughed. "Yes, Charlie. I do know that."

I looked at Valerie, thinking she might chuckle, too, but she stared at the table. Then she whispered, "I have to go."

And before I could stop her, she stood, muttered her thanks and left.

# 26

As soon as I got home, I went to my computer and typed in a search for Javier Solara. The first result that appeared was from Wikipedia.

*Javier Solara (c. 1944 –1990) was convicted of the murder of Marilee Travis, 15, of Timsville, Illinois. Solara, a neighbor of the Travis family, became obsessed after Marilee began babysitting his daughter. After attempting to assault her in his car, he stabbed her repeatedly on a back road behind their homes. Solara was executed in Stateville Prison in 1990 by the State of Illinois by lethal injection at the age of 56.*

I sat there, thought about Valerie's dad. It was just too strange.

I called Maggie. "Did you know that Valerie's father murdered some girl?"

*"What?"*

I told her the story.

"Damn," Maggie said. "Thank God the prosecution doesn't seem to know. It's totally irrelevant, of course, but I wouldn't put it past them to try to introduce it anyway, just to draw a negative inference."

*Just like I'd done today, at my mom's.* "Do you want me to write a motion in limine?" I asked. "To make sure they don't mention it?" *Limine* is Latin for "at the outset," meaning motions in limine are usually brought before trial to limit or prohibit certain testimony or exhibits.

She thought about it. "No. Clearly, they don't know, and I don't want to put it on their radar."

"How's Martin?"

"They say he'll be okay. They're going to discharge him today. Actually, I gotta go, Iz. I'm at the hospital and I see my grandma coming out of his room now."

Maggie hung up, and I thought more about my talk with Valerie, about the way she was twisting her wedding ring and the things she'd said about her husband.

I stood and walked to the dresser in my bedroom. I opened the bottom drawer and dug past some scarves and workout clothes until I found the small navy blue box at the back.

I took the box from the drawer and stared at it a second, then sat down on my bed. Inhaling deeply, I opened it and a tiny moan escaped my lips. There it was. That antique, art deco ring with an emerald-cut diamond, surrounded by other small, square diamonds. The ring Sam and I had seen in a little store on Jewelers Row. He had put it on my finger in a room of the James Hotel, where we were playing hooky from work, pretending we were rock stars. And that day, we were. We had everything we wanted— drinks and food and sex and most of all, each other. Sam and Izzy. Izzy McNeil and Sam Hollings. Mr. and Mrs. Hollings. The possibilities had seemed limitless.

I found my cell phone and called Sam.

He didn't answer until the fourth ring, and then he was laughing, saying something like, "No, I think we have to take a left," to someone in the background.

I knew that laugh. It was Sam's carefree chuckle, the one Sam only made when he was happy, truly unburdened by life. I heard the laughs of other people, too.

"Sam?"

"Yeah. Izzy?" He sounded surprised. "Hold on a sec." Silence grew on his end, the laughter dying away, then, "Hi, I'm back," he said, his voice more quiet, as if he were trying not to let anyone hear. "Sorry. I was on the other line when you called, and I clicked over and I thought… Anyway."

*You didn't know it was me. You wouldn't have picked it up if you had.* Ouch. "I just wanted to say hi."

"I'm glad. How are you?"

"Well, uh, I'm a little messed up, I guess."

A pause. "Me, too. I should have called you after the other night, but I kept wondering if you walking out of the restaurant that day was the right thing to do. And if maybe I should leave it at that."

"Sam, you can't saunter back into my life, saying things, and then drop out again."

"I know." He said nothing else. An uncomfortable moment ruled.

Through the phone, I heard the tinkle of laughter again, sounding like Alyssa and some other woman.

"What are you up to?" I asked.

"Uh, we're going on a boat. Seeing some of our friends." I noticed the use of *we* and *our.* "I'll let you go."

"Don't say that." His words were fast, as if he'd rushed to get them out of his mouth before he'd thought about them. "Hey, guys, I'll be right there," he called away from the phone. After a moment, he continued. "I mean, Iz…" He breathed hard. "Don't say that *yet.*"

"What do you want me to say? What do you want from me, Sam?"

"I want to be able to explain to you what I've been thinking, why I'm having problems with…"

"With being engaged?"

"Yeah."

"Figure it out, Sam." My words came out with a gulp at the end. I was, I realized, tearing up. "Or let it go."

I hung up.

It was morbid, but I slipped the engagement ring out of the box and onto my left hand. I stared at it. In my mind was an image of Sam putting the ring on my finger, and then an image of Sam with Alyssa and their friends. Friends I didn't know, even though I used to know everyone in his life, everything about him.

I pulled off the ring then and pushed it into the box so that the diamonds barely stood above the navy puff inside. Instead of putting the box back in the drawer, I found the safe in my office closet. I opened the safe, lifted my passport, the deed to my condo, my grandmother's pearl earrings, until I found the bottom. And there I stowed the box. Out of sight.

# 27

"Champagne, sir?"

"Oh," Sam said, startled. He blinked and saw the waitress as if she'd just materialized in front of him. How long had he been standing there, thinking about Izzy? "No, thank you," he said.

The waitress smiled. "They're making a toast." She held the tray a little closer to him. "You're the groom, right? You'd better get up there." She nudged her head toward the front of the ship.

Sam felt a swirling in his stomach, remorse and guilt picking up steam, moving deeper inside him. He faked a smile, thanked the waitress and took a glass.

He walked from the stern to the bow, toward the sound of upbeat jazz music, toward the group of thirty or so people who'd gathered here on the boat for him and Alyssa. It wasn't even a boat; it was a *yacht*. A fifty-foot Azimut yacht with three bedrooms, a salon, a full-time captain and staff of three. The ship was owned by Alyssa's boss, who'd taken a liking to her since she'd moved to Chicago to perform research for his company.

Right then, Sam saw Alyssa. She wore a yellow dress and diamond earrings, and a huge smile that made everyone at the party—their engagement party—grin back at her. He wanted to smile at her, too. He wanted to make her happy, the way he'd wanted to make Izzy happy. But for some reason, Alyssa—and his attempt to give her what she wanted and deserved—was not making him happy, something he had been forced to acknowledge recently. And now, nothing could overpower the realization—not the August sun, not the glittering diamonds on Alyssa's engagement ring.

She turned and saw him. Her face beamed even more, and that made his heart feel ripped apart. God, he didn't want to hurt her. He didn't. Was that what he was doing to Izzy, too? Was he just making a disaster of everyone's life?

It was a question he'd been asking and asking, and that question was forcing him to consider his options. There was one in particular, an option he'd never had considered himself capable of, that was appearing more appealing. In part because it would give him some power in his life. And maybe that would help him make sense of everything.

Alyssa raised her arm and gestured at him while a group of women surrounding her turned to look at him. They all waved. "Come here!" one called. "It's time for the toast."

He was hurting all of those people, he knew—or he would eventually if he kept on this course—because they loved Alyssa and if he caused their friend pain, they would hurt for her. That's how it worked. If you were lucky. Izzy was like that. She'd had people who loved her and rallied around her. Was he pulling Alyssa and Izzy and their families into his confused world?

Was it time to take himself out? To take advantage of this opportunity that had presented itself? Because that's what it was—an opportunity, not just an option.

He raised his hand and gave Alyssa and her friends a *one minute* gesture. Putting the champagne glass on a nearby ledge, he took the piece of paper from his pocket. He'd been carrying it with him ever since he'd gotten it, as if he was afraid that without viewing it often, the opportunity would disappear, too.

He unfolded the paper, deeply creased now. He read the document again. He could take advantage of this, he knew. Was it time to do so?

# 28

Lucy took a liking to Theo's friend C.R. He had eyes like dark blue denim and a golden tan. We were at the Matchbox, a teeny bar wedged at the corner of Milwaukee and Ogden.

"What does C.R. stand for?" Lucy asked him.

"Nothing really. Somebody just started calling me that."

"Oh." Lucy blinked.

I laughed. I couldn't help it. Lucy shot me a look to be quiet, so I erased the smile from my face. Theo was at the bar with his business partner, Eric, getting beers.

Lucy wasn't deterred. "What do you do for a living, C.R.?"

"I work with horses."

"Wow, that's amazing." Lucy shot me a look like, *See, these young guys are great.*

He shrugged. "Yeah."

"I'm from Connecticut. I used to ride." Lucy put a hand on her chest. "Do you do dressage?"

"Dre-*what?* No, I drive. You know, buggies. We're supposed to call them carriages."

"Oh." Still determined, she said, "You must be a great rider, though, right? To do that kind of work?"

"Nah. Kind of fell into it."

And that, apparently, was that. C.R. stared blankly across the room.

Lucy nodded lamely and pointedly didn't look at me. She tried again to start a different conversation with C.R.

As she did, I thought about earlier today, after Valerie had taken off so quickly. *What had she been about to tell her friends? What was she about to tell me?* I had followed Valerie to the door, but she couldn't be stopped. I'd called her on her cell phone a number of times, but she never picked up.

Lucy appeared stumped, apparently from another dead-end conversational attempt with C.R. I figured she was probably realizing right then that Mayburn had everything she wanted, everything she needed—stability, money, a good job. Most of all, he was someone she loved. All things I used to think about Sam.

But like a fighter who was almost down for the count but wouldn't give up, Lucy took a breath and actually clapped her hand against her drink glass. "That's great you fell into that kind of work with horses," she said. "How interesting."

"Yeah. Ya think?"

"Yes, definitely."

C.R. turned his body to face Lucy. "What do you do?"

Lucy stalled, and I thought I knew why. I took a sip of my wine, pretended to pay attention to Theo and Eric, who were making their way toward us. If Lucy said she was a mom of two, there would be the inevitable back-of-the-mind question—*how old was she?* The answer to which was about fifteen years older than C.R.

"So what kind of horses?" she said, galloping over his question.

God love her, Lucy kept trying, and with an infusion of a large slug of beer, C.R. finally started contributing to the conversation.

Theo and Eric reached us, and Eric gave me a smile. He seemed like a nice guy, clearly highly intelligent, someone who seemed to be observant of everything but who remained quiet most of the time. He had black hair cut close to his head. His hairline was inching back—he'd be one of those guys who lost his hair early—but he had keen green eyes and a chiseled-looking face with prominent cheekbones, making him also look like the kind of guy who would be handsome for a long time.

"What are you doing for the Labor Day weekend?" Eric asked Theo and me. "Want to see the Sharpies?" The Sharpies were a band Theo and Eric both liked. I was sure they'd already had this talk or that they could easily have it in the office, since Labor Day was still a few weeks away, but Eric was clearly trying to give C.R. and Lucy room to chat. That he was sensitive to other people like that made me like him.

"Dude, maybe we should take everybody to the show?" Theo said. "It'd be good to get 'em out of the office."

"You want to take all of them?" Eric replied. He meant their employees. Theo had been saying that he wanted to do something to reward their group for working hard all summer. I had been impressed that someone as young as Theo would have the management wherewithal to realize that positive reinforcement for employees was important. I thought of Sam, who'd been so happy when he was in charge of staff members at the wealth management firm where he used to work. Now, he was on the trading side of the business and didn't like it.

"Yeah," Theo said to Eric, "let's take 'em all."

Eric looked at the ceiling and muttered a few numbers under his breath. "That'll cost a lot."

They started talking about the ticket prices, about providing food and drink. They spoke in shorthand and truly listened to each other. I understood a little better now how they'd been successful together, both of them talented designers and programmers, with Theo's charisma combining with Eric's business sense. Sam used to be like that with the people at his firm, too. I knew it was something he missed.

*Enough about Sam!* I said to myself. All I'd been doing for the past few days was comparing Theo to Sam, Sam to Theo, on everything from work styles to sex styles. Theo was winning on the latter, I had to admit, but then I was quite sure no one would ever be able to compare to Theo on the sexual front. And could I ever give that up? Even for a deeper relationship, something I had with Sam? I'd never have thought I'd choose sex over a deep connection, but until Theo, I'd never known what was possible.

Lucy and C.R. turned to us, apparently having used up all their conversational potential.

"Ready to head out?" Lucy said.

C.R. seemed to assume the question was being put to him. "Your place?"

Lucy was taken aback, but I wasn't. The quick hookup was how things worked at their age. Hell, it was how things had worked with Theo and me when we met.

"Umm," she said. "No, I can't, I've got…people at my house."

"My place, then," C.R. said.

Lucy sent me a *help* look, but I only shrugged. She wanted the young guys? She was going to have to deal with the fact that most were looking for a nightcap. A personal one.

Lucy pulled out her phone and made C.R. do the same. "Let me just get your number," she said. "I have a really early morning tomorrow." They exchanged numbers, and she promised to call him and make plans for next week.

Before she took off, Lucy whispered to me, "It's like they're from a different planet."

"See, I told you." Now she would be back to Mayburn, I thought.

But she only said, "I love it," squeezed my arm and left.

# 29

On Sunday morning, I picked up my Vespa from Maggie's and drove it to her grandfather's place to talk about the trial. Martin was out of the hospital and feeling better, but his doctor had strictly said he wasn't allowed to try Valerie's case this week.

The Bristols had lived in Bridgeport while they raised their five children and while Martin built his criminal defense practice. But they'd moved recently to a place on the newer near-south side, a penthouse that took up the entire floor of a high-rise on a historic street called Prairie Avenue. Normally, each floor held a minimum of eight apartments, Maggie told me, but the highest floor had been made into a single one for Martin and his wife and the masses of kids and grandkids that were always around. From the penthouse, Martin loved to point out landmarks to the kids, things like the Shedd Aquarium, the Museum of Natural History, Soldier Field. And he could take them out the door to the symphony or the Art Institute.

Maggie's grandmother answered the door when I arrived. She was as tiny as Maggie and just as alive.

She embraced me, standing on her toes the way Maggie

did. "How are you, Isabel? I haven't seen you since...
Well, I suppose since you were on TV."

"I'm fine, thanks." Usually, it was awkward to run into
someone I hadn't seen in a while, especially people who
knew that last year my fiancé had disappeared and I had
been suspected in a friend's murder. Hence the TV stuff.
But Margaret Bristol, after whom Maggie was named,
didn't look uncomfortable at all. I suppose when your
husband has put away a few mass murderers and represented a few others, you get used to running across the
occasional awkward situation.

"He'll be glad you're here," Mrs. Bristol said. "You
know he likes you very much, Iz. And he's grateful for
your help with the trial."

"Well, I'm grateful for the work." I put a hand on her
arm. "How is he?"

She looked down the hall then back at me. "Impossible," her grandmother said. "We took him to the hospital,
and they said it was stress, exhaustion, dehydration. I'm
practically shoving fluids down his throat. Trying to make
him eat. Mostly, I think it's emotional. He's clearly having
a hard time dealing with something. He's always gotten
distant at the beginning of a trial, but this is different."

"What do you think it is?"

"I don't know." She shrugged one shoulder. "But I suppose that's how life is. Even after fifty years of knowing
someone, you still never know everything about them."

"I understand that." I didn't know everything about
Sam. And yet I liked that.

Mrs. Bristol smiled and pointed a finger down a marble
hallway. "They're in the sun room."

The room at the end of the hall was small, filled with
white-and-blue couches all facing toward a few tables, and

beyond that, massive windows overlooked the museum campus and the currently teal-colored Lake Michigan.

It was hot in the room. The sun streamed through blinds, which were halfway down the window, and yet Martin Bristol wore flannel pajamas and a matching robe. Maggie, wearing white jeans that came to her knees and a blue tank top, sat at his feet and held a huge trial notebook as she ran down questions for upcoming witnesses.

"Hi, Iz," Maggie said.

Martin echoed, "Hello, Isabel!" We shook hands.

I couldn't help but glance over his shoulder, out the window again. "Great view, Mr. Bristol."

Martin followed my gaze toward the museum campus. "Most of that wasn't here when I was a child." he said. "It grows up around you, like kids grow around you." His gaze dropped to Maggie. "Just like grandkids…" He sounded rather bleak.

"Marty, don't get all sentimental," Maggie said.

He shook his head. "I wouldn't dream of it. Now, let's talk about the trial." His kind, keen eyes met mine. "Are you ready, Isabel?"

For a moment, I was at a loss for words. How could anyone be ready for a major trial that, a few days before, they didn't know was coming? But as Martin's replacement, I didn't want to scare him.

"I'm taking it a day at a time," I said. "Tomorrow is Detective Vaughn."

"I hear you have some history with him," Martin said.

"Oh, yes." I gave a single nod and an angry glare escaped my eyes.

"Good," Martin said. "Take that emotion into the courtroom and take him down."

"That's the plan." I didn't say that I knew Vaughn

would probably be an excellent witness. Our showdown had the makings of a bloody battle.

We went silent. All I could think to say was, "I spent some time with Valerie this weekend."

For the first time, Martin Bristol seemed to brighten. His spine straightened; his hands gripped the arms of the chair. "How is she?"

"I suppose the same. She's scared. She said she didn't kill Amanda."

Martin Bristol sat back and nodded very slowly. "And what do you think?"

Maggie, who was paging through a transcript and taking notes, groaned.

I pointed at her. "My friend tells me that it doesn't matter."

"Normally, it doesn't, certainly not at first. In most instances, you're not talking about guilt or innocence right away, it's about information. You're the information pipeline to the legal system. You have to explain to your client what they're charged with, what that charge means, what the sentence could be."

"And what happens after all that? What if the defendant tells you they're innocent?"

"It's complicated. If your client tells you they're innocent, the situation you face then is to analyze the evidence against them, and explain whether it's overwhelming or something you can defend against. You never know at the beginning. You truly don't. You look under every rock for the evidence. You ask—is it possible they have the wrong guy? And if so, how can I show that? If the evidence really is too mountainous to overcome, you explain that to your client. If the guilt is *so* manifest then all you can do is mitigate at that point. You might agree to a natural life sentence. Or if it's something like murder, maybe you argue their act doesn't warrant first degree. Maybe the circumstances around the crime help explain it." A pause. "In this case, I do believe Valerie."

We sat in silence for a moment. Then I had to ask, "Martin, why did you take this case?"

I saw Maggie go still.

When he said nothing, I continued. "Valerie had another lawyer, right? A good one. Jayne Krepps?"

Martin nodded. "After I heard about Valerie's case, I asked to meet her. After talking to her, I knew Valerie didn't do it. I *knew* it. And I wasn't sure if Jayne understood that."

"So sometimes it does matter to you—the innocence or guilt?"

"Yes."

"You took the case pro bono. Why?"

"I learned Valerie was taking out a loan with ridiculously high interest in order to pay Jayne." He shook his head. "She couldn't afford it."

"Sounds like you're getting sentimental, Marty," Maggie said in a light tone.

He smiled. "Don't underestimate me, dearest Margaret."

They both laughed. A light moment. But I had a question I just had to ask. "If Valerie didn't kill Amanda, then who did?"

Maggie closed the trial book and leaned back on her hands, waiting for her grandfather's answer.

"It doesn't matter," he said.

"But you said that it did matter to you."

"What mattered to me was that I felt she did not kill Amanda Miller. Who did is not really of interest."

"I know that's technically true. We don't have to prove

who killed her. We only have to prove that they don't have evidence beyond a reasonable doubt that Valerie did."

"Correct."

When nothing else was forthcoming, I said, "I don't know how you do this. Don't you have to know—morally—who did it? Even if you don't have to ultimately prove it?"

Martin Bristol gave a short shake of his head. "This is not about morality. Do I think it's moral that someone may have killed her best friend? Of course not. Do I think that an accused person deserves, like all citizens, to have counsel? To make sure her constitutional rights are upheld? To make sure she gets the correct due process we are all entitled to? Yes."

I sighed. "Civil and criminal law are so entirely different. In a civil lawsuit, there isn't such a shield between attorney and client. We want to know *everything*."

Martin Bristol stared at me with a reddish, tired tinge to his eyes. "Izzy, I need you to try this case to the best of your abilities. You don't need to know who killed Amanda. You just need to prove that Valerie didn't."

None of us said anything. Martin's words posed a silent question to me: *Can you handle it?* The case wasn't going to resemble a civil suit. So could I get on board or not?

"Okay," I said. "I'm in."

# 30

On Monday morning, I was wide-awake at 5:00 a.m. and sitting on the couch in my living room, surrounded by paper. With Theo asleep, I went over the notes I'd made from the talk with my father and those I'd taken during my conversation with Martin and Maggie yesterday, while I crafted and recrafted my cross-examination of Detective Vaughn.

For each point, I searched for some way to sneak up on Vaughn and get him to admit things. Then I pretended I was Vaughn—I tried to jump into his mind and think of how he could dodge my questions, then ways I could pin him back down. I studied Vaughn's grand jury testimony and later his testimony in a motion filed on Valerie's behalf. Unfortunately, there wasn't much there, since testimony like that was brief and relatively pro forma.

An hour later, light from my bedroom hallway poured into the living room, startling me. I glanced up. Theo stepped into the room, his body covered in nothing but a loosely wrapped towel.

"You're up early," he said, making his way to me. I moved some of the transcripts and he sat.

"Do you ever wear clothes?"

"Every day. But around you? Not so much."

I laughed. "What about around other women?" I had no idea why I said it. I shook my head. "Ignore that question."

He shrugged one shoulder, looking a little amused. "I can answer it."

"It doesn't matter. I'm really not a jealous person." It was true. Except for Alyssa and Sam, I had rarely been jealous. "Or is the right word *envious?* Would I be *envious* if you were always naked around other women or would I be *jealous?*"

Theo pursed his beautiful mouth a little and looked straight ahead. "Hmm. Well, I'm the one who dropped out of college, but if I had to guess I'd say they're both kind of the same, but envy is worse. Envy means you would take something away from someone else."

"So the question is whether I would take you away from another woman?"

"That's a good question." He turned to me, smiled. The towel around his waist slipped a little.

I scooted toward him, wrapped my arms around him. "I would," I whispered into his mouth. "So I would be envious."

"We don't want that." He kissed me.

A moment later, he was pulling off the T-shirt I'd slept in, and I was climbing on top of him. But then I caught a glance of the transcripts.

"Wait!" I said. "I can't."

"Can't?" He caught one of my earlobes between his lips and gave it a gentle suck.

I pulled away, pointing to the transcripts. "I *cannot.*" I yanked the T-shirt back over my head. "Do you know who I'm cross-examining this morning?"

"That asshole Vaughn."

I smiled. That was the way I referred to Detective

Vaughn—an exception to my no-swearing rule—and I liked that Theo had picked up the lingo. Theo had also been interrogated by Detective Vaughn after Jane had been killed. "Exactly. This is my chance to get him back for both of us. To destroy him!"

Theo blinked at my vehemence, then burst into laughter. I couldn't help it. I did, too. He pulled me back into his lap and hugged me. "I thought that giving you a little action this morning would calm you down."

"But I—"

"I know, I know. You don't want to be calmed down. I can see that."

I told him I needed my anger, my excitement, to be at the top of my game. "If this had been a civil case, Marty and Maggie would have deposed Vaughn for hours by now. Without that, I'm flying blind, and Vaughn is going to try and shoot me from the sky."

With that reminder, I extricated myself from Theo and reluctantly went to shower.

When I got to the courtroom, I told Maggie about the sky/shooting metaphor.

She crinkled her nose. "No, no. It's not like that at all. It's more like a bullfight."

"Who's the bull?"

"He's the bull."

"So I'm the puny guy in tights with a red cape?"

"Listen to me. You're the bullfighter, and he's the bull. You've both been here before. The prodding and taunting of him is part of your profession. Just know he's going to charge back and try to kill you."

"So far, this isn't helping."

Maggie put a hand on my shoulder. "When the bullfighter lets himself get angry or loses his focus, the bull seizes on it and *rams* him." She smacked a fist into the palm of her other hand. She leaned closer. "So don't let him piss you off. Don't let him fluster you. Or even better, let him *think* he's pissing you off, then go in with your sword."

"For the kill." I started bouncing on my toes a little like a boxer.

"For the kill."

"Got it," I said, then again, "Got it." Suddenly, I stopped and looked at Maggie. "Doesn't the bull usually die?"

She nodded.

I smiled.

Just as I was expecting Vaughn to be led into the room, the judge tossed off a quick question from the bench. "Any housekeeping matters to take care of before the first witness?"

"Yes, Your Honor," Ellie Whelan said, standing from counsel's table. Ellie, in a navy blue suit, stepped up to the judge. "Your Honor, we have a motion in limine."

The judge frowned. "Why wasn't this motion heard prior to trial beginning?"

"We apologize, Judge. We just learned some information yesterday that we felt was highly pertinent and which must be addressed before today's testimony."

Ellie looked excited, practically clicking her heels together. "Our motion has to do with prohibiting counsel for the defense—" she turned and pointed directly at *me* "—from cross-examining Detective Vaughn."

The judge looked confused.

Ellie pushed on. "Specifically, we're referring to Isabel McNeil, who only entered an appearance in this case last

Thursday. As a result, we only learned this information over the weekend and this morning."

"What information is that?" The judge sounded irritated.

"Ms. McNeil was investigated by Detective Vaughn."

The courtroom went silent. The judge's eyes shot to mine. Next to me, I saw Maggie hang her head, then bristle and shake it back angrily.

"Ms. McNeil was a 'person of interest'—" Ellie made air quotes with her hands "—on the Jane Augustine case, just a few months ago. I'm sure you've heard of it, Judge. A local broadcaster was killed."

The judge's eyes stayed on mine.

I bit my lip. *Mother hen in a basket.*

Ellie Whelan wasn't done with her argument, which meant it wasn't our turn to talk yet. I glanced at Maggie and saw her give me a *Don't say anything* look. I felt relieved. I hadn't seen this curveball coming, and despite myself I felt embarrassed. I wasn't sure how to respond.

"Ms. McNeil was investigated by Detective Vaughn for that murder," Ellie continued. "She clearly has bias against him, she is hostile to him, and she should not be allowed to question this witness."

Now I was no longer embarrassed, just pissed off and ready to talk about it. I stood and opened my mouth, but Maggie stood with me and shot me a *Don't* look.

"Your Honor," Maggie said, "this is an inane and ridiculous attack on my cocounsel. Whether I have received a ticket from a police officer or had any other involvement with the police on an unrelated manner has no correlation whatsoever as to whether or not I might cross-examine them."

"Well, this is a little different, counsel," the judge said, but he was still looking at me. "I remember that case, and it was a rather big one."

"Big, small, it doesn't matter, Judge. The point is that, as lawyers, we are able to put our personal issues aside and do our job, just like you, Your Honor. Every day, you put aside personal judgment in order to sit in with an unbiased look at your courtroom and your cases." I liked the buttering up she was doing. And from the way the judge finally turned his full attention to Maggie, it appeared he might, too.

Maggie continued on, arguing other points, asserting the state was floundering for advantage because of their weak case, her voice growing, points punctuated with stabs of her finger into the air.

When she slowed for a second, Ellie Whelan tried to pipe in with a comment, but the judge held up a hand to her and looked at me. "I'd like to hear from you, counsel."

I swallowed hard, then spoke up. "Your Honor, I was a witness in the case concerning Ms. Augustine. I was never a suspect."

I had found Jane dead, I told him. Then I paused a moment. I couldn't stop the torrent of images that always hit me when I talked about it—of smiling, confident Jane at the anchor desk; the snapshot of Jane, happy, on a Chicago roof deck, days before her death, her hair hanging in shiny sheets of black on either side of her face, framing her mauve-blue eyes; Jane strangled with a red scarf, her head beaten; Jane's blood, pooled around her...

I forced my mind back to the present. "I met with the police on a number of occasions to try and establish who had perpetrated the crime," I continued. "And as Your Honor probably knows, the person who killed Jane was identified within weeks of her death. I believe that person has entered a guilty plea, and the only matter remaining is sentencing." I took a breath and shot a glare at Ellie Whelan. "The fact is, that entirely unconnected case is being used to try and halt the administration of justice in *this* case. As my cocounsel said, this is ridiculous."

I caught the anger swooping up inside me and threw a figurative bucket of water on it, dropping my angry tone. If I let myself go any further, I'd be proving the state's point—that I couldn't be impartial in matters relating to Vaughn.

Ellie Whelan tried to jump in. "If I may, Judge—"

I held up my hand. "Counsel, I'm not finished." I shot her a *Don't mess with me* glance and was gratified when she shut up. "Judge, I am generally a civil litigator, and I have been doing a lot of watching and learning over the past few days. What I've observed about the criminal justice world—" I waved my hand around the courtroom "—is that all of you seem to know each other very well." I pointed at Ellie. "Counsel here clearly appears in front of you nearly every day on other cases, and yet we're not throwing up a motion in limine saying she shouldn't be able to handle this case, because you two have met before." I pointed at Tania now, and then Maggie. "I'm also willing to bet that both the state and even my cocounsel have run into some of these detectives before on other cases or they probably will in the future. But will that prevent them from doing their job? No. Of course not. The fact that an attorney knows a witness does not prevent them from cross-examining them." I actually wasn't sure about the case law here, but it sounded right, and so I continued. "For Ms. Whelan to suggest that I cannot handle the task I have been given this morning because I have met Detective Vaughn in the past is not only incorrect, it is insulting. I am a lawyer, Your Honor. And I'd like to be able to do my job."

Ellie Whelan couldn't keep her silence anymore. "Judge, this motion…"

But the judge interrupted her. "No further argument. Based on what I've heard and Ms. McNeil's personal assurances on this matter, the motion in limine is denied. Counsel, call your witness."

# 31

Valerie was brought into the courtroom for the day's testimony. I smiled reassuringly at her, and she returned the smile with a grateful nod, but then she looked away. I'd hoped we might continue our conversation from Saturday, but it clearly wasn't going to happen now.

As we waited for the state's attorneys to fetch Vaughn and put him on the stand, the courtroom door opened again.

"It's Q!" Maggie said.

Sure enough, there was my former assistant, dressed in tan pants and a blue jacket that nicely set off his black skin.

"Do I have time to say hi?" I asked Maggie.

"Yeah. Tell him hi for me, too."

I pushed through the Plexiglas and hurried to the back where Q was still standing. "You're here!" I gave him a hug.

"Of course I'm here."

I'd texted with Q this morning while I was working on Vaughn's cross, hoping the fact that Q and I used to work together on trials would get my mojo rolling. It had, and Q said he'd come watch.

He looked around the courtroom now. "Who are the big players?"

It was what he always used to ask, and I pointed out Valerie, told him about the state's attorneys.

"How's your jury?" he asked.

"Good, I think."

Q sighed and ran his hand over his head. He'd never gotten used to the fact that he was balding and decided to shave his remaining hair off. *I'm still a hairy beast in my mind,* he used to say. "I miss the law," he said now.

"You do not. You never wanted to be in it. You want to be an actor."

"That dream has died."

"Well, don't let it. You've got time now to go on auditions and take classes."

He shook his head. "It died because I'm not really that into it anymore."

"What *are* you into?"

Another shake. "All I know is I miss working. I miss working with *you*. I miss all the trouble you were always causing."

"I wasn't *causing* trouble." The truth was, trouble usually found me. Either I didn't code my billable hours correctly or my client entertainment receipts were too large because Forester loved the best restaurants and the best bottles of wine. It used to rattle me when the powers-that-be pointed their fingers in my direction, but I'd gotten used to it. I gradually learned that the partners were calling me to the mat because it was disconcerting how much work I brought in as a young associate. They simply wanted to make sure I had it together and that I could handle it.

"So we're going to see Detective Vaughn this morning," Q said. "I hope you kick that jackass's ass."

I smiled. "God, it's good to have you here."

Just then, Ellie and Tania walked into the room with

Detective Vaughn. The smile slid from my face, and I hurried ahead of them to the front of the courtroom. When I reached our table, I glanced at Vaughn, a guy who was probably in his early forties. As when I'd met him before, he was wearing casual pants and a button-down shirt, but he'd lost the snazzy running shoes he usually wore in favor of brown loafers, and he'd added a jacket.

As he made his way to the witness stand, my mind sorted through the times I'd seen or spoken to Vaughn before—when he came to my office after Sam had disappeared and snidely insinuated I knew more than I did; when he questioned me after Jane had died and let it be known he thought it was me who'd done it; when he was at my home with a search warrant, taking glee in his uniformed officers pawing through my closets and my drawers.

The memories pissed me off, and I dropped my eyes from him as he took the stand. I shuffled through my notes, and put a couple of exhibits in a file. This was a classic trial attorney move—act like the witness is nothing to you, even if they are. Out of the side of my vision, I saw Vaughn sitting down, adjusting the mike in front of him and Ellie Whelan standing to direct him. I took more time organizing things on the table, still ignoring them both. Maggie knew what I was doing, and she turned and spoke with Valerie to let me gather my thoughts.

To distract myself a little, I glanced through the Plexiglas at the gallery, searching for Q again and hoping for the goofy smile he'd probably make to lighten the moment. But before I found his face, I spotted two other people I knew—my father, sitting near John Mayburn. They'd met very briefly when my dad returned to town, to life. Mayburn had done some digging on Vaughn and Valerie's case, and even though he'd given me the information over the weekend—information I was about to use—he said he wanted to be here this morning, too, a fact I'd forgotten. And although I'd gotten my dad's impressions on Vaughn's cross, he hadn't asked what courtroom I was in or what time Vaughn would take the stand. But then again, my father rarely asked anything. He simply knew.

My dad and Mayburn shook hands, as if just recognizing each other. They both looked at me then. My dad, elegant in a suit that looked Italian, like most of his clothes, gave me a *Go get 'em* kind of nod. Mayburn held a quick thumbs-up.

I turned back and looked in the direction of Vaughn and found he was watching me. Our eyes met. He didn't look nervous to see me. In fact, he looked pleased. He cocked his head to one side a little and smiled as if to say a mild, *Hello, again.*

Ellie started questioning him, took him through his background, then got right to the point. "Did you have any part in the investigation of the death of Amanda Miller?"

"Yes, ma'am."

I felt like guffawing. I'd met Vaughn a few times, and he wasn't a "ma'am" kind of guy. That talk was clearly for the jury's benefit.

Ellie led him through how he became involved in the case, the steps he took to investigate. All the while, Vaughn was the picture of a well-bred officer. Ellie started asking more pointed questions, and soon, the state was hammering away at Valerie Solara, pointing out all the evidence that had highlighted her as the killer. Like the fact that Valerie had been cooking with Amanda the day she died, teaching her the recipe she would eat that night. In fact, it was a Mexican dish that had been handed down through Valerie's family. The women had made two batches of food. The one that Amanda had eaten from had killed her.

It got worse. Valerie had also tried to seduce Amanda's husband, Vaughn said.

"How do you know that, sir?" Ellie asked.

"She said—"

I stood and interrupted him. "Objection. Hearsay."

"It's an admission against interest, Judge," Ellie said.

The judge thought about it for a second. "Overruled."

Vaughn threw me a smirk, then continued, saying that under questioning, Valerie had admitted to him that she had once hit on Zavy.

Ellie asked who else he had questioned, and Vaughn said that Bridget, a close friend of Amanda and Valerie, told him that before Amanda died, Valerie had asked where she could get information on poisons.

"Do you have an opinion as to who caused Amanda Miller's death?" Ellie asked.

I stood. "Objection,"

"Foundation?" the judge asked.

I didn't really have a great cause, but I'd wanted to slow the impact of Vaughn's testimony. "Calls for speculation."

"I'll rephrase," Ellie Whelan said. "Sir, with your experience in law enforcement for over two decades, having solved hundreds of crimes, do you have a professional opinion as to the perpetrator of the death of Amanda Miller?"

I'd made things worse. Now, Vaughn sounded like the most stellar detective of all time.

"Sorry," I murmured to Maggie.

She shook her head. *Don't worry about it.*

"Yes, I do have an opinion," Vaughn said. "It was Valerie Solara."

"Why would Ms. Solara want to do that?"

I had to do it. I stood again. "Objection. Calls for speculation."

Ellie Whelan didn't have a quick response this time.

"Sustained," the judge said.

But it had been a direct exam, and Ellie knew it. "Nothing further," she said, with triumph in her voice.

By that time, after hearing all the evidence against Valerie, I felt a little sick about representing her. But I kept thinking of how Vaughn had once added up evidence against *me,* deciding *I* had killed someone.

Sometimes it's a nice move for a lawyer to stand and introduce themselves to the witness on the stand, to say something like, *Good morning, detective, I'm Izzy McNeil, and I represent Valerie Solara in this case. I have just a few questions.* The jury likes to see people act cordially, at least at first, and this gives the witness the impression you might not have too many hard questions.

But there was going to be no politesse between Vaughn and me. I had no qualms about showing I had only tough queries.

"Detective," I said without introduction, "you explained to the jury that the evidence in this case all pointed to Valerie Solara, is that correct?"

He paused, studying me, a small smirk on his face. "Yes."

I squinted at the police records in my hand, as if confused. "Well, let's take a step back here. Initially, you considered Amanda Miller's husband, Xavier Miller, correct?"

"Yes. In homicide investigations, it's standard to look first at the spouse. Basically, you start inside and work your way out. So generally we'll look at family first, then the next ring of people like neighbors and—"

"Thank you, Detective. I don't know what you need to do generally. I'm asking you a specific question. The next person you suspected was the Miller's live-in nanny, correct?"

"Yes."

"A Ms. Sylvia Zowinski? That was her name?"

"Yes."

"And you considered her not just because Ms. Zowinski was on the 'inside,' as you put it. There were other reasons you investigated her, correct?"

He paused. He was trying to figure out how much I knew. In addition to what my father had noticed about the records, Mayburn had also found some dirt.

While I waited for Vaughn to answer, I glanced at the gallery again and saw my father and Mayburn leaning in to speak to one another. It gave me the best idea. I tucked it away for later. "Detective, you had other—"

Now he was the one to interrupt, with a terse, "Yes. Yes, we looked at the nanny."

"That wasn't my question." I said this like I was being very patient with a small child. "There were other reasons *why* you wanted to investigate Sylvia Zowinski, correct?"

"Yes."

"She had a criminal record under a different name, didn't she?"

"Yes."

"Convictions for—" I looked at my notes as if consulting a huge scroll of Sylvia Zowinski's former crimes "—fraud, right?"

"Yes."

"And embezzlement?"

"Yes."

"And impersonating a corrections officer, correct?"

He almost sighed, but held it in. "Correct."

"So, Detective," I said, striding toward the witness box, starting to feel the high that only comes with a good cross, "it's your testimony that you suspected first Mr. Miller, then Ms. Zowinski, and ultimately Ms. Solara, is that correct?"

Vaughn grunted.

"Detective, you'll have to answer out loud for the jury."

Shooting me a derisive glare, he leaned toward the microphone. "Yes."

"Who else did you suspect?"

He paused. He was smart to do so. He was, in his head, reviewing anything he'd said at the grand jury, any testimony he'd given at a motion on this case. "That's it," he answered.

I scrunched up my face and stared at the notes I'd taken from my discussion with my dad. "I don't think that's right." I looked up at the judge. "May I approach the witness?"

The judge nodded.

The jury looked interested now.

I walked up to Vaughn. We were so close I could smell his cologne, which if I didn't hate him so much I might admit was appealing in a clean, beachy kind of way.

He looked me up and down and made a face as if disgusted at what he found there.

"Sir," I said, "showing you exhibit number sixteen, these are the general progress reports that you made on the day after Amanda Miller died, correct?"

Ellie Whelan stood. "Objection, foundation."

"I'm laying my foundation, Your Honor, if counsel would let me ask my questions."

"Overruled." The judge looked at the detective. "You can answer."

"Yes."

I took him through what the report looked like, the fact that it was a form created by the Chicago Police Department.

"And in these progress reports, these GPRs," I said, "you made notes for yourself, which were later the basis for your typed reports, correct?"

"Yes."

"And you suspected three people."

"Ultimately, yes."

"I'm referring to the day after Ms. Miller died."

"I can't remember exactly what day everything happened, but ultimately, yes, there were three suspects."

"You testified that it wasn't until two days after Ms. Miller died that you first considered Ms. Solara's involvement, isn't that right?"

He paused. He couldn't get around what he'd said in his direct testimony. "Yes."

"And yet on the day after the death, you had three suspects, according to your notes, correct?"

"No." He paused. An anxious look crossed his face. I was acting very, very confident and any witness who testified a lot, as Vaughn had, knew the signs of an impending catch when an attorney was about to snare you. "I don't believe so," he said, hedging.

"Detective, can you look closely at the notes you made?" I handed him my copy of the GPRs.

He perused them with apparent concentration.

"Now, Detective, what is the notation that you see there?" I pointed at the notes.

"It's a number three."

"Correct. You wrote a number three in parenthesis, yes?"

"Yes."

"And that notation is just above and to the right of the word *suspects*."

He said nothing.

"Is that right?"

He cleared his throat, and threw in a "yeah" at the end.

I glanced at the state's attorneys' table and saw Ellie Whelan and Tania Castle frowning. On direct, Ellie had taken Vaughn through his investigation in a more general way. Now I was making it precise.

"Detective Vaughn, I'd like you to think back to after Ms. Miller died. Specifically, *the day* after she died. On that date, you had three suspects in mind, isn't that correct?" I crossed my arms and stared boldly at him, daring him to disagree with me.

He glanced at Ellie Whelan, who couldn't do anything except look right back at him.

"Take your time," I said, gracious now.

Vaughn waited another few seconds, looking down at the records without touching them. He then leaned toward the microphone. "We had three suspects on that day."

"And in addition to Mr. Miller and Ms. Zowinski, please tell the jury who the third suspect was on the day after Amanda Miller's death."

I glanced at the jury. I had them. Some bent forward, waiting for the answer.

"There was a neighbor," Vaughn said.

I gave a curt nod, like, *Yep, that's what I thought*.

At the state's attorney's table, Tania and Ellie were whispering fiercely. A neighbor had been mentioned in the notes as a witness, but not as a suspect. And yet Mayburn had surveyed the area the Millers lived in and a number of people not only remembered the case, they wanted to talk about it. The cops were asking a lot of questions about a particular neighbor, and that neighbor had been taken into a station for questioning.

"Please tell us the identity of that neighbor," I said.

"I don't recall his name. He was just someone we wanted to converse with."

"You don't recall his name?"

"No."

"Would your notes help your recollection?"

He seemed to almost sigh. "Probably."

"May I approach, Judge?"

"You may."

Again, I walked up to Vaughn and handed him his general progress reports.

He took his sweet time looking at them. "The neighbor's name was Dominick St. John."

I gave a big nod, like *There we go.*

"Please tell us why you wanted to talk to Mr. St. John."

Vaughn blinked once. Then again. "He's a doctor."

"Oh, so you remember him, then. Good. What kind of doctor is he?"

"I believe he is an internist."

"And did you want to talk to him in his capacity as an internal medicine doctor?"

"No."

"Tell us why you wanted to talk to Dr. St. John."

He had the sense to affect a bored air. "The nanny mentioned that Mr. and Ms. Miller had been fighting with a neighbor."

"In fact, she was seen fighting with that neighbor, Dr. St. John, on the day Amanda died, correct?"

"Yes."

"You learned this from other neighbors."

Vaughn gave me a loathing, laserlike look.

"Is that a *yes,* detective?"

"Yes."

"In fact, you learned that the Millers and Dr. St. John had been in a feud over some property issue for years, correct?"

A sigh. "Correct."

"Specifically, what kind of property issues did the feud concern?"

"I don't know."

I put my hands on my hips. "Why don't you know?"

He sighed with frustration. "We didn't need to. We learned everything we needed about Valerie Solara."

"Two days after that."

"Yes."

"But on the day after Ms. Miller died, the first day you were on the case, you had three potential suspects, one of which included the Millers' neighbor."

"Yes, but—"

"But you didn't look into the specific disagreement that the Millers and the neighbor had?"

"No."

"Let me make sure I understand this. You don't know what that disagreement was about?"

"Property."

"You don't know specifically."

"No."

"You don't know if the resolution of those property issues would have meant a good deal of money for either Dr. St. John or the Millers, do you?"

He inhaled. I didn't know the answer to that question,

either, not yet, but then, I wasn't the one on the stand. "Detective?"

"No."

I nodded. "Because it wasn't important. Isn't that right?"

Vaughn opened his mouth. His eyes flashed with anger.

But I took back my copy of his notes and turned around. "No further questions," I said before he could answer.

Ellie stood and went through a redirect to rehabilitate her witness, showing how thorough Detective Vaughn and his brother detectives had been. But as far as I could tell, I'd done some damage to the state's case, hopefully giving the impression that the cops either rushed the investigation or were hiding something.

When Vaughn left the stand, he threw me a look, one of abhorrence.

I gave him a big, shiny grin. He stalked from the room.

# 32

The judge announced a fifteen-minute break, and the jury filed out. Q came forward and hugged me, whispering that I'd done *"fabulously,"* then he took off.

Valerie stood and came to my side. "You were excellent. Thank you."

"Of course. So, about this weekend…"

"Yes, I wanted to say thank you. And I'd like your mother's address to send her a note. That was lovely of her."

"Sure. You took off pretty fast." *And without telling me what you were about to reveal to Amanda and Bridget that night.* I wanted so badly to know. But I didn't want to push her.

"Yes, I apologize." Nothing else was forthcoming.

"That's okay. We'll do it again. Get together, I mean."

"Sure."

I could tell she was like an animal about to bolt for the safety of the deep woods, so I said nothing else about that topic. I turned and pointed to Mayburn. "That man is an investigator I use sometimes to help on cases. He came up with a lot of material that I used with Detective Vaughn. And so did my father." I pointed at him.

"He's…kind of an investigator, too. Would you like to meet them?"

Valerie peered around me, something anxious in her eyes, but she nodded. "Yes, okay."

Maggie, Valerie and I walked to my dad and Mayburn. "Thanks, you guys," Maggie said. "Amazing stuff. We had an investigator on the case, and he didn't come up with information that the neighbor had been a suspect."

"No problem," Mayburn said.

My dad murmured. "Of course."

I introduced them to Valerie, both of whom shook her hand and asked polite questions about how she was. Very little flustered my dad or Mayburn, and the sight of a beautiful woman charged with murder probably only registered as a beautiful woman. Valerie seemed to feel their relaxed way toward her and even smiled a little. Eventually, she excused herself.

When she was gone, I thought of the idea I'd had while I was crossing Vaughn. I pointed to my dad, then Mayburn. "You two could make a great team."

I purposefully raised this topic in public, because I knew both would reject the suggestion in private. Before they could say anything, I spoke up once more. "You should work together."

"I don't think so," my dad said. "John seems to have a nice operation going on his own."

"Yeah, that's kind of how I like it."

My dad nodded at him, like he completely understood.

"I don't mean *together,* together," I said. "Just divide up tasks. C'mon, we really need your help in this case."

"We do," Maggie said. "You've already gotten us some info on Dr. St. John, but we need to look into him further, since the cops didn't, and we should find out what we can about the nanny, too."

"And Mayburn is already researching all the other players in this case," I said. "Plus, Maggie's firm can't pay that much."

Maggie nodded. "My grandfather took this case on for free. We're paying Izzy on it, because we needed her to step in. We'd like you to do the same, but we can't pay what Izzy tells me you're used to, especially since we already paid one investigator."

"And neither of you wants to shake down the whole case," I said. "But at the risk of repeating myself, we really, *really,* need your help." I'd taken Vaughn down a notch, but the state still had a lot of great evidence against Valerie. No one said anything for a second, so I continued, "Mayburn, you're trying to change your lifestyle, maybe have more time in case Lucy comes around…" I trailed off. It was kind of a low blow, but it was true. "And Dad, you're not sure what you want to do, and you don't know how things really work in Chicago. And you're sort of in the same business, so even if it weren't for this case, it would make sense to team up."

"Good point," Mayburn said, half under his breath.

My dad and Mayburn looked at each other, as if for the first time.

"Good," I said. "It's decided. This will be your test case."

# 33

He thought about it all the time now—about the night when he'd gone to the house to make it real.

No. Speak the truth. He'd gone to the house see death, to see another human being die.

He was led into a room. Brown plastic molded chairs, cement floors painted cement-gray, the walls made of large yellow-colored brick.

Along the left wall were telephones. He kept looking at them. The phone at the very end was labeled. Although he couldn't make out that label, he didn't need to. He knew what that phone was intended for. It was reserved for a savior.

He looked around. There were people here, but no saviors. They were all out for blood, out for death.

He thought about the girl, too. Thought about her all the time, in fact, although he supposed she wasn't a girl anymore. No, she had continued to grow, while the other, the one who had been killed, would always be fifteen.

"All right," a man said, his voice gravelly, ominous, "let's go."

Finally, he let himself look toward the front of the room, at the man with the gravelly voice, and more importantly at the man whose life was about to end. He hadn't thought that man would be able to see him, since he was sitting toward the back. But he was wrong. The man stared at him, kept staring, challenging him, his eyes telling him, *You know.*

After a minute, the ominous voice said once again, "All right, let's go." And then it started.

That look stayed with him. It was part of him now. He saw those eyes every night.

# 34

The next detective took the stand, and Ellie Whalen stood to direct her witness. At first, she took him through the same sort of questions she'd asked Vaughn.

But then she put down her notes, crossed her arms and said, "Okay, detective. Let's talk about the food." She glanced over at Valerie then looked back at the detective. "You spoke to the coroner after Amanda Miller was murdered, correct?"

"Yes, that's correct."

"What did the coroner say about the cause of death?"

Maggie stood. "Objection. Hearsay."

"Sustained."

Ellie paused to rethink her question. "Did *you* ever learn the cause of death for Ms. Miller?"

"Yes. I read the autopsy report," he said. "The cause was…"

But Maggie jumped up again. "Objection, Your Honor. It's still hearsay if the detective read it."

"Counsel misconstrues my statement," Ellie said.

"No, counsel does not," Maggie retorted.

She and Ellie went back and forth, arguing and sending each other scathing looks. In the end, Maggie lost and she sat down, giving a low huff that only Valerie and I could hear.

"The cause of death," the detective said, "was cardiac arrhythmia caused by food that had been laced."

"When you say 'laced,' detective, what do you mean?"

"Two batches of Mexican food were made on the night of Amanda Miller's death. In one batch of food was a high amount of a drug. It was essentially mixed into the food."

"And did Ms. Miller eat that food?"

"Yes, and she died after eating it."

The court reporter requested a break to fix a problem with her machine, and I leaned toward Maggie. "Mother father, this isn't good," I whispered to her.

"*Mother father?* Is that a swear word replacement?"

"Yeah."

"For *what?*"

"Mother fucker," I said, dropping my voice even more.

"See! You just said it. You *always* end up saying the 'bad' words. So let's just quit this."

"No. I'm trying to make myself a better person."

Maggie rolled her eyes and sat up as the judge called for the state to continue their questioning.

"Okay, let's take a step back for a second," Ellie said. "What kind of food are we talking about here?"

"As I said, it was a Mexican dish. Specifically, it was called chicken *mole*."

"Okay, and please tell the jury who prepared that food?"

"Amanda Miller and Valerie Solara."

"From whom did you learn that, Detective?"

Maggie jumped up again. "Objection. Again this is hearsay."

"If counsel will permit the witness to answer, she will see that this is an admission against interest."

"I'll allow it for now," the judge said.

"Thank you, Your Honor," Maggie said, as if she'd won the objection. But she sat down with another under-her-breath huff.

"From Valerie Solara," the detective said.

"Do you see Ms. Solara in the courtroom today?"

"Yes."

"Can you stand and identify her, please?"

The detective, a big guy, groaned a bit as he got to his feet. He looked directly at Valerie and pointed to her.

The eyes of everyone in the courtroom shot to our table and to Valerie. It was an awful feeling. A detective, standing there and pointing, made even me feel guilty. I glanced at Valerie to see how she was doing.

She blinked and blinked again, looking startled.

Maggie made a soft growling sound. "I've seen The Point a million times," she whispered, "but I still hate it when they do it."

The detective sat down, and Ellie Whelan perused her notes, letting the silence fill the room for a few moments. "Now, Officer," Ellie went on, "in your twenty-six years of detective work, have you ever known anyone to commit suicide by poisoning their own food?"

"No."

"Is there any reason to think in this case that Amanda Miller poisoned her food in order to take her life?"

"No."

"If Mrs. Miller did not place that poison in her own food, then who did?"

"In my professional opinion, it was Valerie Solara."

"On what do you base that opinion?"

"A few things. For one, it was Valerie Solara's recipe.

She'd learned it from her father. For another, she was teaching Amanda the recipe, so we know she was directing the preparation of the dish. Also, Xavier Miller saw her putting something blue into one of the batches of the chicken *mole*."

"Objection!" Maggie called.

"Sustained."

Ellie moved on as if she hadn't noticed. "Detective, what color is the drug you spoke about, the drug that killed Amanda Miller?"

"Blue."

"Now, Detective," she continued, "in your line of work, do you deal with motives for crimes?"

"Absolutely. That's our bread and butter."

"And what would Ms. Solara's motive be to do such thing to Amanda Miller?"

"We learned that she had, essentially, tried to seduce Mr. Miller before the death."

"Objection, hearsay," Maggie said.

"Admission against interest," Ellie answered.

"Overruled."

"When you say she tried to seduce Mr. Miller, you are referring to Amanda's husband, correct?" Ellie prompted.

"Correct. Xavier Miller. We concluded that Valerie Solara wanted her friend to die so that she could take her place in their relationship."

"Objection," Maggie said. "Speculation."

"Sustained. The jury will disregard."

Maggie sat down. "Finally, I get sustained," she muttered.

But the damage had already been done. "That will be all, Detective," Ellie Whalen said before she sat at the state's table with a satisfied look on her face.

Maggie was out of her chair in a second. "Detective, you just told us that there was no reason to believe Amanda Miller killed herself. But you learned that Amanda Miller was suffering from depression at the time of her death, didn't you?"

"That's correct."

"We know that because you wrote that in your notes, right?"

"Yes."

"You learned that depression had come on quite recently, is that correct?"

"Yes, it had started about a month before her death, but—"

"Thank you, Detective," Maggie said, cutting him off. "You learned the depression was severe, didn't you?"

"I don't recall."

"Well, let me refresh your recollection." She looked at the judge. "Your Honor, may I approach?"

"You may."

Maggie made her way over to the witness stand. "Showing you what has been marked as Exhibit number seventeen. Detective, those are your notes, correct? The general progress reports you made in this case?"

"Yes."

"Why don't you read those to yourself to refresh your recollection about what you learned about the severity of Mrs. Miller's depression?"

The detective took his time. Then he put the notes on the railing that surrounded the witness stand.

Maggie picked them up. "You learned her depression was severe, right?"

"Yeah."

"That's the word you wrote—*severe*. Is that correct?"

"Yes."

"Thank you," Maggie said in a voice that indicated she was done with that topic. She wasn't going to specifically draw the conclusion that Amanda Miller had, in fact, poisoned her own food, but she was going let the jury wonder about it.

Maggie continued with her cross. She used the information Mayburn had dug up about the disagreements the Millers had with their neighbor.

"Detective, where did that neighbor live?" Maggie asked.

"He lives just to the north of the Millers."

"So his house is *directly* next door to the Millers."

"That's correct."

"The name of this neighbor, please."

"Can I see my notes again?"

Maggie glared at him a little. She thought that the detective knew the neighbor's name just fine but was trying to tweak her by making her trot over with his notes.

Maggie stood next to the detective while he looked at his notes, all the while glancing at her watch.

Finally, the detective said, "Dr. Dominick St. John."

"And what is the approximate distance between the Millers' house and that of Dr. St. John?"

The detective shrugged. "I didn't measure it. Maybe twenty feet."

"Pretty close, huh?"

"I don't know. Define *close*."

Maggie let it go. "And you learned that the St. Johns and the Millers had once been good friends."

"Correct," he said. "But then they had some dispute over control of an association of sorts, some neighborhood kind of thing." It was clear the detective didn't think much of the neighborhood "thing."

"In addition—" Maggie lifted the police records to

show him she had knowledge of this information and he'd better go along with her "—you mentioned here that the St. Johns and the Millers often left their doors open during the day, isn't that right?"

"Yes. The kids are all apparently friends, and they go back and forth between the houses."

"From your investigation, did you determine what time the Mexican food was prepared?"

"Between three and five."

"That's 3:00 to 5:00 p.m. right? So, during the day?"

A grunt. "Yeah."

"Did you determine whether the Millers' house was locked or unlocked at that time?"

He made a wry face, the look of a witness who knows a good point is about to be scored by the opposition. "We believe it was unlocked."

"Later that evening, at the time of Mrs. Miller's death, was the house locked or unlocked?"

Another wry face. "Same answer, counselor."

"The house was unlocked."

"Yeah."

"Thank you, Detective."

# 35

I left the courtroom to use the restroom but stopped short when I got into the hallway. There was Detective Vaughn.

"You're still here?" I said. Though we'd never spoken outside an official capacity—he as a detective, me a witness—in a screwed-up way, Vaughn and I had been through much together. Enough that I didn't feel the need for pleasantries.

He peered at me with his forest-green eyes under thick brown brows. "I was waiting for you."

My stomach turned. No good had ever come of Vaughn waiting or looking for me.

He held up his hands in a show of surrender, as if he had read my nervous thoughts. "I just… I wanted to talk for a second."

I narrowed my own eyes, suspicious, said nothing.

"So—" he nodded toward the courtroom "—you did a good job in there."

I was so surprised at his words that something seemed to stick in my throat. I coughed. I had never heard, nor ever expected, a compliment coming from Damon Vaughn.

But then of course he had to take it away. "I kinda let you score some points," he said.

"You *kinda* let me? I took you down, dude. Admit it."
I didn't say the word *dude* much. Possibly I had picked it
up from Theo. Either way, it felt okay.

He shrugged. "You did a good job." He cleared his
throat. "I also wanted to talk to you because, well, I'm
trying to make amends."

"What does that mean? Are you in AA or something?"

A short laugh. "Probably should be. No. Getting a
divorce." He raised a hand, and in what looked like a
nervous gesture, he brushed through his rough brown
hair with it. Although his body was lean, his features
were coarse—his nose thick across the bridge, his jawline wide and straight. Put together, the whole picture of
him was that of someone manly, someone strong. And
yet his expression now was one mixed with pain and
embarrassment.

"Oh. Sorry." I actually felt a little bad for him. Breaking up with Sam had been one of the more excruciating
times of my life, and we hadn't even been married.

Vaughn shrugged again. "It's okay. I guess. But anyway, I've been looking at my behavior over the years
and…I guess, well, I guess I'm sorry."

I took a look behind me, then back at him. "You saying
you're sorry to *me?*"

"Yeah. I think I might have been a little rough on you
back then." He shrugged again. "There were a lot of reasons. I mean, hell, the evidence I had…"

"The *evidence?* This is you sounding sorry?" My hair
suddenly felt hot on my neck, and I shook it back over my
shoulders.

"No, I am." Vaughn nodded. "Really. I'm sorry."

"Did a Chicago police officer just apologize to me?"
I said sarcastically. That felt good, too. I wasn't often

sarcastic. "Let's get a court reporter out here. We need someone to witness this."

His green eyes glared a little. "I said it once. I won't ever say it again. There it is."

I thought about it. I scoffed for good measure, then said, "Okay. I'll take it." I didn't like giving in so easily, but I was shocked at how good it felt to have Vaughn saying, essentially, that he believed me now. I hadn't known I needed his…what? Forgiveness? That wasn't right. His…opinion? No. It was, I suppose, a *belief* that he knew I was innocent. And now that I'd learned of that belief, I could let it erase the tiny cache of my own embarrassment that I still, apparently, carried around. I hadn't known the shame was there until now, but just as fast, with Vaughn's apology, it was gone. And it felt good.

We stood in an awkward silence. It seemed a farewell of sorts.

"Well," he said.

"Well."

"If you ever need anything…" He picked up his left hand, then let it drop, in some sort of strange half salute that made me think he'd gotten the gesture from a TV show and had copied it in a mirror. "Yeah," he continued. "So let me know." Another TV-detective hand gesture. "I'm pretty good at making problems disappear or taking care of them quickly."

"I'm not sure I know what that means."

He didn't explain.

I took a step toward him. He almost looked a little nervous.

I held out my right hand.

He looked at it. Shook it. And walked away.

# 36

From a doorway down the hall, Valerie watched Izzy and the detective. A minute earlier, Valerie had slipped out of the courtroom, skirting around them and went to the restroom. When she came out she saw them shake hands. Now the detective turned away, walking the hall-way with officious, succinct hits of his heels.

Valerie turned herself and headed toward the empty courtroom, the one where she always went during breaks or before court started. There, she would meet a bored law clerk from the Bristols' office, someone barely older than her daughter, and that clerk would, essentially, babysit her. It was an embarrassing situation. But Valerie couldn't handle the stares she got in the main courtroom—from Amanda's friends, and from people she didn't know but who all looked at her with a certain mix of insatiable curiosity and hatred.

She was almost to the quiet courtroom, her sanctitude, when a door opened. The men's room. She kept her head down and tried to dodge around the door, but the person actually put out a hand, as if to block her. It was only then she looked up.

Her mouth opened. Nothing came out. Finally, she said his name. "Zavy."

She hadn't come face-to-face with him for nearly a year. She had only seen him in court, where he always avoided looking at her.

"Valerie," he said. He wasn't avoiding her now. He was staring at her. "I thought I would feel anger toward you," he said. He shook his head. "But it's only pity."

She stalled, her mouth open, her whole body frozen, and yet someone was screaming—one long, loud tone in her head. Finally, she managed to speak around it. "Excuse me," she said. She stepped around him this time, trudging, zombielike, that voice still screaming, toward the empty courtroom and her law clerk babysitter, where she could sit in silence. And she would try not to think about Xavier Miller.

# 37

"Counsel, what's up next?" the judge asked from the bench.

"We have a snafu," Ellie Whelan said. "Sorry, Judge." She threw a smile at Maggie and me that made it clear she wasn't truly sorry about whatever she was about to say. "We planned for two other detectives to testify this afternoon, but we've determined that we don't need them. We'd like to call the coroner."

"He's available?"

"Yes. He was in the courthouse for another case."

"Son of a bitch," Maggie muttered, then addressed the bench in a loud voice. "Your Honor, we request a continuance. Counsel had originally indicated to both the court and to us that Dr. Rosen wouldn't be called for a few days."

The judge sighed, gave a small glare at the state's attorneys, then addressed Maggie in a tired voice. "Counsel, I've got a jury that just waited through a lunch break to hear testimony. We've got to keep this trial moving. No continuance." He looked at the state's attorneys. "Don't let this happen again."

"Yes, sir."

"When will Dr. Rosen be here?"

"He's here now," Tania Castle said, speaking up.

"Judge, we need some prep time," Maggie said.

"Fifteen minutes." The judge stood and left the bench.

I turned to Maggie, my eyes wide. "Are you *kidding* me? He's just going to let them call an *expert* witness with no notice?"

"Dirty trick," Maggie said, glaring at the state's attorneys over my shoulder. "But that's how it goes around here."

I said nothing, stumped. Never, ever would this have happened in a civil courtroom, where the lawyers realized that it took a hell of a lot of time to prep for the cross of a highly trained physician. "It's ludicrous," I finally blurted out. "I mean, surely, we can do something. Let's ask again. Let's get the judge out here. Let's..."

"Hey, Lawyer For Hire," Maggie said, cutting me off. "This is how it goes around here. You never know what'll come flying at you."

"And so now a forensic pathologist is flying at us?"

Maggie looked at her watch. "You just blew one of our fifteen minutes." She sighed. "The truth is, there's usually not much to cross a coroner on."

We spent the next fourteen minutes looking through Dr. Rosen's testimony from the grand jury and found Maggie was right. There wouldn't be much material with which to pick apart his direct testimony. And that testimony wasn't going to be pretty.

The coroner was a man who looked very, very tired. From his testimony about when he'd gone to college and medical school, it sounded like he was in his late forties, but his skin was as gray as the corpses he worked on. His eyes were bloodshot slits.

Maggie leaned over and whispered in my ear, "They work these guys like dogs. They have huge backlogs of cases."

"Doctor," Tania Castle said to the coroner, "in connection with your duties, did you have occasion to perform an autopsy on the body of a woman named Amanda Miller?"

"Yes, I did."

"And did you take notes or produce any kind of report regarding your examination of the body?"

"I took notes and then I wrote what we call a postmortem report."

Tania marked the report as an exhibit and approached the witness. She took the doctor through how the autopsy was performed, how they weighed the body and measured the length of it. He described his external and internal examinations.

"And what did those examinations reveal, Doctor?"

"The internal exam was unremarkable. The external exam showed some bruising about the wrists."

"What would have caused that?"

"I received information that Ms. Miller had fallen on the night of her death and her husband had caught her by the wrists. The bruising could be consistent with that."

"So your initial opinion as to the cause of Amanda Miller's death?"

"Inconclusive."

"Doctor, what is a toxicology screen?"

"It's testing of blood, urine and gastric contents to determine the presence of drugs or other toxicants that might be present in the body."

"Is that routinely done?"

"It's often done in cases like this with an otherwise healthy person and no evident cause of death."

"What did the toxicology screen reveal in this case?"

"Nothing initially."

I looked at the jury and saw some of them giving each other puzzled expressions.

"What happened next with respect to your examination of the body of Mrs. Miller?"

"At the urging of detectives, we ordered additional toxicology to look for one drug in particular."

"What drug was that?"

"Propranolol. It's a beta blocker, which means that it blocks the effects of adrenalin on the cardiovascular system. It lowers heart rate and blood pressure."

"And what are the most common medical uses for Propranolol?"

"Hypertension and cardiac arrhythmias."

"Do you know why the detectives requested a tox screen for Propranolol?"

"Because Mrs. Miller had been in possession of the drug. Apparently, she did a lot of speaking at charitable engagements and she used Propranolol for stage fright." He looked at the jury. "The drug is also used for anxiety. At some point, the detectives or Mrs. Miller's husband realized that the Propranolol she usually had was missing."

"What did the toxicology screen show?"

"A large dose of Propranolol in her system."

"Doctor, why didn't the initial tox screen show that?"

"It's not included in the basic screening. We can't test for the presence of every drug. It's far too expensive."

"Doctor, based on your training and experience, did you reach an opinion as to the cause of Mrs. Miller's death?"

"Yes, I did. She died as a result of cardiac arrhythmia, brought on by the large amount of Propranolol in her system, which was ingested from the food she had eaten that night."

"Do you have an opinion to a reasonable degree of certainty as to how the Propranolol got in the food?"

"Objection," Maggie said, standing.

"Judge, I'm not asking who did what here," Tania said. "I just want the doctor's opinion from his review of the body."

"Overruled," the judge said. "Continue, counsel."

Tania restated her question.

"Yes, I do have an opinion," the doctor said. "An additional review of the stomach contents showed that a number of Propranolol tablets had been crushed and then mixed into the food she ate."

"What happens when that amount of the drug is in the body?"

"Cardiac arrhythmia can occur, which causes the BP and heart rate to drop dramatically, and the person can slip into shock and die."

"And is that what occurred here?"

"Yes."

"And the Propranolol, what form does that come in?"

"Tablet."

"What color are the tablets?"

"Blue."

"Would you say it's the same shade as blue cornmeal?"

"I've never seen blue cornmeal. I don't cook."

"Thank you, Doctor. That will be all."

Tania sat down.

"Cross?" the judge said.

I looked past Maggie to Valerie, who was hanging her head, eyes closed. I wanted to tell her to look up. I wanted to tell her she looked guilty, but Maggie and I had to talk fast about what to do now.

We huddled together. "I don't think there's anything," I said.

"I don't, either," Maggie said, "but I hate to not cross a witness who was so harmful to us."

We thought for a second.

"Counsel?" the judge said.

Maggie's eyes went bright. "I think I have something," she whispered.

She stood but didn't move around the table. "Just one question, Doctor. Would a physician, an average internist, know about a drug like Propranolol and what dosage would be lethal?"

Tania stood now, too. "Objection to relevancy."

"Judge, there has been testimony that the Millers were in a feud with their neighbor, Dr. St. John, who is an internist. Since the witness is also a physician, I want to ask him what the average internist might know about this drug."

"I'll allow it," the judge said.

"Thank you, Your Honor." She looked at the witness. "Doctor, should I repeat the question?"

"No, I remember it, and the answer is yes, an average internist would know about a drug like Propranolol and what dosage would be lethal."

"Thank you, Doctor. Nothing further."

# 38

"Am I even married to Spence?"

My mom and I were in her bedroom. I sat on the bed, talking with her as she changed clothes for the evening, something she did nearly every night whether she and Spence were going to the opera or merely having Charlie and me for a visit, like they were that night. I, on the other hand, hadn't done this since I was a kid—watch her get ready. Well, the truth was, with her depression, she sometimes wore the same clothes for days back then. And so when she changed at night, I knew she was in a good mood. "What are you talking about?" I asked. "I was at your wedding."

My mother disappeared into her walk-in closet. She called out, "But I was still married, technically, to your father."

I tried to think about this through the eyes of the law. I'd never encountered a dead-then-not-dead-husband scenario in my legal career. "I'm sure you're married. You believed, reasonably, that your husband was gone."

My mom stepped out of the closet, threading a black patent-leather belt through the loops of her white wide-legged pants. She halted a moment, seemed to be remembering something. "Spence was my Onassis. I felt like Jackie Kennedy."

I wanted her to talk more, but she said nothing, just continued to fasten her belt, then went to the large mirror where she always stood to refresh her makeup. "That's not a bad thing," I ventured. "That you felt like he was your Onassis."

"No. God, no. It saved me. But it required me to give up what I thought I knew, that your father was alive, that your father and I were meant to be together." She sighed. "*Meant to be together.* I'm too old for these things."

"You're not too old for anything."

She looked at me now. "No, of course not." I got the feeling she was saying it more for me than for herself. "But really, this idea of two people being two halves of a whole, it seems silly to me that I bought into that."

I didn't know what to say. *I* believed that. And as I watched my mom, I realized I didn't want her to think differently. So much of my life, my belief system, I guess, was based on that idea.

My mother seemed to sense my unease. "Don't listen to me."

"You dressed, Mom?" Charlie called then from the hallway.

"Yes, hon, come in."

"Don't listen to me about what?" Charlie said, loping into the room. He wore jeans and a shirt with the sleeves rolled up. He fell onto my mother's bed with a tired *ummph.*

My phone rang. *Mayburn.* I hopped off the bed and stepped out of the room to answer it.

"Hey, Iz," he said. "Your dad and I—we got some information on Sylvia Zowinski."

"Who?"

"The nanny for the Millers."

"Great. What kind of information?"

"Her husband is a bad guy," Mayburn said.

"Sounds like she's a bad guy, too, with all those things she was convicted of."

"That's the thing. She got convicted, but it definitely appears her husband was the mastermind behind the whole thing. Looks like she finally got the balls to leave him, and that's when she took the job with the Millers. She was with them for a few years and had no other criminal problems."

"Where's the husband now?"

"Can't find him."

"Any reason to think he might have wanted to kill Amanda Miller? Or that she did?"

"Not sure. We know the husband wasn't happy about his wife leaving and going to work for them. But as I said, she had worked for the Millers for some years and there were no incidents that we know of."

"Have you talked to her?"

"She left the country."

"Whoa. Really?"

"Yeah. She's from Honduras—Zowinski was her married name. Her real last name is Cordova. She told people in the Millers' neighborhood, after Amanda died, that she was going home to be with her family."

"Or was she running from something she did?"

"But what's the motive?"

"Maybe she was running from something her husband did."

"We'll keep looking into it, but as of right now, we've hit some dead ends."

Despite the message, I liked hearing him say *we*. "How do you like working with my dad?"

"Well, since it's the first day, it's hard to tell."

"What's your impression?"

"That he's a bit of a cold fish."

"Oh, and you're so warm and fuzzy?" I felt a little defensive. *I* could certainly complain about my father. But I didn't want anyone else to.

"You're right." Mayburn laughed. "It's going fine. I'll talk to you later."

I went back into my mom's bedroom and crawled on the bed next to Charlie. "How was work?" I asked him.

"Great. I love it."

My mom, who was threading gold earrings through her lobes, gave me a happy *how-crazy-is-that?* look.

"What were you guys talking about before?" Charlie said, propping some pillows behind his head. "Two halves of a whole?"

"We were discussing two people being right for each other," I said.

"We were talking about me getting old," my mom said.

"You're not getting old," Charlie scoffed.

"It's true." I pointed at my mom. "Look at her. She's more beautiful than ever."

My mother blushed, something she did not normally do.

I sat up. "You know, you *do* look really good." My mother looked remarkably...*what was it?*...refreshed, I guess.

"Yeah," Charlie said. "Have you been getting a lot of sleep?"

My mother half shrugged, seemed sheepish. "Something like that."

I looked closer at her. "What's going on with you?"

She shrugged again, but she was looking down. My

mother had always been the most honest of people, even with her emotions. *Especially* with her emotions. She had never been able to hide a moment of melancholy or anything else that she felt. I always wished she had some sort of filter. But now, she was clearly holding something back, and I didn't like the feel of the shield she seemed to erect.

"What's going on with you?" I asked again.

My mother looked at the ceiling now, appeared to be trying to glean some guidance from the heavens. Finally, she spoke. "I went to the dermatologist," she said. She explained that her dermatologist had done various "procedures," and she was considering others.

"You mean surgery?" I said, surprised. My mother's best friend, Cassandra, had undergone a number of "touch up" procedures, and my mother had always sworn she wouldn't do the same.

"No, of course not. I just had some things…done. A little of this, a little of that."

"What does that mean? Like Botox?"

She nodded. "And a few other things." She looked at Charlie and me, and I could see she was nervous for our reaction.

"Have at it," I said. "I'm in full support."

Charlie spoke up. "I'm not."

My mother studied him. "Charlie. You're judging me? *You?*"

We both knew what she meant. For one thing, Charlie was just about the least judgmental person we knew. For another, he had milked a worker's comp settlement into two years of sitting around and doing mostly nothing, which my mother and I never judged him for.

Charlie looked confused, as if he, too, was surprised to find himself saying this. He eyed my mom. "I just think you don't need to do anything. Aging is a natural process, and you're gorgeous." He put his hands to his face and patted the skin under his eyes. "I'm getting lines, too. They're natural."

My mother and I burst out laughing.

"You don't have lines!" I said.

"None!" my mother agreed. She turned and looked in the mirror. "You have no idea what it's like to age physically. Especially when you're a woman. It's such a strange thing. In my mind, I'm smarter, more aware than I've ever been, but this shell that I wear I'm…well, it's disintegrating. That's the only way to say it."

"And that's natural," Charlie said.

"So what if it's natural?" She sounded annoyed. "Does that mean I shouldn't address it? Diabetes occurs naturally, and if it does, you take insulin. If you get heart disease *naturally* because you eat too much steak or you have high blood pressure because you eat too much cheese, they treat it with medication or surgery. If your teeth are dirty, *naturally,* from eating, you brush them."

I said nothing, surprised at what was essentially an outburst from my normally sedate mother.

"But you don't have diabetes or heart disease," Charlie said.

"If I did, I would take something. What I do have now is aging, so why shouldn't I do something about it?"

"I don't know," Charlie said, sounding less sure of himself now. "You always said you would never have anything done. And I just think you're beautiful already."

My mother smiled and laughed, a particularly happy, tinkling laugh she'd always had yet rarely used. She walked to the bed and kissed Charlie on the forehead. "Thank you," she said simply.

"Where are you all?" we heard Spence call.

He entered the bedroom a few seconds later, looking surprised to find us there. "Why aren't you in the kitchen?"

"We were just chatting," my mother said.

"Yes, but…" Spence seemed to falter. It was true; he wouldn't have usually found Charlie and me in my mother's room. "I have things ready," he said simply. I could picture the bay window in the kitchen downstairs, the table loaded with snacks and wine.

"I was just telling Charlie and Izzy how much I dislike getting older," my mom said.

Spence's eyebrows drew together. He ran a hand through what was left of his graying hair. He looked entirely…what was the word? *Disquieted.*

And indeed, this was a new side of my mother we were seeing. Was the therapy making her open up, making her change? Was it my father's appearance in town, and back in our lives, that was causing her to have a tougher time with aging?

"Well, I…" Spence shifted back and forth, looking distinctly uncomfortable in his own bedroom.

"Let's all go downstairs," my mother declared, striding across the room to kiss him on the cheek.

"Yes, let's," I said, standing, wanting to make Spence feel better.

"Yes, let's," Spence said, echoing me. But his words sounded hollow.

## 39

"State your name for the record, please."

"Xavier Miller."

"And your address?"

Zavy shifted forward in his seat toward the microphone, stating an address in downtown Chicago.

Ellie Whelan, dressed in a pale blue suit, looked up from her notes. "And how long have you lived there?"

"Eight years."

"Who do you live with, sir?"

"Generally, my two daughters. My stepdaughters. But they're staying with their aunt for a while."

"Why is that, sir?"

"Because of…" Zavy Miller picked up a hand and trailed it around the courtroom. His eyes landed on Valerie's, then went back to Ellie Whelan. "Because of all this."

"And has anyone else lived in that house with you and your stepdaughters?"

"Yes. Previously my wife lived there also. Before she died."

"And who was your wife, sir?"

Zavy Miller looked very handsome, wearing a navy suit and a silk tie. He brushed a hand through his blond hair. "My wife was Amanda Miller."

"How long were you and Amanda married?"

"Six years."

"So, Mrs. Miller had two daughters from a previous marriage?"

"That's correct. But I adopted them after we were married."

"Why is that?"

"Their father had a substance-abuse problem and lost custody of them."

We heard someone in the courtroom murmur, *Aw.*

Zavy continued. "I became very close with them after Amanda and I met."

"And how old are your stepdaughters now, sir?"

"Tessa is twelve, and Brit is nine."

"Brit is Britney?"

"Yes."

Ellie Whelan turned a page of notes and asked a few more questions about Zavy and his stepdaughters.

I leaned close to Maggie. "He's a good witness."

"Excellent, unfortunately."

"Let's take a step back," Ellie Whelan said. "How did you and Amanda meet?"

He smiled. "We met at a theater downtown. We were seeing the same matinee. Tessa was only five at the time. She had wandered away from her mother, and I helped her find her mom."

"Jesus," Maggie whispered. "He's friggin' St. Anthony."

"Which one is that?" I asked.

"The saint who helps find lost stuff."

Maggie's family was decidedly Catholic, while I hadn't been raised with any particular faith. I found the saint stuff fascinating.

The room was silent, the jury paying close attention. "And how long did you and Amanda date before you were married?" Ellie asked.

"About a year. We were very much in love." His voice seemed to break a little at the end.

Ellie shrewdly consulted notes, letting that bit of emotion linger.

I heard a cough from Valerie, and I looked at her. She wore a black wrap dress with tiny checks of silver, her hair pulled back in a loose knot. She stared at Zavy, her eyes intense.

Right then the courtroom door opened and someone slipped inside and into the last row. People went in and out of the courtroom all the time, and usually I didn't pay much attention, but something made me look closer. And then I saw a man with golden hair, a man with olive-colored eyes.

"Holy shit, there's Sam," Maggie whispered. "What's he doing here?"

"I don't know," I said, my voice holding a tinge of nervousness.

Sam settled himself on the bench and let his eyes sweep the courtroom. They landed on mine. We both stared intensely. Then he smiled.

"Everything okay?" I mouthed.

He gave me a thumbs-up and a big smile. He had come to court to support me, I realized. Just like he used to when I represented Forester Pickett. I had always assumed Sam came back then because he also worked for Forester. But now here he was, far from his office, nothing connecting him to this trial. Except for me.

I blinked with surprise and pleasure, and turned back to Zavy Miller.

"Did your wife ever suffer from mental health issues?" Ellie Whelan was definitely a smart litigator. She was "fronting" the deceased's depression, knowing from earlier that this issue would rise again.

Zavy nodded, his eyes sad. "She had some problems with depression. It was recent—just a short time before she died."

"Do you know the reason for that depression?"

"She was trying to figure that out with her doctor. I'm not quite sure how much to say here.…" When Ellie Whelan didn't offer him any help, he added, "They were discussing premenopausal issues."

"That's fine, thank you," Ellie said. "Was Amanda taking any medications for this depression?"

"Yes."

"And how was that working?"

"She said it was helping."

I stood slightly. "Objection." Since I would be handling any cross-examination of Zavy, I was the one who was supposed to object. "Hearsay," I added.

"The statement was made by the deceased," Ellie said.

"And that statement does not exclude it from the hearsay rule."

Maggie gave me a tug on my jacket and whispered, "It does in a criminal action."

*Shazzer.* Another difference between civil and criminal.

I wanted to say, *Never mind,* but since that wasn't exactly legalese, I sat and said, "Objection withdrawn."

I glanced at Sam, who gave me another thumbs-up, as if my objection had been a brilliant legal maneuver rather than a bust. I couldn't help but smile again. Strange how natural it was to have him there. For a moment, I replaced him in my mind with an image of Theo—tattooed, long-haired, sexy-as-hell Theo—sitting in the courtroom instead. But that didn't seem natural at all. Theo felt completely removed from my professional life, and it was hard to imagine him playing a part the way Sam always had.

Ellie moved a little closer to Zavy Miller. "Sir, you mentioned your wife said the medications were working to alleviate her symptoms."

That wasn't exactly what he had said, but I didn't want to object again.

"Correct."

"Sir, based on your intimate knowledge of your wife and what you knew about her condition, was she depressed enough to take her own life?"

"No, certainly not."

Ellie Whelan nodded, then walked to the podium and put her notes down. She looked at her witness. "I need to ask a personal question, sir. How was your relationship with your wife?"

"Wonderful. We were very happy." Again, his voice had a crack in it.

I looked at the jury. Most appeared sympathetic. One woman blinked her eyes and squinted like she might tear up.

Zavy cleared his throat as if embarrassed. He lightly put his fist to his mouth while he did so. Then he looked up at Ellie.

"Do you need a minute, Mr. Miller?" Ellie asked.

"No. Thank you. I'm fine."

"Sir, directing your attention to the night of December second of last year. What were you doing on that night?"

Zavy stared straight ahead, but it didn't look as if he were focusing on anything in particular. He almost seemed to shudder, then he looked back at Ellie. "That night I had dinner with Amanda."

"And where did you have dinner?"

"At home."

"Were your daughters there?"

"No, they both had playdates. They were with friends."

"Did you and Amanda make dinner together?"

"No. She wanted to surprise me with Mexican food because it's one of my favorites."

"So your wife prepared the meal?"

"Yes. Well, she and…" His voice stopped. His eyes went to Valerie. This time they stayed there.

"Sir," Ellie prompted, "did anyone else prepare the meal with your wife?"

"Yes. Valerie Solara."

"Do you see Ms. Solara in the courtroom today?"

"Yes." His eyes still hadn't left Valerie.

"Can you point her out, Mr. Miller?"

Zavy lifted his index finger and pointed to Valerie.

"Sir, can you stand and do that again so that the entire courtroom can see?"

Next to me, I heard Maggie growl, then she said under her breath, "The Point. *Again.*"

I whispered back. "Should I object? It's not like he saw her stab his wife or something. It's probably not appropriate."

She shook her head no.

Zavy Miller stood, pointing to Valerie, then sat down again. I looked at Valerie. She tugged on a silver rope necklace around her neck. I tried to give her a message with telepathy. *Don't do that. You look uncomfortable. You look…guilty.*

As if she'd heard me, she dropped her hand, but still she looked straight at Zavy and he back at her.

"Now, Mr. Miller, how do you know that Valerie Solara assisted Amanda in preparing the Mexican meal that night?"

His eyes went back to Ellie Whelan. "Because I came home that afternoon from work and I saw them."

"You knew Valerie Solara before that time?"

"Yes, I'd known her since I met Amanda."

"And how would you characterize Amanda's relationship with Valerie Solara?"

He raised his eyebrows and exhaled. "Well, they *were* good friends."

"What do you mean by that, sir?"

"Well, she killed her, so…"

I stood. "Objection!"

"Sustained," Judge Bates said.

Once again, Ellie Whelan didn't blink. "Do you know how long Amanda and Valerie have been friends?"

"Maybe fourteen, fifteen years."

I leaned toward Maggie. "Can I switch places with you so I can be near Valerie?"

She nodded and slipped from her seat, letting me take it.

I gave Valerie what I hoped was a reassuring look.

"And had you become friends with Valerie?" Ellie asked Zavy.

"I *thought* I had."

This time Ellie didn't ask what he'd meant by his tone. "Can you tell us about your friendship with Valerie Solara?"

"Well, she was one of my wife's best friends. She and Bridget."

A couple of jurors looked at the people in the gallery as if searching for Bridget. She wasn't there because she was expected to testify later.

"We were all close," Zavy continued. "I became friends with her husband, Brian. When he got sick, Amanda and I tried to pitch in and help her."

I looked at Valerie. Her jaw was set in a straight line.

"Is that true?" I whispered to her. "Did they help you when Brian was sick?"

She nodded, not taking her eyes away from him.

"Do you know what kind of illness Brian suffered from?" Ellie asked.

"Objection," I said without standing.

Judge Bates turned to me. "Basis?"

"Relevancy."

I didn't really care if Zavy told the jury what illness Brian had. I simply wanted to mess with Ellie and throw her off her rhythm.

The judge knew it. He paused, giving me a look before he turned to Ellie. "I'll allow it."

"What kind of illness did Brian have?" Ellie asked.

"Lou Gehrig's disease."

"Returning your attention to the afternoon before your wife died, can you tell us more about what you saw when Ms. Solara and Amanda were preparing dinner?"

"It was chicken *mole*. Amanda told me it was a recipe that had been in Valerie's family, and she wanted to learn how to make it. Amanda did that a lot—cooking lessons and stuff like that."

"How much time did you spend with your wife and Valerie while they were making dinner?"

"Maybe thirty, forty minutes. I sat in the kitchen with them and we all chatted while they cooked."

"Did you see anything strange when you first came into the kitchen?"

"Objection," I said.

"Sustained."

"Did you see anything out of the ordinary?"

"Yes. Right when I walked in."

"What was that, sir?"

"Well, Valerie was by herself then. I guess Amanda was in the bathroom or something. And Valerie had... what do they call it?...a mortar and pestle. She had ground something in it, and she was putting that into one of the dishes."

"What do you mean by 'putting that' into one of the dishes?"

Zavy made a gesture, as dumping something out. "It was something blue, kind of powdery, and she was pouring it into one dish and then using her hand to make sure all of it got in there."

I stood. "Objection. The witness is making an assumption as to what was in the mind of the defendant."

"Granted."

"Let's back up," Ellie said. "When you said 'something blue,' what did you mean?"

"I wasn't sure what it was. I asked her, and she said it was blue cornmeal."

"Objection, hearsay," I said.

"It's not offered for the truth of the matter asserted," Ellie said.

"Overruled."

Ellie continued. "Did you have any further conversation about what she *said* was blue cornmeal?"

I really wished there was an objection for snotty insinuation by counsel. But since that wasn't on the books yet, I stayed silent.

"No. Valerie was an excellent cook. We'd had her Mexican food a number of times, so I trusted her." He sent Valerie a look that appeared sad, as if to say, *Yes, I had once trusted her.*

"And, sir, when you say she was pouring it into 'one of the dishes,' what did you mean by that?"

"They were making one dish, both technically chicken *mole,* but they said they were doing two versions of it. One would be a little spicier for Amanda. I have some minor digestive issues, so I don't eat food that's too spicy."

"And did you and your wife often create two versions of a dish for that reason?"

"Yes."

"After you spoke with your wife and Ms. Solara that afternoon, where did you go, sir?"

"To the gym. And briefly back to my office to pick up something."

"What do you do for work?"

"I'm an investor in various businesses, so I have a small office, and I make my own hours."

"When did you return to the house?"

"About an hour and a half later."

"Was Ms. Solara still at your home at that time?"

"No."

"How long after you returned did you and Amanda eat dinner?"

"Maybe an hour or so."

"Tell us about the dinner itself."

Zavy shifted forward. He exhaled audibly, adjusted his gray silk tie. "There's not much to tell. We ate. We talked about the kids. Tess had a play at school coming up, and we discussed that." He shrugged. "It was just... normal."

"Did you try both batches of the chicken *mole?*"

"No, I just ate the one."

"Did Amanda try both that evening?"

"No."

"Which batch did Amanda eat from?"

"She had the spicier one."

"How did you know which was spicier, if you didn't try both?"

"The dishes looked the same, but they had put a few sliced onions on the spicier one so we would know which was which."

"Did anything peculiar happened during dinner?"

"No, not at all."

"Was there any food left when you were done?"

"A little, but we put it down the disposal because we were planning on driving to our second home the next day."

"Where is that home?"

"Fontana, Wisconsin."

"What did you do after dinner?"

"We washed the dishes. Then we watched TV for a while."

"Did your children return?"

"No, they were both staying overnight at their friends' houses. Amanda had wanted it to be just us because we would be with the kids for a week at the lake."

"What happened next on that evening?" Ellie asked.

Next to me, I saw Valerie drop her head. When I glanced, her eyes were on her lap.

"We went to bed around ten, and then..." Zavy coughed, sounded like he was choking. He was, I realized, crying. He cleared his throat and shook his head. "I'm sorry."

"Do you need a break, Mr. Miller?" Ellie said.

"No. No, I'm fine."

His eyes strained, he lifted his head higher. "We went to bed that night, and then Amanda got up to use the restroom and...it was like her legs went out from under her. She sort of stumbled and fell."

"What did you do?"

"I helped her up from the floor."

"How did you do that?"

Zavy pantomimed a pulling gesture. "She was reaching her hands up to me for help, so I grabbed her by the wrists and pulled her to standing. She was breathing fast and said she was dizzy. I said we should go to the E.R., but she didn't want to."

"What happened then?"

"She said she felt weak and exhausted, and she just wanted to go to bed. I was worried about her, so I looked up *weakness* and *dizziness* on the internet, then ran out to the drug store to get her some medications."

"Mr. Miller, do you have any medical training?"

"No."

"So you were relying on what you read on the internet as to what might help Amanda?"

"Well, no, not really. I couldn't figure out what might be causing her symptoms. I just got anything I could think of, some Tylenol, some Tums, some iron pills, because she said she had been anemic once while she was pregnant."

"Was Mrs. Miller pregnant on the night she died?"

"No."

"Did any of the medications help?"

"She took the Tylenol. She said she did feel a little better, less dizzy, but I think she was trying not to worry me. It kept coming and going, the dizziness." His eyes were pained. "She looked so confused, so scared. I started saying that maybe we should go to the hospital. But then I found her on the floor of the living room. And she was..." His head sank toward his chest.

In my own chest, my heart went out to him.

"Dead," he said finally. His head stayed low. When he finally lifted it, there were tears trickling down his cheeks.

The courtroom was silent. Ellie let the moment hang.

She asked some clarifying questions, and Zavy testified more about looking for his wife, about finding her on the floor, about calling 911, about the efforts to revive Amanda. He talked about how the coroner had later told him that Amanda's food had been laced. He'd also told Zavy that he could have died if he'd eaten the same batch of food Amanda did. He talked about her funeral and the children she'd left behind.

Ellie Whelan raised a finger and cocked her head like she'd just remembered something. "Mr. Miller, let's go back in time for a second. You told us about how you and Amanda aided Valerie Solara when her husband was sick, is that right?"

He nodded.

"You have to answer out loud, please."

He leaned toward the microphone. "Yes, that's right."

"And during the last year of Brian's life, did you spend much time with Valerie and Brian?"

"Yes. They didn't live too far from us at the time. Amanda or I would often stay overnight there, because Brian needed care around the clock and we wanted Valerie to get some sleep."

"Did anything out of the ordinary ever happen during that time?"

"Objection," I said.

"Overruled."

Ellie repeated the question.

Zavy cleared his throat, gave a dodging glance at Valerie. "Yes. Something did happen one night."

"Please tell us about that."

He moved a little in his seat, looked uncomfortable. "Well, I was staying at their house, and Brian needed his airway cleared in the middle of the night. I took care of it, and when I left his bedroom, Valerie was standing in the hall."

"What time of the night was this?"

"Maybe two or three in the morning."

"Did Valerie and her husband share a bedroom at that time?"

"No, the master bedroom had been turned into a hospital room, essentially. When we were there, Valerie stayed with her daughter, Layla, in her room."

"And where would you stay?"

"In another guest room."

"What happened when you encountered Ms. Solara in the hallway that night?"

More shifting around in his seat. "We talked a little about Brian and what was going on with him. Then I went to move around her to go to bed, but she stopped me."

"How did she stop you?"

"She put her hand on my arm. And then she sort of pulled me toward her."

"What happened then?"

"She tried to kiss me."

An intake of breath from a few of the jurors.

"What did you do?"

"I pushed her away. Gently. But she kept trying to kiss me. She said she loved me."

I could feel some kind of energy pouring off of Valerie. I glanced at her, had no idea how to read the steely gaze she directed at Zavy.

Zavy spoke some more about how he'd rejected Valerie, how he'd felt bad for her, but he'd never been attracted to her. He had loved his wife.

"We need to talk before I cross," I whispered to Valerie. I needed to find out if what Zavy was saying about Valerie's seduction—*alleged* seduction, I should say— was true, as well as the details of that night.

But the opportunity to cross wasn't coming anytime soon. Zavy's testimony went on, the state's attorneys milking it for all it was worth before turning to the issue of Propranolol, the medication Amanda took occasionally and which, ultimately, killed her. She took it for stage fright, Zavy said, testifying just as the coroner had. She occasionally made speeches in her course as a board member for various charities. When she did so, she got extremely anxious and would sometimes take a tablet of Propranolol. She often refilled the prescription, even when she didn't need to, simply to have the medication on hand for the future.

Finally, Ellie said the magic words, "Nothing further," and sat down.

"Any cross examination?" the judge asked.

"Yes, Your Honor," I said, "but we'd request a short break first."

The judge looked at his watch. "Let's take a break now. I've got a settlement conference."

I looked into the courtroom gallery, my eyes finding Sam's. I turned to Maggie and Valerie. "I'll be back."

# 40

I made my way to Sam, noticing the small gallery was more crowded than it had been when we started the trial.

When I reached him, he was smiling shyly. I hadn't seen that look since the day we'd met at Forester's party years ago. We'd been standing on Forester's green lawn, behind his house, during the annual Pickett Enterprises' picnic. I had shaken Sam's hand. He had those martini olive-green eyes. And he had given me the exact shy but delighted smile he was giving me now.

"What are you doing here?" I said. Then I quickly added, "It's great to see you." It was the truth. I had felt my own smile somewhere inside me since I'd seen him enter the courtroom.

Sam shrugged. "I don't know. I was just excited for you when you told me about the trial. I had an appointment that was west of the city, and..." He shook his head. "Actually I didn't. I just wanted to see you, see how things were going."

That was exactly what he used to say every time he came to visit me in court. *I just wanted to see you, see how things were going.*

I was flooded with a rush of memories—Sam and me

on my rooftop deck, him playing the guitar; Sam and me at the James Hotel when we got engaged; Sam and me in the bleachers at a Cubs game, sweating happily in the sun. But the euphoria of those memories, the ones which came so fast, were followed by flashes of not-so-happy memories, ones that were feelings more than images— the despair when Sam had disappeared; the wondering if he was dead; the confusion of whether I had known the real Sam Hollings or someone else altogether.

But then I blinked, took in his shy grin and all the good memories came back. And all I felt was happiness at seeing him.

"And I just wanted to let you know," he said, "that I *am* figuring it out. But I don't want you thinking about us now."

*Us,* I thought. *Us.* I had to admit, I liked the sound of it.

"Just focus on the trial," Sam said. "On your job."

"Well, thanks," I said. Out of the corner of my eye, I saw Zavy Miller and I gestured with a thumb. "That's the widower of the deceased."

"Yeah, I could tell. How is Maggie going to cross him? Nice Maggie or mean Maggie?" Sam had watched Maggie in court, too, and he knew she could tailor her affect to the witness.

"She's not. I'm crossing him."

Again his eyes were excited. "Great. Good luck."

"Thanks." I looked at Sam and his green, green eyes. "So, shouldn't you be at work?"

"Yeah…" He laughed a listless laugh. "But work is…" He shrugged. "It's work."

"Still?" After Forester had died, Sam had been forced to take a job in the trading side of the business. He had told me that he spent his days studying volatility software, itching his index finger toward the mouse, waiting for the right moment to make the right trade at the right price. He missed his old job as a wealth management advisor. He missed dealing with people. He had loved working with Forester and his other clients, loved discussing their futures, their todays, and the ways they could best make their money work for them.

Another shrug. "Yeah, it's a job. It's just not an important one like yours." He looked around the courtroom.

I did, too. Was I doing something important here? I supposed so. I was helping to ensure someone's constitutional right to a trial by jury. But was I also defending someone who had murdered her friend? Zavy's testimony was eating at me.

"So, do you think Maggie will give you more of these cases?" he asked.

"I hope so. I do like being back in the law."

Sam's eyes searched mine. "I know. I can tell."

"You can?"

"Yeah. Yeah, definitely."

I liked that he saw me, understood me. I wondered if Theo could say the same. But probably that was too much to expect of Theo. We'd only been together months, whereas Sam and I had years in our collective storage closet.

"I should go." I looked at my watch. Five minutes of the break was gone. But something made me want to keep standing there in the light of Sam's gaze.

Just then my dad appeared behind Sam. And what followed was an incredibly uncomfortable moment.

I'd been engaged to Sam. I'd been about to marry him. But back then I hadn't known that my father was alive. The two had never met. I had no idea what to say.

I pointed at my dad, then Sam, then back again at my dad. "Christopher...Sam...Sam...Christopher."

The two men shook hands. I could see recognition immediately in my father's eyes. He knew who Sam was. Of course he did. But Sam clearly didn't know who he was. He knew *about* my dad, he knew he'd returned to our lives. But he didn't know what he looked like. And the name Christopher, such a common one, didn't seem to register.

"Nice to meet you," Sam said with a friendly voice.

Just then Maggie came up to say hi to Sam, and he turned to talk to her.

"Izzy," my dad said, voice low. "Mayburn and I made the rounds last night."

"I know, I talked to him."

"No, after that. We went looking for the doctor who lived near the Millers, but first we talked to everyone who was in the neighborhood. And we found out that there wasn't just one shouting match between Amanda and Dr. St. John. There were a number. One of them was at a block party. Another was in front of Dr. St. John's house. There were a couple more, too. Do you want all the info?"

"No, that's enough for now. That'll give me something to cross Zavy with, without the jury thinking I'm beating him up."

I was about to turn away when my dad stopped me, a hand tapping my shoulder.

"Do you want me to watch her?" he asked.

"Her who?"

"Valerie."

"Watch her like, do I want you to do surveillance on her?"

"No, watch her in court."

I was confused now. "What do you mean?"

"Izzy, I'm a psychologist. And when I was around—" meaning, *When I was alive...* "—I was a police profiler."

"Right. So?"

"I'm trained to study people, to figure out the type of person who commits a certain type of crime and ultimately the specific person who committed a specific crime. I've been watching her the whole time, actually. But I need a little bit more to form a professional opinion. Do you want that opinion?"

"On whether she did it?"

He nodded.

I didn't hesitate. I nodded, too.

Maggie walked away and Sam stepped back up to us. I took them both in—Sam, right next to my dad, shoulder to shoulder. Sam's blond hair looked bright, youthful, compared to my dad's graying brown hair, a vague color that seemed as if the vitality had been bled from it.

"I have to talk to Valerie," I said.

Both nodded. Neither moved. Awkwardness reigned.

"Okay," I said. "So...I'll see you later."

Sam smiled at that. My dad didn't.

Not knowing what else to do, I turned and walked back through the Plexiglas.

When I reached our table, I looked over my shoulder and stopped, my mouth parted a little in surprise at what I saw.

Sam and my dad were talking.

# 41

Maggie and I took Valerie into the order room, the one where we'd talked to Martin that first day of the trial.

Valerie seemed to read my thoughts. "How is your grandfather?" she asked Maggie.

"Thanks for reminding me. I want us to call him. He seemed pretty rested when we talked this morning. He asked that I let him know what Zavy testified to."

Valerie nodded. "Let's call him."

Maggie hit a button on her cell phone and turned on the speaker. Her grandmother answered then quickly put Martin Bristol on the phone.

"Hello, ladies." Usually, his voice was booming, lawyerly, take-charge. But this voice was smaller, weaker. "How was the testimony of Mr. Miller?" he asked.

Maggie nodded at Valerie to answer.

"It was difficult to listen to, Marty," she said. "But it was essentially what we expected." Her eyes moved to Maggie, who pushed the phone a little closer, then gave Martin a full rundown of the testimony, told him we were about to prepare for cross.

"Excellent," Martin said. "Well, it sounds like you have everything taken care of." He cleared his throat. "And that's good. I'm feeling a bit stronger—" we all shot each other glances; he didn't sound stronger "—but I have to do some research on a few old cases of mine."

None of us said anything. It wasn't typical for lawyers to dredge up old cases just for the heck of it.

"Research?" Maggie asked.

"Yes. But I'll be keeping my eye on you ladies. In fact, I'm about to call the Illinois Crime Lab."

Maggie's eyebrows moved together in a confused expression.

"The place where they do DNA testing?" I asked.

"Yes."

"Was there any DNA in this case?"

"No."

When he didn't continue, Maggie frowned a little. "There was no DNA of importance," she explained. "There was DNA from Valerie and Amanda in the kitchen because they prepared the meal. There was also DNA of Zavy and Amanda and their kids all over the house. Exactly what you would expect. No one is introducing any DNA evidence in this case, because there's no value added. Right, Marty?"

"Yes, exactly right. As I said, this has to do with another case. A case I handled years ago."

Maggie's brow dropped lower over her eyes. When no one said anything, she spoke up. "Okay, well…let us know how things go on that."

"Will do," Martin said vaguely.

After we'd turned off the phone, Maggie looked at Valerie and me. "He's never done anything like this before. I can only imagine that he must be feeling his age again, what with being sick and all. He must be reviewing his life, reviewing his work."

A sad silence settled into the room. All of us looked down at the round, fake-wood table, thinking of the Martin Bristol we knew—the powerful Martin, the sharp Martin, the firmly-in-the-present Martin.

Valerie exhaled loud. "It doesn't sound like he's coming back to the case."

"No, it doesn't." Maggie reached out a hand and patted Valerie's. "I'm sorry."

Valerie gazed down at the table. But then she looked up at Maggie with a grateful expression. "It's all right." She looked at me. "I think you're both doing a good job. I'm very glad to have you. Thank you."

"I'm glad to hear you say that," I said. I looked at my watch, then moved a little bit closer to her. "Because we need to talk about what Zavy said." I took a breath. If Martin really wasn't coming back, Maggie and I had to step it up.

"Why do you dislike Zavy?" I asked Valerie.

Her eyes flashed with intensity, then something faded. "I can't...I can't talk about it."

I touched her forearm lightly. "Let me ask you something different. Did you like him before the trial, or does your dislike of him have to do with the case?"

I glanced at Maggie. The concerned look she'd had for the conversation with her grandfather stayed in place. But she looked at Valerie to answer, too. Valerie's face turned away from both of us. She stared out the small window where white clouds danced in the powder-blue sky like a painting, looked very much like someone who wanted to escape.

"Valerie," I said, "I have to go back to the original question. Please tell me why you dislike Zavy."

She turned back to me. "Why do you think I dislike him?"

"It seemed obvious to me from the way you were staring at him."

"He cheated on Amanda."

"Oh." I understood that. If Bernard cheated on Maggie, I'd be pissed.

"With whom?" Maggie asked.

Valerie shook her head roughly. "It doesn't matter."

"Was it you?" I blurted the question before I even knew I was thinking it.

Maggie groaned.

"No!" Valerie said. "It was *not* me."

"Did Amanda know about this affair?"

Valerie's eyes filled with anguish. "Yes." She said the word *yes* like a hard kernel.

"Does this have anything to do with Amanda's death?"

Valerie shook her head, her mouth pursed, as if holding back words, causing the skin around her face to tighten more than it already was. She was such a beautiful woman, but now she looked contorted with...what was it?

When she didn't answer, I asked, "Is there anything at all about Zavy's affair that I should use to cross-examine him?"

She shook her head firmly back and forth. "No."

"Plus, we don't want to go after a grieving widower," Maggie said. "Even if he isn't grieving as hard as we think."

I thought of a friend of mine who used to have extramarital affairs. "Sometimes people cheat for different reasons," I said. "He may be grieving more than we think."

Valerie made a small sound. Was it a scoff?

"Does anyone know about this affair of Zavy's? Like the prosecution?" I left unsaid, *Because that would be one hell of a motive—not only did you want your friend's hus-*

*band but you wanted to keep him away from the woman he was sleeping with.*

"No," Valerie said emphatically. "*No one* knows." She cleared her throat. "Amanda wanted it that way."

Silence in the room.

I glanced at Maggie. She was staring at Valerie with narrowed eyes. She looked at her watch. "We don't have that much time. Let's move on."

I gave Maggie a nod. "All right, well, even if you didn't have an affair with Zavy, we need to talk about whether you tried to kiss him that night."

More silence.

Maggie cleared her throat but said nothing. This was my witness, so she was letting me take the lead on the prep.

Valerie stared at the table again. I thought maybe we'd have to prompt her, but finally she nodded.

"So you *did* try to kiss him?"

"Have you ever watched someone you love die?" Valerie asked. Before we could answer, she kept talking. "Brian was young, too young. The disease was killing him. And watching that was killing me. I wasn't doing well mentally. I was getting only a few hours of sleep at night. At the most. Many times, I never slept. Even when Amanda or Zavy came to help me, I often *couldn't* sleep. I couldn't relax. I was just mentally…not good."

"What happened that night with Zavy?"

She shook her head. "It was momentary insanity. I didn't want Zavy. I never have." She shuddered as if the thought of him repulsed her. "I was bleary from lack of sleep. I couldn't tell up from down. I wanted some kind of comfort. I wanted to obliterate everything."

I knew what she meant. I nodded at her to continue.

"We were in the hallway, and suddenly, I was trying to kiss him."

"And he didn't return the kiss?"

"No." Her mouth formed a bitter, straight line for a moment. "It took a second, but he pulled back and then I realized what I'd done. I turned away. *Right* away. It was nothing like what he said. I never told him I loved him." Another shudder. "I didn't keep trying to kiss him, and he didn't push me gently. He just pulled back, and I was relieved that he'd stopped me. I told Amanda the next morning."

"What was Amanda's reaction when you told her you had tried to kiss Zavy?"

"It didn't make her happy, but she knew what my life had been like. She knew I was losing it slowly." She made a small, rueful smile. "Or maybe not so slowly. Things were uncomfortable for a little bit, but Brian was going downhill fast. As I said, it was horrific to watch him die, and Amanda forgave me. She kept helping me. She was my friend." Her eyes seemed to come alive then. She looked at Maggie and me. "Like you two. I see what kind of friendship you have. I am envious of it. I miss Amanda so much."

"What about Bridget?" I asked. "Are you still friends with her?"

Her mouth formed another rueful shape. "No. Because she believes I might have killed Amanda."

I looked at her. It was exactly what I was wondering.

# 42

Because our client didn't want us to discuss Zavy's affair, and because it was, as far as we could tell, irrelevant to the trial, I had little to work with for the cross-exam of Zavy Miller. Still, when court resumed, I stood and took him through various questions, mostly for clarification. Also, it might not look good to the jury if we had no points to make, even if that was the truth.

"What pharmacy did you go to for medications on the night the decedent died?" I asked.

"CVS."

"Where is that located?"

"At the corner of State and Division."

"And is that the pharmacy your family normally used?"

"Yes."

I looked at my notes. "You said your wife was exploring her depression with a professional, is that correct?"

"Yes."

"Was that with a psychiatrist or a psychologist?"

"Objection," I heard Ellie call from behind me. "This is irrelevant."

"I'm just exploring the issue of the decedent's mental

state, which is within the scope of the direct as counsel herself raised it."

The judge gave me a nod. "Overruled." He looked at Zavy. "You may answer."

"Both," he said. "She was seeing a therapist and also a psychiatrist who she had seen before. The doctor who prescribed the Propranolol."

I didn't want to talk about the Propranolol so I moved on. "Sir, you have a neighbor named Dominick St. John, is that correct?"

"Yes."

"And you and your wife have had disagreements with Dr. St. John, is that right?"

"Yes, I guess you could call them that."

"What would you call the incidents?"

A pause. "I guess 'disagreements' would be right."

I took him through the basis of the problems with Dr. St. John, and in doing so, Zavy described the issues they'd had. Essentially, the main disagreement had to do with some properties in the neighborhood that were being zoned for business use. Dr. St. John had vehemently opposed the zoning, wanting the neighborhood to remain strictly residential. Amanda was the board president of the neighborhood association, and she wanted to bring money to their area in order to make a host of luxury improvements, things like old-time streetlamps, benches, sculptures, small parks, all of which cost money.

"Some of your neighbors said the disagreement had gotten so heated, they called it a 'feud.' Is that right?" I asked.

He shrugged. "I'm not sure what they called it."

"Well, on more than one occasion, Amanda and Dr. St. John were seen and heard screaming at each other, is that correct?"

"I'm not sure."

I decided to take a stab in the dark to make Zavy understand that I had solid info. "You were with your wife when she got in a shouting match with Dr. St. John at a neighborhood meeting, weren't you?"

"Oh. Well, yes, I was."

"And there were other occasions where the two were seen yelling at each other, correct?"

"I wasn't always present, but yes, I did hear about that."

It was about all I could do for the time being. Reluctantly, I gathered the few notes I had. "Thank you, Mr. Miller. Nothing further."


Court was adjourned for the day due to issues the state was having scheduling their witnesses. I looked immediately to the gallery, but Sam was gone. I felt a pang in my belly at the loss of him. Was I willing to give him up entirely?

Maggie had dodged to another courtroom to take care of something on a different case. The state's attorneys had already gone to their offices, the judge to his chambers. And Valerie and I found ourselves alone at our table.

I turned to her, and I brought up Zavy's direct testimony. I told her honestly that it had hurt our case.

She nodded, digesting the information.

I put my notes in my bag, then looked at her again. I thought about the talk with my dad. I wanted his opinion of Valerie but I also wanted to form my own. "Valerie, could you bring me in a little bit? You were telling me the other night about something you were going to divulge to Bridget and Amanda. Could you finish the story? If it helps with this trial at all, I want to know." I paused. "I *need* to know."

Valerie moved her seat away a little, not saying anything. She reached back and grasped her long, dark hair, untying it from the knot it was in, pulling it over one shoulder. She then twisted the length of hair with both hands, as if turning over the thoughts in her head, spinning them around and around, trying to decide where they should land, what she should reveal.

"I'm not sure," she said finally. She closed her eyes and opened them again. "There is so much to tell, but I don't know what is important to this case." She looked around the room. "To this trial…"

"Mom," I heard someone call.

I turned and saw a striking young woman making her way toward us. She reminded me of a deer. She had thin legs and big, brown eyes. Her hair was the color of Valerie's but longer, with a wash of copper-color over it. Her skin was lighter than her mother's, making her look delicate despite her height. Her clothes contributed to the delicate look—a short ruffled skirt made of a diaphanous gray and a pink, baby-doll T-shirt.

"Izzy," Valerie said, "have you met my daughter, Layla?"

I stood and shook her hand. "I've heard a lot about you. It's nice to meet you." Valerie had told me that Layla had graduated high school a year or so ago and she was doing well at DePaul University.

"You, too." She held my eyes for a minute, then, as if it were uncomfortable to do so, they dipped down. It was the same thing I'd noticed in some of Theo's friends. But then, those friends were probably only three years older than Layla.

I thought of Sam, age-appropriate Sam, in the courtroom earlier, then forced the thoughts away for now.

"Layla," I said. "It's a beautiful name." I glanced at

Valerie. "Is that like the Layla from that Eric Clapton song?"

"Actually, it's an African name," Valerie answered. "My mother's, originally."

"Grandma La," Layla said. She and Valerie smiled at each other.

Layla looked at her watch then. "Are you ready, Mom?" she asked. "I have to meet the group for my 3-D Animation class."

Valerie nodded. She looked at me. "Layla is a digital media major."

"Is that right?"

"Yeah." Layla smiled big. "It's really cool."

"Good for you." I didn't know the girl but I felt relieved that she had something to make her happy, especially when her mother faced a murder charge. The thought made me feel cold. I felt bad suddenly that I had been pressuring Valerie to tell me more than she was ready to.

"Gotta check something," Layla said, holding up her cell phone. "I'll meet you outside, Mom."

Valerie watched her daughter leave the courtroom, a concerned look on her face. I couldn't blame her. We both knew Layla could lose her mom. And very soon.

Then I thought of Valerie saying she was envious of Maggie and me, of our friendship. It was so sad, that statement, which made her sound as if she didn't have a friend in the world. I suddenly counted myself very, very fortunate. Whatever mistakes I'd made in my life, whatever low points I'd hit, I always had my friends and family. What's more I always *knew* I had them—people I could call, people I could fall apart with—and sometimes that knowledge was the best thing of all, a life vest to buoy me through choppy seas. No matter that her father was a murderer, no matter what *she* had done, Valerie deserved that, too.

"Valerie," I said, facing her. "I am your lawyer. But outside of trial, if you ever just need a friend…" I shrugged, not knowing how to say it. "Well, I can be that. I'd like to be that."

She blinked. I thought she might cry. Then she just said simply, "Thank you," and then again, "*Thank* you."

# 43

The yelling. The shouting. It started as soon as Maggie and I reached the street outside the courthouse. I'd found Maggie in the courtroom she'd gone to and when she was done, we left together.

"How dare you!" we heard now. "How *dare* you!"

Both of our heads snapped to the right. We saw a man with too-dark hair, like a wig, a large paunch and a very angry red face. He wore a suit, so he looked like he could be a lawyer, but what was this?

The man stormed up to us. "How dare you come into my neighborhood and malign me to my neighbors? You have ruined my reputation with your sordid accusations!"

Maggie held up a hand. "Whoa, whoa. Who are you?"

"I am Dr. Dominick St. John." He emphasized the word *doctor*. He shook a finger in our faces as his voice rose again. "And I am the one who will be suing you for slander! Your people have come into my world, into my neighborhood and implied that I might have killed Amanda Miller. I've been getting calls from journalists! If they put *anything* about this in the newspapers or on the internet—*anything*—I will also be suing you for libel!"

His voice grew louder with each word, and spit flew

from his mouth. Behind him, I saw a bunch of young guys stop to watch the show.

I wanted to say, *Gee, you must have a nice bedside manner,* but the man was starting to freak me out. "Doctor," I said, "please calm down."

His eyes veered to mine. "Do *not* tell me to calm down. I will not calm down!"

"Yes. You will," we heard an authoritative voice say from behind us. My dad.

Christopher McNeil stepped up to us. The good doctor, in what seemed an instinctive manner, immediately stepped back. My dad was someone to be careful of. That much was clear. It was something everyone could feel.

"Sir," my father said in a low voice, "in no way have you been slandered. In no way have you been libeled. And if you persist in speaking to these young women in this manner, I will walk in those doors—" he pointed at the courthouse "—and grab one of the numerous police officers. And then the papers will have something very specific to write about. Your arrest."

Dr. St. John looked flustered.

My dad jumped in with two more words before he led us away. "Goodbye, sir."


"He's not a bad guy," my dad said as we drove out of the parking lot.

"Dr. St. John? Are you kidding me? That guy seems mental."

"He *is* mental. In a sense. He's under the care of a psychiatrist. But that's not who I'm talking about."

"Wait, how did you find out confidential information like that—that he's seeing a psychiatrist?"

"He's being treated for an anxiety disorder. There's no history of violence in his record."

I noticed he hadn't told me how he got the info, and I could tell he wasn't going to. "He's going to be even more mental when he gets served with a subpoena to testify in this case."

My father looked at me through his copper-framed glasses, concerned. "You and Maggie are calling him as a witness?"

I nodded.

"I'll keep an eye on you two when you're out of the courtroom."

It was something I was getting used to, so I just nodded again. Then, "So who were you talking about when you said he's not a bad guy?"

I fiddled with the vent, looking for more air-conditioning, which wasn't seeming to make a dent in the heat. My father didn't look hot, though. Maybe it was from all his years in humid Italy. Or maybe he was just a master of the never-let-'em-see-you-sweat mentality. Both were probably true.

"Sam," he said.

I looked at him. As usual, his face was placid.

"That was the guy I was engaged to. And all you can say is 'He's not bad'?" I laughed.

My father didn't.

I stopped. "Just as an aside, do you laugh at anything?"

My father's eyes moved around a little as if searching for the answer. His mouth crunched up. "Not really."

"Do you know how sad that is?"

He shrugged. "What's there to laugh about?"

"Do you remember when I was young, when we were a family? You used to laugh all the time. You had this mischievous look on your face like you were always ready to crack up."

"Well." A pause. "Well. That was someone else. That was a different life."

"But you *have* to laugh. Every chance you get."

"I gave up laughing long ago." My heart hurt for him.

"Have you spent any time with Charlie lately?" I asked.

"He's busy with the radio job."

"True." But Charlie knew how to make time for the people important to him. I wondered how he was doing with the issue of my father.

"So, what did you talk to Sam about?" I asked.

"Not much."

I fought the urge to ask more, let the silence hang there. And it worked.

He started talking again. "I was just asking him, since he knows you well, what he thinks about me being here. About me being, well, back in your life."

"That's the passing conversation you had? Now *that's* funny." When he didn't laugh, again, I looked out the window at a pack of teenagers hanging out on someone's front stoop. "What did Sam say?"

"He said that he thought you needed someone, a sort of father figure if you will, since Forester passed away last year."

I was touched that Sam got that. "He's right."

"So you're okay? With…uh, with me being here?"

"With you being alive? Yeah, sure." I sighed. "My life is so weird," I said, half under my breath.

"Mine, too."

We both laughed at that.

# 44

When I got home, I did some research Maggie had asked for, then I scoured the internet for information about Dr. St. John. As my dad said, there didn't seem to be anything that indicated violence in his history. In fact, he'd been named one of the best doctors in the city by *Chicago Magazine* ten years ago.

After an hour, I received a text from Mayburn. I found the nanny. She's back in Chicago looking for a job.

Yes! I wrote back. I'll get the subpoena for her. You get ready to serve her with it. She's coming to court.

I let Maggie know, then started working on the subpoena. Theo had gotten to my place about ten minutes before, and I heard him moving around in the kitchen. When I looked up, he stood in the doorway of my office with a pitcher of iced tea.

"You are so sweet," I said.

He walked in and handed me a glass.

"You know how to make iced tea?" I asked.

He chuckled. "I wanted to do something for you. Plus, iced tea isn't that hard."

"I know, but I guess I just didn't expect it from you."

"You say things like that a lot."

I thought about it. I supposed he was right. I often commented about how he seemed older than he was, more mature. "Does that bother you?"

"No. I'm tough to bother." He leaned down over me, his soft hair falling onto the sides of my face like a light curtain. He kissed me. God, those lips. Then he stood. "I'm heading up to Wrigley if it's cool with you."

"You have tickets?"

"Nah, C.R. and I are just going to watch the game at Murphy's."

It was such a young thing to do—watch the Cubs game *next* to Wrigley Field, without going inside. Maggie and I used to do that when we were in law school.

"So how is C.R.? Has he talked to Lucy? I haven't spoken with her."

"Yeah, and he's into her."

"Really? Have they seen each other?"

"Yeah."

"What did they do? What do they talk about?" I realized it was probably the same thing people wondered about Theo and me.

He shrugged. "I don't know."

"You don't know?"

"That's not what *we* talk about."

"Weird. You're friends, but you don't talk about your dates, what happened on them?"

"Hey, you're friends with Lucy, but you don't know, either."

"That's only because I'm on trial right now, and I haven't kept in touch like I normally would. Under normal circumstances, I'd know all the details."

He seemed to think about this. While he did, I let my eyes sweep up his body, taking in the white T-shirt that had some kind of red design on it, which seemed to bleed in a sexy way into the skin of his arms, tattooed with other designs.

"I *should* ask C.R. about him and Lucy," Theo said. He nodded as if agreeing with himself. "You know, sometimes when I'm around them I act all casual and shit, like those guys do, because they're my buddies and I'm their age, but I'd like..." He drifted off as if lost for words.

"What?"

"I don't know."

"You want friendships that are a little deeper?"

"Yeah. Exactly."

"You've got Eric."

"That's true. But Eric and I talk about work all the time. *All* the time. When we're done with that, we don't have much energy to be buddies."

I understood that. It was how I'd felt about a number of lawyers I'd worked with at Baltimore & Brown—I realized they were interesting people I'd like to know better, but as litigators we got so much of each other at work. "I can do that for you," I said. "I can be a friendship that's deeper."

"You're more than that."

"I know. But I can be the friend part, too."

He met my eyes, and I saw an appreciation there. "Thanks."

"Anytime."

An hour and a half later, as I sent an email to Maggie about my research, my mom called.

"Hello, Boo," she said, using the nickname my father had given me as a kid. I noticed she used it more often these days. "I was thinking we should go out and get a glass of wine. Perhaps the Elysian Hotel?"

"Now?"

"Yes."

I pulled the phone away from my face and stared at it, then returned it to my ear. "Really?" My mother had rarely called me last minute about *going out*. Overall, she preferred to be in her house where she was most comfortable.

"Are you too busy with the trial?" she said. "I should have thought about that."

"Actually, I'm at a good breaking point." I didn't mention that I was also curious to see if there was a reason for this different behavior of hers—this desire to step out. "I'll meet you in twenty."

The Elysian Hotel was a vast stone building occupying a city block on State Street. It boasted a massive cobblestone drive that hearkened to an estate in Europe, so different from the other newer hotels in Chicago, which tended toward the sleek and modern.

Inside the lobby, a large soapstone bust of a man dominated the place. Staircases on either side of the sculpture twisted upstairs to a snug, dark bar.

My mother sat on the leather banquette against the wall, and I took a chair to the other side of the tiny table. The waitress soon delivered two glasses of Sancerre, which my mother was delighted to find on the wine list.

"Isn't this nice?" she said, raising her glass to toast me.

"It is," I said simply. "What's going on with you? You don't usually ask me to meet you out."

She lifted her shoulders and smiled. "I suppose that's true." Another lift of her shoulders. "I feel I have a different outlook on life right now."

"A good one?"

"Very."

When she didn't say anything else, I asked, "How is Spence?"

"Well…" She sounded unsure. She looked me in the eyes. "Spence told me that he stopped by your place over the weekend."

"Yes. Did he tell you why?"

She nodded. "I know this is very disconcerting for him. I'm going through a time, a rather interesting, wonderful time actually. I feel like I'm learning to know myself much better than I ever have before."

"Because of Dad. Because he's back in town."

"Technically, yes. But it's more to do with…" She shook her head and seemed unwilling, or unable, to continue.

*It's more to do with what?* I wondered. Did it have to do with feelings she had for my father? Or was it the concept she had mentioned to me last week—that she could trust her instincts again because she had been right, and he hadn't been dead?

"Have you seen him?" she asked.

"Yes, he's been coming to trial, and he's been working a bit with Mayburn." I stalled momentarily when I realized my mother didn't know Mayburn's name; I'd only told her of our work relationship generally, when I absolutely had to. I'd listened to Mayburn's advice—okay, not advice, but commands—not to let anyone know I did work for him on the side. It would, he said, take away the whole reason for me, an average Northside girl who could slip into everyday situations like the mom's crowd on a playground or women's locker room, to handle work for him. And so as uncomfortable as it made me, few people knew I worked for him.

"I did see Dad after you mentioned it on Sunday," I said. "I went to his apartment."

"Oh." Her eyebrows raised. "I admit, I've been curious. What's it like?"

"Nondescript."

"I suppose that's fitting, isn't it? He probably doesn't really know who he is at this point."

She said it in a gentle way, and I knew she meant the statement to be a kind one. We were both silent for a second.

"So getting back to you and Spence..." I said.

The waitress delivered mixed nuts in a silver dish. We munched on a few, and my mother looked pensive for second. "You know, we're not that good," she said.

My stomach sank.

She seemed to sense my reaction. "Let me explain, Boo." She sighed. "I've been struck now, more than ever, about how each person goes through different lives within their one lifetime."

My dad had said something like that when he had driven me home that day. Spence had mentioned something similar, too.

"Do you know what I mean?" my mom asked.

"I think so. But what do *you* mean?"

"Well, I've gone through a number of lives, haven't I? After all, I was one person when I grew up in Michigan. I was another person after I met your father. I was yet another person when I became a young mother."

I saw what she was getting at now. "And you were quite another person after dad died."

She looked at me. "Yes, that's right. And I don't know if I have ever said it but I'm sorry. I'm sorry that the person I was then was not able to take care of you the way I should have."

"I've never been angry about that. I've always understood."

She nodded. "Yes, you've always been very empathetic, even as a child. I appreciate that."

"Thanks." I was touched. "But you and Spence now?"

My mother shrugged. "I am a different person again now that your father is alive. Spence doesn't seem to like that person."

"Mom, he loves you immensely."

"Of course he does. But it's not about how much he loves me. It's a matter of adaptation—whether he can acclimate to who I am now, whether our relationship can do that."

"And so what do you think?"

She dipped two elegant fingers and her thumb into the silver dish and pulled out an almond. She looked at it for a moment, as if not entirely aware she was holding it. Then she looked at me. "This is one of those situations, Isabel, where the cliché is true—only time will tell."

# 45

"We're going to a hotel." I pushed my cell phone closer to my ear and looked around to see if anyone was near. But the courtyard of the Elysian was deserted, save for a valet and a waiting cab across the way.

"What?" Mayburn said. "Who is going to a hotel?"

"Sam and me." My body tingled as I said it. With excitement, with trepidation, with guilt.

Mayburn whistled, then laughed. "Thanks."

"For what?"

"I haven't laughed in a month." As if to try it again, he laughed once more. "Shit, that feels good."

"Okay, glad it's amusing. But we're not going to a hotel as in a *hotel*." I told Mayburn how, after my drink with my mom, Sam had called, talking about our engagement at the James Hotel. He didn't want to go there, he'd said. He knew things weren't exactly the same between us, yet he wanted to show me they were still similar. He wanted us to meet someplace where it was just him and me. He suggested the Peninsula Hotel Bar a few blocks away from the Elysian. None of the reasoning quite made sense to me. It sounded romantic, yet it made me wonder if he was hiding us from Alyssa or anyone she knew. But that wasn't worrying me like it normally would. Instead, I was, quite simply, craving information from him; I wanted to know if he had, as he said he would, "figured things out."

"So I'm ready for your help," I said to Mayburn now. "You promised that if I needed advice, you'd give it to me."

"Yeah, I thought about our conversation after we talked," Mayburn said. "You're right that I do a lot of infidelity cases. Or suspected infidelity cases. But they're on behalf of the person who *suspects* cheating. It's the wife at home, and her husband travels a lot for work. So I tell them to pay attention to certain things, like when their partner stops calling them pet names or can't look them in the eye or when suddenly the spouse has new interest or when the wife is rushing you off the phone or changing their eating habits or that kind of thing."

"Okay, so what should I look for with Sam?"

A pause. Then, "McNeil, you're the one he's cheating with."

"We're not cheating! It's a drink. And if anything, he's still cheating on *me* by being with Alyssa."

"What? You want him to be by himself because the two of you broke up? You want him to go on without you and—"

"Yes," I said, interrupting him, "I want him to go on, celibate and lonely, without me."

"Hmm. I wonder if that's what Lucy wants for me."

"No," I answered immediately. "Lucy is way nicer than I am."

"That's true."

"So seriously, just give me something."

"Do you want a Tru-Test?" he asked.

"What's that?"

"It checks for sexual fluids."

"Ew. No! What would I do with that?"

"Help me out, McNeil. What do you want here?"

I thought about it. "I don't know. Just a primer. A way to fish around for information or whether or not it's forthcoming."

"I've taught you that stuff already," he said. "And," he added grudgingly, "you've learned it well. An investigation is like a puzzle—"

"Yeah, yeah, you have to put the pieces together."

"That's right. And often you don't know which piece will be important until you see it. Keep your eyes open. And when you see a puzzle piece..."

"Pick it up," I said for him. "Got it."

Sam and I sat on a slouchy velvet couch nearly hidden by swaths of sheer fabric that billowed from the curtain rod over the windows. The light was low and warm. I'd been to the Peninsula bar before and found the place too dark, maybe a tad staid. But now the room seemed to ooze sexiness, warmth and ease.

Sam and I sipped at our glasses of Blue Moon. I tasted the sweet orange Sam had squeezed into my beer.

When we'd first arrived, Sam told me he'd realized something. Since he and I broke up, he'd lost his job as a wealth management advisor and he'd lost Forester, who was his father figure...essentially he'd lost everything he identified with in life. He'd gotten engaged to Alyssa, he realized, because he wanted something to identify with. But he had been wrong to do so. He wasn't in love with Alyssa. He loved her, but he was *in* love with me.

*I still love you,* he said.

Now, I thought of something that had been troubling me—something I never really spoke at length to Sam about, but something I should have made sure he understood.

"Remember," I said, pushing my beer glass an inch away, "when I was getting a little…I don't know, a little strange before our wedding."

He didn't hesitate before he answered. "Yeah, you were cranky and distracted. I thought the wedding planning was just making you crazy."

"It was. But not just because it was a lot to deal with."

"You had a huge job at the same time," Sam pointed out.

"Yeah, but it wasn't just that, either." I pulled the glass back and stared into the golden ale. "There was another reason I was unhappy." I looked at him. I really didn't want to hurt him. But if we were going to have these conversations, we needed—or at least I did—to be entirely honest.

"Tell me." He didn't look afraid.

So I did. "I felt like the wedding was going too fast, and it was beginning to feel like someone else's wedding."

He nodded. "It got bigger than we expected. That was my fault. You never wanted all the bells and whistles."

"No. But you and my mom were both so into it. The whole thing was fine at first, but then it just started spinning and spinning and we were hardly spending time together, and I was overwhelmed at work, and…"

Sam stared at me as I let my words die away. "How much of your hesitation about the wedding had to do with me?"

"I told you, it was all the hoopla, combined with working a lot and—"

"I understand," Sam said. "But I'm asking you something specific. And now more than ever, I need you to think about this. How much of that time had to do with *me?* About the fact that you weren't ready or maybe didn't want to marry me?"

"None." I answered fast. It was an easy answer.

Sam's face looked excited but not sure he entirely believed me.

"I swear," I said. "The planning was making me nuts and work was making me nuts and I felt like I was growing up too fast, like I'd gone from law school graduate to a nearly married, nearly partner of a law firm. And then you brought up moving to the suburbs…"

Sam laughed and put his hand over his face. "I knew that wrecked you! And I really didn't want to move. Someone at work said there was this house in Winnetka that someone had to sell fast, and so I brought it up to you, but I really didn't want to move, I swear." He laughed again, then stopped abruptly.

Sam's hand slipped into mine. Sam's warm hand. That hand. I knew that hand.

"Iz, I just wanted to marry you. That's it. I loved you so much, I wanted to tell everyone. But I didn't need to do the big wedding. I just needed you." His other hand went on top of mine. "That's all I still need."

I didn't reply. He didn't seem to mind.

We sat in wonder at the make-you-gasp recognition that we were at a crossroad. A big one.

"There's so much to think about," I said to Sam, letting my head loll on the back of the couch.

"I know. But we don't have to do it now."

I took a big breath, looked at him. "That's not what you used to say."

"I know. I always wanted to nail things down. But that was only about me needing something to hold on to."

"Don't you still need that?"

"No." He picked up his glass. He handed me mine. "I only need you. But I don't need any big discussions. We don't need to define this." He paused, looking at me, as if he were soaking up every feature. "Let's just have some fun."

I clinked my glass against his. "Here's to fun."

And then we dropped the topic of us. Instead, we talked about college football, which was about to start. We talked about his family and mine. We ordered more Blue Moons. I told him about how strange it was to have my father back in my life. We ordered more Blue Moons. We told stories to each other that we'd heard before. Sometimes often. But our new status as…well, as people who just want to have fun, that made those stories fresh again. We howled with laugher. *Remember,* we said between laughs. *Remember when…* We ordered more Blue Moons.

Somewhere in there everything slowed, as if the universe, kindly, wanted to give us a bit of a break.

As Sam spoke about the rugby team he'd been coaching, the golden bar lights shined through his blond hair, making it look like a halo.

I looked at Sam. I looked at his eyes, his ears, his nose, his chin. Finally, I looked at his mouth. That sweet mouth I used to kiss, wanted to kiss forever. As a man, Theo was sex on a stick, no doubt about it, no competing with him on sheer, animalistic hotness. But suddenly I could remember Sam's bottom lip on mine, then his whole mouth, gently sucking.

So the next moment, when Sam leaned toward me, I didn't lean back. When Sam put a gentle finger on my chin and coaxed me toward him, I didn't resist. When he kissed me, I forgot where I was. When his tongue went inside my mouth, I groaned.

When he said, *Let's get a room,* I said… "Yes."

# 46

"Jesus," Sam said in my ear, his voice hoarse, heavy. "Jesus Christ."

The door banged shut as we moved, like one clutching mass, into the room. We stood, our mouths together, rough and gentle at the same time. A relief, a release.

Sam nudged me until I fell on my back on the bed. His compact weight fell on top of me, and I cried out. I couldn't help it. That weight felt like a part of me that had been excised and had now returned. I squeezed him around the back, kissed him harder. We started groping then—thrilling, exhilarating and yet so, so familiar.

*You're back,* I kept thinking. *You're back.*

For an hour, it felt, we went on like this, the room's temperature rising, the air between us crackling and living.

I tugged at Sam's belt.

"Yes," he said. "Fuck, yes."

The curse word sent an excited jolt through me. I made my fingers move faster, opening his belt, the quick *zzzzzzzzzzzzzz* of the zipper, tug-tugging at his jeans, shoving off his jacket, unbuttoning his shirt.

And soon Sam was standing before me, naked. He didn't look ashamed that I was still fully dressed. In fact, he squared his shoulders, let his arms fall back, faced me, as if to say, *I'm here. All of me.*

I fell to my knees, some force compelling me there, one hand reaching for his hip bone, the other reaching for him. I put my mouth over him.

"Ooooh," Sam said, then, "Wait." He was groaning, half chuckling. "I can't believe I'm going to say this, but wait for a sec. This is not romantic, but I've needed to go to the bathroom for, like, two hours."

I fell back against the side of the bed. Laughed. This, too, felt familiar. Sex, I remembered, when you had it with someone often, wasn't always scripted and perfect. There were moments of absurdity—how could there not be? And there were matters of timing and reality, like this.

"Go," I said, laughing again, waving a hand.

Sam closed the door and I sat. Panting.

When I caught my breath, I looked around. *How surreal, how insane*, I thought. *This is the person I used to live with at this time last year. And now we are half strangers, half soul mates in a hotel room.* Through my eyes, I took everything in. The moment felt…well, momentous. Why, I didn't know. I was getting better about not caring.

One of Sam's socks was next to me. I picked it up. *I used to wash these socks.* I picked up his jeans next. They were my favorite pair of his, he knew. We'd bought them at a store on Halsted near Webster. *They make your ass look great,* I'd said. Sam had worn them out of the store. We'd gone to the Athenian Room for Greek salads and saganaki.

I lifted the jeans, remembering how the saganaki was lit, how the flame shot to the sky, and we had looked at each other smiling, feeling the same thing.

I was about to put the jeans down, when I noticed the corner of a white piece of paper sticking from a pocket.

I heard Mayburn's voice. *An investigation is like a puzzle. You have to put the pieces together. And often you don't know when you can pick up a piece until you see it. Keep your eyes open. And when you see a puzzle piece...*

"Pick it up," I said.

I glanced at the bathroom door. I heard the toilet flush and water running.

No time to think or debate. I pulled the paper from the pockets. It had been folded a number of times; its creases were soft.

I opened it. Read it. A thousand thoughts like arrows stung my head.

Still, the water ran in the bathroom. I read it again.

It was a document from the *Panamanian Registry*. The information there indicated that a corporation owned a piece of property in Panama.

The name of the corporation was Pickett Enterprises. Forester's corporation. The one I used to represent.

Names of two attorneys were listed at the bottom left. Panamanian lawyers, it appeared. That didn't surprise me. Forester used local counsel for any international business he had. I read the address of the property and got a jolt of recognition.

But it was the information on the bottom right that really surprised me. No, *shocked*. That's a better word.

*Owner of the corporation,* it said.

And below that?

*Samuel Hollings.*

Silence filled the room as the sound of water from the bathroom stopped. In a minute, the door would open. Sam would step out.

But I wouldn't be there for that.

I stood, snatched my purse off the floor. And with the paper still in my hand, I left.

# 47

A trial is a tornado. Thousands of pieces of information—such flotsam—whirl around and around and around. They spin and twist. The tornado grows with each day, with each new bit of information you put into the jury's consciousness.

All a trial lawyer can do is reach out into the swirl, and grasp one piece of information here, another one there, and try to put them together into a cohesive line of questioning for a witness, a thorough argument for a judge, a satisfying closing for the jury.

The real trick, though, is that the trial lawyer has to pretend the swirl doesn't exist. Because the truth is, that swirl can overwhelm. It can wrap you in its clutches and spirit you far away. Even in sleep, it spins and spins, sometimes even faster.

It was the swirl that woke me up that Tuesday night and would not let me fall back to sleep. The document I had taken from Sam made it all so, so, so much worse.

Over and over I went through what that Panamian document could mean. When Sam disappeared last year, it was at the request of Forester, who had received death threats, likely from someone in his family or his camp. If he died suddenly, he told Sam, he had a last request—he wanted Sam go to Panama, where they'd been buying a number of properties, and liquidate them. The Panamian system of ownership of property via "bearer shares" made sales simple to arrange and difficult to trace. That way, a large portion of his estate would be held up and the estate could not be dispersed, which would give time to determine if someone had intentionally harmed Forester, and if so, who.

Forester had been Sam's father figure, and he did as Forester asked. He did so two months before our wedding. Once I learned he was okay, once I learned why he had done what he'd done, we tried to put it back together. That hadn't been successful, but always, always I felt Sam was an honorable man. I never doubted that—not before and not after.

But now this document indicating that he owned a property in Panama. I'd checked the document when I'd gotten home, and it was recent. Why would Sam own property in Panama *now?* I could have asked him. He'd called at least ten times and texted as many since I'd taken off—*Where are you? What happened?* And then, likely when he realized the document was missing, *Let me explain.* But I didn't know if I trusted the answer he would give.

I turned and looked at Theo's sleeping form. He was faced away from me and curved into himself, his broad back slowly rising and falling with his breath. I heard a soft rattle, a tiny snore at the back of his throat. I thought of waking him. But his sleep seemed so deep, and really what would I talk about? Sam? Panamanian property? The trial? What did I expect Theo to do with those random mental shards?

I thought of Maggie. Although she hated to be woken up, she had always made it clear that she would do so for me, and the truth was Maggie had seen me through many a sleepless night. But I couldn't shake Maggie from the under covers of her sleek bed and ask her to listen to my rants about Sam or hear me meander through an upcoming cross-examination, feeling my way down one path, then another, waiting for her murmur, *Oh, that's good* or *I'd leave that alone*. That was what Maggie and I always did for each other when we were on trial. But we'd never been on trial together. I needed Maggie to get her sleep— if not her beauty sleep, then surely her brain sleep.

I got up and wandered through my condo. I felt the need for some fresh air, some space for all the information and thoughts about the trial and Sam and Theo that were cramming the confines of my brain. I thought about my roof deck. It was one of the best things about my place—it was all mine, while the other tenants had a balcony or a patio. The problem with the roof deck, however, was that you couldn't simply stroll outside, sit down and enjoy the weather. You had to make the trek upstairs. You had to be serious about spending some time there.

But on that deck, life was a little quieter, it was all a little more simple. And that was exactly what I sought.

I went up the back stairs with my roof keys. I pushed open the door up there and stuck a brick in it to keep it open. I stood, taking in the sky, which was a queer yellow. There was an ominous light from somewhere in the city.

An iron table and chairs were on my deck. I took a seat on one of the chairs and thought of all the time Sam and I had spent on that roof. Often, he had his guitar, and he would play songs he'd written, or songs he loved, while I lazed through a magazine or just gazed at him. Sometimes the sounds from the street below would be minimal. Other times, during a street fair or a busy weekend, a packet of indistinguishable voices would drift up, joined by the sound of music from someone else's apartment, the honks of cabs.

I looked up at the sky, thinking how strange a color it was—that soupy yellow making me wonder if it were real or if I were asleep and dreaming that I was bathed in that weird light.

I forced my thoughts away from Sam and returned them to Valerie and Zavy and Amanda. As a litigator, when you were on trial, that trial had to take the number one spot in your life, no matter what else was going on.

I tried to imagine what it was like to live in the Gold Coast, as Valerie had, and then be forced to leave that wealthy enclave and move west of the city after your husband died. Had she been jealous of Amanda, who still had her house in the Gold Coast and her handsome husband? Valerie had been clear today—she had hit on Zavy. She said she'd apologized to him and to Amanda. They'd forgiven her. Was that true? Even if it was, what if *she* hadn't forgiven Amanda for being the one who had everything? Valerie had talked about being mentally unstable when Brian was dying. Had she stayed that way? Had she removed Amanda from the world so she could try to regain a husband and that Gold Coast life?

"How are you, girl?"

I jumped and spun around. *Theo.* I hadn't heard him coming up the stairs. "What are you doing up?"

"I'd ask you the same thing. I woke up and you were gone." He wore jeans but he was shirtless, as he was so often in my dreams, and thankfully, in my reality.

He took a few steps toward me and sank into a chair. "What are you thinking about?"

"Ah, nothing. Just the trial." I waved one hand, as if to dismiss the whole thing. I thought about Sam then—Sam today, Sam up here on my deck in days of yore. If it had been Sam sitting in front of me now, I would have told him about my warring thoughts about Valerie.

But then something dawned on me. Maybe it had come time to see if Theo could handle such a discussion.

Half an hour later, the swirl had slowed, seemed more manageable somehow, the bits of information grouped closer together, more clear. Theo had not only listened, he had asked great questions. Not legal or professional questions, like those I might have heard from Sam or Grady, my friend from Baltimore & Brown, but commonsense questions, questions that made it clear where the story I was trying to tell had gaped or faltered.

I sat back in the iron chair, settling back into the warm, August night air, as well, and I looked at Theo, smiling. "Thank you."

"Sure."

We went downstairs, and as we entered my apartment, our arms were around each other, hands already groping. I heard the tinny sound of my cell phone ringing in my bedroom. Sam, probably. I ignored it. It rang again. I went to find it, thinking maybe Maggie couldn't sleep, either. But it was a number I didn't recognize. Yet when you're on trial, every call could be important.

I answered it.

"Izzy?"

"Yes."

"Oh, hi, Izzy. It's Valerie. Is there any way you can come over?"

# 48

The address Valerie had given me was farther west of the city than I had imagined. I drove through quiet Logan Square to get there. Logan Boulevard was a wide avenue with trees down the middle. On either side stood old Victorian mansions with turrets and wraparound porches next to sturdy brick homes that had been turned into apartments.

I kept moving until I found Valerie's street. The street itself was nice with well-tended bungalows, but I worried for Valerie and Layla in terms of the rather rough-and-tumble avenues that surrounded it.

I got off my Vespa and nervously looked around, hoping the bike would be there when I returned. Just to be safe, I got out my lock, squeezed the brake lever and clamped the lock over it.

I hurried toward Valerie's address, a bland, four-story building with tan aluminum siding. The entryway was a dim, sallow-looking place with meager orange light. According to the buzzer, only two apartments were in the building, which probably meant each occupant had an upstairs and a downstairs.

Valerie buzzed me in. The hallway inside matched the foyer, lit low and with an eerie bulb. But then Valerie opened her door, and I stepped into a small kitchen. A table was set with two bamboo placemats across from each other, a few flowers in a lime-green vase in the center. The flowers looked like those that grew in an errant manner on city streets, weeds technically, but somehow in this cozy apartment they were perfect additions to her table.

The rest of the kitchen was constructed inexpensively with plain, older yellow appliances and linoleum countertops, but it was pleasing—low lit, with jars of oatmeal, flour, chilies, sugar, candies and other assorted items along one wall.

Valerie wore jeans cuffed at the bottom and a white T-shirt. The shirt was fitted and I could see she had a trim body beneath the dresses she'd worn to court every week. Her dark hair was loose, no makeup adorning her face. She looked beautiful. And very, very sad.

Valerie gestured at one countertop, where she had placed a pot of coffee and a few cookies on a plate. "Would you like something? It's not exactly the spread that your mother was so gracious to put out."

I laughed. "No one does a spread like my mother or Spence. I'll have a cookie, and just some water if you have it." As she poured me a glass, I looked at my watch. Three in the morning. "What are you doing up?" I asked.

She took her coffee and my water to the table and gestured at me to sit. "I'm so sorry to wake you. I was just going to leave you a message." She brought the plate of cookies to the table and sat down, too.

"Don't be sorry. Like I said earlier, I was awake. I was actually sitting on my rooftop, thinking about the trial."

At the mention of the trial, Valerie looked pensively at the table, saying nothing.

I wondered why I was there. "Where's Layla?"

Valerie's eyes flashed with something—what?—but when she looked up at me, they dimmed. She glanced around. "She's still out."

"On a Tuesday?" When she said nothing, I offered, "Well, she is a college sophomore, right?"

Valerie nodded.

For something to do, I picked up the oatmeal cookie she'd given me and broke it in half. "So why did you ask me to come, Valerie?"

"Because I was…" A helpless shrug. "I was lonely, and you said something about being my friend."

"I'm a good friend," I said. "It's something I pride myself on."

She smiled, then it faded. "I was thinking of how good it felt to talk to you the other day. I haven't spoken about my father in so long. In fact, I've only spoken about him a handful of times since he was executed."

"That must have been terrible."

"It was. For a long while, I really believed he would be freed." Valerie took a sip of her coffee. "The execution didn't happen for years and years. His case would be appealed and then sent back and then appealed some more. I could hardly follow the ups and downs, but each time his conviction was upheld, each time he was closer to death, my trust died a little bit. And then it just…" Again that faraway expression. "It just went away."

It sounded as if she had come to terms with it. "And now," she continued, "it seems I'm due for the same fate. At least the prison part of it. Sometimes that makes me wonder if I deserve it. Is it somehow scripted ahead of time, this curse on our family?"

I didn't know how to answer. Did she wonder if she deserved it because she was guilty? "How old were you when he was executed?" I asked instead.

"Twenty-four." She sighed. "Then my mom died, and I got pregnant with Layla soon after. Two Solaras dead, another created. Layla's father took off for Florida shortly after we found out I was pregnant. He helped when he could, but he wasn't ready to be a father, and I was fine with that." An inhale of breath. "She's my world." Her eyes suddenly became animated and stared into mine in a beseeching way. "Izzy, I can't lose that world. You *have* to help me."

I told her I would. I asked her questions. What had happened that night she went to reveal something to Amanda and Bridget? What was she going to tell them? But even though her eyes remained anxious, her demeanor aggrieved, she wouldn't tell me any more. She had, I realized, merely wanted comfort. And so I asked her about other things—things that girlfriends would talk about. Where had she gotten that silver necklace she'd worn that day? Had she been to the new discount clothing store on Southport? Had she seen any exhibits at the MCA?

Before I left forty-five minutes later, I hugged her. She clung to me, and so I squeezed her back even tighter.

"Thank you," she said, over and over. "Thank you. Thank you."

I told her it was no problem. That I was happy to do it. But I left knowing nothing more, feeling more confused than ever.

# 49

The next morning, as I made my way through the glass doors in the courtroom, bleary from lack of sleep, Maggie came out of the order room, talking on her cell. She gestured me toward her before I'd even dumped my bag at our table.

I wanted to tell her about Sam and me at the hotel, about the Panamanian document, about my visit to Valerie's last night. But before I could speak, Maggie put her hand over the receiver and said in a low voice, "It's my grandmother."

She glanced at the state's attorneys, then turned her back, speaking into the phone. "Did you see any of the case names?" A pause. "What? Are you sure? Was it spelled the same?" She shook her head. "I don't get it. Was it just one file?" Another pause. "Okay. I'll talk to you later."

She spun to face me, a puzzled expression on her tiny face, and placed the phone on our table. She looked around. The state's attorneys were at their table, organizing exhibits. The bailiff prowled the front of the courtroom, looking at his watch. Maggie dropped her voice even lower. "My grandmother says Marty's not doing good."

"Oh, no."

"Yeah, she's really worried. Everyone is. He's acting even more peculiar…"

The judge came in the room, and we all turned, our hands behind our back. He stepped up to the bench. "Greetings, everyone. We're going to be efficient with our time this morning. I have a meeting with the chief judge at eleven."

"We're ready to go, Judge," Tania Castle said.

"As are we, Your Honor," Maggie replied. "We'll retrieve our client." She picked up her cell phone and texted her clerk to bring Valerie from the empty courtroom. "So anyway," she whispered to me when she was done. "My grandma says Marty is almost manic. He won't stop reviewing old cases. It's like he's getting ready to retire or…" She squeezed her eyes shut and then open. "Or like he's getting ready to die."

"Don't say that. Don't jump to any conclusions."

"I know. I know. But listen to what my grandmother just told me. One of the old files he pulled had the name 'Solara' on it."

*"S-O-L-A-R-A?"*

"Yeah."

"Was there a first name on the file?"

"No. She said that it was simply marked with the word *Solara*. When she tried to look closer, he got upset. He gathered the materials, said he was going to the library."

"The one in your office?"

"No, the law library at the Daley Center."

"Really?" Most lawyers used computers to look up cases and statutes, and so attorneys didn't often utilize the sprawling law library at the downtown courthouse unless they really needed to tuck themselves away. Or they were researching old materials that weren't digitalized.

"And now he won't answer his phone, she says," Maggie said. "I mean, *what* is going on?"

"Could this be Valerie's case?"

"It was an old Redweld folder that he pulled from their basement storage."

"What about Valerie's father's case? Did he work on it?"

"That's what I'm wondering. My grandmother said in his early days of the law, when he was a state's attorney, he didn't often tell her the names of defendants on cases he was working on. The *victims* were his clients, he felt, and his responsibility was to them or their families. So he always used the victims' names when they talked about his work. After he started working as a defense lawyer, he changed it around, of course. The defendants were his clients now. My grandmother doesn't remember hearing the name Solara before Valerie's case."

I thought back to this weekend, at the Bristol's penthouse when we spoke about the case. When I'd asked, *So sometimes it* does *matter to you. The innocence or guilt?* Martin had looked at me, paused, and solemnly said, *Yes.* I had assumed he was speaking of Valerie.

Valerie came into the courtroom then. Maggie greeted her, then strode across the room to talk to the state's attorneys.

"Thank you, Izzy, for coming over last night," Valerie said.

"Of course." I paused. "I wanted to ask you something. Do you remember who the state's attorney was on your father's case?"

She looked startled for a second. When I didn't explain, she seemed to think about it. "Yes. Emmet Lambert."

"Oh."

"Why do you ask?"

"No reason, I guess." But I had a strong, *strong* feeling about this I couldn't ignore.

Maggie came back to our table. "Mags," I said, "can you handle this morning on your own? I want to find Martin. I have a hunch about something."

She bit her bottom lip, thinking about it. Valerie looked confused.

"Someone should make sure he's okay, don't you think?" I said.

Valerie nodded.

I looked at Maggie. "Can you handle the witnesses by yourself?"

Maggie's eyes rose to the ceiling and made a ticking sound with her mouth, as if reading off a mental list of witnesses in her head. "Okay, sure. Some of them are essentially repeats of earlier testimony. So I'll be repeating earlier crosses. Then we have the EMTs. Yeah, I can handle it."

"Call your first witness," the judge said. "Now, please."

I picked up my bag from the table, and left the courtroom.

# 50

The Daley Center, the site of much frenetic activity in my previous lawyerly life, now seemed like a calm island after the crazy energy of 26th and Cal. I took the elevators to the very top and entered the library. From the thirtieth floor, the south side of Chicago was visible, along with Lake Michigan, a glistening cobalt-blue today. This view, I'd always felt, was one of the best in the city.

I showed my ID to security and entered the main part of the library—bookshelves along either side surrounding wood tables where researcher-types, law students or lawyers huddled over books and laptops. Even though the bookshelves were high, they were placed far enough apart that nothing could overshadow the view of the lake. However, with the August morning sun already blasting inside the floor-to-ceiling windows, the place was growing warm.

I glanced around the space, not seeing Martin. I knew the library had back rooms and errant halls. Slowly, I picked my way up and down one aisle, then another and another. As I reached the more hidden sections of the library, the lake wasn't evident, the windows smaller, the air cooler.

I turned a corner, and finally I saw him. He was

hunched over a stack of opened books, a pile of documents and a notepad. Usually, if Martin was working, I saw him in a full suit, his hair coiffed, his tie clip gleaming. But he was in a shirt now, which looked too big for him, no jacket, sleeves rolled up. With his head bowed over his work, I could see his pink scalp through his white hair.

"Martin."

He looked up, mouth round and open like a fish. "What?" Then, "Izzy?"

I walked to the small table where he sat and pulled up a nearby chair. I set my bag on the floor and sat down.

"The trial?" He sounded bewildered. "What's happening?"

"Everything is fine. Some additional detectives today, and some emergency medical personnel."

"Okay, so…" Deep concern showed in his eyes then. "Is it Maggie? Is something wrong?"

"No, she's great. You've trained a good lawyer in your granddaughter."

He smiled. "Well, she comes by it naturally, and not because of me. She's just wired the right way."

"She is."

Quiet.

"So Martin…" I picked my hair off my neck and let it fall back on my shoulders, feeling hot at the thought of making an accusation at Martin Bristol. "You were an assistant state's attorney in the late 1970s."

Like a good trial lawyer, he gave nothing away. No indication of whether he was confused or knew exactly where I was heading. "Yes."

"You were a newer lawyer at that time."

He gave me a single nod. "That's true. After high school, I followed my father into machinery parts sales.

I quit fourteen years later because I was miserable, and then I went to law school."

"And then you became a state's attorney."

Another nod, very slow and cautious this time.

"And then you worked on the Javier Solara case." There had been no mention of Javier's attorneys on the internet yesterday, and Valerie had said the prosecutor's name was Lambert, but then why would Martin be studying an old file with the name Solara on it?

When he said nothing, gave no reaction, I continued. "You must have been…" I trailed off doing the math in my head. "You must have been a second chair at Javier's trial?"

"Third." He cleared his throat. "Third chair."

I nodded. "So what's going on, Martin? I know you're opposed to the death penalty. Are you haunted by the fact that you sent someone to that fate?"

A heavy sigh. "I *am* against the death penalty. I lobbied to overturn it in this state. Because the system costs entirely too much, because it's not a deterrent to others, because…well, there are a lot of reasons."

"But back then? During the Solara trial?"

"Back then I was okay with it. Particularly when we were dealing with someone who brutally stabbed a young woman full of promise."

"So what happened? Why this?" I gestured at the notes in front of us.

Martin Bristol looked at me in a way he never had before. He had always respected me, always treated me amazingly well. But I had never felt that I was on his level, not personally, not intellectually, not professionally. His kind heart and open nature had allowed me into the world of the Bristol family when I became Maggie's friend.

And yet now, Martin Bristol looked at me like someone he needed, like he needed me to step up to his level.

"You can tell me," I said. I wasn't sure precisely what I was encouraging him to divulge. But obviously something was there.

His eyes searched mine, for reassurances, it seemed.

I stared back. Then, to give him a break from what seemed an internal struggle, I glanced down at his yellow legal pad.

Over the years, so many things had changed with the law, with life, but Martin Bristol had probably used such yellow pads since he'd begun practicing.

It was hard to read his writing, particularly upside down, but I could see two columns he'd created—Evidence For, one said, and Evidence Against. Below the headings were notations.

I looked back up.

"Javier Solara," Martin said, "was innocent."

# 51

Executions like Javier Solara's happened at midnight in the "death house." At least that's what the public defenders office called it. Martin's bosses at the state's attorney's office had often mocked that term, but he had finally understood it the night when he went to Solara's execution— the night when he wanted to make it real.

1990. Joliet, Illinois. Home of Stateville Prison. In the daylight, when one pulled up to the place, it looked almost quaint, like a college campus. But there was nothing charming about it. The place housed thousands and thousands of inmates, the kind of people Martin had helped put away since becoming an assistant state's attorney, people who deserved to be there.

But he wasn't so sure that was true of Javier Solara. Initially, Martin had been excited about the case. Yet as it went on, as the evidence was analyzed, he'd had his doubts. He'd wanted to voice his concerns more than once to Emmet Lambert, the lead attorney. That wasn't so easy to do because Emmet Lambert was one of the most revered state's attorneys in the office, in the state even. He'd been there longer than anyone, through different bosses and different judges and different mayors. But finally, Martin had gotten the courage to discuss with Emmet some of his hesitancies with the Solara case—like the fact that Javier Solara simply *owned* knives that were *possibly* the same type as the one that killed Marilee Travis. That didn't seem persuasive to him. He mentioned a few inconsistencies with state evidence. He started to turn to other points, but Emmet became angry. He told Martin he'd had enough of his insubordination. He let it be known that if Martin wanted to move up in the office—hell, if he just wanted to keep the job—he should respect those who came before him.

Martin held his tongue after that. He had two kids by then, and the legal market was tough. But he thought about the case often. Thought about the fact that no witness could tie Solara to Marilee Travis at the time of her death. Sure, there were witnesses who'd seen him that day on his own property, near the Travises' place, and later there were people who'd seen Marilee returning from school, walking, and Solara picking her up, giving her a ride the rest of the way. But nothing more than that. Some hairs from Solara and his cap were found near the scene on the Travises' back property, but only near the scene, not *at,* and again, the Solara and Travis properties abutted each other. There was no evidence of Solara on the body of Marilee Travis, but the police's theory was that such an absence was due to the fact that the crime happened on a chilly November day. Solara was seen earlier wearing gloves, probably would have had them on when he killed her, too. That's what Emmet had said, as well. A grand jury had believed him, for what that was worth. And at the trial, Solara's defense lawyer was completely outmatched by Lambert.

More than anything, it was a feeling Martin had that Javier was innocent. But everyone was convinced otherwise, and people were happy that someone was being held responsible for the murder. So they tried the case, and Javier Solara was not only found guilty, he was sentenced to death. But luckily—if you could call it luck—death sentences took forever, sometimes never happened, because of the lengthy, required appeals process involved.

For a while, Martin was satisfied to keep an eye on the case from the sidelines, letting other attorneys fight for Solara's rights and his innocence. But then all the appeals were exhausted, and it came to that night—the night Javier would be executed, the night Martin went to the house to watch it all.

As a former state's attorney on the case, Martin had been invited to view the execution. Emmet Lambert was dead by that time, and the second attorney on the case had retired to Florida a few years ago, so Martin went there on his own, walking across the Stateville lawn in the eerie, moonless night, toward the death house.

Never before had he felt such dread. When the cacophony of formless cries started—the inmates shouting from inside the jail, which apparently happened every time an execution was carried out—the feeling intensified. You couldn't tell what the prisoners were yelling, but the anguish could be felt, the anger.

The house was small, its only purpose was to kill, and there was no way to avoid what was about to go on inside. People nodded when he entered, glanced at his name badge and expected him to know what to do.

Eventually, he was led into a room. He sat on the plastic chairs lined in rows. Elevated at the end was a glass wall showcasing another room, this one smaller, maybe ten-feet by six-feet. The same big yellow bricks that made up the walls in the viewing room covered the walls in there, too. The same linoleum was on the floors. Hanging overhead was an exhaust fan with chipping paint, a remnant of the old days when electrocution was the preferred means of killing. The other accoutrement in the room was more current—silver bars on the walls from which IV bags could be hung.

Martin stared at the phones on the wall, particularly the one at the end, the red one that was labeled and reserved for the governor should he want to intervene. For years, Martin and his fellow state's attorneys had feared the idea of the red phone, didn't want some politician mucking up years and years of work by the state. But now he stared at the phone and its cherry color. He tried to ignore the other spectators filing into the room—appellate prosecutors, select members of the press corps. *Ring,* he told the phone in his head. *Ring.*

When it didn't, he looked around, and recognized some of the other people in the room. Marilee Travis's family. It seemed morbid, but then who could blame them? Their daughter had been brutally killed. Who wouldn't want the person who had done that to die? Especially when you knew for certain that the man about to be wheeled in on a gurney had done it.

But what if you didn't know for sure? If Martin was true to his previous profession of assistant state's attorney, he wouldn't admit that a wrongful conviction ever happened. The party line was that state never made mistakes, or if they did, they were small, inconsequential. They were rendered against people who, if they had not committed this crime, had certainly committed others. They were doing a service by getting such people off the street.

He had believed that for a long while, except for this one kernel of doubt about Solara. Yet now, he was on the

defense side. Now he understood better how mistakes
could be made. And here he was, ready to watch a man
being killed and hoping—*praying*—the red phone would
ring.

# 52

I was, I realized, completely enraptured by Martin's story. My breath felt shallow. But he stopped talking. He stared at the yellow notepad, eyes cloudy.

I almost wanted to look away from the misery emanating from him. I'd never expected to see or feel such a thing. I didn't know if I wanted to, if I could handle it.

His mouth was closed tight, head slowly moving back and forth, saying, *No.*

I fought the impulse to stand and simply leave him, leave the library and the courthouse and forget that I'd seen such intense pain.

But as quick as that impulse came, another followed. I knew I couldn't leave him. In fact, I had to share his experience, to hear it. The fact that Martin was a pillar of society, a well-respected member of the bar, didn't mean that he never had problems, and it certainly didn't mean that he was immune from needing help.

"Can you tell me the rest of the story?" I asked.

No response.

"Please," I said.

He looked up, looked into my eyes, and I read his gratitude there. I nodded in acknowledgment. And then Martin Bristol started talking again.

\* \* \*

Martin remembered looking at his watch that night. Ten minutes to midnight. Behind the glass window, a door was opened, and Javier Solara was wheeled in on a gurney. His head had been shaved by then. There was no sign of his full black hair. He was thin—a far cry from the short but strong man he'd been when he was accused of killing Marilee. Javier was already strapped to the gurney, lying still, sheet up to his neck. But his eyes were open.

The warden asked if he had any last words.

"Yes," Solara said. The room was miked, audible in the spectator's area.

And then the most extraordinary thing happened. Solara turned his head, and he looked *right* at him. "I want to say these words to him," he said.

A confused warden pointed to Martin to make sure he'd understood properly.

The warden left Solara's side and entered the spectator area to talk to Martin. "You don't have to do this," the warden said.

"I want to do it," Martin said.

The warden led him down that hall again and then to the right. They pushed open the door and then, Martin was on that stage of sorts, Solara looking up at him.

He glanced at Solara's body, ensuring he was still strapped, then he leaned forward, offering his ear.

"Innocent," Solara said. His voice was gruff, as if he smoked cigarettes constantly, but there was something gentle about it, something very human.

Martin felt himself leaning farther toward Solara.

And then Solara spoke again. "I will die innocent."

Martin reared back. It was something out of his nightmares. Was this man he'd helped put here, this man who was about to be only a shell of skin cells, telling the truth?

Martin turned to the warden. "Perhaps we should wait…" he said.

The warden gave an abrupt shake of his head. "No one stops this show unless that phone rings. You know that."

"He claims he's innocent."

The warden made a gruff sound, almost a cough. "Yeah, a claim of innocence. How many times you heard that?"

Martin didn't answer. Truth was, he'd heard such claims from many defendants. But this one seemed different. And this one—this *man*—he was about to see killed. Martin was led back to the gallery. Again, he stared at the phone. He tried to think of Marilee Travis who had been so ruthlessly murdered, her life ending in terror. But when he looked at the gurney, that's what he saw on Solara's face, too. Terror. Solara looked through the glass and continued to look right at Martin; right at him.

"We've started the first shot," the warden said. One injection was to render unconscious, one was to paralyze, the last would stop the heart.

Javier kept looking at him. That was how Martin thought of him suddenly, as "Javier" instead of "Solara." Javier continued staring at him, challenging him, telling him, *Do something.* And yet there was nothing to be done. The warden had been right. At this point, only the governor could stop the death.

He waited for Javier's eyes to close, for that look to just go away. *Go away.* But Javier's eyes stayed open, fixed on Martin. Martin glanced at the warden, then the medical engineer who was administering the drugs. Both looked a little confused. Martin's gaze shot back to Javier. No change. Still it yelled, *Help!* Still it shrieked, *I am innocent!* He heard the other message Javier was giving him. *You did this. You could have stopped it.*

Then the most horrible thing happened. Javier's body bucked against the restraints, convulsing and writhing, his body moving so violently the gurney moved with it.

"Oh, God," he heard a women's voice say. Someone else in the visitor's room began crying.

The warden and medical engineer froze for a moment, then the warden forced Javier's body back to the gurney, laying over him to stop the gurney from moving, shouting at the medical engineer. More people were talking now, yelling for help.

The second shot was given, and just as swift, the spasms stopped. And then the room went silent. But Javier's eyes were still open, still staring at Martin. It seemed that the man could see into him, into his deepest thoughts, and so Martin stopped saying, *Go away,* in his mind and instead started saying, *I'm sorry. I believe you. I'm sorry.*

The third drug was started. Still, the stare. And then at last, finally, his gaze fell shut.

Yet that gaze would stay with Martin. Forever. It was part of him now. It grew worse when he learned that likely the first drug Javier was given didn't work properly, which was why Javier remained awake, which likely meant he was actually conscious during the horrifying and excruciating process of having his body paralyzed, and maybe even when his heart was violently, ruthlessly stopped.

Lately, having taken on Valerie's case, Martin saw that look even more often—every day, every night, in particular when he lay down and tried to close his own eyes.

# 53

I neared the courthouse, my right hand pulling as hard as possible on the Vespa's gas.

Driving south on Ashland, then Ogden, I heard my phone bleating from my bag. Ignoring it, I turned the Vespa onto California and sped toward the parking garage. My phone rang again and again and again. I tried to fish it out with my hand so I could glance at it at a light, but I couldn't find the damn thing. Finally, I pulled over to the side and searched out the phone. I looked at the display and saw all the calls had been from Maggie. There was also a text message. Call me!!

I popped up my helmet off my head and dialed her number.

"Where are you?" she demanded.

"About two blocks away."

"Just so you know, the press is here," she said before I could tell her that her grandfather was following me.

"Really? Well, you thought the media would pick up the story sooner or later."

"Yeah, a ton of media has been coming to the courtroom all morning. At first I figured that word of the case had spread. But then I realized Valerie's case wasn't the story. *You* are the story."

"*I'm* the story?" I blinked in the August sun. "What the helicopter?"

A pause. "Really?" Maggie said. "You're going to give me a swear word replacement now?"

"Yes."

"Say it."

"No."

"What the *hell?*" Maggie said for me.

"Exactly. Why am *I* the angle?"

"The minute the judge took a break, they started asking questions about you. Their angle, apparently, is 'Izzy McNeil, a woman suspected of murdering her friend, is now representing a woman charged with killing her friend.'"

"Whoa. That's a good angle."

"Iz!" Maggie made an irritated *grrrr* sound. "I don't want you giving any interviews. I don't know why, but my grandfather has been adamant about no press."

"I think I know why." Martin didn't want the press digging too deep around Valerie's case. They might find out that he had once helped prosecute her father.

I turned around, but I didn't see Martin's car. Maybe he'd already passed me.

"What do you mean?" Maggie asked.

"I'll explain. Or he will."

"He's coming?"

"Yes."

Maggie made a tiny *yay!* sound. "Okay, back to the media. Marty will be fine. The press will see him, but he won't say a word. He'll just walk in with his mouth closed."

"I'll do that, too."

"No, the press can't see you come in. We're in the home stretch of the state's case, and I don't want anything to throw us off our game. I don't even want any shots of you coming into the courthouse. Not just yet. My grandfather always says you have to be the one to control the message."

"Okay. Is there a back way into the courthouse?"

Maggie groaned. "They used to let attorneys use it, but now it's the judges' parking lot. You're going to have to go through the front door. I guess you're going to have to disguise yourself."

"Disguise? How would I do that?"

"I don't know." She was truly irritated now. "The press will be all over you. My clerk just went outside and said they're literally *waiting* for you."

"I suppose I could keep on my helmet."

"Maybe that'll work. Stuff all your hair under it." She sighed. "That damn hair."

"*Excuse* me?"

"Sorry. Gotta go, Iz. The break is over."

I kept driving. Soon I saw the press. The news vans were lined up and down the street, a glut of people with cameras and microphones on the steps of the courthouse. Martin was nowhere to be seen. I turned the Vespa around, pulled over again to put my hair under my helmet.

The problem was, I simply had too much of it. Maggie was right. "Damn hair," I muttered.

I sped back down the street, dodged into the parking garage right before the courthouse, and parked, managing to avoid any suspicion from the press. But I seriously doubted whether the helmet was going to do it when I walked up those steps.

As I turned off the Vespa, I saw two guys walking slowly toward the stairway. Was that a camera one of them was holding? I froze, but they kept walking, didn't even notice me. Not press. They slouched by in their baggy clothes and baseball caps.

One of them wore a big hooded sweatshirt, despite the August heat. I had an idea. I took a risk.

I took off my helmet, and, inching a few steps forward, said, "Hey, guys."

Both responded with wary looks.

I smiled big. It felt as false as it was. I decided to simply go for it. "Can I buy that from you?" I pointed at the guy on the left, the taller one, and his black Chicago Bulls sweatshirt.

They looked at each other, then looked back at me with suspicious eyes.

"Your sweatshirt," I said, then felt I needed to give some explanation. "I love the Bulls."

No response.

"I'm from out of town, and I really want a Bulls shirt." I sounded like a lunatic. I pulled my wallet out of my purse. "Fifty bucks?"

"Make it sixty," the guy said without flinching.

Before I could counter, he raised the sweatshirt over his head, pulling it off.

I scrambled in my bag, praying I had enough cash, and unearthed three twenties. I handed him the money, and he swapped me the sweatshirt.

"Thanks." I put the sweatshirt over my head, yanked the hood up.

The guys were still standing there, staring at me. I realized I could get mugged or worse. I had long learned from Maggie that the presence of the courthouse at 26th and Cal had never stopped anyone from committing crimes in or near it.

"That'll be it," I said, sounding clipped and decisive.

Surprisingly, they seemed to appreciate that and moved on.

Once they were gone, I put the helmet on top of the hood. With the black skirt, black sweatshirt and silver helmet, I must have looked crazy. Although no more so, I told myself, than anyone else entering the halls of 26th and Cal. But I didn't look like me, and that was what I needed.

I sailed through the media—past the news vans with the satellites on top and the bored camera guys and the reporters talking on their cell phones, all of them straining their eyes and necks over my head. I felt invisible in my hoodie and helmet, and for that moment, I very much liked it.

# 54

I made it inside the door of the courthouse, my eyes darting around, pleased not to see any press. But then I felt it.

My heart started to hammer, despite my mental warnings toward it. My face began to flush. Under the hood and helmet, my scalp was suddenly scalding hot.

I dodged across the lobby and pulled off the helmet, then tore off the sweatshirt. I could tell that the air-conditioning was turned up—the way they do in so many office buildings—making it bone-cold, but the frigid air couldn't touch my heat. It turns out, Maggie's fears were coming true—I was having one of my heat attacks.

I stood for a moment, trying to force cool air into my lungs, ignoring the sweat that started to course down my back, soaking the shirt under my suit. Glancing around the lobby, I was glad no one seemed to notice me. People pushed past, looking for courtrooms, asking questions of sheriffs who stood guard around the lobby. I spied a sundry shop in the corner. I dodged over there, feeling more sweat pour down my back.

The man behind the counter looked at me, up and down, then once again. "Are you okay?"

"I will be, if you have some Benadryl." I remembered

how one of my sweat attacks had happened right as I was about to go on air for Trial TV. The only thing that had halted it was a dose of Benadryl.

The guy behind the counter shook his head. "Are you kidding?" he said with a scoff. "You know what kinda drugs you can make from Benadryl? You can make *meth* from that stuff. You think they're going to let us sell that in the courthouse?"

"What about some aspirin? Anything that would reduce inflammation?"

He nodded and sold me a small packet of aspirin. I took them and chugged them down with a bottle of water from my bag, while I chastised myself for not carrying Benadryl in every bag I owned. I'd done that for a while, but then the attacks had dropped off and I'd hopefully assumed that they were gone for good. Silly, silly girl.

I stood there a second, hoping for a stalemate, but my blood was still boiling, my face even more red and pulsing. I would sweat through my suit if I didn't get a grip. And Maggie wouldn't want me to try a case with her anytime soon if I showed up like that.

I looked at the guy across the counter. He had started to squint at me. "You okay?"

"No. Medical condition."

He squinted some more, his face concerned.

"Please," I said. "Isn't there some Benadryl *somewhere* around here? Maybe someone has some leftover in a drawer from the flu last year."

He shrugged.

I pointed my face. "Look at me. I'm having an allergic reaction."

"To what?" His eyes were concerned now.

What should I say? *I'm allergic to big events, to fear, to trials?* The sweat attacks had been difficult to predict, except that they always correlated with extreme anxiety piled upon more anxiety. The problem was, the sweating only made the anxiety worse. Now, in my head, fears of being recognized by the press warred with thoughts of that document in Sam's pocket and then with my concern and sadness for Martin and finally, most importantly, for Valerie, my client. "Seriously," I said to the guy behind the counter. "Can you please ask someone if they have anyone have any Benadryl?"

He looked a little annoyed, but then he seemed to notice a new flushing of my face. I could feel it. I imagined it purplish in color. "I'll see what we have in the back," he said.

He disappeared behind a small door, gone for at least ten minutes. When he returned he held a silver foil strips in his hand, and I saw a little pink Benadryl underneath the plastic coating on that sheet.

"*Thank* you," I said. "Thank you."

I put a twenty on the counter. When he held out his hand, I snatched the packet, ripped it open and gulped the Benadryl with one swig of water.

I used the restroom outside the courtroom to clean myself up. By the time I'd done that, the Benadryl was taking effect, making my body temperature slide back to normal, introducing coolness and calm, for which I've never been more grateful.

When I walked into the courtroom, reporters lined the first few rows, but there were no cameras since they weren't allowed in Illinois courts.

The judge wasn't on the bench. I didn't see Maggie or Valerie or Martin. But my father and Mayburn were in the last row, right next to each other, like two friends who'd worked together for a long time. They were talking when I first walked in, speaking low, but they didn't look at each other when they did so. The sight almost made me giggle.

I wanted to tell them what I learned from Martin, but not until he told Maggie and Valerie. I suspected the three were in the order room, and that conversation was happening right then.

I dodged over to my dad and Mayburn and asked them for an update. They whispered fast, speaking over one another, talking about how they were still looking into Dr. St. John, the nanny and a few other leads.

"Can you two fit in one more assignment?" I asked when they were finished.

They nodded.

I reach in my bag and pulled out the document I took from Sam. I showed it to them. Both read it, showing no expressions. Finally, my dad handed it back.

"Will you investigate that for me?" I asked. "It looks current, but I need to know if that's accurate. And I need to know if it means what I think it does."

Mayburn had worked with me through Sam's disappearance. And my dad, although I didn't know it at the time, had been watching from the sidelines. So they both knew about the possible importance of the document. Yet both seemed to know to hold their comments until they had further information.

"Okay?" I asked.

They both nodded again like silent twins.

Just then one of the reporters noticed me and made a beeline. Others followed and soon the lot of them were hurrying toward me. But the sheriff appeared, and quickly he escorted me away from them with a few pointed elbows and a gruff, "Step aside! Officer of the court."

He led me through the Plexiglas door, past the counsel

tables, and to the order room. The judge wasn't on the bench. Clearly, Maggie—or Martin?—had convinced the judge to continue the break.

I opened the door to the order room, and slipped inside. No one turned to me. I looked at Martin, could see that he was clearly in the midst of telling Maggie and Valerie his story.

And then Valerie's voice rang out, louder than I'd ever heard her. "So you just let him *die?*"

# 55

Silence. I heard myself inhale and exhale. I shot a look at Maggie, who appeared stunned by the whole scene.

Valerie stared at Martin, her eyes confused, a little wild. "You just let him *die?*" she asked again.

We heard a burst of discussion from outside the room, then silence reigned again.

Martin's face was lined with what looked like absolute grief. I noticed again how much weight he had lost over the past few weeks.

But then he sat taller, rolled his shoulders back. "I did."

There was a gap in the room, a pocket of quiet and uncertainty; none of them seemed to know how to fill it.

Martin spoke up. "I wasn't as certain then as I am now of Javier's innocence, but I had a sense about the case. I thought the evidence against him was underwhelming. And although I couldn't have stopped it at that point, I let him die without doing anything else. And I will go to my grave with the guilt of that."

Maggie put a hand to her mouth, but she was surprisingly quiet. Even she could be stumped into silence, I supposed.

Valerie glared at Martin, but then the anger drained

from her expression. "I don't want you to live with that," she said. "It's not your fault he was arrested. It's not your fault they believed he was the one."

"I've spent years since then collecting evidence of his innocence. I became fairly certain after I learned about a man named Mickey Harwick."

"Mickey Harwick," Valerie repeated, recognition and surprise coming over her face. "He was a handyman in our town. He would go house to house looking for work. He used to do a lot of work at the Travises' house."

"That's right," Martin said. "And he was arrested for killing two teenage girls in the town next to yours. The murders took place about ten years after Marilee died, and he wasn't arrested until much later, but the weapon was a construction knife used to cut around pipes and doors. It had a rounded edge." He paused. "And he's discussed other murders while in jail. One sounded exactly like Marilee's."

No one said anything.

"Almost right after that," Martin continued, "I saw that you had been arrested. It was like God had given me a chance to absolve my guilt by helping you, Javier's daughter."

"What happened last week?" Maggie said, finally speaking up, "when you suddenly didn't feel good?"

Martin gave her a small smile. "Margaret, I know you think I'm capable of anything. I appreciate that. I thought I was, too, but apparently we were both wrong. I worked so hard on this case, and my body betrayed me. I suppose this is what happens with age—the body gives up before you want it to. It wouldn't let me go forward anymore." He sat a little taller. "I am feeling better, though. It's why I had the energy to leave the house today, to go to the law library."

"Does this mean you'll come back on the case?" Valerie said.

"I think it would be negligent of me to do so. I'm still not myself. My energy is still minimal, I'm having a hard time thinking. I keep going over and over your father's case. I want to make sure that evidence is compiled both on your father and Mickey Harwick, and all my doubts are in writing, so I can turn the case over to an innocence project, someone who will see if there is any DNA evidence available, any new evidence or witnesses who were missed. Someone who might exonerate your father. That is what I have to do before I die."

Maggie looked wounded. "Don't talk about dying."

"C'mon, Magenta," he said. I remembered Maggie telling me he used to call her that when she was a kid. "We're Irish. We don't fret over dying. Normal part of life."

Maggie's brow furrowed. I could tell she was thinking hard about all this. "Do we have to tell the judge this? I mean ethically?"

I thought about it. "I don't think so," I said. "The reason a lawyer is given work by a certain client, or why a lawyer goes after that work is only relevant if there's a conflict with the underlying lawsuits."

"I believe Izzy is right," Martin said. "We need to go forward with the trial." He looked at Valerie. "We need to get you out of this mess. Especially if you truly are innocent."

Valerie didn't hesitate before she said, "I am."

# 56

There's nothing worse than a witness on the stand who is *slaughtering* your case while you have to keep a straight face, giving the impression you couldn't care one whit about what they're saying. Inside your stomach, the contents heave. Inside your head, you scream *Shit, shit, shit!* And yet the placid, almost bored look you force onto your face says to the jury or the media, *Not impressed. Not a bit. And you shouldn't be, either.*

That's exactly what happened when Bridget Shanahan took the stand for the state.

At first, it was simple enough. Tania Castle, looking very pleased with herself, asked Bridget to introduce herself. Tania then took great pains to draw out Bridget's history as a surgical nurse, making her seem like an angel of mercy who would never, never, never tell a lie. And she did a good job of it. Bridget appeared to be a sweet, kind, smart woman. She had light brown hair that was thick and full, and made her medium-size self seem smaller. She had a quick smile that she shot at the jury whenever she was nervous, which seemed to endear her to them.

When Tania asked whether Bridget had an occasion to speak to Valerie a week before Amanda died, she looked pained. "Yes."

My pulse picked up. Was this the conversation Valerie had started to tell me about over the weekend at my mother's?

"And what did you talk about on that day?" Tania asked.

"The poison lady."

Many of the jurors developed confused expressions. I tried to hide mine.

"Can you explain what you mean by *the poison lady?*" Tania said.

"I'm writing a mystery novel in my spare time. Or I'm trying, anyway. I'm kind of lazy." She shot a chagrined face at the jury and a few chuckled appreciatively. "Anyway, I met this woman they call the 'poison lady' at a mystery writers' conference. She's a pharmacist, and apparently she helps authors figure out causes of death for their plots. I saw her speak on a panel called 'How to Kill Your Character.'"

"What is the name of this pharmacist?"

"Betty Payton."

"And you had discussed this woman, Betty Payton, with Ms. Solara before the conversation you're talking about, right?"

Maggie stood. "Objection."

"Basis?" the judge said.

"Leading."

"Granted." The judge looked at Tania. "This is your witness, counsel. No leading questions on direct."

Tania wasn't as good as Ellie at acting like a ruling against her was a good thing. She stalled for a second, then faltered trying to ask another question. Finally, she said, "Have you ever spoken to Valerie Solara about the woman you call 'the poison lady' after that conference at which you saw her speak but before the conversation we're talking about?"

Maggie sat and made a tiny laugh at Tania's clumsy attempt to get her question free of objections.

"Yes."

I glanced at the back of the small courtroom. People had flooded into the gallery. Spectators crowded themselves onto the benches, even packed themselves around the edges of the courtroom, jammed against the walls. The back of the gallery was at least two rows deep of standing-room-only people, most of them craning their necks.

Everyone in the front of the courtroom tried to ignore this, but it was nearly impossible. I'd always known that a trial was a theater production of sorts, but now it truly felt like that; all of the players waiting for their cue to take the stage; members of the audience ready to be entertained.

Bridget testified about how, at one of their Tuesday-night get-togethers, she'd told Valerie and Amanda about the poison lady because she'd found her fascinating. "I told them, 'Can you believe this woman knows about a million ways to kill someone?' But neither of them had seemed interested at the time."

"Did that surprise you?" Tania asked.

"No, I was always going on and on about the book I was trying to write and the conferences I went to. Just like Valerie and Amanda would go on about their kids. That's how it is when you're best friends, you're like family…" She paused and sent a heartbroken look Valerie's way. "You listen to all that. That's what you do for each other."

At the mention of "family," I glanced at my father again, sitting alone in the third row of the gallery, wearing a tailored light gray suit. No sign of Mayburn. I wondered about my dad's opinion of Valerie, the psychological opinion that he'd said he needed more time to form.

I often found myself looking at him over my shoulder when something new happened at trial—some new bit of evidence introduced—to see what he thought. I knew if he dipped his head to the side in a grudging way, that meant Maggie and I had done simply okay handling that part of the trial. But when he closed his eyes and nodded in a long, solemn fashion, I could tell we'd scored big points. Maggie had begun to rely on him, too. *He's better than any jury consultant I've ever had,* she'd said.

As Bridget talked about the poison lady and Valerie, I kept looking at my dad. When his gaze met mine—with no reaction of any kind—I raised my eyebrows. *Anything?* I asked him with my eyes.

He gave a slow shake of his head. *Nothing yet with this witness,* he seemed to be saying.

Suddenly, I found myself wondering what he did during the times he wasn't in court, the times when I didn't see him. Did he ever venture into his new city for his own pleasure? Had he made any friends? I seriously doubted that second one. It made me sad.

"So, bringing your attention back to the conversation you had a week before Amanda died, why were you talking about the poison lady?"

"Valerie asked me about her."

*Uh-oh.*

"Were you surprised when Ms. Solara mentioned the poison lady?" Tania asked Bridget.

"I was. It had been a while since I'd gone to that conference, and I hadn't spoken about her since."

"What did Ms. Solara say when she mentioned the poison lady?"

Maggie stood. "Objection. Hearsay."

The judge looked at Tania for her response.

"It goes toward the present state of mind of the declarant, Ms. Solara, at that time."

The judge looked back at Maggie.

"Your Honor," she said, "Ms. Solara mentioning a woman whom her friend had discussed previously does not indicate *anything* about her state of mind."

But apparently the judge wasn't sure about this objection because he looked back at the state. Tania had moved to the state's table, and she and Ellie had their heads together, Ellie whispering something.

Tania stood. "The present state of mind exception can also be offered to prove future conduct."

"I'll allow it," the judge said.

Tania smiled and stood a little taller, looking at her witness. "What did Ms. Solara say when she mentioned the poison lady?"

"Valerie asked whether I knew her real name and whether I knew how to get ahold of her."

Maggie groaned, but when I glanced at her, her face was bland, almost bored, like the good trial lawyer she was. I dialed up my own fake-boredom, ignoring the *pound, pound, pound* in my chest. So this was what Valerie had wanted to reveal? That she was looking for information about poison? Or at least someone who could bring her that information? Not good. Not good at all.

Some of the jurors had raised their eyebrows at the testimony, others leaned toward the witness.

"And what did you say to Ms. Solara when she brought up the topic of the poison lady?"

"I told Valerie that the woman's first name was Betty. I didn't remember her last name at the time. I told her she could probably find her on the internet."

"And the week after your conversation, Amanda Miller was dead, is that right?"

Bridget sighed loudly. She looked pained, as if she didn't want to have to answer the question. "Yes."

*Ouch.*

"No further questions."

Maggie only had a few points to make, so she walked toward the witness, hands behind her back to further her nonchalance. "To your knowledge, Ms. Shanahan, did Valerie Solara contact this pharmacist, Betty Payton?" Maggie was smart not to refer to her as "the poison lady." It had too evil a tone.

"I have no knowledge that she ever did."

"Thank you." She took another step toward her. "Ms. Shanahan, you and Amanda and Valerie, you said that you three were best friends, isn't that right?"

"Yes."

"You were almost like family."

"Yes." She nodded fast.

"You never saw Valerie make any advances toward Xavier Miller, did you?" It was a stab in the dark, I knew, and I hoped it would go our way.

"Objection," Tania Castle said. "Covers material not raised on direct."

We all looked at the judge, but he was staring nervously at the gallery.

Finally, the silence seemed to register, and the judge looked back to the state. "I'm sorry, counsel," he said to Tania. "I didn't hear your objection." It was a failure few judges would admit in open court while a court reporter sat in front of them and media jammed the gallery. His eyes went back to the gallery, on all those reporters and spectators. We all stopped to follow his gaze. People continued to push in through the doors. Tania repeated her objection.

"Overruled," the judge said, without waiting for argument on the point. Then he looked at Maggie. "Counsel, how much examination do you have left?"

"Just a few questions, Judge."

He nodded. "Ask them."

Maggie shifted back and forth on her feet. I sensed she didn't feel as good about her stab-in-the-dark question, now that so much time had passed, but she asked it again anyway. "Ms. Shanahan, you *never* saw Valerie make any advances toward Xavier Miller, did you?"

"No," she said emphatically. "Never."

"To your knowledge, Valerie loved Amanda Miller very much, correct?"

"Oh, yes. They were as close as two people could be."

Maggie paused, and I knew she was thinking. Then she glanced at the gallery, looking to the third row at the end, looking to my dad. He gave her a single nod. *Ask it.*

"Ms. Shanahan," she said, turning back to the witness, "do you believe that Valerie Solara could have killed Amanda Miller?"

"No," she said quickly, a shot of relief in her eyes, as if thankful someone was finally asking her *the* question. "No, I really don't. I believed it at first, I suppose, because the police said it was true. But there has to be some other explanation."

"No further questions. Thank you, Ms. Shanahan."

As Bridget stepped from the witness stand, the judge gestured to his sheriff and whispered something. The sheriff, the new one who had been kept in his quiet box for most of the trial, stepped from the bench with his chest puffed out. He walked in front of the bench and declared in a booming voice, "This honorable court will adjourn to new quarters!"

The murmurs from the gallery were so loud we could hear the collective grumbling through the Plexiglas.

The sheriff continued to boom, explaining that the trial would be taking a break and would move to a larger courtroom upstairs, which could accommodate everyone. "And all members of the press are required to register with the clerk of this court, Ms. Beverly Hannah," he added, his voice ringing. He paused to gave a steely stare to the reporters.

Ms. Beverly Hannah, the clerk who sat to the judge's right, blushed. The judge gave the gallery a curt nod, then stepped off the bench and disappeared into his chambers.

Maggie walked back to our table. "Holy shit," she said. "We're moving to another courtroom, which means the judge and state's attorneys and public defenders in *that* courtroom will have to come down here."

"Is that a common occurrence?" Valerie asked.

Maggie laughed. "No. It'll piss off a whole boatload of people. But it's good for us. That's one of those big courtrooms." She almost rubbed her hands together. "One of the good ones."

The press was apparently also pissed off about the move, as well as the registering requirement. We saw them erupt into discussion. Meanwhile, Martin sat calmly in their midst, listening. He looked at us, and although his face was sad, there was something different from when I'd found him at the library. As if relief were making him still.

He stood then and pointed upward, mouthing that he would see us upstairs.

A few rows behind him, I saw Valerie's daughter, Layla, looking around, concerned.

The clerk turned on the audio, and the voices of the media members flooded the front of the courtroom. *What did he say? What's going on? The court is moving. Why? This is ridiculous! We're public citizens, too. We have a right to be here as much as anyone else. Why should we have to register?*

Ellie and Tania, the state's attorneys, suddenly left their table and moved toward the gallery.

"Oh, Jesus, are they making a statement?" Maggie said, her voice tinged with alarm.

"What would they say?" I asked.

"No idea."

Valerie's eyes went big, scared.

Ellie and Tania opened the door. Ellie took a little step ahead of Tania and cleared her throat. "Attention, please," Ellie said.

But Ellie only announced, in a few sentences, they would follow the judge's orders. She encouraged everyone to do the same.

"Phew," Maggie said.

Ellie closed the door and walked to our table. "Did you call the press?" she asked Maggie.

"Hell, no. I don't want press here."

"We don't, either." They both looked at me.

"What?" I said, defensive, but they turned and left.

I glanced at my father, who stood still, looking at me. He wanted to talk, I could tell. He looked at Valerie, then back at me and gave a slow nod. He had, apparently, formed his opinion about her.

# 57

As Maggie and Valerie left, I told them I'd meet them in a minute, then I gestured my dad toward me. Waiting for him at the front of the room allowed me to avoid the press that streamed the other way, heading for the larger courtroom upstairs.

When my father reached me, he adjusted the lapel of his light gray suit, then his copper-rimmed glasses. He was, I realized, hesitant about something.

"What?" I said, then immediately regretted it. Why didn't I speak to him like a normal daughter to a normal father? Why didn't I ask, *How are you?*

But if my father noticed or cared, he didn't show it. "Do you want to know my professional analysis of your client?"

"Yes."

He took a step forward and placed his bag on the table. It was a slim, leather briefcase bag in a rich brown-red.

My father looked at me, nothing in his face changing. "She's guilty."

I flinched. I couldn't help it. "Are you saying that because of her father?"

"No. Mayburn and I just learned about that, and we were going to tell your team."

"You all knew this?"

"Yes. As of today, we know that Marty was the third chair prosecutor on Javier's case. He believes Javier was innocent."

My father didn't act surprised. Had he figured out that part, too? "Where is Mayburn?" I said.

"Doing what you asked."

*Looking into the document I took from Sam.* I almost asked my father what he thought; I almost confided in him about what had happened with Sam as of late. But I realized I was scared of what he might say. I wanted to make my own decision about this.

"Why do you think Valerie is guilty?" I asked instead.

"I used inductive profiling from other murder cases, particularly poisoning cases. Then I also utilized deductive strategies, examining what we know about the crime scene and the victim. And as you know, I've also been studying her behavior."

"And based on all that?"

"Based on all that, I believe she's guilty. Do you want me to tell you about each of those areas of analysis?"

I looked at my watch. "I do, but there's no time. I have to be upstairs."

He nodded. Seemed placid, calm. But I was nothing of the sort. *How can I represent her if she's guilty? Do I believe my dad's analysis, trust him?*

"Are you *sure?*" I asked.

No response.

"I need to know. Are you 100 percent sure?" I asked.

Another pause. "No. First of all, you have to remember when I was a profiler—well, the feds don't call it that, but anyway..." He looked around at the now nearly empty courtroom, no one near us, then back at me. "That job largely involved systematic, analytical processes with larger sources of data."

"That means nothing to me."

He cleared his throat. "My job was to gather and scrutinize information about crime patterns and trends so I could help plan where to place resources for the prevention and suppression of criminal activities."

"So you weren't involved in analyzing individual suspects?"

"I was. But certainly not as frequently. It wasn't my main job."

"Okay."

"Also, I haven't done a voice stress analysis on Valerie, which is usually very helpful. I've barely heard her speak at all."

I thought about it. I heard my own words to Valerie just the day before. *I* am *your lawyer*.

"Thanks, Dad," I said to him.

He acknowledged my gratitude with a single nod.

"I've got to get upstairs. See you there?"

He studied my face, then he nodded again.

# 58

A pebble in his shoe. That's all she was. A pebble with red hair, who seemed to be looking for more, asking for more, when the fact was everything was already the way it was supposed to be. Valerie was on her way to a penitentiary, it seemed clear. The bright future he'd envisioned after Valerie was gone shined at him like a mecca in the distance. He could see it—the time when everything would be perfect.

Except there she was, this red pebble and her people, who were sniffing around. He could practically feel them at his back. He wanted to tell her to butt out, leave everything alone on the path to his mecca. But there she was, with her inquisitive faces, with her people poking their fingers into things. Those people—he knew they were her investigators, saw her talking to them in the courtroom—had spoken to every single one of the neighbors, had been digging around into his past.

No one had to be hurt, if she would just go away.

But what if she didn't, he asked himself? Well, he had done it once to save his life, to have a shot at mecca. He had removed a pebble. It hadn't been easy. Some might think it was, but they would have overlooked his agony. So he didn't want to do it again. Not at all. He wished people knew that. This "problem" they thought he had was not a problem at all. It was just a preference, really; it was as simple as that, and he'd never hurt anyone with that preference. Never. This notion that his intent was somehow evil was absolutely untrue. Untrue! He wanted only happiness. Not just for himself but for everyone involved, the people he loved.

So no, even though the opportunity had simply presented itself, he hadn't enjoyed what he'd had to do, the removal of a metaphorical pebble from his shoe. But he deserved happiness, and he would do what he had to. And so yes, if he needed, he knew he could do it again.

# 59

I took the stairs to the new courtroom, not wanting to see any press at the elevators. I pulled out my phone as I climbed. There was another text from Sam. Red Hot, please call me. Then one from Mayburn that said essentially the same thing—minus the "Red Hot" part. I stopped on a landing and dialed Mayburn's number.

He started talking as soon as he answered, as if he knew I wouldn't want the pleasantries. "Sam owns a corporation. Its main asset is a property in Panama."

This was what I'd feared, but still his words hit me like a slap. "Is it one of the properties that Forester Pickett used to own?"

A pause. "Yeah."

"How long has Sam owned it?"

"Since last year."

"Since Forester died?"

"Right."

Another slap. "Mayburn, Sam was supposed to turn over those properties back to Forester's estate after we figured out who killed him."

"I know." There was a weight to Mayburn's words, as if he were very, very sad for me.

"How much is it worth?"

"Four million."

"Jesus." I tried to think it through. "Why would Sam still own it?"

Mayburn said nothing, but I think we both heard the same answer in our heads. *Because he's a thief.*

When I got to the new courtroom upstairs, the crowd was worse. Way worse. The floor where the room was located was much nicer—the ceilings high and edged with marble molding, the doors to the courtroom rimmed with black marble and copper plates. And the courtroom was much grander than the other—with the marble wall behind the judge's bench, columns cut into it, the rest of it decked out in old wood and copper finishes. But because there was no Plexiglas protecting this courtroom from the gallery, reporters soon swarmed toward the railing separating the counsel's table from the crowd, taking advantage of the fact that the judge wasn't on the bench yet.

To add to the situation, the sheriffs hadn't yet swapped posts. *This* sheriff was definitely old school, the kind nothing could fluster. He sat on a chair near the bench, arms crossed over his ample belly. He looked ready to use his gun should anyone storm judge's chambers with a machete, sure, but he wasn't about to exert himself for much less than that.

When I reached Maggie and Valerie, I stopped, silent, hearing my dad's words. *She's guilty.* Valerie, meanwhile, was blinking madly at the oncoming members of the media.

"Is Layla here?" Valerie asked me. "Did she follow us?"

"She was in the old courtroom when the judge

announced the move," I said. "I'm sure she's on her way up."

We searched the gallery with our eyes, but it was difficult to see through all the press. They kept calling questions to us, their words hitting and joining together so that I couldn't concentrate on just one.

"Let's get Valerie out of here," Maggie whispered to me as she texted something on her cell phone. "Doesn't look like we're starting up anytime soon."

We turned and walked, skirting by the old-school sheriff, who gave Maggie a bored, "How are ya?"

"Hey, Paulie," she said. "Taking my client out for a sec."

Another bored nod.

Maggie led Valerie and me behind the bench into the area that housed the sheriff's quarters and judge's chambers. She took a left and led us down a narrow hallway toward a door at the end.

But before we reached it, we saw an empty prisoner's cell. "That's the bullpen," Maggie said. "That's where they keep people who aren't out on bail." She mentioned these few sentences casually. She was so accustomed to this world, nothing was foreign to her.

But Valerie looked at the cell with obvious horror.

I put my hands lightly on the small of Valerie's back, guiding her toward the end of the hallway.

When we got there, Maggie opened it a crack, and outside we saw a law clerk standing, waiting. Clearly, Maggie's firm knew all the secret hallways and passageways of this old courthouse.

We moved Valerie to a courtroom down the hall with a few people in it, but no judge on the bench. Maggie spoke to her law clerk, issuing instructions. She turned to Valerie. "We'll be back for you as soon as trial starts up, okay?"

Valerie nodded, looking weary but calmer being away from the reporters. "Where's Martin?" she asked.

"I'm sure he's on his way. Probably running into people he knows." Maggie studied Valerie. "How are you doing about…about everything he told us?"

Valerie answered more quickly than she usually did, sounded more sure of herself. "There are a lot of feelings churning around," she said, "but mostly I feel relieved. I *knew* my father didn't do it."

It was almost like my mother's reaction to knowing my father was alive. Although it roused up feelings, mostly it validated what she had always felt in her gut.

"I can't wait to tell Layla," Valerie said. "Please keep an eye out for her."

As soon as we stepped outside the courtroom, at least seven reporters were there, peppering us with questions.

Maggie closed the door quickly behind her, trying to hide the fact that Valerie was there, and that seemed to work. No one tried to push past us and open the door. They just shouted questions, phones outstretched to record our words. "No comment," Maggie kept saying. "No comment." But after a moment, I focused in on their questions. And realized, they were all about me.

"Izzy, what does it feel like to be accused of killing your friend and now represent someone accused of the same thing?"

"Do you think your client did it, Izzy?"

Maggie and I pushed through them, and all I could think was, *I wish Jane were still around.* Jane could have instilled some order in this crowd. Or she could have told me what to say.

I got stalled in an eddy of more reporters coming down the hallway, all of them asking questions. "Why did you take on this case, Izzy?"

"Was it to prove that you didn't kill Jane Augustine?"

Maggie held up her hand. "As all of you know," she said loudly, glaring around the group, "my cocounsel was never a suspect in the Jane Augustine case."

I'd technically been a *person of interest,* which felt about as bad as being a suspect, but I kept my mouth shut.

"And as all of you know," Maggie continued, even louder, "the real perpetrator of that murder was caught and is now behind bars. We will not be addressing that case any further, and I know you will be respectful and do the same."

Whether it was the admonishment or the fact that we'd finally thrown them some scraps, the pack of press broke apart a bit. We pushed past them and hurried toward the courtroom. They followed us, a few still throwing out questions, but they seemed appeased. For now.

Back in the newly assigned courtroom, the judge still wasn't on the bench. My dad stood at the front of the room, at the railing near our table. I could tell from his look that he had something to say. Was he going to tell me not to represent Valerie? Would he give more evidence of what he believed to be her guilt?

"What is it?" I said when I reached him.

He paused, glanced around.

I led him inside the railing and to our table, away from the trailing media.

"I need to give you another professional opinion," he said.

My heart sank. "About Sam? I know he technically

still owns property that was once Forester's. Mayburn told me."

He shook his head.

"What then?"

"Look at the daughter."

"What daughter?"

"Valerie's daughter. Layla Solara."

I glanced at the courtroom. Layla still wasn't around. "What do you mean? Where is she?"

"Last I saw, she was outside the old courtroom. But I'm talking generally about her. Has she been interviewed?"

"I'm not sure. I have to check with Maggie. Valerie has been trying to keep her out of this as much as possible."

"But she's in it."

"What do you mean?"

"I'm not sure exactly, but she knows something. Or she's hiding something. I can just tell."

"Like you can tell about Valerie's guilt?"

"I'm more sure about this. After we talked, I left the courtroom and saw Layla go in an empty courtroom down the hall."

"The one where Valerie has been sitting during breaks?"

He shook his head. "Different one. Opposite side. Farther down." He described where the courtroom was. "I followed her, and talked to her."

"And?"

"I didn't get anything out of her of substance. But trust me, she's giving off a more guilty affect than her mother."

I said nothing, mulling it over.

"What about Layla's background?" my father asked. "Did someone look into that?"

"I didn't think so. She's so young."

"That doesn't mean a thing."

"Maybe not."

He seemed to think for a moment. "I'm on it." He turned and left.

# 60

Twenty minutes later, with Valerie back in the courtroom, the judge addressed the jury, apologizing for the move and reiterating how they were performing the most important public service possible. He directed them to pay strict attention to the trial, even though it had grown more complicated.

As he spoke, the back door opened and in walked Layla. She was dressed in another ruffled skirt, this one pink, and she wore expensive-looking shoes, ballet slippers with a hint of a sparkle. Her hair was pulled back, with little makeup on her radiant skin.

I looked past her to see if my dad was behind her, but I didn't spot him.

Layla squeezed into a bench.

At the front of the room, the judge paused and looked at the state's table. "Call your next witness, counsel."

Ellie Whelan declared that a pharmaceutical expert witness would take the stand. A short man with large tortoise-shell glasses walked through the courtroom and sat in the witness chair. Ellie led him through a direct exam that, while truly boring, further explained the mechanics of the drug, Propranolol, and the pharmacist's opinion that numerous tablets had been crushed and put into the Mexican food ingested by Amanda Miller the night she died.

We wouldn't be calling an expert witness in opposition, because there was no real disagreement on the use of Propanolol, but when Ellie was done, Maggie took the pharmacist through a few questions we might need for background later.

Soon, the pharmacist was done, and he left the stand.

"Next witness, counsel?" the judge said.

"Your honor, at this time, the state rests."

"Sweet!" Maggie whispered under her breath.

The judge looked at Maggie and me. "Counsel, will you be calling any witnesses for the defense?"

"Yes, Your Honor, but they aren't here right now. We'd ask that court be adjourned until tomorrow."

The judge turned his gaze to Valerie. "Ms. Solara, do you intend to testify in your defense?"

Valerie looked at Maggie. We'd talked about this, and we thought that Valerie would not make a good witness, too nervous and skittish, although we hadn't exactly put it like that to her. Maggie gave Valerie a light squeeze of the wrist, telling her to go ahead.

But Valerie had never spoken in the courtroom. She opened her mouth. No sound emerged. There were some murmurs from the press.

"Silence in the gallery," the judge ordered. He looked at Valerie. "Ma'am, you do understand that you have a right to speak in your own defense, but it is not required?"

She coughed a little, as if to get her voice working. "Yes, Your Honor, I understand."

He looked at the jury. "The fifth amendment of the United States protects witnesses from being forced to incriminate themselves. It is the right of every citizen *not* to have to answer questions. We all have a right to silence, if we choose."

He looked back at us. "Ms. Solara, have you and your attorneys determined whether you will testify in this case?"

Maggie gave her another squeeze on the wrist, this time in a show of support, it seemed.

"Yes, I have," Valerie said. "And no, Your Honor, I will not."

Murmurs, questions from the crowd in the gallery. The judge ignored them, looked at the jury. "Very well. Ladies and gentlemen of the jury, no inference of guilt or any other inference is to be drawn from Ms. Solara's decision not to testify on her own behalf. I'll instruct you further on this at the close of the evidence." He crossed his hands on his desk. "Ms. Bristol, how many witnesses will you be calling and how much time do you need for them?"

"Two or three witnesses, Your Honor. We expect them to be short."

"Do you anticipate we'll be able to close tomorrow?"

"Yes," Maggie said.

"Very well." The judge dismissed the jury with admonishments not to talk amongst themselves or to anyone else about the trial. "Especially not to any members of the media." He glared at the reporters in the gallery, then stepped down.

"How are *we* going to avoid the press?" Maggie said under her breath. "Right now they have no footage, just my statement on paper. I don't want to give them anything else to run on the news about you."

I glanced at the gallery and saw the reporters chomping at the bit—bags collected, cell phones, voice recorders and notepads ready. "Then we're not going to avoid the press. Not exactly." I turned back to Maggie and gestured in the direction of the bench. "Follow me. I have an idea."

I called Q from the hallway behind the judge's bench. "Hi, what are you doing?" I said.

"The same thing I'm always doing these days. Watching *The View* on my DVR and contemplating suicide."

"Put down the razor blade. Can you get to 26th and Cal in thirty minutes?"

"Why?" He'd said only one word, but I could tell his voice was excited, his interest piqued.

"I need you," I said. "I want you to act as a publicist for the trial. Just for the afternoon. Sort of an acting job. And then tomorrow, I need you to do a real job and run our trial graphics."

Maggie, standing next to me, shook her head no. *We don't need that,* she mouthed.

I put my hand over the phone for a moment. "Yes, we do, Mags. We need to go splashy and big and knock this thing out, especially since we don't have a ton of witnesses and especially since the press is here. Trust me on this?"

Maggie exhaled hard, but she nodded.

"Are you kidding?" I heard Q saying excitedly through the phone.

"Not kidding. We need you. Thirty minutes?" I gave him the number of the courtroom.

"I'll be there in twenty."

We met with the judge on scheduling matters. When we got out of the chambers, Q was in the courtroom, tapping his foot in anticipation, but at the same time, entertaining Valerie with stories about how he and I had worked together in the past. I couldn't believe it, but I saw

Valerie laugh, genuinely, her hand covering her mouth. With Q in a gray suit, his bald head gleaming under the lights, and Valerie in an ivory dress, setting off her brown skin, they made a striking pair, people who appeared as friends already. About half of the media was still in the gallery, watching them and jotting notes, waiting. The rest would be waiting outside with their cameras, I knew.

Q, Maggie, Valerie and I huddled up. I looked around and found Martin, who stood at the side of the gallery, as if wanting to leave the case to us now. I gestured him toward us. "Please," I said.

Quickly, Martin was at our side. We all leaned in together.

"Here's the plan," I said.

When we were done, Layla walked back in the courtroom again. I wondered where she had been. She came over to her mother and linked arms with her. "We should get you out of here, Mom," she said. "People are saying the media is camped outside the building."

I was touched by her apparent sweetness, but I wondered what my father had meant about her knowing something. Or hiding something. I wondered if he had found out anything about her. What could there be to find, though? She was a nineteen-year-old girl. But I kept hearing my dad's words—*guilty affect*. I would watch her, I decided.

"I think we have a way out," I said to Valerie and Layla. "In a minute or two, you'll follow me downstairs to the lobby and wait until I give you a signal."

Valerie nodded, not asking for more details than I'd already given her, which I liked. She trusted me, I saw.

Their arms still linked, Valerie put her hand on

Layla's arm and looked with wide, sad, scared eyes at her daughter. "Shall we do dinner tonight?"

I knew she was thinking that this might be one of her last nights of freedom. We would likely close the case tomorrow. Which meant that the jury would start deliberating. Juries are highly unpredictable animals. They could deliberate for ten minutes or ten days. Valerie could be headed for prison as soon as tomorrow night, if they found her guilty.

But Layla didn't seem to understand this. Or maybe she didn't want to, something I could understand. "Tonight is my trivia night," Layla said.

"Oh, that's right." Valerie's voice had grown hard, despite her sweet tone—a brittle candy shell. "I know you love that."

"I'm going to run to the restroom," Layla said. "Be right back."

As she left, her mother turned to me with an expression that seemed...helpless.

I wanted to say, *It's going to be okay. You are going to be okay,* the way I would have yesterday or the day before that. But we were too close to the end of the trial now. I didn't know that anything would be okay.

"Layla does this trivia thing every week with friends," Valerie said. "It's something that makes her feel normal, I guess, when our life has been nothing but."

I nodded. "Sure. I understand."

I looked at my watch. We'd given Q and Martin enough time to uphold their part of the plan.

We took the elevators downstairs. When we got there, Maggie's law clerk was waiting, and we directed her to take Layla and Valerie into an alcove. Then I inched toward the front door.

\* \* \*

Q and Martin were holding a press conference on the plaza of 26th and Cal. Every reporter strained to hold out a microphone, every cameraman shined their gleaming electrical eye at the pair.

Some of the courthouse workers had gone to the doors to hear them, and with a number of the doors propped open, Q shouting his words, we could hear perfectly.

Q, stepping easily into the role of publicist on behalf of Bristol & Associates Law Firm, read a statement about the trial that we had whipped up in the courtroom.

"The state," he said, sounding a bit like Jesse Jackson, the Early Years, "says this trial is about friendship, or the failure of it. They say it's about envy, seduction. Well, those are simply words meant to inflame the jury. They have no physical evidence tying Valerie Solara to the crime. Nothing!" He scoffed. "That's nearly impossible in today's day and age, and yet the prosecution has nothing." He punctuated the air with a rolled-up sheaf of papers. "We will be providing the media with statistics on the percentage of crimes that produce physical evidence in our contemporary times. It will be high. I'd ask everyone who wants that information to step forward when we're done and give me your contact information."

Hmm. That last hadn't been part of the script. It sounded okay, I supposed. And I knew Q. If he said he'd do it, he'd do it. He'd find the research and provide it. And it would buy more time at the end of his little speech.

Q kept talking and introduced Martin, who basically gave a similar talk, in a more subdued way. There was nothing new the two were adding, technically, but with the press so hungry for "news," every attention was focused on them. Maggie stood nearby, as if ready to contribute something, although I knew she planned to say absolutely nothing.

I turned and sought Maggie's law clerk who was hiding in the alcove with Valerie and Layla. I pointed to a side door, mouthing, *Go, go.*

We watched them leave fast, skirting the edges of the press. They made it across the street. *Yes!* No one had seen them.

I looked at Mags. "Go," she said. "And then I'll be following soon after you."

I nodded. "We need to catch up about Sam," I said.

"News?"

"Yeah. Bad news."

"Oh, honey." Maggie gave me a quick squeeze of a hug. "We'll talk later. You better go."

I dug in my bag and found the hooded sweatshirt I'd bought in the parking garage. I yanked it over my head, pulled my hair inside it, then added my helmet atop it. And quietly, my face downward, I pushed through a revolving door and slid down the side of the crowd, no one noticing me.

# 61

Theo and I walked into the club. Techno music pounded despite the mostly empty confines of the place. Laser lights swirled through the darkness. Later, the place would be insanely packed, Theo and C.R. had said, as if that were a good thing, but now was the time to get cheap drinks.

We walked farther into the club and into one of the deep seating pits that was sunk into the floor, circular, padded with colorful pillows. To me, it seemed the kind of decorating you might see in a college dorm, albeit a high-end one, but I kept my mouth shut.

We perused the bar menu, and I pointed out an item to Theo. "Blue Moon. That's what Sam used to drink."

Theo glanced at me, a little question in his eyes, and when the waitress came he ordered a Heineken.

Just then C.R. and Lucy arrived. They slid into the booth with us and ordered drinks. We all started chatting. Theo and C.R. seemed pleased by the club. And Lucy, in a miniskirt and a tank top, looked like she not only fit into the place physically, but was as pleased with it as the boys. And that's exactly what Theo and C.R. seemed to me right then—boys.

I'd been dealing with a murder trial for weeks, with

someone's life in the balance. And Sam had returned, throwing my own life's balance out of whack. I should have been happy for the levity in the room and with the group. C.R. and Theo ordered more drinks, kidding with each other, and joked with Lucy as C.R. tickled her and kissed her neck. But somehow it all made me feel weary, older.

I kept thinking about my dad's words. *Look at the daughter.* I kept thinking about Valerie saying that Lucy was at a Trivia Night tonight.

While the boys and Lucy laughed and called to people at the next seating pit, I pulled out my phone and ran a search for Trivia Nights in Chicago. There were more than a few. Since Layla went to DePaul, I started focusing on a search for just that area, in the Lincoln Park neighborhood. I found a couple, but only one that held their trivia games that night—Paddy Long's Tavern.

I piped into the conversation. "Who wants to do some trivia?"

My suggestion was met with blank stares.

I explained that a bar on Diversey had trivia that night. I looked down at my phone and then mentioned the drinks specials for good measure.

"Yeah, sure," C.R. said, looking around the place. "It's kinda lame right now anyway. We can come back later."

Soon, we were in another cab, pulling up to Paddy Long's. In front, a few small trees and plants guarded patio tables. White lights hung from the leaves of the trees, and people sat at the tables laughing and talking. A striped awning hung over them.

Inside, the air-conditioning blasted onto at least a hundred people taking up the tables, peering at trivia cards, then consulting their tablemates and neighbors about it, writing down answers, calling questions to the host. Occasionally, cheers of celebration would erupt from a table.

"I guess it's like bingo," Lucy said.

"I guess so," I said.

Neither Theo nor C.R. responded. I wondered whether anyone today still played bingo and if those two knew what it was.

A group got up from a table on our right, vacating it. We slid in.

I glanced up at the TV over the bar and saw a rugby game. "Sam played rugby," I said.

Theo gave me a glance, but I was saved by a waitress who brought drink menus and trivia cards.

Lucy, C.R. and Theo immediately got into the spirit, writing down correct answers and consulting us on others.

"Which country first gave women the right to vote?" the host called out from a microphone.

"New Zealand!" Lucy cried.

"You're so smart." C.R. gave her a fake punch on the arm. "How did you know that?"

"Oh, I think I was probably a suffragette in a past life," she said.

"Like that song, 'Suffragette City'?"

"Yeah, I love Bowie," Lucy said.

"Nah, that's by Ziggy Stardust."

"Well, sure, but it's Bowie."

CR's eyes crinkled. "What do you mean?"

"Ziggy Stardust *is* David Bowie."

"I don't think so."

"I'm pretty sure." Lucy shot me an *Is-he-kidding?* look.

I tried not to laugh and took a sip of my beer. Meanwhile, my eyes searched the place for Layla. Small lights dangled over each table and over the bar, but the gaps in between were dim and it was hard to distinguish one person from another. The bar stretched back and back. I couldn't see the people at the end.

Still, I looked over people's heads, craned my neck. Was that her, with the long hair? No. Was she with the group of girls on the left? I squinted and studied them as best I could, but finally decided, nope, no Layla.

"What does that suffragette song even mean?" C.R. said.

"I think it's about being addicted to a woman," Theo said. His hand slipped onto my lap and up my thigh. "I get it."

"But what's a suffragette?"

"It's a woman," Lucy said. "Someone who thinks she should have the right to vote."

"What does voting have to do with it?"

The trivia host raised his mike again. "What does the term *prima donna* mean in the opera?"

"A fucking bitch!" C.R. said. He laughed, as if he'd gotten the right answer.

"Hey, let's get another beer," Theo said, pulling C.R. from his stool.

The smile had already slid from Lucy's face. "He doesn't know what a suffragette is and he thinks *prima donna* means fucking bitch."

"He's young." It was the only thing I could think of to say.

Lucy sighed. Her shoulders sank in her white tank top. "I'm not so sure I want young anymore."

"Mayburn is an adult," I offered.

She looked up, but her face bore a tinge of the distraught. "I think maybe I need to be alone for a while."

"Alone, how?"

"Like alone with my kids. And my divorce lawyer. And my therapist. And my priest. And my house. Alone."

She sounded rather certain. And very sad.

"Do you want to leave?"

An exhale of breath. "No. I'll stay. I know you and Theo want to."

"Are you kidding? I want Theo home, in my bed, so I can get up early tomorrow for the last day of trial." *So I can go to sleep and not think about Sam. Or maybe so I can sneak up to the roof and call him to confront him.*

But I reminded myself that I'd dragged the group there for a reason. I heard my dad's voice again. *Look at the daughter.*

"Luce," I said, "let me go to the ladies' room, then we'll go."

She gave a glum nod. Apparently, her foray into the world of younger men had come to an abrupt halt.

I got up and walked slowly toward the back, my head swiveling as I looked for Lucy. That wasn't her in the corner, and no, not that girl by herself. Maybe "trivia night" was just an excuse Layla gave her mom so she could head somewhere else. She probably shouldn't even be here, since the drinking age was twenty-one, and Layla was nineteen.

And then I saw something familiar. A shift of black-brown hair over one shoulder, a chin lifted into the air as a woman laughed. I kept moving toward her, walked slowly between the tables, not wanting to draw attention. Everyone was so intent on the trivia and listening to the host that it wasn't hard.

I came closer to the table with the woman. She was with a guy, their heads inclined, laughing. I'd nearly reached them. I got a shot of excitement because *yes,* it was Layla. She and the guy were consulting one of their trivia cards.

But my excitement quickly tapered. My dad had said to *look at the daughter*. Here I was looking at her, while she played an innocuous game of trivia. What was there to see?

I stopped slightly behind a table of people. I was about to turn away when I focused on the guy. *Wait a second*. I knew that guy. Or I thought I did.

I took another step closer, careful to stay obscured by the surrounding table.

Yes, I knew that guy. Yet he was not so much a guy; he was a man.

That man was Zavy Miller.

# 62

In the cab on the way back to my place, I texted Mayburn. Need background info on Zavy!!

Then I texted my dad. Anything on Layla? He answered quickly. Nothing of interest.

My head reeled with a million questions. *What were Zavy and Layla doing together?* He had been a father-figure to her, from what I'd heard, stepping in when Valerie's husband, Brian, was sick and after Brian died. So was Zavy just supporting Layla during a tough time? Taking her out for a night to get her mind off her mother's murder trial? But then why had Layla told her mom she was going out with friends, plural? Or maybe it was simple—maybe she *was* going out with friends and they had cancelled, and she'd called Zavy. But they had looked…intimate. Like people on a date.

"What is it?" Theo asked. He slid closer in the backseat of the cab and put his hand on my knee.

As it always did, his touch calmed and inflamed me all at once.

I told the cabbie to drive slow as he neared my house. I scanned the streets for any members of the press.

*Please, please, please have lost my address,* I willed the media. *Or please think this isn't a big enough story.*

Wish granted. No media outside. Maybe they were all home analyzing Q's data.

I called Maggie, but it went right to voice mail.

Anxious to do something, anything, I started getting ready for bed. Theo trailed behind me. A minute later, when I opened a seldom-used drawer, I came across a piece of paper.

"Sam's," I said, looking at it. An old practice schedule for the high school rugby team he worked with.

I felt Theo's silence before I really noticed the gap in the air.

I looked across the bed. He was naked—so big and tall and perfect-bodied and naked—that I just stared for a second. He could always reduce me to silence.

But then I noticed he was just looking at me sort of strangely.

"What?" I said.

He moved, slid under the sheet and pulled it up to his chest.

"What?" I said again.

"You keep bringing him up today. Sam."

I got in bed and pushed our bodies together. But Theo only looked at me, expressionless, then moved his beautiful self slightly away. "We've never really talked about him before," he said. "But it looks like it's time to do that."

"I know." I thought about it for a second. "You know we were engaged. Then he disappeared last year. Then he came back, and we couldn't get it together so we broke up."

Theo studied me, almost sadly. "Why couldn't you get it together?"

I thought back to that time. "Too much had happened for me to forget and move on right away. I wanted us to work at getting our relationship back together, but Sam wanted us to be together already. He wanted it to be done and for us to be perfect the way we used to be."

Theo looked at me some more. "I assume you've had therapy for this."

I laughed, but he didn't laugh with me. "Are you serious?" I asked. "What do I need therapy for?"

Theo didn't respond.

"Look," I said, "he disappeared. I understand now why he did that. Why am I the one who needs to get therapy just because I couldn't trust him right away?"

Now he answered fast. "Because it's the same thing that happened with your dad. It seems to me you've got some recurring issues flowing around here."

"What's that supposed to mean?"

"Your dad disappeared. He 'died' very violently and very suddenly when you were little. Then later you met Sam. It sounds like he was one of the first guys you ever really trusted or fell in love with."

I nodded.

"And then he disappears suddenly, just like your dad. It makes sense that when he came back you wouldn't trust him. And you wouldn't trust the whole situation. You don't trust him to stick around."

*And I'm not sure I trust Sam now—Sam, with a four-million-dollar property he has no right to possess.*

But I wanted to trust Theo. I needed to, if we were going to keep going, keep being together. And so I told him everything.

I told him about Sam getting engaged to Alyssa but willing to call it off. I told him about seeing Sam for drinks at the hotel and the Panamanian document. I left out the part about making out in the hotel room. If Sam and I had ended up sleeping together, I would have had to tell Theo, but I wanted to keep the conversation about Sam's return to my life. And what I was going to do about it. Theo needed to know. He deserved to be a part of that decision.

Theo watched me as I talked. When I finished, he reached out a hand and smoothed my hair away from my face.

"Are you pissed off?" I asked him.

He shook his head no. "I'm sad you couldn't tell me before."

"I'm sorry. I—"

"No, don't be sorry. I understand it. I just wish I could have been there for you before now."

I scooted closer to him and wrapped my arms around him. "Thank you," I said into his chest, my words muffled.

"I still think you need therapy."

"You think I'm crazy."

"Hey, therapy is not just for people who aren't friends with their head. I've had lots of therapy."

I pulled back a little to look better at his face. "I'm surprised. Why?"

He stared at the ceiling for a second like he was trying to remember. "When I decided to leave college after my freshman year to start my company, my dad said it was okay, me dropping out. He was really supportive. But my mom was scared for me. She said the only way she would support me was if I went to a therapist for a while." He shrugged. "I really liked it. I figured out a lot of things about myself."

"Like what?"

"Like sometimes I'm trying to be like *my* dad. For a lot of different reasons. Sometimes I'm trying to be like him so I can give my mom some piece of him, even though he left her. Sometimes I'm trying to be like him because I want him to notice me and I wish they hadn't split up. That he hadn't left. Sometimes I'm trying to be like him because he's smart, and I can learn a lot." He shrugged. "Just things like that."

"Interesting."

"Yeah, the process is kinda cool."

"No, not the therapy. I mean *you're* interesting."

He looked at me. "You think so?"

"Yeah, I think so. I think you're a renaissance man. You're big and strong and manly and you do all that surfing and heli-skiing and whatever. And you're smart, too. Not just book-smart, but smart enough to start and run your own company." I started twirling a strand of my hair. "And then you're sweet, too, and you know when to admit you need help, like the therapy, and you're cool enough to make sure you got something from it. And you're such a great boyfriend that you just listened to me tell you my ex-fiancé wants to get back together with me."

He took the strand of hair, coiled it softly in his finger, then gently placed it on my head, away from my face. I almost said that Sam used to do that. It would have been true. But I did *not* want to talk about Sam anymore. I needed to talk *to* him about the document. I needed to decide what to do about that whole scenario. But I didn't want to deal with any of that now. And Theo seemed okay with that. He kissed my forehead, stroked my hair again.

Then he stopped. "Hey," he said, "did you just call me your boyfriend?"

"Yeah, I guess I did."

He said nothing.

"That all right with you?"

"It's cool. And I guess that would mean you're my girlfriend."

I liked the sound of that. "Yes, that's what that would mean."

He kissed me then, really kissed me, and there went the world. "My girlfriend," he said into my mouth, like he was trying it out. "My girlfriend."

# 63

I woke up at the crack of dawn, slunk downstairs and peeked outside, relieved that once again the press was nowhere to be seen.

I ran upstairs, got ready and was just about out the door again, dressed in a short-sleeved lavender suit, when Mayburn called.

"Hey," he said. "Can you grab coffee so I can tell you about the background checks?"

"You know I don't do coffee."

"You're a freak."

I snorted.

A sigh from Mayburn. "Fine, can you grab a green tea with soy milk and Splenda so I can tell you about the background checks?" He paused. "Or are you still drinking *decaf* tea?" he said with scorn.

"I'm off the decaf wagon because of the trial."

"Well, that's something."

Twenty minutes later, Mayburn and I were tucked into two purple velvet chairs in a Starbucks. The window behind us looked onto the intersection of North Avenue and Wells Street, traffic starting to pick up as people headed to work.

Mayburn placed a slim stack of paper on the table

between us and patted it. "Aside from this, there are no records for Zavy Miller."

"What do you mean?"

"I have him back to…" Mayburn's voice trailed off. He lifted a few sheets of paper and flipped through them. "Let's see, I have documentation on him marrying Amanda. That's the first year I can find anything about him. That's the first year he got credit cards, a very large business loan, and then a home mortgage with Amanda. Before that, it appears, he never existed."

I felt my face crease with confusion. "Xavier Miller can't be that common of a name."

"It's not. What I found was easy to locate. I just can't find him before that time."

I picked up the other papers, glanced at them, saw notations for *Xavier J. Miller*. "What's the initial *J* stand for?"

"Jennings."

"Not common, either."

"Nope, but even with that name, my search results are the same. Xavier Jennings Miller appeared in Chicago, at least on paper, ten years ago. He met Amanda a year later and then from what I can tell they got married pretty quick."

"Yeah, that's what he testified to at trial. Where did he live before that?"

"I don't know. There's nothing. But I'm trying some other avenues, and I'm hoping to have something soon. I just wanted to tell you what I knew so far."

"Ask my dad to get on this."

"I don't think I need him here, I just have to—"

"Seriously," I said, interrupting him. "Get him on it. He's lived under different names, lived so many different lives. If anyone can figure out who Zavy Miller really is, it's him. Plus, there's something else." I told him about my dad being suspicious of Layla, and about seeing Layla and Zavy together last night.

"Wow. I'll talk to Christopher." Mayburn thought about something. "Sorry about what I said the other night about him being a cold fish."

"It's okay. Wouldn't you be, too, if you'd gone through what he had?"

"Yeah. Probably."

I thought of the two of them on the courtroom bench, sitting near each other. "How has it been? Working together?"

He nodded, a sort of surprised expression on his face. "Gotta say, your dad's good. He notices everything, and he seems to be able to slip into places without people really noticing him."

I thought about how my father had watched me for much of my life. I'd never noticed him, either.

"I guess that's true," I said. "Well, except for Dr. St. John. He sure noticed him."

"Yeah, we both went up and down that neighborhood. Didn't think we'd need to be too quiet. You hear anything else from the good doc?"

"Not so far."

"We're keeping an eye on him."

"Thanks."

"So. I haven't heard from Lucy," Mayburn said.

I blinked at the topic change, then, "I'm sorry."

"Yeah, me, too." None of his usual sarcasm rose to the surface. His face actually looked pained.

For the first time since I'd known him, I leaned forward and touched John Mayburn. We had never hugged, never even shook hands except the first time we'd met. We existed as two people who worked, in some ways, very intimately with each other, but rarely had any physical contact.

But I saw now that he needed support. And maybe affection. I put my hand on his. I saw him fight the instinct to pull away. When he didn't, my heart ached for him.

"Thanks," he said, looking down at our hands. "Sorry I keep bringing this up."

I gave his hand a squeeze, then sat back. "I'm not. I understand. Hell, I might understand better than anyone. Sometimes, you can be the most perfect couple and still have the worst timing."

Mayburn nodded. "You make any decisions about Sam?"

I thought about Theo, about our talk last night. "Not officially. But things are really good with Theo. And I don't know if I need the complications of Sam and all his craziness." And yet with those words, I felt a deep pull of sadness. It was so damned confusing. "I have to talk to Sam about that document, but I've been so busy with the trial. And I guess I've been putting off confronting him. No matter what happens with us, I want to think of him as a good guy. The way I always have."

"Yeah, it's amazing when you think the person you're with is one of the best people you know. I think Lucy's the best."

I patted his hand again. "I know you do. You just have to decide—do you have the time and the patience to wait for her?"

"What if I wait and she still doesn't want a relationship anymore?"

"I don't know."

"In the end, all I really want is for her to be truly happy."

I thought about telling him what Lucy had said to me

about wanting to "go backward," to meet some of Theo's friends so she could feel younger and forget the decidedly adult struggles she faced in the future. Then last night, she had said she wanted to be alone.

"There is no way around the timing issue," I said to Mayburn, "and it seems she wants some room. If you push her right now, you'll lose her. Period. You've found the person for you. I think she has, too. But it's apparently too overwhelming for her to move from one intense relationship situation into another. It would be overwhelming for the kids, too. If you love her, think of her and the kids right now. And if ultimately you can't, then…" I shrugged. "I don't mean to make light of this, but if you can't, then you can't."

"I can," he said simply.

And that, I thought, was the real definition of love.

# 64

Even after meeting Mayburn, I was still going to be early for court. I just hoped the media wasn't early, as well. I hopped on the Vespa and headed west on North Avenue, then south on Ashland, speeding toward 26th and Cal.

*Damn.* Two news trucks were parked right in front of the courthouse. I stowed the Vespa in the parking garage and yanked the Bulls sweatshirt out of my bag, pulling it over my helmet. Once again, I looked like a jackass. Once again, I didn't care because I sailed past the trucks with no problems. I yanked off the whole ensemble as soon as I was through the doors, and thankfully, there was no sweat attack this time.

When I got to the courtroom, Q was there, dressed in a navy blue suit and a yellow tie.

"Q!" I called.

He hugged me quick when I reached him at the front of the courtroom. I wanted to tell him about Sam, but he held up a hand. "Not now," he said. "Lots to do…" Then he moved at lightning speed about the place, as if he had spent a lot of time in a criminal courtroom. He played with two laptop computers on our counsel's table, then he jumped up and adjusted audiovisual equipment and a screen that had been erected on the wall behind us, facing the jury. The state's attorneys came into the courtroom and eyed him warily.

I introduced Q as our "trial graphics expert" then turned away before they could think of something to object to about his presence. I lowered my voice and pointed to some equipment. "Where did you get this?" I asked Q.

"From Maggie's law firm. It's even better than the stuff we had at Baltimore & Brown. They must have paid top dollar for it and never used it."

"You know, we only have a few witnesses and then closings."

"I know. You should've called me earlier." He tried to sound irritated, but his face wore a smile. I could tell he was glad to be working. "Here's how it's gonna go," he said. He rattled off a bunch of exhibits that he'd loaded into the machine.

When he began muttering at the machine, apparently having trouble with a document, I looked at my watch. There was time to make the phone call.

Following the path Maggie had led us the day before, I went behind the judge's bench into the warren of halls back there until I reached the empty bullpen. I stared at it for a second, saying a silent prayer that Valerie didn't have to live the rest of her life in a cage. And yet, if my dad was right—that she was guilty—then maybe she deserved such a fate. I felt overwhelmed suddenly. I didn't like—didn't *want*—to be the arbiter of someone's future. I could almost hear Maggie then. *You're not deciding innocence or guilt. You are giving your client the best defense, a defense everyone in this country is entitled to.*

With that, I turned my back on the bullpen and walked a few feet away. I leaned against the wall and I dialed.

"Sam," I said when he answered. "It's me."

\* \* \*

Five minutes later, I'd heard everything I needed to. Yes, Sam admitted, there was still one Panamanian property in his name. Yes, it was one of the properties that Forester had asked him to transfer to his name upon Forester's death and then sell. For over a year, he'd thought that property, like the others, *was* sold and the money turned over to Forester's son, Shane, once the mystery surrounding Forester's death had been solved.

But then he'd heard from the real estate agent he'd worked with in Panama that a mix-up had been uncovered. The shares of the company that owned the property had been turned over to the buyer, as per custom, making that buyer the owner of the company and its assets. But before the buyer could take over the residence, that buyer was convicted of a crime and therefore, the shares reverted to the previous owner—Sam. He'd found this out right after he'd gotten engaged to Alyssa. It served to remind Sam of the life he used to have—with me, with his job as Forester's wealth management advisor—and he realized how far away he felt from the person he'd been then.

"I didn't like it, Iz," he'd said. "Not at all. I don't know if you can understand what it's like to be so disappointed in yourself. To feel like you've gone backward in life."

"Are you kidding?" I retorted. "After you disappeared, I lost my fiancé and my job on top of losing Forester. I know what it's like to go backward, my friend." The words were said with some scorn. "So if you found this out weeks ago, why haven't you turned the corporation over to Shane?"

Quiet.

"Why, Sam?" My heart hurt as I said the words. He

wasn't the man I thought he was; he didn't have the integrity I'd always believed I'd seen in him.

"Iz," he said. "It's hard to explain." He sighed.

I pushed the phone closer to my head. I wanted to hear his explanation. I wanted to think the best of Sam, even if this was really and truly the end for us.

But just then I heard the door to the courtroom open and a voice yell, "Iz?" *Maggie.* Heels *click-clack*ed on the cement floor, then Maggie appeared in a gray pinstripe suit with a teal silk blouse. She'd styled her hair and wore more makeup than usual. She rubbed her hands together when she saw me. "Last day of trial!" she said. "Let's go!"

"I have to run," I said to Sam.

"No, don't."

"I'm on trial, Sam. I'll talk to you later." But I'm not sure if either of us believed it.

# 65

Before we went back in the courtroom, I finally got to tell Maggie about the document I'd found in Sam's pocket, along with what I'd learned from Mayburn and what Sam had told me just now.

"Wow." Maggie shook her head. "Wow. I didn't see that coming."

I looked at her, waiting for some pronouncement, some advice. But Maggie only said, "Sam's got some balls, huh?"

"I guess that's one way to put it."

"What's he going to do with it? With the property?"

"We didn't get that far in our conversation."

Maggie reached out a hand and stroked my shoulder in sympathy. "I guess that'll be the big tell, huh? He fesses up and he's the Sam you always knew."

"And if he doesn't?"

Maggie raised her eyebrows, seemed stumped into silence.

"Enough about this," I said. I needed to tell Maggie about seeing Layla with Zavy and about the dearth of the information about him.

"Girls!" we heard Q shout into the hallway. "I need you."

"One sec," I called.

"Now!"

We made our way back to the courtroom. "The state's attorneys keep asking me questions about the exhibits," Q whispered. "And I don't know the rules here in the world of criminals."

Q explained the exhibits to Maggie, following it up with some questions about the testimony she intended to illicit.

Maggie answered, then listened as Q explained some other exhibits and offered suggestions of when they could be utilized during testimony.

"This is great," Maggie said. "Why didn't we do this earlier in the trial?"

I shot her a look. "I *told* you to do this earlier."

"Sorry."

"No worries, girls," Q said. "I'm here *now*."

Maggie looked over at the state's table and grinned a little. I could see what was coming. After the show we'd put on yesterday in front of the media, the state had countered by giving interviews to the evening news stations, calling the case against Valerie "rock-solid" and the defense "laughable."

I'm not a fan of taunting. Maggie, however, was different. She adjusted her suit and sauntered over to the state's attorneys' table.

"It's going to be a new show in here now," she said. "A different show. How should I explain this? We're stepping it up. A lot. You guys ready?"

Tania blinked at her, but Ellie only scoffed.

"Seriously," Maggie said. "I'd get ready if I—"

But then the door opened. We all glanced toward it. Someone large entered the room, someone with dark hair, wearing an orange golf shirt.

Maggie gasped. "Bernard!" She clapped her hands.

She hustled toward the back of the room, ignoring the press who'd arrived and were now turning in their seats.

"Who's the Samoan?" Q asked me.

"He's Filipino."

"That's the French horn player you guys met in Italy?"

"Yep."

Maggie was hugging Bernard, as he lifted her off her feet.

The sheriff came into the courtroom, announcing, "Court is about to begin!"

Maggie came back to the front of the courtroom. "That's my boyfriend!"

Ellie smirked. "I can see that."

"He said he came in last night to surprise me, but he got in late, and didn't want to wake me up, so he just checked into a hotel." She sighed. "What a good boyfriend."

Ellie rolled her eyes. "Jesus, where are we? Queen of All Saints grade school?"

"I don't care what you think," Maggie said. "I don't care about anything. That's my *boyfriend*."

I sat at the counsel's table, stunned. I had seen Maggie through many boyfriends, but she never used the word so many times, not in a year much less in a few sentences.

She looked to the back of the room. Bernard, with his huge self and his inky, shaggy black hair, had settled into a seat near the back, but because of his height he could be seen clearly. He waved at Maggie, smiling big. She did the same.

"Okay, Mags. We're all glad that your *boyfriend* is here," I said. "But we have to get back to work. And I need to talk to you about something."

But then the press hushed as Valerie was led through the back door by Maggie's law clerk. Her hair was pulled back in a severe ponytail and her normally warm, dark skin somehow appeared cool and grayish as if it had been bled of vitality by the last week as she was on trial for her life.

The judge came through the chambers' door as Valerie sat. "Let's go," he said simply. He nodded at Maggie. "Counsel, call your witness."

Maggie stood. "Your Honor, the defense calls Elizabeth Payton."

The poison lady.

## 66

Elizabeth Payton had trim dreadlocks to her chin and horn-rimmed glasses. She wore a cardigan sweater over a summer dress.

Maggie asked the witness to state her name, then buttoned her suit coat. "Thank you. Do you go by Elizabeth?"

"My friends call me Betty."

"Ms. Payton, can you explain your profession to the jury?"

"Sure, I'm a pharmacist."

"Do you work in a pharmacy?"

"No. I used to after I graduated college, but now I work for a drug company in a lab."

"Do you also serve as an adviser for authors and writers?"

"Yes, I do."

"Have you ever been called 'The Poison Lady'?"

She smiled. "Yes, that's my nickname now."

Q pushed a button on his computer and the screen behind us sprang to life, showing a blowup of a magazine article. *Poison Lady Kills 'Em with Kindness,* the headline read.

The jury perked up.

"Ma'am, have you seen this before?" Maggie pointed to the article.

"Yes, that's a piece a writing magazine did on me."

"What was the article about?"

"How I'd always wanted to be a writer, but never had the discipline. So what I do instead is consult with writers, often mystery writers, who have something happen to their characters—illness or death—and need to have it explained. Pharmaceutically. Or when they're trying to figure out a plot and they might be able to use my pharmaceutical knowledge." She shrugged. "I don't know how it got rolling, really. It's sort of a hobby of mine."

"Do you charge for these services?"

"No."

I looked at the gallery. The reporters were sitting forward in their seats, scribbling notes.

"Did you ever appear on a panel called 'How to Kill Your Character'?"

Q clicked a few more buttons, and a different image popped to life, a program conference brochure showing a panel named just that. "Yes, I have. A number of times. That's a program from one of the conferences."

"Objection," Ellie Whelan said, sounding irritated. "Counsel hasn't asked to admit these 'exhibits'—" she made air quotes with her hands "—and I would object to such admission."

"Granted."

"No problem, Your Honor."

I nodded at Q, who quickly made the screen go black. Q and I had done this many, many times—flash something illustrative, then taking it down when an objection was drawn, knowing the impression had already registered with the jury. In this case, these weren't exhibits that could make or break our case, but we had a number of objectives in mind. First, after a week of watching the trial every day, we wanted the jury to wake up and get them to pay attention. Using a TVlike screen always helped with that. Second, we wanted to show that Betty Payton was legit as a poison expert. And finally, with our graphics, we wanted to distinguish ourselves from the state, to show how professional we were, how serious we were about Valerie's defense.

Maggie crossed her arms and looked at the witness. "Please tell me, Ms. Payton, about the 'How to Kill Your Character' panel."

Betty Payton adjusted her glasses, then pointed to the screen where the program had just been. "Sometimes at these conferences, they'll call it something different, but that's generally my function—I go to writers' conferences and help devise creative ways to kill people." She laughed, but only a few jurors followed suit.

"That's quite a hobby," Maggie said, now drawing chuckles from the jury. "Now, Ms. Payton, I want to ask you a very pointed question here. Do you know someone named Valerie Solara?"

"I know of her, but I've never met her."

"How do you know of her?"

"Because I have been subpoenaed to appear at this trial."

Q, who clearly wished he could have been here at the whole trial, with more experts requiring exhibits, tapped on his computer, causing a subpoena to appear on the screen.

The judge shot Q a stern look and so did Maggie. I elbowed him, and the subpoena disappeared.

Q looked at me. "I love being here," he whispered.

"I can tell," I whispered in return.

"I want back into the law," he said.

Now Maggie sent both of us a look, and we went quiet.

"Other than through this trial," Maggie said to the witness, "do you know of someone named Valerie Solara?"

"No."

Maggie took a moment to let that sink in, pacing back and forth, then eventually to our table.

She pointed to Valerie. "Is this woman familiar to you, Ms. Payton?"

"No, she is not."

"Did you ever get a call from someone named Valerie Solara?"

"No."

Maggie went on, asking if Valerie Solara had contacted her through email or by mail or through Facebook or through any other fashion. "No," Betty Payton answered to each query.

"Okay, well, let's take out the name Valerie Solara." Maggie said. "You do, I suppose, get calls and emails from different people about your hobby."

"Yes."

"Has anyone ever contacted you asking about how to kill someone with the drug Propranolol?"

"No."

"And did you ever offer anyone information on how to kill someone with Propranolol?"

"No. Through all the years I've been doing this, I've never discussed Propranolol as a means of death, surprisingly."

"Why are you surprised?"

"It's a relatively common drug. And it would be a simple and effective means of killing someone."

Maggie asked a bunch of questions about the drug and

why people would take it. She asked if some people took it for stage fright, which Ms. Payton said they did.

"It really would be quite a simple thing to do," the witness added. "It's a very crushable tablet, and although it has a bitter taste, if masked by strong-tasting food, you would never know it's there." Maggie glanced at her notes, but in the meantime, Betty Payton spoke up again. "There are actually many drugs like this. For example—"

From the bench, the judge spoke up. "Ms. Payton, we don't need to know additional ways to kill someone pharmaceutically. Although we certainly appreciate your knowledge." He looked at Maggie. "Counsel, let's move on."

Maggie nodded. "Ms. Payton, you said that you had never considered Propranolol as a means of death, despite its effectiveness. In your opinion, would an average person know that Propranolol could be effective in that manner?"

"I wouldn't think so, no."

"Who would have the requisite knowledge to understand how Propranolol could be used in this way? Another pharmacist?"

"Yes."

"Or a doctor?" *Like Dr. St. John.*

"Yes."

Maggie paused. She glanced at the jury. "Thank you, Ms. Payton," Maggie said. "Nothing further."

The state didn't take long crossing the witness. They simply used her to bolster the testimony of their own pharmaceutical witness.

Once Ms. Payton had stepped down, the judge looked at us. "Next, counsel."

Maggie looked at her watch. "I apologize, Your Honor.

I took less time with Ms. Payton than envisioned. Our next witness should be here in half an hour."

"Very well, let's take a break."

I turned to Q. "Hang out with Valerie for me? Keep her occupied while I talk to Maggie?"

"You got it, Red."

He walked to Valerie. "Come on, Val. The white girls need to chat."

She actually smiled and followed him toward the front of the courtroom, away from the crowd.

Maggie headed toward the gallery, waving at Bernard.

I grabbed her arm. "Mags, I gotta talk to you. It's about Valerie's daughter, Layla."

"What about her?"

We both looked at the gallery and saw her sitting in the back row. She was dressed in a demure pink dress. She stood and left the courtroom, as many of the spectators were doing.

"I saw her last night," I said.

Bernard came up, leaning over the iron railing that separated the gallery from the courtroom. "You were *so* good," he said to Maggie.

"Really?" She stepped toward him and, on her tiptoes, gave him a quick hug.

"Mags," I said. "I hate to interrupt, but can we chat?"

"Just give me five minutes," she said to me, gazing up at Bernard.

I sighed and looked around. Q was talking, Valerie was nodding, looking interested or at least distracted from her trial. Should I tell her about seeing Layla with Zavy? Maybe it was simple, and it wouldn't even matter to her. Or maybe it would upset her, and push her over the edge emotionally.

Layla, I thought. I would talk to Layla.

I took a step, but there were a number of reporters in the gallery, some staring at me, as if waiting. I turned around and left the courtroom through the back, and peeked my head out into the hallway. Press milled around, lawyers rushed to other courtrooms. No sign of Layla.

I stepped back, trying to think. I knew that Valerie had waited before trial in an empty courtroom downstairs this morning. And my dad had seen Layla go into a courtroom yesterday. Maybe she was there now.

Scooting into the hall and through the stairway door, I descended three flights of steps. I opened the door when I reached the right floor, and sure enough I saw Layla, way down the hallway, walking away from me. There was no mistaking her height, the pink dress or the swing of her hair.

"Layla!" I called.

A clerk stepped out of nearby courtroom and shushed me.

"Sorry," I mumbled, hurrying after Layla. But she was walking fast.

Layla passed the courtroom where Valerie always waited and kept going. She stopped abruptly and opened the door of another room down the hall, disappearing inside.

I hurried after her. When I reached the door she'd opened, I looked in the windows, through the small anteroom, and into the courtroom. I saw a vacant judge's bench, an empty gallery. Court was definitely not in session.

I opened the door and stepped into the anteroom where the walls were plastered with sheets of paper, listing the cases to be called.

Making sure to grab the door with the lock, I began to

pull open the next set of doors to go into the courtroom itself. But I'd only opened it a crack when I saw them.

I froze.

Zavy Miller stood, his back against a wall to the far left. In front of him was Layla. Their arms were around each other. Layla dug her fingers into Zavy's blond hair and grasped the sides of his face. *Were they...?* Yes. Layla Solara was kissing Zavy.

I held my breath and inched the door closed so only a sliver was open. But I could still see them. Oblivious to anything but themselves, they kissed like lovers—lovers who knew each other well, but were still fervent about each other.

I blinked with shock.

Soon, their bodies were pressed together, their mouths open wider in hungry kisses. Zavy grabbed Layla by the upper arms, pushing her against the wall. I leaned forward a little, ready to bolt in the door if there was some kind of assault going on, but Layla only groaned and lifted one of her legs around Zavy's waist, pulling him closer.

# 67

Climbing the stairs, my breath was a little ragged and not just because I hadn't worked out in a week. I kept seeing Zavy and Layla locked together.

I tried to piece together what I knew of Xavier Miller from earlier testimony and other things I'd heard. He was in his mid-forties, an investor. He lived in the Gold Coast. He had two stepdaughters to whom he claimed to be very devoted.

Slipping in the back door of the courtroom, my eyes searched and found my father. I made a beeline for him.

But I was interrupted by reporters, blocking me, calling out questions. "Izzy, how did you think the testimony went today?"

"Tell us why you decided to take this case?"

Another guy stepped up. "Izzy—"

But then my dad was at my side, holding up a hand. He gave the reporters a ferocious look. "You will step back. *All* of you. Now."

I was about to tell him to save his breath. The Chicago media could be intense.

But the reporters responded, moving away.

"Nice," I said. "Thanks."

We huddled up at the side of the courtroom. "How did you know?" I asked.

"Know what?"

"About Zavy and Layla."

"What about them?"

"They're together. Like, as a couple."

My father showed more emotion—surprise—than usual.

"You *didn't* know?" I said. I explained what I saw.

"No. I just knew she had a lot of intense energy coming off of her. I could sense it. Initially I thought that was natural, since her mother is on trial, but then as I watched her, I noticed some kind of sneakiness. She was always looking over her shoulder, always slipping out of the courtroom at odd times and then back in, looking pleased. I just wondered what was happening with the girl. I had no idea it was this." A look of distaste crossed his face, but then it was gone just as fast.

"Did Mayburn ask you to look into Zavy's background? Did he tell you what little information there was on him so far?"

He nodded. "I'm looking into it now."

"How are you looking into it if you're here?"

"I have people. I have ways." He said nothing else.

"Okay, well, could you hurry up those people and those ways? I need to know..." What was it I needed? "I just need to know if there *is* anything to know about Zavy. Please."

He nodded again, then left without pleasantries or any kind of segue.

I glanced at our table and saw Valerie still talking to Q. She briefly looked from him to me. Normally, at a time like this, I would give her a thumbs-up or a reassuring smile. But now all I could do was look at her, wondering.

What was going on here? Should I tell Valerie what I saw? Or did she already know? Was it possible there was some screwed-up mother/daughter plot at work here? Had Zavy turned down Valerie's advances and so she'd planned Amanda's death? And then…what? Trotted out her daughter? But why? Because Zavy had money? It seemed a weak reason to kill a woman who had clearly been Valerie's friend for some time.

I gave Valerie a brief, false smile, then went up to Maggie and Bernard. "Sorry, Bernard, but I need her."

"Sure," he said good-naturedly. He kissed Maggie on the cheek and turned away.

"What's up?" Maggie said, her eyes scanning my face.

"We *have* to talk."

I took a deep breath and launched into the story, whispering fiercely how my father had told me to look at Layla, how I'd seen her last night with Zavy and again today in the empty courtroom.

By the end of my tale, Maggie's mouth was hanging open. She said nothing. Very un-Maggie-esque.

"Oh, holy mother of Elvis," I said, "is this something that you didn't want to know? Like one of those criminal lawyer things I don't get?"

"No, no, no," she said, recovering her voice. "You had to tell me." Her eyes strayed over my shoulder to Valerie.

"Okay. What now?"

"Come with me."

I followed Maggie through the gallery, where the reporters hushed, waiting. We went to where Martin Bristol was standing.

"Marty," Maggie whispered. "We need your help." He opened his mouth, probably to tell us that we were doing fine, that we could handle it, but then Maggie piped up again. "*Big*-time," she said.

We walked with Martin to the side wall as I'd done with my dad, and leaned in to whisper. Once again, I told the story. "So what should we do?" I asked Martin when I was done.

Martin Bristol didn't hesitate. "We should tell Valerie. Immediately. This is possible exculpatory evidence. We must inform her. And we have to consider calling Layla and Zavy to the stand." He turned around, looked at the sheriff, who seemed to be readying himself for the judge to take the bench again. "And we need to continue the break from this trial," Marty said.

"I'm on it," I said. I hurried to the sheriff and spoke to him, explaining we needed a short extension of our break. He clearly thought our witness wasn't there yet, and although I wasn't sure about the location of the witness, I didn't correct him. "And can we use your sheriff's chambers for a quick conference with our client, sir?"

I thought he might like the use of "chambers" and "sir," and I was right. He gave a quick bow and magnanimously drew an arm toward the back, as if to say, *What's mine is yours*.

The chambers were ivory, but the paint was thick, as if it covered hundreds of old layers of paint under it. Like the courthouse itself, the place felt as if it held secrets that would probably never be told.

"Valerie, let me summarize," Martin said. He glanced at me, I nodded and he began to talk in his confident, soothing voice. At first, Valerie's face was skittish, her eyes darting from Martin's to mine to Maggie's, then back again. But when Martin told her about me seeing

Zavy and Layla last night and again today, her face went rigid with obvious anger. The muscles of her neck stuck out like cords. Her jaw tightened, moving back and forth. Her hands clenched and squeezed one another.

Put simply, Valerie Solara very much looked like someone who could kill.

# 68

Valerie Solara said only one word. "No."

Her face was no longer contorted with anger, but it was still set rigidly, with...determination? And with... what?

When no one said anything, she spoke up again. "I will not allow you to call my daughter to the witness stand." She shuddered, as if it were unthinkable. "And not Zavy, either."

Martin began to run down the pros and cons of calling Layla or Zavy to the stand. Meanwhile, I kept thinking, *Why aren't we talking about whether Valerie knew about Layla and Zavy? Why aren't we asking what in the hell was going on here?*

I drew Maggie aside. "Let's ask if she knew about Layla and Zavy. What if this is a part of a plot? What if she *did* do it?"

Maggie's eyes narrowed. "Izzy," she whispered, "that's not our job right now. We were hired to represent her in this murder trial to the best of our ability and to show that the state did not prove guilt beyond a reasonable doubt. There's *nothing* we need to hear right now, except whether we should explore Zavy and Layla's relationship in an open courtroom. This information could help free Valerie.

It would be another piece to show the jury that the cops rushed to judgment, when there was a lot more going on behind the scenes than they knew. But if she won't allow us to do that, that's the end of the discussion."

I felt Valerie's eyes on mine. Her expression asked for help—no, *begged* for it. But how was I supposed to help? I had no idea what was going on or what to do. I'd told Valerie I would be her friend. Had I been her friend by telling her about Layla and Zavy?

Maggie and I moved again to Valerie and Martin. "So, we'll proceed as planned?" Maggie asked.

Martin nodded. "That's right. Get your next witness."

But none of us moved. We all stood and looked at each other.

"You're sure?" I said to Valerie.

She nodded vigorously. "I am. I won't put my daughter at risk. *She* is innocent. She is innocent," she repeated. Then Valerie's mouth set itself in a straight line.

When we stepped into the courtroom, my eyes found Layla in the gallery. She sat, face downcast and placid, as if she hadn't just been making out with Zavy Miller, the husband of the woman her mother was accused of murdering. A man who had once been a father figure to her.

I looked then for Zavy Miller. With his testimony over, he had no longer seemed important to the trial. I found him now in the back, behind a news reporter I recognized from ABC7. Zavy scrolled through his BlackBerry, looking like an average businessman checking in with the world. But *was* he an average businessman? I let my eyes roam the courtroom. I didn't see Mayburn or my father.

I reached in my bag under the table to see if there were any texts or messages from either. Nope.

"For the defense?" the judge said.

I stood. "Thank you, Your Honor. The defense calls Sylvia Zowinski."

A woman in her fifties made her way to the stand. She was heavy, and she walked slowly, as if each step caused pain. When she got to the stand, she glared at the judge, then sat down, glaring some more at me and the other lawyers.

I asked her to state her name and took her through questions about her work experience in the child-care field, ending with her stint as a nanny for the Millers.

"Are you still employed with the Millers?" I said.

Sylvia Zowinski had graying brown hair that hung long, obscuring her face. She shook it away in an awkward kind of gesture. "No. After Amanda died, the kids went to live with her sister, so Mr. Miller could sort everything out."

"Where did you go?"

"To visit some of my relatives."

"And so your job ended at that time?"

"Yes."

"Ms. Zowinski, I apologize for having to ask you this, but it's important to this case. You have a criminal record, don't you?"

She let her hair fall in her face again. "Yes."

I gave Q a nod. He typed a few things on his computer, and Sylvia Zowinski's rap sheet appeared on the screen, blown up to about five feet big.

The jury all stared, reading it.

"Ms. Zowinski," I said, "do you recognize that document?"

"Yeah. It says what crimes I got on my record. They're not even supposed to be there."

"Why is that?"

"They were supposed to be expunged."

Ellie Whelan stood from the state's table. "Your Honor, we object to the display of this document. What probative value does it have here?"

The judge looked at me for my response. I'd already made my point, so I gestured at Q to take it down. "I'll move on."

I looked at my own copy of her rap sheet. "Ma'am, you have been convicted of fraud, is that right?" I nodded at Q, and a copy of the order finding the witness guilty of fraud appeared.

"Yes," she said.

"Twice."

"Yes."

I looked at Q. He removed the first order, then showed another one, finding her guilty of the same thing.

"Ma'am, you've also been convicted of embezzlement, having to do with a job as an office manager, is that right?"

"I pled guilty to that because it was costing me too much money. I didn't have that kind of money to pay you lawyers," she said bitterly.

"But you did plead guilty to embezzlement, correct?"

Q removed the order and put up a guilty plea.

"Yeah," she mumbled, looking at it.

I asked her questions about her convictions, drawing out the details. Then I looked at my notes. The main reason to call Sylvia Zowinski was to show that the cops should have looked at her as a suspect, especially with her background. We would try to do the same thing with Dr. St. John, who we were calling next.

I glanced at the rap sheet again. There were other crimes there, but some were older than ten years—which meant they weren't usually admissible—or they were misdemeanors, which were also generally excluded from evidence.

I looked up. "We have no further questions for this witness, Your Honor."

But we couldn't stop the state from asking her questions.

"Ms. Zowinski, you worked with the Millers for a number of years, correct?" Ellie Whelan asked.

"That's right."

"You got the job because you were recommended by the nanny who'd worked for the Millers before you."

"Right."

"And in the long time you lived with them, did you ever see Mrs. Miller harm herself?" Ellie was trying to discount any suggestion we had elicited earlier in the trial that Amanda might have killed herself.

The witness looked confused. "No."

"And in the time that you worked for the Millers, how was Mrs. Miller's mental status, that you observed?"

"Well, being a mom is hard, but she was always good about it. Never yelled or anything like that."

Striding confidently toward the witness, Ellie buttoned the coat of her black suit, trimmed with red piping. "Ma'am, working as closely as you did with Amanda Miller, did it seem possible to you that she would have committed suicide?"

"Objection," I said, standing. "Ms. Zowinski is not a mental health professional."

"I'll withdraw the question," Ellie said.

"You don't have to do that," Sylvia Zowinski said, "because I can tell you, Amanda would never leave her girls."

Ellie Whelan thanked the witness and sat down.

# 69

Dr. Dominick St. John was still fuming at us. Which was great for two reasons. First, we wanted him mad. Second, we could use his anger to convince the judge he should be an adverse witness, one we could essentially cross-examine if needed, even though he was our witness.

Seeing the doctor again, I could tell now that his hair was definitely a wig, dyed a sort of chestnuty-brown color. His face was almost the same hue. He was either a supertanner or he needed to prescribe himself some blood pressure medication.

Maggie asked about where he lived, whether he knew the Millers, whether he was on the neighborhood association board along with the Millers. Maggie then zoned in on his house, how it was right next door to the Millers', asking a series of questions about that.

He answered each through gritted teeth. He glared at Maggie, and every once in a while turned his eyes to me to do the same.

Maggie kept going. "You and Zavy Miller, the two of you had gotten into disagreements about zoning and whether small businesses should be allowed in the area, is that right?"

"It is." He explained their disagreements, drawing out

details of who said what and at what meeting. "Then I found out that *Xavier*—" he continued, saying the name in a mocking way "—had money in some of the businesses that were attempting to locate to our neighborhood— some bars. *That's* why *Xavier* wanted to get the alderman to have it rezoned."

The courtroom door opened. Mayburn came in and stood near the back, a few rows behind where Layla sat.

"And did you disagree with that course of conduct?" Maggie asked.

"Of *course*. Have you seen where we live? It's historical. It's beautiful. It's elegant. It's the one of the most *pure* neighborhoods in the city."

I glanced at Mayburn, expecting him to roll his eyes or make a face at the pomposity of Dr. St. John, but instead he wore a somber expression. He met my eyes, then raised his eyebrows. *We gotta talk.* My dad soon entered the courtroom, as well, standing near Mayburn, and although he didn't change his expression, I could feel the same message from him.

"Did you let Mr. Miller know that you were unhappy about the rezoning attempt?" Maggie asked.

"Of course." Dr. St. John sat up taller and touched lightly at his hair, as if to make sure it was still there. His face contorted. "It was infuriating, because he wouldn't listen to reason. All the other neighbors said to me, 'We want you to fight this. This is a battle worth going to the mat on.' And so I returned the assault from Mr. Miller." He made it sound like the Battle of Gettysburg.

"How did Mr. Miller respond?"

Dr. St. John's reply sounded like a snarl. "*Xavier* Miller acted completely unprofessionally." He stared at Zavy from the witness stand. "He ignored my letters and my repeated attempts to discuss the matter, and so finally I had to bring in legal counsel."

"What did the attorney do, the one you retained?" Maggie asked.

"We threatened Xavier with legal action. It was the only way to get his attention."

"How long ago was this?"

"A little over a year ago."

"And so you had occasion to see Amanda Miller during the time that you and Mr. Miller were disagreeing on the zoning."

"Yes," he said with obvious distaste. "I've already testified to that."

"Now I'm asking for specifics. Under what circumstances did you see Mrs. Miller?"

He looked Maggie up and down, as if disgusted by what he saw there. "Neighborhood meetings."

"You and Amanda Miller got into some shouting matches, is that correct?"

Dr. St. John took a breath and seemed to calm himself. Now that we were accusing him of shouting, he didn't look like he wanted to do it any longer. "Yes."

"During one shouting match did you ever say, *'I could fucking kill you'*?"

He blinked. "I'm not proud of that language."

"Is that a 'yes'?"

"Yes, but…"

"I just needed a yes or no answer. Thank you, sir."

Maggie moved on like it was no big thing. She strolled back to our table, sifted through some notes to let the statement linger. But it was big.

Ellie Whelan knew it. She stood. "Hearsay, Judge. We'd request that the jury be admonished to ignore the witness's statement."

"Overruled. It's not being used to prove the truth of the matter asserted."

Maggie permitted herself the tiniest smile as she looked at some notes. "Doctor," Maggie said, facing him again. "In addition to the arguments at the neighborhood association meetings, did you ever have an altercation with Mrs. Miller on her lawn?"

Maggie moved away from our table, began to pace in front of him.

The doctor paused. "Yes."

"What were you fighting about?"

"I wouldn't say we were fighting."

Maggie stopped moving. "Were you shouting?"

"Yes."

"About a week before her death?"

"Yes, but only because she came at me, screaming, when I walked my dog by her front lawn. Honestly, I'd never seen her like that." He made a shocked face, as if remembering. "Even at the neighborhood meetings I'd never heard her raise her voice. But she verbally attacked me, and of course I had to defend myself."

I wondered what had been going on with Amanda in the week before she died, when a woman who sounded like a calm, kind person went into a rage on her front lawn.

"Of course," Maggie said, echoing the witness. "No further questions."

Ellie Whelan led Dr. St. John through a series of soft-ball questions meant to show what a perfect citizen he was. Then he was excused.

As he walked by Zavy, he stared, challenging Zavy to stare back, but Zavy dropped his gaze to his lap. The reporters scribbled furiously.

When the doctor was gone, I felt a certain weird sense coming over me, one I recognized as a feeling I often got at the end of a trial. At first, there was relief that it was nearly over. The other sense that always hit then was anxiety, because the whole thing would soon be turned over to the jury or judge, someone other than you. You were nearly done, and yet there was so much that had to happen, so much you couldn't control.

"We'll take a five-minute break before we have our closing arguments," the judge said.

Reporters went in the hallway to call in their latest news. Meanwhile, my dad and Mayburn walked to me.

"We need to talk," Mayburn said.

"What is it?"

"Something on Zavy."

Right then, Martin walked up to us. I quickly introduced them.

"Mr. Bristol," my dad said, "we were just about to update Izzy on some news."

Maggie, Q and Valerie joined us.

"Okay for everyone to hear?" I asked Mayburn.

He hesitated, stared at Valerie for a moment, then nodded.

We all huddled up, and my father spoke.

Zavy Miller was really Xavier Jennings, he said. He had been arrested twice in New Orleans for sex with a minor. Both of the young women were in high school. Fifteen and sixteen years old.

No one said anything for a second.

"Was he convicted?" Martin asked.

My father looked at him. "I'm on that right now. I should know soon, but John here——" my dad gestured at Mayburn "——said you would need to know this as soon as possible."

"Hell, yes," Maggie said. "Zavy being arrested for having sex with minors means little in relation to whether he could've killed his wife, but it just goes to show the lazy police work on this case. We *have* to get an extension and see if we can put in evidence of his prior convictions."

"Absolutely not." Two strong words from Valerie. As if to test them out, she said it again. "Absolutely not."

"Valerie…" Martin said. "Your father was innocent. If you are, too, we have to make sure we show everything that points that way. We may not be able to get Xavier's crimes admitted—there are rules about past crimes coming in during a current trial—but we have to try. It goes to show that the police honed in on you. They didn't look at the doctor, the nanny. They didn't know about Zavy's history."

"If we show his history," Valerie said, "then there is a chance his…relationship…with Layla might come out. Isn't that right?"

*What* was *their relationship?*

"Yes," Martin said. "If the city investigates, there's a chance they could find out about it."

"Then, no," Valerie said. "The answer is no."

Maggie tried to talk her into it, but Valerie was visibly upset. "I am trying to protect my daughter," she whispered fiercely. "Doesn't anyone understand?"

"*I* do." It was my father. He looked at Valerie. "I understand."

No one said anything for a moment, and we felt the weight of the eyes in the gallery.

"I'm not sure if this is anything," my father said, leaning farther in so no one else could hear, "but I've been thinking about something else." He reached in the pocket of his tan suit and pulled out a rolled-up sheet of paper.

He opened it. "This is a blueprint of Amanda and Zavy's house. With all the litigation about the zoning, it was readily available." Without pausing, he told us how we might use it.

I felt like saying, *This is crazy. We don't know the whole story of our client. Or of the victim's husband. We have to know the whole story before we decide anything!*

But then I had a flash of realization. Was this a trait of mine—needing to know everything about a situation before making a decision? It seemed so. And that trait had made me thorough, but it also held me back sometimes. Like when Sam came back to town. I wanted everything neat and tidy before I could say, *Okay, let's do this again. Let's be us again.* Maybe I just needed to jump in sometimes, when I didn't know it all, but I knew it felt right; when I felt I needed to be a lawyer; when there wasn't time for the whole story.

I looked at Valerie as my father explained what he thought. I met her eyes, which asked me, *What should we do?* She trusted me, I could see that. She was looking to me for guidance, and this was my *job*.

"I think you've got something here," I said to my dad. I turned and put my hand on Valerie's wrist. "Let Maggie do this."

"I don't think…" But Valerie's words died away. Still, she looked at me for help, for me to guide her, which is what I'd been hired to do.

"Listen to me," I said. "Maggie can do it. We recall Zavy to the stand. Like my dad said, we won't touch the arrests in Louisiana. We won't go anywhere near his relationship with Layla or even his wife. We'll just use this." I pointed to the blueprint. "That should add to the reasonable doubt. If there is *any* reasonable doubt, the jury will have to acquit you. But it shouldn't be enough to trigger an investigation against Zavy, if that's what's worrying you. You need to get out of this murder charge, but you don't want to shed too much light on Zavy. Because it could shed light on your daughter. Is that right?"

"Yes."

"Maggie has the skill and the finesse. Let her use it."

Valerie hesitated. Then she nodded.

"Mags," I said, "let's do it."

# 70

We convinced the judge that we needed to recall Zavy for very brief testimony. He took the stand and was sworn in once again. The questioning of a victim's family members or that of a plaintiff was ground that we needed to tread lightly. The jury was likely feeling sympathetic toward Zavy Miller. If we verbally beat up on him in an effort to cast doubt on the state's case, the jury might become defensive on his behalf. They might want to cast a guilty verdict just to prove a point.

Maggie adjusted the collar of her teal blouse. She asked a few simple questions of Zavy, clarifying some of his earlier testimony.

After a few more softballs, she turned to the notes she'd taken from a discussion with my father. "Sir, you said that your wife was very weak on the night of her death, correct?"

"Yes."

"You wanted her to go to the hospital, but she wouldn't go, right?"

"Yes."

"And when you found her collapsed, she was in your living room, correct?"

"Yes."

"That's where she was when the ambulance arrived, right?"

"Yes."

I could hear my dad's voice. *If a woman was that dizzy and weak, why would she be in the living room? Why wouldn't she be in bed?* It was a tricky line of questioning, but we had to show, anywhere we could, that the cops and the state hadn't put the whole picture together. They'd jumped to conclusions and then shoved the facts toward their version of the events.

"Sir, you said on direct that you were in the bedroom, but when your wife didn't return, you went looking for her. Is that what you testified to?"

"Yes."

"And did you tell the police this?"

"Yes."

"Why was your wife in the living room?"

He shrugged. "She was going to get something in the kitchen, and—"

"I'm sorry to interrupt you, but let me ask you something. What was she looking to retrieve in the kitchen?"

"I…" He paused, seemed to be thinking. "I don't recall."

"Something to eat?"

"No. Well, I don't think so. We'd eaten that Mexican food."

"Did the police ask you why she was going to the kitchen?"

"No."

"If she was so ill, so weak and dizzy, why didn't *you* retrieve the item from the kitchen that she needed?"

"I don't recall."

"And if she went to retrieve something in the kitchen, why was she found in the living room?"

"Well, if you'd let me finish my answer before, I would have told you."

He was irritated. And he was showing it to the jury. Irritation is one of those emotions that can present themselves differently on various people and more importantly, it can be interpreted in very different ways.

"I'm sorry," Maggie said to Zavy. "I'll let you finish your answer, but let's back up a moment. Just so I'm sure I understand…" She handed him a document. "Sir, do you know what this is?"

He studied it. "It looks like a blueprint of my house."

"Objection," Ellie Whelan said, standing. "We've never seen this exhibit."

The judge looked at Maggie for a response.

"We just obtained the blueprint today. I'll be laying the foundation for it through Mr. Miller's testimony."

"Continue," the judge said.

Ellie sat, looking nervous. She and Tania had no clue where we were going with this testimony.

Maggie looked back at Zavy. "Does this accurately represent the dimensions of your home, and the location of the various rooms of your residence?"

"Yes."

She asked him a few other questions, then handed out the extra copies that the law clerk had made to the judge and state's attorneys. "Mr. Miller, please finish your answer about why Amanda was in the living room."

"It's rather simple. I think she stopped in that room, maybe to turn off the lights or something."

"Was she near a light when you found her?"

"No."

"Did the police ask you why she had gone into the living room?"

A pause. "No."

"Looking at the blueprint, where is the master bedroom?"

He pointed at a large room at the top-right of the blueprint. Maggie asked him to turn it so the jury could see.

From the corner of my eye, I saw Q scowl. It was the kind of exhibit he would have loved to flash on the courtroom wall, but there hadn't been time to scan the blueprint.

"This is the kitchen, correct?" Maggie said, pointing to a room at the bottom left.

"Yes."

"And this is the living room." She drew her finger from the kitchen to the other side of the house, the bottom right.

"Yes."

"Mr. Miller, you testified that your wife was weak and dizzy, correct?"

"Yes."

"Asked and answered," Ellie Whelan said.

"Sustained."

"She was so ill, you wanted her to go to the emergency room," Maggie said.

"Yes."

"Asked and answered," Ellie said, but Maggie just moved on.

"She was so ill that you went to the pharmacy to get her some medicines you hoped could treat her."

"Yes."

"Did the medicines you purchase have any effect?"

"Like I said before, she seemed a little better at first."

"But you said her weakness and dizziness seemed to come and go, correct? So she continued to be ill."

"Objection," Ellie Whelan said. "What is meant here by 'ill'? This isn't a medical witness."

"No, it's not," Maggie said, facing the judge. "There is no medical witness because Amanda Miller was not afforded medical attention that evening, a fact the detectives did not investigate. I'm simply asking Mr. Miller for his layman's impression on his wife's health, since he is the only witness to that."

"Counsel is misstating the evidence," Ellie said.

"Overruled," the judge said. He looked at Maggie "Be careful, counsel. Do not make statements about testimony not in evidence."

"Thank you, Judge." She looked back at Zavy. "Mr. Miller, you told us your wife stumbled that night, right?"

"Yes."

"Was that typical for her?"

"Not at all."

"She was dizzy."

"Yes."

"She was very weak."

"Yes."

"Asked and answered," Ellie said in an irritated voice.

"Move it along, counsel," the judge said.

Maggie didn't blink. "But you left her alone to go to the pharmacy."

He paused, as if realizing maybe that hadn't been the smartest move. "Yes," he said.

"She was still ill when you got home."

"She said the Tylenol helped."

"And yet after that, she still experienced dizziness."

"Yes."

"She still experienced weakness."

"Yes."

"And you don't know why she was in the living room when you found her."

"No."

"Thank you, sir. Nothing further."

# 71

Ellie was passionate and fiery as she started her closing argument. "Who are they kidding?" she said to the jury, her voice rising. She pointed at Valerie. "This woman killed Amanda Miller. Poisoned her. And then her legal team comes in here and insinuates that Amanda might have killed *herself.* Or that her neighbor killed her. Or that the nanny killed her. Or that her husband didn't get her enough medical care. *Who are they kidding?*" Ellie threw up her hands and snorted with a look of disgust.

I had to admit, viewing her purely as one litigator to another, Ellie Whelan was doing a kick-ass job so far.

"Do we really believe that Dr. St. John killed his neighbor over a property feud? That's ridiculous." She shook her head. "And do we really believe that just because someone like the nanny, Ms. Zowinski, has a criminal record that she would kill her boss? That she would murder a woman whom she liked very much, and whom she saw as a devoted mother, and whom she worked with for years?"

I tried to catch Valerie's eye, but she was too focused on Ellie. Meanwhile, my mind started racing away from the argument, thinking about everything we'd learned lately. I tuned back in when Maggie got up to do her closing. She was as passionate as Ellie had been.

"They ask, 'Who are we kidding?' Well, who are *they* kidding? They have not proven their case and they *know* it." She stalked in front of the jury, meeting each of their eyes, pulling them in. "I notice they didn't mention the concept of reasonable doubt. Well, I'd like to talk about it. It's very, very important in this case. In any criminal case.

"What is reasonable doubt? You won't get jury instruction on it. You know why? Because it can't be defined. You know it when you see it. You know it when you *feel* it." She stopped in front of the jury box, right in the middle. "And we all feel it in this case." She paused and took a breath.

"The cops, though?" she said. "They sure didn't feel any doubt. They thought they had their perpetrator. And granted, that is the cops' job. We give them salaries so they will find the bad guys in our society. But that pressure can cause tunnel vision. A nice woman in the Gold Coast was murdered. The public was crying to find out who did it. The cops decided it was Valerie Solara. Then they ignored other suspects that they *knew* about. Tunnel vision is a known phenomenon in criminal justice, and it happened in this case."

She started pacing again. "Let's talk about Valerie Solara. Valerie loved her friend. Very much. Everyone you heard from told you that. Now, did Valerie once, when faced with the grief of losing her husband, make an inappropriate advance toward Mr. Miller, her friend's husband? Yes. Fine. But how in the world do we get from that mistake…" She made a gesture with her forefinger and thumb to show what a small thing it was. "To this?" She waved her arms around the courtroom. "If a small mistake like that can lead you to being tried for murder, then we all better be very, very careful about our mistakes in this life."

Maggie went on, reviewing the testimony and nitpicking every bit of it until it seemed the state had almost no evidence against Valerie Solara. But my focus was fading again, because I kept trying to piece it all together. Was Maggie right that Zavy having been arrested for sex with minors meant little in relation to whether he could've killed his wife? If there was a chance he had, why wouldn't Valerie simply want to say so? Was it really to protect her daughter? Or was she somehow giving consent to Zavy's relationship with Layla?

All the questions swirled in my head. No answers came. And I reminded myself to focus, to be Valerie's attorney.

When the closing arguments were over, the judge read the jury their instructions and then they disappeared into a back room to decide Valerie's fate.

"I want to go home," Valerie said as soon as they were gone and Martin had joined us at the table. Valerie turned to Maggie. "You did a wonderful job up there. I should have said that first. Thank you. But now, I want to go home."

"The jury may have questions," Maggie said.

"You told me the jury could take hours or even days."

"Technically that's true," Martin said. "Juries are completely unpredictable in terms of their timing, but they're usually anxious to get back to their real lives."

Again, Valerie spoke up. "But if they decide I am guilty, I could be taken into custody immediately."

"Yes," Martin said. "Yes, that's right."

"Then I want to go home. Even if it's for an hour."

No one said anything for a second. My mind swirled.

On one hand, I understood completely the desire to be home one last time, just in case. On the other hand, we clearly didn't know everything about Valerie or her life. Or that of her daughter.

"Valerie," I said. "Is there any chance you are planning on leaving town?"

Maggie shot me a look. *We don't ask that question.* I remembered once that Maggie told me she wasn't entirely disappointed if someone she was representing disappeared because she could imagine a better life for them.

But if Valerie Solara was a flight risk, I wanted to know. I had a duty as an officer of the court to ask it.

"No." Her voice was just as firm.

Valerie turned away, and it was clear there would be no further discussion. My heart felt singed with pain for her—for the abject fear she must be suffering from. I wished so desperately I could do something to alleviate it.

"Valerie," I said.

She turned and stopped.

"Do you want me to go with you?"

Her eyes welled up. "Thank you. But no. I want to be by myself."

The ache in my chest surged again. "Okay."

No one else seemed to know what to say. It felt suddenly like the most awkward and sad moment I'd ever witnessed.

As she walked away, I watched her, but when she got to the door, my eye caught on someone else. Someone standing just inside the door, looking around, eyes searching. Someone blond.

"Sam," I said.

# 72

"Do you remember what you were like then?"

I took a deep breath, fought not to feel defensive.

"I knew you couldn't help it," Sam said, still able to read the expression on my face, despite our time apart, despite the fact that he had, apparently, become a different person. A person who would consider taking possession of a multimillion-dollar property that wasn't his.

But we weren't talking about that now, sitting in the back of an empty courtroom. We were talking about the months before our wedding, when I had acted, Sam said, like I didn't like him anymore. Like I didn't want to get married.

My defensiveness died away. "I know I was probably hard to get along with. I was so overwhelmed with work, so overwhelmed with the wedding."

"You never wanted that big wedding."

"But you did. And I loved you."

I think we both noticed the use of the past tense, although neither of us commented on it.

"It didn't feel like you loved me then. All I felt was you pulling away."

"No." Once again, an ache in my chest, this time for the pain that must have caused Sam.

"And then Forester died, and I was in Panama. I have to tell you something, Red Hot. I felt good when I was there. I mean, I was so worried about you, I could barely eat, and I was distraught about Forester, but I felt like I was needed when I was there."

I nodded. I understood.

"When I got the document saying I still owned the place in Punta Patilla, I remembered what it felt like to feel good."

"You don't feel good with Alyssa?"

"Not like it should feel. Not like it did with you."

I shifted on the seat and faced front, staring through an open glass door at the empty judge's bench. "How much did getting that document have to do with you wanting to get back together with me?"

"I don't know. I just know that I remembered what it felt like to be with you, to feel strong and wanted."

"Sounds like you know what would be good for you."

"I do. "

I turned again, looked deep into his green eyes. "Did you think about what's good for me? Did you think about that when you took off for Panama? When you decided to drop a bomb on me and tell me that not only were you engaged, but you would leave that engagement for me? Did you ever really think about what any of that would do to me or how it would affect me?"

Sam's mouth opened, but no sound came out.

"Because isn't that what love is supposed to be?" I asked. "Aren't you supposed to look out for the person you're in love with, just as much as you do for yourself? That's what I thought when we were in love."

"Is that what you were doing when you were pulling away from me? Was that for me?"

"The fact that I hadn't said anything yet was for you, yeah. Hell, yeah. I didn't want to dump something on you that might have to do only with me. I was trying to figure it out."

"How about bringing me into it? Isn't *that* what a relationship is about?"

His voice had gotten a little stronger, and I was about to raise mine, when, from out of nowhere, I started to cry.

Sam looked startled, then he moved to me fast and put his arms around me. "Oh, Iz," he said, pulling me closer.

He hugged me, and I hugged him and pretty soon, I could feel his back moving, his sharp intakes of breath. Sam was crying, too. The air was quiet but for an occasional gulp of breath.

"Hey, what's going on here?" A man's voice.

We raised our faces and saw a pissed-off-looking bailiff.

"I'm sorry," I said. "I'm on trial upstairs and we—"

"I don't care what you're doing. You can't do it here."

Sam followed me into the lobby and outside. Thankfully, the press was all inside or in their trucks. Once in the plaza, I moved to the left, toward the handicapped ramp that scrolled around the side of the plaza, part of it out of view. I stopped when I reached that part and leaned my back against the cement wall.

It was steamy hot outside, a scent of Mexican food and cigarette smoke surrounding us. Sam stood in front of me, eyes worried, pained. Over his shoulder, I saw cars snaking down California Avenue.

"Iz," Sam said, his voice heavy, sad. But he spoke nothing else.

Finally, I did. "I have a question for you. If I said I

needed time, if I said I had to sort out some things in my life and I wanted you to wait for me, what would you do?"

"You'd be with me at the end of that time?"

I paused. "I wouldn't be able to say that."

"Then, I don't know, Iz. I mean, why would I wait?"

I thought of Mayburn, saying he'd wait for Lucy to make up her mind. I thought of how evident it was that he loved her tremendously.

I looked at Sam and wondered if I could say the same thing here. Did he love me like that?

Then a better question appeared. Did I love *him* like that—right now, and not based on our history?

The answer came fast.

# 73

Feeling the heat of the air and liking it, Zavy Miller strolled down Oak Street, a few Barney's shopping bags in hand, his seersucker jacket over one arm. He'd purchased a steel cuff bracelet that he knew Amanda's daughter, Tessa, would love, and a flouncy skirt for Brit that the salesperson swore someone of nine would die for.

He couldn't wait for them to come home from Amanda's sister's place. He would care for them; he would love them. And he truly, truly did love them, even if no one understood. It *was* love to him. Even when his fatherly affection turned into a lover's passion, he would never force that passion on them if they didn't want it. He had never, ever done that, wouldn't.

He moved to the window of the next store, pausing for a moment to study pink pearl earrings Tessa would appreciate. He checked his watch. The closing arguments should be done by now. The case was probably being given to the jury. He hadn't wanted to be there for the closings. He had seen all he needed.

Getting called to the stand again—he hadn't seen that coming. Hadn't imagined the line of questioning about the living room and why Amanda had been there. But they hadn't taken it further than that. He had feared they had other evidence, too. But they hadn't, for example, gotten a surveillance video of the CVS pharmacy, which would have shown he never went there that night. They hadn't asked him anything about the bruises on Amanda's wrists.

It had been terrible to lose Amanda. Because she was a wonderful woman. She was. But life was simpler now, especially as he looked to the future with the girls, as he prepared them, the way he had Layla.

He marveled at how solutions for some of the greatest problems in his life had been found out of nowhere. He had come so close to losing everything. And then? Then the universe swept in and made it right. Now, there was one more step to be made, a decision twelve people would have to make, but he knew they would make the right one.

Zavy moved to the door of the store and pulled it open.

## 74

"So where are we going for cocktails?" Q snapped his briefcase shut when I came back to the courtroom and made my way to the counsel's table. "I'm ready."

When I didn't say anything, he raised an eyebrow and looked closer at me. "Sheesh, looks like you could use a drink. What the hell happened? Is it this case? Is it getting to you?"

"The case is getting to me, but it's not just that." I looked over my shoulder and saw Maggie and Martin sitting near the jury box, deep in conversation. She'd told me Bernard would be at the CSO for the rest of the afternoon, and she looked relieved to have some time alone with her grandfather.

I looked back at Q. It would take too much to tell him the whole story about Sam, and I didn't have the energy to analyze it, as I knew Q would want to.

When I'd answered my own question—did I still love Sam at this moment? Did I want our relationship to grow from there?—the answer was a quick no. And I think Sam felt the same, even if he wouldn't admit it.

Grief washed through me as I thought of that last embrace in the August heat.

"I'll tell you soon," I said to Q. "But will you wait with

me here? Just wait for a while." I simply wanted to stop moving. To sit and let everything settle in.

Q's eyes were filled with concern, but he nodded and put his briefcase on the floor. "Of course."

And so we waited, and we waited. We texted Valerie that there was no news. We called a law clerk from Maggie's office to pick up the audio-visual equipment. We went downstairs to the so-called Gangbanger's Café for bottles of water.

When we returned to the courtroom, the jury still wasn't back. The state's attorneys were gone, probably somewhere else in the building already working on another case. Maggie and her grandfather were still deep in conversation.

"Iz, let's play Would-You-Rather," Q said. We settled into chairs at our now-empty counsel's table and began the game that we often played to pass time—when we were in a car on our way to a deposition or waiting for the verdict, like we were now.

Usually, Q asked me ridiculous questions. *Would you rather pole dance naked around a lamppost in public or pole dance naked in front of the executive committee of the firm? Would you rather have your eye fall out at random times or have uncontrollable, constant drool?* But this time, the questions were different.

"If you had the choice," he said, "would you rather work for Maggie and Martin or go back to Baltimore & Brown?"

I answered quickly. "Maggie and Martin."

"Would you rather work for Maggie and Martin *or* another big firm that was going to pay you the exact amount you made at Baltimore?"

That one I had to think about. I'd made a lot of money at my old firm, more than any other associate, and I was in dire need of cash now. Still, the game acquired absolute honesty. "Maggie and Martin."

Q ran through a whole series of similar questions, asking me if I'd rather work for the Tiffany's store on Michigan Avenue, or for the Chicago Bears, or as a cabaret singer, or as a Vespa salesperson and a million other professions. Or would I rather work for the Bristols?

Every time I answered the same. "Maggie and Martin."

Finally, Q stopped the game and nodded to where Maggie and her grandfather sat, their heads inclined. "Sounds like you need to ask for a job interview," Q said.

"I told them I would help them out whenever they need it."

"Would you rather work for them full-time or part-time?"

"Full-time," I answered without hesitation.

"Well, there ya go."

I thought about the past week, being on trial with Maggie. I thought about how we communicated so easily, the way we divided out tasks as if we'd been doing it forever. I had loved it. And I loved the times when we worked with Martin.

I looked back at Q. "If the firm has room for a trial assistant or a graphics coordinator or whatever, are you in?"

Q looked around the room, as if he were going to mull over the question, but then he looked back at me fast and answered loudly. "Yes."

Forty minutes later, Q and I were still talking to Maggie and Martin, working out the details of our entry into their firm. I was excited in a way I hadn't been for a long time, and not just because I would have a regular paycheck again, starting Monday. The excitement came from the fact that I was getting back into the law, and more than that, I would get to work every day with my best friend, Maggie, and my second best friend, Q.

Martin Bristol seemed thrilled about the new additions to his firm. Since I was coming into their practice, he said, he would slowly begin taking a step back.

"Grandpa," Maggie said, dropping the use of his first name for once. "You're not old enough to retire. Mentally, you're still at the top of your game."

He gave curt nod. "Thank you for saying that. I will need those mental faculties because although I won't be working as much at the firm, I will be working on the matter of Javier Solara."

"What do you mean?" Q said.

Martin filled him in on the case of Valerie's father. "Yesterday afternoon, I contacted the Center of Wrongful Convictions at Northwestern."

"They investigate people in jail who might have been wrongfully convicted," Maggie said.

"That's right. I will be working with them to clear Javier's name. I'll be working very hard, I suspect."

All of us went silent.

"Sir," Q said, moving forward in his chair a little bit. "I think you're a very honorable person, and I'm honored to be working for you."

I looked at Maggie and saw that she had tears in her eyes as she studied her grandfather. She vaulted out of her sitting position and hugged him tight around the neck. He smiled and returned his granddaughter's embrace.

Mayburn came in the courtroom then and walked up to us. "Anything new on Zavy?" I asked him.

"Not yet, but I'm supposed to meet your dad here." He

pointed at the other side of the gallery. "You want me to sit over there and wait for him?"

"Certainly not," Martin said. "Izzy and Q will be working with our firm now, and it's my hope that you will do more of that, too."

Mayburn smiled, one of the first smiles I'd seen in weeks. He nodded, took a seat.

Just then, the door opened and we all turned. There was Lucy DeSanto, standing in the door surrounded by what seemed like a ring of sunshine. She wore a navy blue dress and white espadrilles. She looked very pretty and very adult, not at all the way she looked last night with Theo and C.R.

She walked to us. "Hi, all," she said. "Izzy told me you would probably get a verdict today, so I came to support you, to see if anything has happened yet." She looked around the courtroom, taking it all in the way people do when they haven't spent much time in a courtroom.

"That's so sweet," I said, standing to hug her. "The jury is still out. Wait with us."

"Okay," she said. She looked at Mayburn and took a few steps toward him. "Can I sit here?" She pointed to the spot on the bench next to him.

Mayburn couldn't hide the longing on his face whenever he was in Lucy's presence and it was palpable now. "Of course." He stood.

But before she stepped into the bench, she looked at him. "I came to support you, too."

Mayburn seemed not to know how to respond. "Thanks. That's…that's nice."

Maggie, Martin and Q began to talk again, sensing the need for Mayburn and Lucy to speak by themselves. Yet I couldn't help but listen.

"John," Lucy said, her voice low, "I have to tell you that I don't want to get back together. Not right now."

A pause of disappointment. "That's okay," he said finally.

"But I would love for you to have breakfast on Saturday. Just a casual thing."

No pause this time. "Yeah," he said. "Yeah, definitely."

I felt elation for them, which was quickly followed by sorrow. Sam and I wouldn't be doing that, wouldn't be spending a little time together to see how it went. We were out of time.

The sheriff entered the room.

"All rise!" he boomed, although there was no one but our little group in shouting distance.

The judge came into the room and to the bench. "We've called the state's attorneys." He looked at our small knot of people. "And I need you to get your client back here, please. We have a verdict."

# 75

Valerie was hunched over, her fingers folded, her face resting forward on them as if she were praying.

"Ladies and gentlemen of the jury..." the judge said, his words slow, weighted. "Have you reached a verdict?"

The foreman stood, an older man with keen eyes. "Yes, we have, Your Honor."

"Please hand me the verdict."

The foreman passed the verdict to the person on the left, who passed it on down the row of jurors. Most of them looked tired, a few looked disgruntled. No one looked at Valerie.

Finally, the verdict forms were handed to the sheriff. Chest puffed up, the sheriff took slow, deliberate steps toward the bench, almost as if he were performing some kind of military march.

I scooted close to Valerie, put a hand on her back. She was slumped forward, but there was an incredible amount of energy coming from her body, which was hot.

The sheriff handed the verdict papers to the judge, who read them, then cleared his throat.

"In the matter of the *State of Illinois v. Valerie Solara,*" the judge read, "the people find Valerie Solara..."

Valerie sat up. She stared at the judge, as if she'd already heard bad news.

"Not guilty of first-degree murder."

A loud cry from Valerie, as if the sound had shot from her throat. Scuffles and murmurs from the press in the gallery, many of who scampered out to report the news.

Valerie fell forward again, crying hard. And Maggie and I moved to our client and wrapped our arms around her.

We sat in Valerie's apartment, Maggie and I on the couch, Valerie in a chair across from us. The chair had a wood back and its cushions were covered in a textured, red fabric. It looked like an expensive piece of furniture, one made for some home other than this.

After the verdict was read, Maggie and I had walked over to Ellie and Tania to shake their hands. None of us said anything, just gave each other nods.

When they'd left, we suggested a big dinner out, but Valerie, wiping her eyes, said she wanted to go to her apartment, and she wanted Maggie and me to go with her.

"I'm so glad," Valerie said now. "I'm so relieved at this verdict, but…it's…well…" She looked from Maggie to me and back again. She sat up straight, breathing in, seeming to breathe in strength. "This is not over."

"Valerie," I said, "you were found not guilty. *Not guilty.*"

She nodded. "Yes." The movement of her head stopped. "But…" She fell silent.

Maggie and I glanced at each other. *What's going on here?* I asked her with my eyes.

*No idea.*

I looked back at Valerie. "Where is Layla?"

Valerie hadn't allowed Layla to be in the courtroom for the reading of the verdict, in case it went the other way. *I don't want her to hear the word* guilty *about her parent,* Valerie had said. *I know what that's like. It stains you.*

"She wasn't here when I got home," Valerie answered. "She sent me a text that she went to get me my favorite meal from Salpicon, a Mexican restaurant on Wells. They make a *sopa de tortilla* like my father did."

"So she knows about the verdict."

"No."

Maggie and I exchanged another glance.

"Call her," Maggie said. "Tell her it's over."

"It is not over." Valerie shook her head, looking despondent. She looked at me in a beseeching way.

"Valerie," I said, "is there anything you want to tell us?"

Maggie sent me a warning look.

"Mags," I said, "isn't it true if she wants to talk to us now, she can speak about anything she wants?"

Maggie looked at Valerie. "I suppose."

"Well, I don't think Valerie is going to tell us something that would require us to go to the judge," I said. "Something like...well, that you killed Amanda Miller?" It was out of my mouth. I couldn't hold it back.

"I didn't," Valerie said fast, fierce.

Maggie gave a one-shouldered shrug. "Even if you did kill her, that wouldn't cause us to go to the judge. Telling us of a crime in the past is still covered by attorney-client privilege."

Valerie stared at Maggie, seemed to be digesting her words. Then she blurted, "I didn't intend to."

Silence in the room.

"Not her," Valerie said. "I didn't mean to kill her."

And then some of the pieces fit together. Then others clicked, locked in.

"You meant to kill Zavy," I said.

She nodded. "We both did."

"You and Amanda."

"Yes."

"Because of his relationship with Layla?"

"More than that. There's more."

"Is this about his arrests in New Orleans?"

She shook her head. "We didn't know about that." A pause, as if she were making a large decision. Finally, she looked at me and spoke. "Remember when I told you about that Tuesday night, when I went to talk to Bridget and Amanda?"

I nodded. "You had something to tell them."

"That's right." She took a breath. "Can I talk about this now?"

"Yes," Maggie and I said at the very same time.

# 76

That Tuesday night, about a year and a half ago, Valerie said, she had decided she couldn't keep quiet anymore.

All that week, she had been going over and over the events in her head, thinking of what she'd seen. Or what she thought she'd seen.

She'd had a spring barbecue party earlier that week, inviting Amanda, Zavy and their kids, as well Bridget and her boyfriend at the time and another family Layla knew from school. Valerie said she was a nervous hostess, always cooking up a storm but relying on her friends to keep the conversation flowing and the other guests satisfied. Yet it had been a lovely time. Valerie had even begun to relax, to stop worrying that people would think about the wonderful house she used to share with Brian and compare it unfavorably to the apartment they were in now. But no one seemed to notice.

By the time things started to wind down, Valerie was happy. She'd gone upstairs to find Layla before everyone left. The party was meant to be a support for Layla, a way to be around other families, instead of just the two of them, as it had been since Brian's death. But sometimes her daughter's grief of losing her father sprang up during such times. Layla had told Valerie that sometimes it hurt her to see families who were still whole. Valerie understood and respected Layla's emotions. She would give her time when she saw Layla disappear, as she had that night. Then she would go upstairs and often find her sitting on her bed, sometimes just staring at the floor or zoned out in front of her computer. But always she required her to come downstairs when the party was over, insisting that Layla say goodbye to their guests, as Valerie's mother had taught her.

When she'd gotten to the top of the stairs that night, she'd seen Zavy. The stairs were carpeted, and apparently he hadn't heard her because he didn't turn. Valerie opened her mouth about to say something, but a movement caught her eye. It was Zavy's elbow jutting back and forth.

*What is he…?* Valerie started to think, but then the movement made his body turn just a little, and she could see. He was touching himself. Rubbing himself on the outside of his pants. *He's masturbating.*

She thought to turn around, to leave the embarrassing situation alone, but then she saw that his attention was focused on Layla's barely open door. Looking past him through that crack, she could see Layla sleeping on her bed, lights on. Layla's head was to the side, pillowed on a sheet of her long hair, and her legs were splayed out, the way they were so often when she slept. She was wearing a dress, and that dress had slid up her legs, revealing a slice of white panty.

Valerie must have made some kind of sound, because Zavy turned, his hand dropping to his side. He looked startled for a moment, then his face slid into an oddly casual expression.

"Hey," he said. And then he slipped into the bathroom.

Valerie stood frozen, listening to the sounds of silence

in the bathroom, then running water. She wanted to pound on the door and then pound on Zavy's face, but the whole thing had happened so quickly.

Confused, frightened, angry, she woke Layla, brought her downstairs and within minutes the party had entirely broken up. Valerie was terse with her guests, and soon everyone was gone, Zavy leaving with a jovial, "Great to see you guys!" that belied anything amiss.

The next Tuesday night with Amanda and Bridget, once they'd finally gone into Bridget's blue living room, Valerie had looked at them. "I'm just going to say it," she said.

They nodded. That was how they had always worked—*just say it.*

When she paused again, her friends looked a little confused, waiting for her to divulge whatever it was.

Finally, she said, "At the party on Saturday night…"

More nods.

She told them that she'd found Zavy watching Layla sleep.

"Sure," Amanda said. "He loves Layla like he loves his own kids. He was probably checking on her."

"That's kind of what I thought. At first. But he hadn't heard me come up the stairs. He didn't know I was there. And he was…" Her voice died away.

"He was what?" Amanda said, a puzzled expression on her small face. She brushed away her hair that flipped up at the ends, and peered at Valerie.

Valerie closed her eyes in order to speak the words aloud. She told them what she'd seen.

"That's crazy!" Amanda said.

Valerie eyes darted to Bridget's. She shook her head, too, as if in utter disagreement.

"I know what I saw!" Valerie said.

Amanda put her drink on the coffee table with a hard plunk. Wine sloshed over the sides, but no one moved to mop it up. Amanda leaned forward so that her thin body strained toward Valerie's, her eyes alive with anger. "Zavy *adores* Layla! But only as a daughter."

Valerie shook her head. "I didn't want to believe it. I didn't want it to be true but—"

"Does this have to do with the time you hit on him? Do you resent Zavy?"

"No!"

"Then you're being ridiculous! You yourself said, you only saw him from behind."

"I'm…" Valerie thought back to that night. "I'm pretty sure," she said, but her voice was now nearly a mumble.

Amanda's face softened a bit. If Valerie read her right, which she usually did, it was an expression of sympathy.

Bridget spoke up for the first time. "Honey, you've been through a hell of a lot since Brian died. You don't get over those things quickly. It's natural you're going to be overprotective of Layla. She's what you have left of your family."

Valerie blinked fast, an attempt to clear the pain from her mind. As always, the reminders of her losses made her wince.

When she opened her eyes fully again, Amanda spoke. "Look, Bridget is right. And trust me, if Zavy did that, I would kill him myself. But he is not that kind of a guy."

"I didn't think so, either," Valerie said, "but—"

Bridget held up a hand. "Zavy is a great man, Valerie. We've always said that. All of us."

Valerie shook her head, small at first, then she felt herself shaking her head in bigger arcs. She hadn't thought the hard part was going to be convincing her friends to believe her. The hard part, she had thought, would be simply telling them.

Amanda soon excused herself with a lame excuse about the charity ball she had coming up that weekend. When Bridget and Valerie were alone, they went over it again and again. Bridget was sure there had to be an explanation. But without Amanda's anger, Valerie grew more and more positive about what she had seen. There was no doubt. Then she was swamped with an overwhelming sense of dread because she knew she would never again let Layla be around Zavy, and she knew that would mean the slow death of her relationship with Amanda. And, because the three girlfriends had been a package deal from the start, things with Bridget would slide, too. That very thought then filled her with grief, as if her friendships with them had been the cork in the bottle that kept her from being overwhelmed—kept her open to the future. Without them, the grief she always held at bay would envelope her.

But Layla was her number one priority. Always had been, always would be.

## 77

Zavy Miller unpacked the presents he'd bought for Tessa and Brit on Oak Street. He considered wrapping them, but he thought it more elegant to simply tie a pink bow around each. He put two on Tessa's bed, the other on Brit's. Then he walked toward the kitchen, thinking that everything would now be returning to normal, or at least the normal that he had dreamed of for so very, very long.

His reverie was interrupted by the ring of his cell phone. He lifted it from his pocket. It was Ellie Whelan, the district attorney. He smiled as he answered it.

Sounding clipped and bitter, she said, "Mr. Miller, I have some bad news."

Zavy had reached the kitchen by that time, the space he and Amanda had designed together. They had been so happy once. They had been happy up until the end. He amended that a little. Something had happened to Amanda before she died. It started maybe seven months before she died. A fight with Valerie, Amanda had told him. Whatever the fight was about—she wouldn't say—it seemed to cause her angst. She started seeing a therapist to talk about it, said she didn't want to speak about it with anyone else, didn't want anyone to think poorly of Valerie. Soon, she was on antidepressants. They seemed to help somewhat. But then that week before she died—the fits of weeping, the slamming of doors. He had chalked it up to oncoming menopause.

Until he had come home that afternoon and discovered Valerie in his kitchen, the guilty look on her face as she scooped the blue powder into the dish.

He shook his head and dispersed those thoughts. He cleared his throat to let Ellie know he was listening. "I'm sorry," she said. "The jury delivered a verdict of not guilty."

He sat at the kitchen table, staring around at the space that he thought would be full of laughter and love after the trial. What would happen to all of them now?

"I'm sorry, Mr. Miller," Ellie said again. Then silence.

"Yes." He waited. *Not guilty,* she'd said. He felt the disappointment pool around him.

Ellie spoke up. "I don't lose a case very often. And I don't like it." Her voice was bristling. "Frankly, I think the jury made a mistake, but my boss doesn't want to do any posttrials on this. This is the end." Still he said nothing and after a pause, she said, "Again, I'm sorry."

# 78

I watched as Valerie tucked her feet under her now, still in the red chair, her posture defeated despite the victory in court. She seemed to grow weaker as she told Maggie and me the story.

The night she spoke to Amanda and Bridget, Valerie didn't sleep. In her mind, her greatest fears had been realized. She knew what she had seen, but her friends didn't believe her. She was back in a place she knew so well—damaged and fearful because of a man. Helpless.

"I had stopped trusting men a long time ago," she said. "I knew that they had the capacity to harm. I never got over my father's guilty verdict and execution. I didn't believe it of him, but I knew I was probably wrong." She laughed a little and looked at Maggie. "I guess I was right to believe in him, though."

"You were," Maggie said. "And Martin wants to spend the rest of his career exonerating your dad's name."

Valerie nodded in a slow, sad way. "I got pregnant with Layla on purpose after my dad died. I think I was trying to create someone I could trust. I knew I wasn't in love with Layla's father—I wouldn't let myself fall in love with any man. I picked him because he was good-looking. I knew he had good genes. And I knew that he wouldn't have any interest in raising Layla. I know that's cruel—to bring a child into this world whose father won't want to be involved. But I also knew I would be a good parent. I wanted to raise her by myself. I couldn't trust anyone, especially not any man."

"But you later married Brian," I said.

Valerie permitted herself a smile. "Brian. It was so surprising. I never thought it could happen. But I loved him. He was a great father to Layla. And then he died." Something ravaged her face, as if she'd seen something horrible. "And then Zavy. It's my fault. It's my fault."

"But how?"

"I trusted him. Brian restored my faith in men, and I let my guard down." She blinked. "Maybe Brian wasn't even the good guy I thought he was, maybe…" Her voice had gotten louder, taken on a quality of a cart heading downhill, with only a second to stop it until it careened out of control.

"Valerie." I leaned forward across the coffee table and put a hand on her wrist. Her skin was soft but cool, almost as light as air, as if it might disappear like froth. "Brian was one thing. Zavy is another."

She looked at me with such sad eyes. Eyes that said, *God, I envy you for that innocence. God, I would give anything to believe you.*

Valerie kept talking. She told us that after that night in the blue room, she didn't see Amanda often and when she did, it was strained. But six or seven months later, after Layla had gone off to college, Amanda knocked on Valerie's door one December day. It was eleven in the morning. She hadn't called before she arrived, and Valerie was surprised to see her.

Amanda stood on Valerie's front porch, shaking a little,

although the December day was unseasonably warm. "You were right."

Valerie looked down at Amanda's hands and saw she was holding a small video camera. She raised her eyes again and met those of her friend. What she saw in Amanda's expression was a volatile jumble of despondency, rage, shock, fear.

"Come in," Valerie said.

As soon as they were in her small living room, Amanda collapsed onto her red chair. She began to sob uncontrollably, her body heaving, her voice like a dog barking. There was so much pain in those cries that Valerie was struck, physically, by the force of them. She didn't know what to do. Any other time she had seen her friend crying, she always knew instinctively to move to her side. But now, she could only watch in horror as Amanda cried with an intensity Valerie had never witnessed, not in anyone. Valerie's fear grew and grew. She didn't want to ask what was making Amanda cry so hard. Instead, she wanted to pull Amanda from the chair and shove her out of the house. She wanted to rewind thirteen years and never meet Amanda.

Instead, she marshaled her strength. "Tell me," she said.

But Amanda couldn't speak right away. It took a full five minutes for her to control her sobs. She tried to speak a few times through her tears, but she would almost choke on them.

Finally, Amanda stood and moved closer to the couch where Valerie sat. In an awkward attempt at sympathy, Valerie stroked Amanda's hair.

Amanda's sobs shuddered to a stop. She lifted the camera and turned it on. It had a small screen on the back about the size of a fist.

There, flickering on the screen was her baby. Layla. Valerie gasped.

Layla was topless, her full breasts proudly bared to the camera. She wore panties Valerie had never seen. Unlike most of Layla's clothes, she hadn't bought them, had never washed them. They were silk. Pink. Hot pink.

Layla was looking into the camera. She giggled. She crooked her finger at the person behind it.

"Come here," she said, laughing some more, a deep, low sexy laugh. An adult laugh.

The camera shook back and forth as if the person behind it were shaking their head.

Layla threw her head back, still laughing. She lay back on the bed—it had a black leather headboard. The room looked like a hotel room. And then she began to stroke herself between the legs over the pink underwear. The panties had only thin strings at the side and a tiny triangle to cover her pubic hair. Layla moaned as she made this action.

Valerie's hands flew to her face, horrified. "Turn that off!"

She heard Amanda clicking a button on the camera. The sound died away. She pulled her hands back and saw the screen was black. "Where did you get that?" she demanded.

Amanda just stared at her.

"Where did you get that?"

"It's Zavy's."

Valerie felt her forehead crinkling with confusion. "What do you mean?"

"I went to his office. I wanted to just drop in and see what he did in there. I almost never go there, but since you told me...you know..."

Valerie nodded.

"Since you told me about that night at the party, it's been on my mind. And I guess I was suspicious. Was he really at the office when he said he was?" Amanda coughed up some tears, a strangled sound coming from her mouth. "Well, he was there," she said bitterly. "I found him masturbating to this video. I left before he knew I was there, then I snuck back into his office when he went to the gym and took the camera."

Valerie leaped from the couch, her arm pointing to Amanda. "Didn't I tell you?" She shook her finger at Amanda's face. "Didn't I tell you? Zavy's sick. Where did he even get this tape of her? He stole it. That's clear." Without a reply, Amanda pushed the Play button on the video camera. There was Layla, still lying back, stoking herself.

"C'mere," Layla said to the camera.

The camera shook back and forth again.

Layla lifted her head up and looked at the camera with a sultry gaze. "If you don't come here, I'll stop." Pointedly, she took the hand that had been touching herself and ran her fingers through her hair—long and tousled and gorgeous. She made a show then of putting that hand down on the bed. One side of her mouth lifted in a suggestive smirk, and she shrugged.

The sound of a man's groan could be heard. The camera was placed on something stationary and then a man entered the camera shot. Zavy.

Valerie gasped and her hands flew to cover her mouth. She wanted to cover her eyes, but she couldn't look away.

Zavy was dressed in jeans and a pastel polo shirt. He nudged Layla with his knee in a familiar way, and she scooted toward the middle of the bed. He sank onto it with her. He stroked her hair, then her jawline. He drew a finger along her bottom lip. She opened her lips farther, then closed them over his finger, sucking on it, looking into his eyes.

He took his finger from her mouth and ran it over one of her nipples. It was Layla who groaned then. He touched the other nipple, then drew a line down her taut stomach muscles.

When his hand reached her pelvis, he stopped, then drew a finger back and forth at the top of her panties. He stopped again. She groaned. Finally, he began to stroke Layla between her legs.

"Do you want me to do it to you?" he said, his voice low and grumbling.

"God, yes," Layla said.

Amanda paused the camera.

"Do they have sex?" Valerie whispered.

Amanda nodded, her jaw working back and forth as if she was grinding her teeth down to mere sand.

"He drugged her," Valerie said.

Amanda shook her head, the muscles of her neck stiff cords. "You saw her. She wasn't high. It was consensual. They both wanted it."

"That's impossible."

Amanda shot her a dismissive look. "I've watched the whole thing, Valerie. They're both very sober, and very into each other. He cheated on me. He *cheated* on me. With Layla!" In silence, Valerie stared at her friend, horrified.

Amanda began to cry once more. They were angry tears, her face flushing red. "I can't fucking believe that he did this."

"He took advantage of her. She's just a young girl."

Amanda's eyes flashed at her. "She's eighteen, Valerie. She's an adult, whether you like it or not. And she knows what she's doing. If you want to see just how much she knows what she's doing, let's look at the rest of this tape."

She made a movement toward the On button again, but Valerie stopped her with a harsh, "No!"

More silence, then Amanda spoke in a flat voice. "He's been grooming Tessa."

"What do you mean?"

"When we met, I fell in love with him because he was so passionate about my children. And now I see, that was exactly what he was passionate about. Not me, not me at all."

Valerie recoiled. "Do you think he did something to Layla when she was younger?"

"No." Amanda gave a harsh laugh. "I think he likes them older than that. He's always talked about how it's so beautiful when girls start to become women. He said he loved teenagers. He 'got them,' that's what he said. And I knew what he meant. Kids that age *always* responded to him. And the girls always flirted with him, and it seemed innocent. But he's always buying Tessa and Brit so many gifts. So many. Like he's wooing them. And he talks to them all the time about how they'll soon have to be adults and learn how to make their own decisions...." A flailing expression took over her eyes. "I don't know how to explain it, but it's like...it's like he's with me because of them. It's like he's been waiting."

"Oh, God," Valerie said.

"I keep thinking of all these other things now—he's been talking about colleges for Tessa, and the schools are always far away from Chicago. He talks about how she should get an apartment rather than live in a dorm. He says he'll visit her often because he has to travel to these places for business. So she wouldn't be lonely. That's what he told her. I thought it was so sweet that he was reassuring her, but now I see what he was doing."

Valerie thought of something. "Remember how he was with Layla in high school? All those gifts he bought her?"

Amanda gave a single nod in grim recognition.

Zavy had bought Layla so many things—an Xbox, a $500 crocodile purse she wanted, pink broadcast-quality headphones. It made Valerie uncomfortable, but only because she couldn't buy such things on her own, and so she let him keep doing it.

"And when Layla went to college, she changed," Valerie said. "I could tell she was in love. She said she had a boyfriend who was older. I thought she meant a junior or something! But that must be when she and Zavy started. She's been so happy." She shuddered with disgust. "She wouldn't let me meet him. It turns out I've known him the whole time."

"Jesus!" Amanda said. "He was waiting for her. Just like he's waiting for Tessa and Brit."

"Are you sure he hasn't...done anything to them yet?"

"I've asked them in oblique ways, and they said no. And my girls don't know how to lie to me. I know every little fib they tell, and they're not lying now."

Valerie felt some relief at that, but it couldn't cool the heat in her stomach, as if her insides were tinged with acid, curling and churning. She put her head in her hands. She felt as if she had lost Layla, as if her little girl was gone forever. She hadn't even experienced that feeling when she'd taken Layla to college that fall. She'd known Layla wasn't a child anymore, but she always felt there was some sweetness to her, some innocence. And now it appeared that innocence was gone. Taken by Zavy.

## 79

"So you decided to kill him," I said.

Valerie looked at me. "Do you understand why? It felt like there was no other option. Layla was of age. Even the earliest we could tell that he'd been with her, when she was first at college, she was eighteen."

"Age of consent in Illinois is seventeen," Maggie said.

"Exactly, so we couldn't press charges. And I didn't want *anyone* to know about them. It would have ruined Layla if it became public knowledge. That stuff stays with you forever and taints you, and it taints how people look at you. I know because of what I went through with my father being arrested."

"But this is different," I said. "No one would have been arrested."

"But if people found out, it would be scandalous. More importantly, if Amanda tried to get a divorce, she knew he would fight her. So she would have to tell the court her beliefs about him grooming the girls, but how could she prove it? She checked with her kids, got them to see a psychiatrist and she was right—nothing had been done to them yet, so there would be no evidence at all to show the court. He really hadn't done anything to them but treat them well. He was waiting for them to turn of age, just like he did with Layla. Amanda didn't want to hide, to pick up and move and run from him."

"A hell of a situation. So how did you decide to use Propranolol?"

"Amanda read about a doctor who had committed suicide with a massive dose of Propranolol."

"And she already had a prescription."

Valerie nodded. "She didn't take it that often, so she had quite a lot."

"So you mixed two different batches of Mexican food? Just like they said at trial? One had the Propranolol in it and the other didn't?"

Valerie nodded.

"Zavy was supposed to eat the one without spice." Valerie nodded. "The one with the Propranolol. Zavy didn't like spicy food. Amanda was always making two batches of everything and she would mark the spicy one with a garnish. When we cooked the *mole,* we marked the spicy with sliced onion on top."

"So Amanda would know to eat that."

"And Zavy would eat the one that was laced," Maggie said.

Valerie nodded. "He never, ever tried the spicy food she made. We thought it would work perfectly." Tears streaked down her cheek.

"And Zavy figured it out?"

Valerie's mouth set itself in an angry straight line, although the tears made crystalline tracks from her eyes. "Yes. I've played it back over and over. I remember when he came in, and he saw me with the Propranolol. We'd just crushed it. Amanda said she was feeling guilty, starting to change her mind, so I told her to leave. I would put the drug in the food."

"But he saw you?" I asked.

"Yes. He came in when I was putting the last of it into the dish. I can remember it perfectly. When he walked in, *I* was feeling guilty then. He was standing right there. And I was about to kill him. I wondered if that was how my father felt before he killed Marilee."

"What did Zavy do?"

"He saw my emotion. I could tell. He sat down. He never did that when we were cooking before. Said he wanted to watch us, to learn. He asked me about what the blue powder was that I'd just put into the one dish. He pointed at it."

"You lied and said it was blue cornmeal."

She nodded. "Amanda nearly freaked out when she came back to the kitchen and saw him. He watched us for a while, talked to us. He asked us how we spiced up Amanda's dish, said maybe he would start trying spicy food someday. We all laughed at that. We were so incredibly nervous. But then everything seemed okay. We talked about other things, we kept cooking and he left. By then we thought it had been *us* who were being suspicious, being strange. We were relieved we were getting away with it."

"So when did he switch the dishes?"

"When he came home later, that's what I figure. He moved the onions on the one that was clean and added the spice, just like we had told him." She laughed bitterly. "So stupid. We underestimated him." She made a choking sound now, as if fighting a sob. "Amanda ate the contaminated one."

Maggie and I looked at each other. Maggie took a deep breath. "Valerie, I hate to say this, but there are two other possibilities. The first is that *you* incorrectly laced the wrong dish."

"No, I wish. I wish it had been a mistake. Right after Amanda died, I thought maybe I had screwed it up, put the drug in the wrong dish, but I know I didn't. We were very, very strict about it when we cooked that day. We'd been over it a million times. We kept the batches away from each other the whole time. And when Zavy left, we finished cooking in exactly the strict way we'd designed, keeping the two separated."

Maggie said nothing, inhaled visibly. "Well, then let's talk about the other possibility."

Valerie was silent. I was, too. The air seemed to pulse with intensity, suddenly, as if there was resistance in the air to whatever Maggie was about to say.

"You have to be aware, Valerie, that…" Maggie took another breath. "That your daughter may have killed Amanda."

## 80

"Shut up!" Valerie barked, two sharp, succinct, loud syllables.

The intensity in the air had increased. I looked from Maggie to Valerie and back again.

"The motivation is there," Maggie said softly, as if to contrast her tone from Valerie's. "Layla and Zavy have been having a relationship, probably her first true adult relationship. Does she love him?"

"Yes," Valerie said through tight lips. "Very much."

"Well, then I think this is a possibility we need to consider."

Valerie sank into her chair. "I'm sorry for yelling. The truth is I considered it myself." She choked on tears, then seemed to will them away. "I can't believe I suspected my daughter, but I did."

"And?" Maggie asked.

"She was at school that afternoon. And after school she was in a music lesson. I've confirmed that she was at both. She has, as you would say, a tight alibi."

"You're sure."

"I'm sure."

Maggie and I said nothing. Finally, I spoke up. "Valerie, you're telling us the truth, right?" She glared at me, but before she could lash out, I talked fast. "You can't blame me for asking. You put yourself through a whole murder trial so that no one would know you and Amanda planned Zavy's death. I know you didn't want to admit to attempted murder on Zavy, but it seems like more than that, you didn't want anyone to know about Zavy and Layla."

"That right."

"So you went through it and refused to allow us to call Zavy or her, in order to protect your daughter, so no one would know about her relationship."

"Yes."

"But maybe you're protecting something greater than her reputation."

Tears streaked down Valerie's cheeks. Quiet reigned again.

Then Valerie Solara stood and walked from the room.

Minutes went by. Maggie and I stared at each other. *What's going on here?* I asked Mags with my eyes. *No frickin' clue,* came the reply from her own.

At last, Valerie walked back in the room carrying sheets of paper. "Here." She handed them to Maggie. "I not only spoke to her teachers and music instructor, I got it in writing from them that she was with them, just in case the state did find out and tried to bring Layla into the case."

Maggie took her time reading the documents. Slowly, she nodded. "These would prove conclusively that Layla was nowhere near the Miller house during that afternoon or early evening." She looked at Valerie. "I'm sorry. I had to ask."

"I understand. As I said, I wondered, too." Maggie handed the documents back to her and she sat.

"Okay," Maggie said. "Let's get back to what really happened that afternoon. If Amanda ate the wrong dish, the one that Zavy switched, she would have known it when she started feeling ill," Maggie said.

"I know." Another wail. "He must have stopped her from getting help. That's why she had the bruises on her wrists. He was holding her down, stopping her from leaving until she died."

"Why don't we turn him in?" I asked.

Maggie spoke up. "Because then Valerie would have to confess to attempted murder."

Valerie nodded. "I can't do that. I can't leave Layla without either parent."

"You ran the risk of leaving her by going to trial on the murder charge," I said.

"Yes, but I couldn't let Layla's relationship with Zavy get out. It would have destroyed her reputation. The media would have been all over the story of two women killing a husband who was sleeping with one of their daughters. She would never be able to outrun the stories."

We all paused a moment, letting all the information sink in.

"What does Layla think happened with Amanda?" I asked.

"She thinks it was an accident. A real accident where no one was trying to kill anyone. She won't believe anything bad about Zavy and she won't believe anything bad about me."

"Did you know she continued to see him? After Amanda's death?"

"I suspected. And then I realized during the trial that they definitely were still together. I just wanted the trial to be finished so I could deal with her and this...*relationship*," she said with disgust.

She covered her eyes with her hand, and we sat in quiet.

My cell phone buzzed, telling me I had a text. "It's my dad."

Outside Valerie's house, the message said. Need to talk about case.

I read it out loud to Maggie and Valerie. Maggie stood from her chair. "I'll get him."

When he walked in the room behind Maggie, he didn't wait for pleasantries or to be invited to sit down.

"There's an old warrant out for Zavy's arrest," he said. "He was convicted of one of those underage sex offenses years ago, but he disappeared before the State of Louisiana could take him into custody."

"What should we do?" I asked.

We heard the front door open again.

## 81

Layla's voice rang through the apartment. "Mom, I'm back! I got the *sopa,* and they had those *tamalitos* you like. And…"

Tall, beautiful Layla walked into the room and saw us. She took a few more steps and dropped the bags of food on the coffee table, her eyes searching us for clues. "Is the jury back?"

"Yes," her mom said. "Yes. The verdict was not guilty."

Layla burst into tears and ran to her mother, falling to her knees and burying her face in her mother's lap. Valerie stroked her daughter's hair.

"Maybe we should go," my father said.

"No," Valerie said. "Layla needs to hear what you told me about Zavy."

At that, Layla raised her head, quickly looking at Valerie and then all of us. "Mom…" she said, in a warning tone, telling her mother to be quiet.

"They know," Valerie said.

Layla's face flashed with anger at her mother.

I spoke up. "Layla, I was at the bar last night, the one that has the weekly trivia. I saw you with Zavy. And then I saw you again in the courtroom today."

Layla's face was wary. "What do you mean? We've been in the courtroom all week."

"The courtroom on the third floor," I said. "The empty one."

Layla's eyes closed for a second. Then she raised her gaze. "I'm not embarrassed about it. You can't embarrass me." Her words were tough, but her face was a mixture of hurt and fear.

I scooted forward on the couch to look at her, still curled up at her mother's feet like a girl much younger. "I would never want to embarrass you, Layla," I said. "In fact, I'm not embarrassed for you at all."

"You think I should break up with him," Layla said. "You think it's something bad, but it's not." She shook her head fiercely. "Love doesn't care about age." The last sentence came out slightly awkward, yet forceful. It sounded like something she'd heard from someone else.

"I understand that," I said. "I'm dating someone who's almost ten years younger than me, closer to your age than to mine. I don't think you have to be the same age to be in love."

Had I just said that...*in love?* I glanced at Maggie, who made a *Whoa* kind of face at me.

Meanwhile, Valerie was sending me a warning stare.

I tried to close my mouth, but I couldn't help but speak again. "But Layla, you should know that Zavy isn't a good guy."

She got to her feet and looked down at us, angry. "Don't say that. He's an amazing person. And what we have together is unique. We're special." Again, they sounded like someone else's words.

None of us said anything. I didn't want to hurt the girl any more than she had been already. But my father, the emotionally ruthless one, spoke up. "You should know that Zavy has been involved with other young women besides yourself."

"What do you mean?"

"Mr. Miller was convicted of having sex with minors when he lived in New Orleans."

"He never lived in New Orleans. I know everything about him."

"He did live there. His name then was Xavier Jennings." My father reached into the inside pocket of his jacket, extracting a sheath of papers. He peeled off the top one, showing it to us, then extended it to Layla. "Here is his mug shot." He looked younger, his hair fuller, but there was no doubt it was Zavy.

My father continued. "He was arrested twice for having sex with girls who were fifteen and sixteen. In both cases, he had rather long relationships with them. One lasted about seven months, one for almost a year. One of the cases was dropped because the young woman refused to testify. In the other one, he was convicted. There's a warrant out for his arrest now."

Layla's face was alive with shock and bewilderment. "That isn't true. It can't be."

My father stepped forward again and silently handed her another piece of paper. "Here's his rap sheet." He pointed to different parts of the sheet, explaining to Layla the dates of his arrest, the status of the warrant, which was very much active.

Distraught, Layla looked at the sheet. A moment went by, then a moment longer. When she spoke, her voice was strangled. "He's told me about everyone he's been involved with."

Somewhere in the room, the sound of a clock I hadn't noticed before—*tick, tick, tick.*

If I had thought waiting for the verdict was intense,

this moment was more so—packed full of chaotic energy. And I felt certain then that despite that chaos, or maybe because of it, Layla needed to know everything. "Your mom and Amanda were convinced he was waiting for Tess and Brit to get older."

"That's bullshit!" Layla said.

"It's not," Valerie said. Her voice sounded strong, clear. She told Layla what she and Amanda had pieced together from Zavy's behavior over the years. She told her about the dinner that night that they'd planned.

"That's not true about Tess and Brit," Layla said. "And he never lived in New Orleans. I would know. I know everything about him." She moaned a little as if in pain. "He fell in love with me because of *me*. He'd never been involved with anyone much younger than him until me. Amanda was two years younger than him, and he said that was the youngest woman he'd dated. Until *me*. He said he couldn't believe it when he realized he was attracted to me, but he couldn't fight it."

No one said anything.

Layla stared at the rap sheet. "But if this is all true..." She looked at my father.

"I'm sorry," he said, "but it is true. It's been verified. He clearly has a history of relationships with younger women. Did he ever come on to you when you were younger?"

"No," she said hurriedly. "I'd known him forever." She glanced over his shoulder at Valerie, who was watching and listening. "We became friends, though, when I was fourteen or fifteen. I realized how cool he was. But nothing ever happened until I was seventeen."

"How long after you turned seventeen?" Maggie asked.

Layla opened her mouth, closed it. Her eyes looked

foggy for a second. "I don't know…I guess about…about a week."

My heart broke for the girl.

"But it wasn't anything physical then," she said. "It was…I don't know…flirty. Adult kind of flirty, I thought. And then when I started at DePaul, then we…" Her voice died.

"I'm sorry to tell you this," my father said, "but he was just waiting for you to be of age, and then to be out of your mother's house. He knew better than to get involved with you earlier than that, because he'd been arrested for this twice before."

"He's doing the same thing now with Tessa and Brit," Valerie said. "Waiting."

"No, he's not!" Layla's voice was loud and raw, but then something washed over her. Her body went limp, like she might faint.

"Layla, sit," Valerie said gently. She stood from the chair and pulled Layla into it, mother and daughter squeezed together, Valerie's arm tight around Layla's shoulders.

"No," Layla said. "No…" Her eyes stared far away. "Oh, my God." She looked at her mom, some kind of recognition on her face. "He told me about the presents he's been buying for the girls. He can't wait for them to come home from Amanda's sister's house." Her hands flew to her face, her hair hanging in sheets. "Now I'm thinking of all these things he said," she mumbled through her hands. "He can't wait until Tessa can go away to college. Since Amanda died, he's been saying he and Brit will probably have to move because she's going to go out of state for some kind of scholarship. Oh, my God, maybe you're right. He'll wait until they're older, but then he'll…"

Layla began to cry again, tears of heartbreak. Her mother tried to console her, hugging her tighter.

Maggie stood. I did, too. "We'll leave you alone."

But Layla shook her head, wiping her tears away with her fingers. Something had changed about her expression; some kind of determination had entered. "Mr. McNeil, can I see that again?" She pointed to the rap sheet.

He handed it to her.

She studied it, exhaling hard a few times, then she pointed toward the top of the sheet. "Is this the number for the New Orleans Police Department, or whoever is supposed to take care of this warrant, or whatever it's called?"

My father looked at her for a moment. "Yes."

"I want to call them."

"If you're serious," I said, "we could call the police here in Chicago. I know someone. They have authority to arrest him, too."

Layla lifted her cell phone. Sniffling, tears still trickling down her cheeks. "Okay. Okay. I'll tell them about the warrant in New Orleans, and that I know where he is."

"What about his other crime, Layla?" I asked.

Valerie looked at me, eyes wide.

"What other crime?"

"What he did to Amanda."

"He didn't…" But then she stopped, her brows furrowed as if she was thinking over everything. "I know you didn't kill Amanda," she said, looking at Valerie now. "You loved her and wouldn't want Zavy to be free to be with me."

"That's right," Valerie said.

"I couldn't believe Zavy would kill anyone. But I didn't

know about New Orleans, either. I didn't know he'd lied to me."

"Layla, stop," Valerie said. "I've been cleared and Zavy will go away for a little while."

Layla's face nearly crumpled. "And then he'll be out again. I won't have anything to do with him, but what about Tessa and Brit?" She squeezed her eyes shut. "I can't leave him out there to just…prey on them."

Valerie stood. "But then everything I fought for will be in vain. Everyone will find out about you and Zavy."

She hugged her mom. "It's okay."

Valerie began to cry.

"It really is okay, Mom. I loved him. And I'm not ashamed of that."

# 82

The doorbell rang, and Zavy stopped his pacing.

He'd been doing that—looping around and around the house—since his conversation with the prosecutor.

Disappointment had filled him, filled the room, the house, when he'd learned Valerie was acquitted. He could drown in it. He had felt the pull, the same way he had in New Orleans, when everything went wrong. When he had made a mistake in the eyes of the law.

But no. He told himself that the universe would right itself again. He knew that. At least Tessa and Brit would be coming home now. But what of Layla? What would happen with them now that Valerie wasn't going away? He felt his heart clench. He loved Layla so much. So much. So much. But he had always known that what he had with Layla would end. It was why he had been preparing Tessa and Brit, preparing himself for when they changed into women. When, in the eyes of the law, they could choose him.

So no, he wouldn't give in to the despair. He wouldn't fall apart. Because the universe *would* right itself again. It would. He kept pacing, planning.

But now the doorbell. *Who was it?* Probably the press, he realized. He thought about it. He would play the aggrieved widower, he decided. He would say something that Tess and Brit could look back on and respect him for, love him for. *We have to trust the justice system,* he would say to the media. He wouldn't look happy about it, but he would add, *I just want my daughters to move forward, to get back to a normal life.*

Valerie wasn't about to tell anyone about his predilections toward Tess and Brit. She had no proof, for one thing. And she certainly wasn't going to tell anyone about him and Layla. She'd already shown how far she would go to hide that.

The doorbell rang again, this time someone hitting it repeatedly—*bang, bang, bang.*

Zavy strode confidently toward the door. He composed a tired, pained, but courageous expression and opened the door, ready for the onslaught of media.

But there were only three men there. Two of them cops. The guy that stood in front of him was about his age. He reached in his pocket and raised a black wallet. He opened it, briefly showing some kind of identification, but Zavy couldn't read it before the guy put the wallet back in his pocket.

A smile lifted the corner of the man's mouth, then disappeared. "I'm Detective Damon Vaughn," the guy said. "Xavier Jennings, you are under arrest."

## 83

*Three months later*

"We're here in the studio today with the subjects of a new *Chicago Tribune* story that broke this morning." The radio host, Tom Easting, looked around the studio at us. His low, inquisitive voice was more familiar to me than his face. "We're joined by Martin Bristol, one of Chicago's most well-known criminal defense lawyers, his granddaughter and law partner, Maggie Bristol, and their associate, Isabel McNeil."

Tom leaned forward on the desk. "As some of you might recall, the Bristols' law firm, along with Ms. McNeil, successfully represented Valerie Solara, a woman who was accused of killing her friend Amanda Miller." He held up his hands, as if an audience could actually see him. "Now, full disclosure here—one of our producers, Charlie McNeil, is related to Izzy McNeil." The host smiled at me. "Is that right?"

I leaned toward the microphone. "Absolutely right. He's my brother." I glanced at Charlie who was in the producers' booth, behind the wall of glass. He grinned and gave me a thumbs-up.

How odd and wonderful it was to see Charlie in his

work environment. Earlier, he had shown us to the green room, pointing out different pictures on the wall of famous people who had sat in the same room before going on the air. He introduced us to the program director, the sales-people, the weather and sports guys.

"Charlie is our best producer," the program director had said when we met before the interview.

I had to stop myself from saying, *Really?* Not because I didn't think Charlie could excel in a job, but I didn't think he would ever *want* to. I had hugged Charlie tight around his middle when the program director left, swelling with pride. I was so happy that I was spending more time with my family. Valerie's trial, Sam's reappearance and my new job had temporarily put me into work mode. But now I was emerging again, growing confident about my professional skills and spending lots of time at my mom's house, seeing her and Spence and Charlie. And Theo was with me most times now. *He's family,* Spence had declared last week.

I tuned back in to the host now, who was also saying flattering things about Charlie. Then he looked at me. "So there was a lot of media coverage surrounding the Solara trial, and it wasn't just because of the case. The media seemed to really like you, Izzy."

"Is that what you'd call it?" I said it with a joking tone, and everyone laughed.

Tom asked Maggie and me more questions about the case.

"We should mention," Tom said into his mike, "that Xavier Miller, the husband of the victim, has since been arrested for that murder. He is in custody awaiting trial, and the State of Louisiana wants to extradite him on statutory rape charges."

"That's right," Maggie answered.

Valerie hadn't wanted Layla to turn in Zavy for murder, sure that it would ruin Layla's life if the story of her relationship went public. But Layla had grown up in that moment in her mother's apartment, as she heard the allegations about her lover. She was still in college now and she'd also gotten a modeling agent. She was busy on "go-sees" in her free time.

Since Valerie couldn't be charged with murder again or even attempted murder—that would have been double jeopardy—Valerie was free, finally. I'd seen Valerie and Layla a number of times recently. They seemed to have become closer. But Layla had told me that Valerie didn't leave the house much because of the press. She hated everyone knowing she had tried to kill Zavy.

I assured Layla that the pressure would die down, people would forget. In the meantime, we had told the radio host, and any reporter or broadcaster who interviewed us on the story, that we wouldn't discuss Valerie, Layla or Zavy in depth.

So the host turned to his left now, adjusted something on a board that was brightly lit, then turned back to his microphone. "Okay, let's get back to the news today," he said. "The *Chicago Tribune* broke a story this morning about Martin Bristol and an old murder case in Chicago. Martin, do you want to tell us about it?"

Marty leaned forward. "I went to the *Trib* because I was ready to admit that I believe I was involved in a wrongful conviction early in my career as an assistant state's attorney."

He explained about Javier Solara, how at the time there wasn't enough evidence beyond a bad feeling, but how it had bothered him his whole life. He talked about how he took on Valerie's case because of her father. "Now, with the help of two innocence projects—the Center on

Wrongful Convictions here in Chicago and the Innocence Project in New York—we have proven through DNA evidence that Javier Solara is entirely innocent."

Martin explained more about the case, answered questions, and then the host took a break.

Charlie came out of the producer's booth. "Going to the green room. Be right back with the other guest."

Maggie and I exchanged smiles at Charlie's professional use of the word *guest*. We both knew the guest well.

As we waited, I glanced at my cell phone, expecting a text from Theo. He was in his business partner's car, en route to a meeting, but I knew he'd be listening.

You rock, his text said.

And then I saw a text right below that one. From Sam. Hey. Just turned on radio and heard you on WGN. You sound great. Hope you are. You deserve a great life.

Just then, the door of the studio opened. Charlie led my mother into the studio and set her up with headphones and a microphone. He hustled back into the producer's booth and his voice broke into the studio. "Five seconds."

"We're back," Tom said shortly, "and we've got another guest, Victoria McNeil. Apparently, it's the McNeil family hour today." We all laughed. "Welcome to the show."

My mother had spent years in the radio biz—as a DJ in Michigan and as a traffic reporter after we moved to Chicago. She angled her mouth toward the microphone like she'd been doing it every day since. Her strawberry-blond hair fell a little bit over her shoulders, and I was struck by how beautiful she was. "Thanks, Tom, for having me," she said into the mike. Her voice was smooth and projected perfectly into my headphones.

"Tell us, Victoria, how you became a part of this story, too."

"I run a program called the Victoria Project. It helps women who are widowed. Last year, the Victoria Project got a very generous donation from an estate. We've been cautious in deciding how to use the money, but now I know I want to put it toward a new arm of the Project."

I glanced at Maggie and we both smiled.

"We will be using ten million dollars to introduce an initiative to help people like the children of Amanda Miller, who find themselves without a mother or a father."

"They're orphans."

"I suppose, technically, but we don't like to use that word at the Victoria Project. These children are fortunate to have other family members supporting them. For example, Amanda Miller's children are living with their aunt and her husband. It's those family members, and others like them, we want to focus on.

"Many charities fund research to cure various diseases—breast cancer, lymphomas, Lou Gehrig's disease. But too little attention is given to the family members who *support* loved ones going through illnesses or the crisis, such as the one the Miller family had."

"So," Tom said, "you're talking about people who have changed their lives to support family members or friends."

"Exactly. We want to give *them* all the help they need. If there are kids involved, as in the Millers' situation, we'll help the kids with scholarships. We'll also provide counseling for families, couples, individuals. And there is so much more we have planned."

Tom continued to ask questions. Eventually, he directed the conversation back to Martin and the juicier part of the story—the execution of an innocent man.

A large window in the studio looked over Michigan

Avenue, since the station broadcast out onto the street out there. A few pedestrians stood listening, some waving at Tom, who would genially wave back without a break in his words.

But suddenly I saw my mom move her face from the microphone and squint out the window.

I turned and almost burst out laughing at what I saw: Spence and my father.

We'd known they were going to be together to listen to us on the radio. Spence was a guy who needed to help everyone. My mother had finally convinced him that, yes, maybe she was a new person, but that new person loved him very much and had no intention of leaving. Once Spence had gotten that message, he'd been reaching out to my father. *We'll be friends in no time!* he said.

We weren't too sure about that—my father had no friends—but he was doing his part, too. He'd agreed to go to their house this afternoon and sit in their bay window and listen to us on the radio with Spence. But apparently plans had changed.

Spence waved broadly now, an even broader smile on his face. My father gave a sideways glance at him, and then, with a grudging look on his face, gave a quick raise of his hand.

I stared at them. Not only had their plans changed—*life* had changed. All of our lives. And as I watched Spence, I realized that life would probably keep on doing that. And that was okay.

\* \* \* \* \*

# Acknowledgments

Thank you so very much to Amy Moore-Benson, Maureen Walters and Margaret O'Neill Marbury. Thanks also to everyone at MIRA Books, including Miranda Indrigo, Valerie Gray, Donna Hayes, Dianne Moggy, Loriana Saciolotto, Craig Swinwood, Pete McMahon, Stacy Widdrington, Andrew Wright, Katherine Orr, Alex Osuszek, Erin Craig, Margie Miller, Adam Wilson, Don Lucey, Gordy Goihl, Dave Carley, Ken Foy, Erica Mohr, Darren Lizotte, Andi Richman, Reka Rubin, Margie Mullin, Sam Smith, Kathy Lodge, Carolyn Flear, Maureen Stead, Michelle Renaud, Kate Studer, Stephen Miles, Jennifer Watters, Amy Jones, Malle Vallik, Tracey Langmuir, Anne Fontanesi, Scott Ingram, Marianna Ricciuto, Jim Robinson, John Jordan and Brent Lewis.

Much gratitude to my experts—attorneys Catharine O'Daniel and Dick Devine, as well as physicians Dr. Richard Feely, Dr. Doug Lyle and Dr. Devon Isaacson.

Thanks also to everyone who read the book or offered

advice or suggestions, especially Pam Carroll, Liza Jaine, Christi Smith, Carol Miller, Les Klinger, Katie Caldwell Kuhn, Margaret Caldwell and William Caldwell.

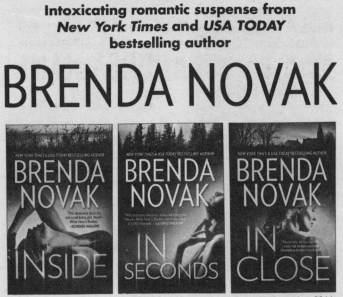

A FAST-PACED CRIME NOVEL FROM

# RICK MOFINA

Tilly's mother Cora pleads for mercy but the kidnappers are clear: if they don't get their $5 million back in five days, Tilly dies. If anyone contacts police, Tilly dies.

After disappearing from his life without a trace decades ago, Cora frantically reaches out to her brother, Jack Gannon, a journalist. Cora tells him about the shameful mistakes she's made—but she guards the one secret that may be keeping her daughter alive.

Meanwhile, a Mexican priest hears a chilling confession from a twenty-year-old assassin, haunted by the faces of the people he's executed. He seeks absolution as he sets out to commit his last murders as a hired killer.

*Time is running out...*

In the U.S. and Mexico, police and the press go flat out on Tilly's case. But as Gannon digs deeper into his anguished sister's past, the hours tick down on his niece's life and he faces losing the fragment of his rediscovered family forever.

# IN DESPERATION

*AVAILABLE WHEREVER BOOKS ARE SOLD*

MIRA®

www.MIRABooks.com

MRM2948R

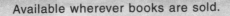

# REQUEST YOUR FREE BOOKS!

## 2 FREE NOVELS
## FROM THE SUSPENSE COLLECTION
## PLUS 2 FREE GIFTS!

**YES!** Please send me 2 FREE novels from the Suspense Collection and my 2 FREE gifts (gifts are worth about $10). After receiving them, if I don't wish to receive any more books, I can return the shipping statement marked "cancel." If I don't cancel, I will receive 4 brand-new novels every month and be billed just $5.99 per book in the U.S. or $6.49 per book in Canada. That's a saving of at least 25% off the cover price. It's quite a bargain! Shipping and handling is just 50¢ per book in the U.S. and 75¢ per book in Canada.* I understand that accepting the 2 free books and gifts places me under no obligation to buy anything. I can always return a shipment and cancel at any time. Even if I never buy another book, the two free books and gifts are mine to keep forever.

191/391 MDN FEME

Name _____ (PLEASE PRINT) _____

Address _____ Apt. # _____

City _____ State/Prov. _____ Zip/Postal Code _____

Signature (if under 18, a parent or guardian must sign)

### Mail to the **Reader Service:**
**IN U.S.A.:** P.O. Box 1867, Buffalo, NY 14240-1867
**IN CANADA:** P.O. Box 609, Fort Erie, Ontario L2A 5X3

Not valid for current subscribers to the Suspense Collection
or the Romance/Suspense Collection.

**Want to try two free books from another line?**
**Call 1-800-873-8635 or visit www.ReaderService.com.**

* Terms and prices subject to change without notice. Prices do not include applicable taxes. Sales tax applicable in N.Y. Canadian residents will be charged applicable taxes. Offer not valid in Quebec. This offer is limited to one order per household. All orders subject to credit approval. Credit or debit balances in a customer's account(s) may be offset by any other outstanding balance owed by or to the customer. Please allow 4 to 6 weeks for delivery. Offer available while quantities last.

**Your Privacy**—The Reader Service is committed to protecting your privacy. Our Privacy Policy is available online at www.ReaderService.com or upon request from the Reader Service.

We make a portion of our mailing list available to reputable third parties that offer products we believe may interest you. If you prefer that we not exchange your name with third parties, or if you wish to clarify or modify your communication preferences, please visit us at www.ReaderService.com/consumerschoice or write to us at Reader Service Preference Service, P.O. Box 9062, Buffalo, NY 14269. Include your complete name and address.

SUS11

# LAURA CALDWELL

| | | | |
|---|---|---|---|
| 32650 | RED HOT LIES | ___ $7.99 U.S. | ___ $8.99 CAN. |
| 32932 | CLAIM OF INNOCENCE | ___ $7.99 U.S. | ___ $9.99 CAN. |
| 32666 | RED, WHITE & DEAD | ___ $7.99 U.S. | ___ $8.99 CAN. |
| 32658 | RED BLOODED MURDER | ___ $7.99 U.S. | ___ $8.99 CAN. |
| 32501 | THE GOOD LIAR | ___ $6.99 U.S. | ___ $8.50 CAN. |
| 32183 | LOOK CLOSELY | ___ $6.99 U.S. | ___ $8.50 CAN. |

*(limited quantities available)*

| | |
|---|---|
| TOTAL AMOUNT | $ _____ |
| POSTAGE & HANDLING | $ _____ |
| ($1.00 for 1 book, 50¢ for each additional) | |
| APPLICABLE TAXES* | $ _____ |
| TOTAL PAYABLE | $ _____ |

*(check or money order—please do not send cash)*

To order, complete this form and send it, along with a check or money order for the total above, payable to MIRA Books, to: **In the U.S.:** 3010 Walden Avenue, P.O. Box 9077, Buffalo, NY 14269-9077; **In Canada:** P.O. Box 636, Fort Erie, Ontario, L2A 5X3.

Name: _____
Address: _____ City: _____
State/Prov.: _____ Zip/Postal Code: _____
Account Number (if applicable): _____

075 CSAS

*New York residents remit applicable sales taxes.
*Canadian residents remit applicable GST and provincial taxes.

MIRA    H HARLEQUIN®
www.Harlequin.com